THE PRETEND FIANCÉ FIASCO

A BRO CODE NOVEL

PIPPA GRANT

Editing by Jessica Snyder, HEA Author Services
Proofreading by Emily Laughridge & Jodi Duggan
Cover Design and Map Illustration by Qamber Designs
Cover Image Copyright © Wander Aguiar

PROLOGUE

The Daily Gossip

By a special anonymous columnist for the Blue Lagoon Gazette

By now, you undoubtedly know that Cooper Rock, baseball player with buns of steel, is marrying Waverly Sweet, his pop star girlfriend, in the little mountain town of Shipwreck this weekend.

We're not here to talk about who's acting as her maid of honor or what they're serving for dinner or how the local sheriff's department will handle shutting the town down with the number of celebrities and athletes destined for the goofball pirate-themed town though.

Oh, no.

We're talking about what really matters.

The treasure.

You want to know what Waverly's colors are or how Cooper's spending his last days of bachelorhood, look somewhere else.

I'm here to give you the real scoop.

To do that, we have to go back in time over two hundred years, to the end of the eighteenth century, when legendary pirate Thorny Rock escaped capture by loading his treasure up in a covered wagon and heading inland from the port of Norfolk.

"Yes, the story I've been told since I was little is that Thorny Rock evaded arrest by hustling inland," Tillie Jean Rock-Cole, Shipwreck's newly-installed mayor and Cooper's sister, told me. "My bedtime stories were about his pirate days and how he settled into life here in the Blue Ridge Mountains. My grandpa insisted Thorny buried his treasure somewhere out here, but to the best of my knowledge, if it's real, it's never been found."

That's right, ladies and gentlemen. The biggest part of the story about Waverly Sweet marrying Cooper Rock is that they're getting hitched in a town where his great-great-something-grandfather, the legendary Thorny Rock himself, buried a pirate treasure.

His family has been hosting Shipwreck's annual Pirate Festival for longer than this author has been alive, but have they been hiding secrets?

Yes, yes, they donated nearly all of the artifacts now on display at the new Thorny Rock Museum in downtown Shipwreck, but did they donate *everything* they had?

According to residents of Sarcasm, a town just up the road from Shipwreck, it's likely the Rock family isn't fully forthcoming when they talk about their pirate ancestor.

I spoke with one resident who requested anonymity because of the supposed truce between the two rival towns, prompted when Cooper's brother, Grady, married a Sarcasm native a few years back. My source said tensions between Shipwreck and Sarcasm remain high, and only partially because of the trash talk about who has the better festival.

"They talk about how they're the best pirate town in the world, but they never mention that Sarcasm was founded by Thorny Rock's cousin, who did the pirating with him," my source said. "We've always thought they're hiding more than anyone at their festival suspects. That's why we started the Unicorn Festival. Because we knew unicorns were the only things that could be more popular than pirates, and we wanted to show them we're not always last."

Pirates and unicorns aside, there's one occasional Shipwreck resident who believes the treasure is still out there.

"Ah, heck, yeah," Beck Ryder, former member of the boy band Bro Code who has a weekend house just above the town proper, said when I caught up with him at Grady Rock's bakery. "Of course I believe the treasure's still out there. How cool would it be to find a treasure? That's like, next level goals for an amazing life, you know? I want to believe in it. I want to believe my wife and kids and I will find it one day."

Ryder says he's been friends with the Rock family for at least a decade, and that Shipwreck is one of his favorite places in the world. His sister is rumored to have fallen in love with her husband while she was in Shipwreck to attend a destination wedding.

That same destination wedding, by the way, is the reason there are wild goats all over town.

Naturally, Shipwreck residents blame Sarcasm residents for nearly ruining their reputation as *the* place for pirate-themed destination weddings by releasing a herd of goats during the ceremony, and naturally, Sarcasm residents deny it.

One thing that can't be denied?

Shipwreck is also a town of love.

Beck Ryder added that one of his former bandmates, Cash Rivers, fell in love with his girlfriend, Waverly Sweet's BFF, the pop star known as Aspen, here in Shipwreck too.

"Oh, yeah, and you know the Wilson brothers are here all the time, between Levi being tight with Waverly and Tripp owning Cooper's team," Ryder continued, referencing two more of his four former bandmates. "It's the best date night when all of us are out here together."

I asked him if Davis Remington, the last former member of Bro Code, ever visited with a lady love as well, and Beck's answer convinced me that he was lying about his knowledge of the treasure.

"Davis Remington? Who's that?"

On point for the men who protect their last band member's privacy, but suspicious when paired with his claims that he hopes to one day find a treasure.

A treasure that Tillie Jean Rock-Cole continues to play coy about. "Despite all of the pirate tales, no one in my family knows anything about where the treasure might be," she told me. "Honestly, if it was ever buried here, it was probably found years ago. Before the internet. When someone could anonymously find a treasure and no one would've known."

One thing is certain—if the treasure *is* still out there, it will be found.

Probably soon.

Because this reporter isn't the only one covering the history of Shipwreck. And the town has the increased tourism to show for it.

"Oh, yes, we have more and more people stopping in every day to ask if we have any secret intel on where the treasure might be," Sloane Pearce, a volunteer at the Thorny Rock Museum, told me. "Ever since Cooper and Waverly announced they were getting married here, we've been slammed. Tourism is up three or four times what it usually is this time of year. People want to find a treasure."

When pressed on if she thought it could be found, she simply smiled. "I guess that depends on if it exists."

Whether it does or not, one thing is certain: this wedding and all of its consequences will be one more story for the Rock family to tell its family for ages to come.

1

Sloane Pearce, aka a woman with just a couple secrets who's mistaken if she thinks glitter is her biggest worry today

IF YOU'D TOLD me when I was thirteen years old that I'd have one of the most important jobs at the wedding of the century, I would've told you good girls don't go in places where jobs like this are required.

I like being thirty-five so much more than I liked being thirteen.

It's way more fun.

"Hand over the glitter bombs, gentlemen, and do not make me get specific about what constitutes a glitter bomb," I say to the twin behemoths that I've just cornered near the makeshift stage in the Shipwreck, Virginia town square where Cooper Rock, local hero—don't tell him I called him that—has just exchanged wedding vows with pop princess Waverly Sweet.

The two men I'm talking to played professional

7

hockey a few years ago down the road in Copper Valley, and if anyone's going to defy Shipwreck's glitter ban, it's them.

Or any one of Cooper's baseball-playing teammates.

Actually, possibly Waverly. There was an unholy amount of glitter involved in the proposal that led to this wedding, and for once, that glitter wasn't Cooper's fault. Directly, anyway.

A few of the locals too. They're sneaky enough to sprinkle glitter and successfully blame it on someone else.

The twins share a look.

"We don't have glitter bombs, do we?" one says.

The other grunts an agreement.

I have to suck in a smile. They're so bad at lying, it's hilarious. "Look, I love a good glitter bomb as much as the next person, but you can't launch them with this much security in town today." On top of half of the professional baseball players in the country and a solid number of professional athletes from other sports being here, there are also a ton of music industry people that I can't name and a not-insignificant portion of Hollywood that I *do* recognize and can name. There are enough important people that the town's been closed since last night. Nobody in, nobody out, without passing a thorough ID check at the roadblocks on either end of town. Wedding guests only.

I try to look sternly at the twins, which is hella difficult. "Imagine you launched a glitter bomb and a piece of glitter got caught in Liv Daniels's eye and she had to back out of her next movie because she was recovering from surgery to try to save it."

8

The slightly larger twin lights up. "Would she have to wear a pirate eye patch in the movie? That would be cool."

The other twin grunts again, I assume in agreement.

So I resort to desperate measures. "I have both of your wives' numbers in my phone."

They share a look, and I'm soon holding an armful of homemade glitter bombs.

Like, a full freaking armful.

I don't know how they were hiding these in their suit pockets. There have to be almost a dozen of these things, all the paper towel tube variety.

I should've picked a dress with pockets.

That would've been more helpful for my job today. Or a large purse. I don't even have room for a phone, much less this many glitter bombs.

"Are you so for real right now?" Tillie Jean Cole, sister of the groom and new mayor of Shipwreck—and also the person who put the glitter bomb ban into effect, which, yes, is Cooper's fault—stops beside us and watches as the quieter of the two twins reaches into his pants and pulls out one more glitter bomb to add to the pile.

I don't want to know what that glitter bomb was touching.

I truly don't.

"They are definitely so for real right now," I tell my friend. "How are you surprised by this?"

She's clearly suppressing a smile too. "You guys. You know how to break into Cooper's house, and you brought glitter bombs to the wedding instead?"

Once again, the twins share a look.

This one suggests there are, in fact, already other glitter bombs hidden at Cooper's house.

The slightly larger twin clears his throat. "I need to go help my lady with the kids."

The other nods. "Yep."

They turn and disappear into the crowd, which is freaking impressive considering their size.

Tillie Jean grins at me. "Did you count how many there are?"

"You may not have any of these for private use." Oh yes, I know exactly where her mind is going. *Will Sloane notice if one disappears?*

Tillie Jean has been one of my best friends since I moved here about six years ago after another wedding that was epic in its own way, even if the memory of why I was here for that one always makes me feel a little awkward. "You already tell people you had to explain to your obstetrician why your daughter was born glittered. I'm not enabling you to break your own ban."

Her blue eyes twinkle in the dwindling sunlight. "You're remarkably not fun today."

"You can think I'm not fun all you want, but I'm having the time of my life. Do you know how many famous people I've gotten to shake down? I will never—*ever*—have this opportunity again in my entire life. I'm living up being the glitter po-po today."

"Are you asking for their autographs while you do it?"

"I would be if this dress had pockets." I pat my hips where pockets belong. "Why does my dress not have pockets?"

"Waverly's dress has pockets."

"I know. I'm jealous."

"Honestly? Me too. *I forgot pockets too*. You'd think being a mom would've made me insist on pockets for this thing, but nope." She fluffs her green bridesmaid dress and grins at me. "Would've been good for food too. Keep up the good work, and make sure you eat, okay?"

"On it all."

She slips away, headed toward a group of Cooper's teammates and their significant others, whom I've already shaken down for glitter bombs, and I get back to having fun.

The well-dressed wedding guests make their way to the dozen or so food tents set up along Blackbeard Avenue. I weave among them, keeping an eagle eye out for anyone who might be planning to interrupt the festivities with glitter bombs, occasionally pausing to breathe in the mingled scents of everything from fried chicken to gyros to butter chicken, all provided by local restaurants with extra help brought in by Cooper and Waverly so the normal restaurant staff can enjoy the wedding too.

It's been an unseasonably warm day, and the mountains beyond Shipwreck are showing off as the sun sets behind them.

It's like the world itself approves of this wedding.

I pass Tillie Jean's husband, Max, who was a joint recipient of the glitter bomb that changed Shipwreck a couple years ago, and he gives me a fist bump. "Good work."

"Tillie Jean shouldn't give me too many more authoritarian jobs. This could go to my head."

"Worse things have happened here." He smiles, and

their toddler daughter grins at me from his arms too, then dives in for a hug.

I catch her and squeeze her little body. "And you're going to grow up with so much mischief that your Uncle Cooper won't dare try to glitter bomb you, aren't you?"

"Dada, ogurt," she replies, reaching for Max, who pulls a yogurt tube out of the diaper bag hung on his shoulder.

I kiss the little squirt on the forehead, pass her back, and continue on my way, because I don't like how some of Cooper's other retired teammates are huddling together near the Scuttle Putt miniature golf entrance.

And I silently high five myself when I successfully collect a half dozen more glitter bombs that I deposit into a repurposed mail collection box.

Waverly's team bought a dozen to put around Shipwreck since they're one way in, no way out without the keys. Though, of course, they were coated with pink sparkle paint first.

As I'm continuing on my rounds, chatting with friends and contemplating a dinner break, I bump into the bride and groom and hug both of them.

"Your dress is gorgeous," I tell Waverly.

"Almost as pretty as she is," Cooper agrees.

And Waverly Sweet, one of the most famous musicians in the world, blushes at the compliments.

"Have your security teams do a thorough sweep of your house before you get too comfortable," I murmur to them. "I've heard rumors."

Cooper's eyes light up. "Really?"

"It's you. Half the people here want to prank you, and

all of them want to do it with glitter or things that make noise."

"Fantastic."

He's smiling so big that it's impossible to believe he's faking it. Tillie Jean told me once that game loves game, and Cooper loves being pranked as much as he loves giving prank.

I lift a brow at Waverly. "You knew what you were getting into…"

"I did, and I do," she agrees. "And you know what? Life's much more fun the Cooper way."

Someone calls Waverly's name, and the happy couple links hands, thanks me again for being on glitter bomb patrol, and heads toward the dance floor that Waverly's crew installed in the town square. During the Pirate Festival every summer, we bury fake treasure and let the festival-goers dig for pirate loot in the town square.

I love my adopted hometown.

Supposedly Cooper and Tillie Jean's great-great-something-grandfather was a pirate named Thorny Rock who gave up life on the high seas as the authorities were closing in. He docked in Norfolk, loaded his treasure up on a covered wagon, and drove inland until he found a great place to bury his loot here in the Blue Ridge Mountains. He founded Shipwreck to be near his treasure, and now I live in a place where it's all pirate, all year round.

There's an added bonus that Cooper's spent his entire baseball career talking up Shipwreck, so celebrities are here on a regular enough basis that the number of famous and important people in town today almost feels normal.

It's fun.

One of my neighbors waves at me as colored spotlights flicker on over the town square. "What's your glitter count?" he asks.

"Twenty-two, but fourteen of those came from the Berger twins."

"I got three more off them myself. And I took three from Libby Rock. *Libby*. Can you believe that?"

Believe that Cooper's mother would launch a glitter bomb at the last of her three kids' weddings, against Cooper?

I giggle. "Yep."

He giggles back. "She's hashtag goals."

"Nobody says hashtag anymore, Grandpa," a teenager mutters as she passes by.

"They do when they don't want to rot their brains."

The teenager gives him a look. "It's called *brain rot*. Not *rot your brain*."

He smiles broadly back. "Wait until you're my age. The kids'll be talking a lot worse than you do. You'll probably call it diarrhea mouth."

Like I said.

I freaking love this town.

I high five my neighbor, and we both go back to sniffing out glitter bombs.

And that's when everything goes to hell.

Well, not *everything*.

Just my day.

Possibly my life.

It takes the form of a six-foot-four, raven-haired, blue-eyed, dimple-chinned, broad-shouldered former high school quarterback who should absolutely not be here.

14

Not anywhere close to here, in fact.

But here he is. Stepping into my path right at the edge of the square.

"*Nigel?*"

The nightmare from my childhood holds out his arms as if to say *who else would I be, you moron?*

You know those times when your body alternates flashing hot and cold so fast that you're not sure if you have a fever or if perimenopause has arrived in blazing-ice glory?

That's me right now.

Nigel Hipplewait should not be here.

He's supposed to be running his grandpa's old church back in Two Twigs, Iowa.

My hometown. The one that I never talk about, and the one that believes gossip, riches, and any music other than gospel music is a straight path to eternal damnation. The one that taught me that no matter what I do, it will never be enough.

That *I* will never be enough.

There's zero chance he knows Cooper or Waverly.

There's zero reason he should be here.

We've had town meetings here in Shipwreck about what to do if an unauthorized person sneaks into the wedding. We're to alert the nearest security person and have the trespasser escorted away for questioning and removal from town.

But what are you supposed to do when the trespasser is someone you've known your entire life, and who your grandma mentioned had just taken over for his grandfather as the town's pastor?

"You can't be here," I whisper.

He does that slow blink like he's irritated, then makes an equally slow show of looking all around the town. "Free country."

"Town's closed for a wedding."

"I'm aware."

"Are you invited? Do you have an invitation? If security asks for your invitation and you don't have it, they're going to kick you out."

Wait.

That wouldn't be a bad thing, would it?

Guilt rears its ugly head at the thought, closely followed by shame galloping in on a dusty old horse that I haven't let out of the barn I thought I'd finally trapped it in not long after I dumped my last boyfriend.

Nigel tosses his hair. It's short, and he still tosses it. "No one's going to question my presence." He peers down his nose at me. "Not like I'm going to question why I haven't seen you with *Steve* all day."

Oooooh, fuuuuuuuuuuuccccckkkk.

"*Rawk! Steve's a dick! Rawk!*" Long Beak Silver, the Rock family patriarch's pet parrot, screeches from the back of a folding chair at the edge of the dance floor.

"Why are you cussing again?" I ask the bird. "Max taught you to say nice things."

"*Rawk! Fuck off! Rawk!*"

I glare at the bird, who's causing enough of a commotion that people are starting to look our way.

People who might realize Nigel's not supposed to be here.

16

They won't realize that, Sloane. They cannot possibly realize that.

Except a rule is being broken by a person who spent a lot of my childhood telling me to follow the rules, and I'm sweating and I'm cold and I haven't had enough alcohol to deal with this, except you don't drink alcohol if you're from Two Twigs, because that, too, is a sure path to eternal damnation.

Which isn't a problem when I'm not in Two Twigs.

But having someone from my past breathing down on me is making it a problem now.

Nigel angles closer, making me want to jump out of my skin. He smells like sweat—the bad kind—and medieval torture devices. "I know the truth about *Steve.*"

"My b-boyfriend?" *Dammit, don't stutter.* The new and improved Sloane Pearce doesn't stutter.

Even when being confronted about the fact that I've spent the past year sending doctored photos back home to my grandmother to make her believe I have a boyfriend so that she won't worry that I'll die alone and childless.

And so that she won't do something extreme.

Like send Nigel to check on me.

"You told your grandma he proposed."

They've talked. Of course they have, but I only told my grandmother that last night.

Shi—shoot—no, *shit*, dammit. This is worthy of cussing, and it's only in my head.

So why is Nigel frowning even heavier at me like he knows I'm cussing in my head?

Screw—fuck this. I lift my head and stare directly at Nigel. "He did."

"And he's not here."

There was a fifty-fifty chance that the man whose picture I've been sending to my grandmother would've been here today. He comes through town regularly, and I know he was on the guest list.

He, however, has no idea that he's my pretend boyfriend.

Fiancé.

Love of my life.

Whatever.

So it's a massive relief that I haven't seen him at all today. "He hates crowds."

It's also a massive relief that I'm nearly certain that statement is true. *Thank you for not being here today, fake Steve.*

"You told your grandma he'd be here with you today."

"He changed his mind last-minute."

"His name isn't Steve, and there's a snowflake's chance in hell that a man like him would date a woman like you. Does he even know the lies you've been telling about him? Actually, does he even know you exist? Give it up, Sloane. It's time to come home and quit behaving like this."

I'm thirty-five years old.

Thirty-five.

And a boy from my childhood is making me feel like that confused, guilty, shame-filled thirteen-year-old who would've been appalled at the existence of glitter bombs all over again. I can't stop the adrenaline rush warring with the emotions that I thought I'd finally mastered.

I pull myself straight, look Nigel in the eye, and say the

meanest thing I can force myself to say at this moment. "That's rude."

"Rawk! Kick him in the nads! Rawk!"

I'd love to, Long Beak Silver.

Nigel shifts a look at the bird. "You need scripture."

"Rawk! You need glitter! Rawk!"

More people turn and stare.

And as I'm glancing around, realizing just how much of an audience we're gathering thanks to the bird, I see something else.

Steve.

My pretend boyfriend. Fiancé.

The man I've been telling my grandmother is the love of my life.

Steve is lingering near the Thorny Rock Historical Museum, which has been a passion project of mine since I decided two years ago that I'm never getting married.

Nigel's half right, half wrong.

Steve is not actually named Steve. He got that part right. But Steve does, in fact, know I exist. Barely, but he does.

What *Steve* doesn't know is the part where I told my grandmother that we're engaged.

And getting married in a week because we just can't wait to start our lives together.

I give it a fifty-fifty shot that if I can manage to explain it to him, he'd go along with the ruse.

Actually, I give it a ten percent shot he'd agree and a ninety percent chance that he'll suggest security escort *me* out of the wedding.

Because apparently, picking the most reclusive

member of a former boy band to be your fake boyfriend means the people you're lying to can still figure out who he really is.

And not telling said reclusive former boy band member that he's your pretend boyfriend—yep.

That's about to bite me in the ass too.

Because Nigel is a freaking hound dog.

He has his teeth in me, and he won't let go until he gets what he wants.

Unless—

"Rawk! Girl fight! Rawk!"

I look at Nigel, who's more or less sneering at me with all of his pompous holier-than-thou pomposity.

Then at the bird.

And then at the glitter bomb in my hand.

I need to talk to *Steve*.

Alone.

And *Steve* is now slipping into my museum with a code for the front door that he shouldn't have.

I'd have to investigate that even if *Steve* wasn't my pretend fiancé.

Also, the freaking *audacity*.

What does *Steve* think he's doing, using the *front* door to break into my museum? Who gave him the code?

Not that I think he'd trash it, but that's bold.

And weird.

And making the hairs on my arms stand on end.

Nigel grabs me by the elbow. "We're leaving. You need to find your moral compass again."

I wrench myself free from his grip without a second thought.

What I do after that—well, I'm going to call it divine intervention that it works.

I shove a loaded glitter bomb at Nigel. "Hold this."

He takes it, probably on instinct.

So I pull the little string that pops it. Directly into his suit.

"Rawk! Contraband glitter! Rawk! Glitter bomb! Rawk!"

Nigel gasps and stares at me.

And then—well, then the twins happen.

"Glitter bombs away!" the more vocal one crows.

I duck.

I dive.

I run.

And as glitter bomb after glitter bomb explodes behind me, I make a dash to the museum.

Nigel can't get in there.

And there's a certain acquaintance of mine in there that I need to see so that I can ask him a very large favor. Probably. After I find out what in the actual hell he's doing in my museum.

2

Sloane

THERE'S pandemonium behind me as I dash to the museum.

I heard Waverly laughing, so that's good. I'll have to apologize to Tillie Jean later.

Probably.

She'll likely forgive me when she hears why I did it. And I'm going to owe her an explanation.

A very long explanation.

I regularly tell people I grew up in Copper Valley but sometimes visit distant relatives in Iowa so that I don't have to answer questions that I don't want to answer. Tillie Jean and a few of my other closest friends know more of the truth now, but not the full truth.

Colored lights rotate over the museum door as I hit the code to let myself into the building. I don't look back to see if Nigel's watching me.

The noise from the crowd tells me a whole glitter bomb party has erupted.

I hope Nigel gets glitter in his eye.

That would be poetic justice.

Not nice, Sloane.

Fuck off, conscience, and let me have this one.

I slip inside and find the foyer empty.

Maybe *Steve* needed to use the bathroom.

Why he couldn't use a bathroom among the very nice portable bathrooms that feel like real bathrooms sitting in trailers on either end of Blackbeard Avenue and just off the other end of the square too, I don't know, but maybe that's why he's here.

I head into the front room, which is full of artifacts about the pirate who ditched sea life to hide his treasure inland, thus founding Shipwreck over two hundred years ago. The Rock family had been keeping all of this stuff for literal centuries, and it's a source of pride and joy for me to have it all displayed now.

Even in the relative darkness, with the room lit only by the gentlest glow from the illuminated light switches and the red exit signs, being around this much history is instantly calming.

Let's be real though—being inside a locked building all alone, away from Nigel, away from having all of my lies exposed in front of the most famous people in the world, is also adding to the calming effect.

Even if I'm getting nervous about what I have to say to the man I'm looking for inside here.

I concentrate on inhaling a long, slow breath as I pass the shadows of a glass case holding a replica of Thorny

Rock's pirate ship that one of Tillie Jean's great-uncles built. I stroll past the darkened silhouette of a painting that Tillie Jean herself painted of Thorny Rock pulling his ship into port in Norfolk back in the day. My shoulders relax and drop as I pass by the stand and case that I know holds a map depicting locations of sea battles that Thorny Rock waged to acquire his famous—and famously missing—treasure.

The museum has three open display rooms, plus a fourth that we're slowly building for an interactive experience and a storage room where we have experts in occasionally to help us with restoration and preservation efforts. With Cooper and Waverly's wedding being basically the biggest news on the internet in the history of history, there's been a lot of interest in Shipwreck itself because of their carefully leaked wedding plans.

Tourism has increased something like five hundred percent over where it was last year, and *Thorny Rock's treasure* has trended at least a half dozen times as a top search on Google in the past few months.

Everyone in the world wants to know everything about not just Waverly Sweet's wedding to baseball's most popular player, but they also want to know how they can find a treasure in said baseball player's hometown.

All the extra attention is exactly why the whole town is locked down for the actual wedding today.

Once I verify that Davis Remington, the real former boy band member whose name is not Steve, isn't in any of the display rooms, I head toward the little nook holding the bathroom, fully aware that stalking a man outside the bathrooms is weird.

Stalking a man outside the bathrooms to ask him to play along with a little charade that we're engaged is weirder.

But if that's what it takes to get Nigel to go home, to believe that this is real, then that's what I'll do.

Davis and I played darts at the Grog one night when I was a little tipsy. I'm pretty sure I let him win. I think. That night's a little hazy thanks to the tequila—okay, *very* hazy—but surely the fact that we played a single game of darts once will count for something. He's even nodded to me a few times since then, like he's acknowledging that he remembers that I'm…fun.

Or something.

I'm halfway to the bathroom when I hear something in a different part of the museum though.

It's a squeak.

And it sounds like it's coming from the storage/workroom.

Like someone's in there, opening a storage drawer.

A shiver ripples through me. "Hello—" I start, but someone's hand clamps around my mouth.

"You're safe, but you need to leave," a soft, vaguely familiar male voice says in my ear. "I'll handle this."

That's not a shiver rippling through my body now.

That's a full-on panic attack.

Who says *you're safe* and means it?

No one. That's who.

I scream against the hand on my mouth and jerk my elbow back, intending to get him in the ribs or the side or maybe a kidney, but my elbow connects with air and I'm suddenly spinning, completely free, the man gone.

There's a crash in the storage room as the door flies open. A flashlight from inside the storage room briefly illuminates a slender person dashing through the doorway, and my brain registers what it also refuses to comprehend.

That's Davis. *Steve* to my grandmother.

I think.

But what—why—*oh my god*.

Something crashes. Something else squeaks.

There's a shout.

A grunt.

Glass breaking.

Call someone.

I need to call someone.

Phone.

Do I have my phone?

Where's my phone?

Fucking dress. *Fucking dress.*

No pockets.

No phone.

No phone.

I rush toward the storage room, heart pounding, and arrive just in time to see the back door swing open and a dark figure dash into the night as a second figure goes flying.

But not toward the fleeing figure.

No, this person is flying like they slipped on something.

Arms windmilling.

Body sailing backward.

Back hitting the floor.

There's a grunt—a manly grunt—and I'm in motion again.

I slap on the light switch, and the man on the floor squints at me.

"What the *fuck*?" I yelp as I confirm at least one paranoid suspicion.

Heat courses from my scalp, down my forehead and over my eyelids, from my nose to my cheeks and ears, then spreads to my jaw and neck.

My heart tries to hammer itself into my breastbone.

My knees wobble and my stomach rolls over at the sight before me.

Today was supposed to be the best wedding ever.

And it's just gone completely sideways.

A wedding crasher who made me start a glitter bomb war. My imaginary fiancé wiped out on the tile after breaking into my museum. And a separate dark-clothed figure fleeing my storage room.

The exit door clicks shut.

"I'm *safe*?" I yelp as a man I very much should not yell at blinks at me once more from the floor, then pulls himself to sitting.

He looks at the door to the outside world that the second person escaped through, then down, his gaze going toward the shattered coffee mug and the spilled coffee with a smear in it where his boot hit it, then looks at me again.

Swear he's thinking about getting up and running after whoever just fled here.

You know. While he might have a concussion.

That wouldn't be even more problematic than the break-in happening at all.

I order my sarcastic side to hush as I dash around him to the back door and fling it open, peering out into the night.

No lights back here. Just the shadows of the backside of the water park across the alleyway. It's closed for the winter.

"Don't—" Davis starts but cuts himself off with a grunt.

Dammit.

Dammit.

I have to pick between dashing into the night to track someone who could've gone any direction around the corner of the building and tending to someone who might have a concussion.

Davis's brown manbun is lopsided. His beard is still thick, but less bushy than the last time I saw him, like he trimmed it for the wedding. And his brown eyes stare at me blankly.

I've decided after most of my occasional encounters with him over the past few years that his blank look doesn't mean there's nothing going on in his head.

Rather, it means he's trained himself well to not give any clues as to what's going on in his head.

But in this situation, I don't trust blankness.

In this situation, I actively dislike blankness.

Nurse Sloane takes over from Freaking Out Sloane, and I squat beside him. "Are you hurt?"

He blinks, and a different blankness schools his features. This isn't *I'm knocked out* blankness.

This is *I'm letting you see nothing* blankness.

"No."

I study his eyes—definitely more alert, if still guarded—then make a quick visual inspection of the rest of the man who used to be my shameful secret boy band crush.

More heat courses through my body.

That's not all he is now, even if he doesn't know it.

I think.

Probably.

Rumor around town is that he just knows things.

That's probably why I picked him. The risk of telling stories about a man who has a way of *knowing* things. That, and he only stops by Shipwreck occasionally to visit Beck Ryder, one of his former bandmates who's had a weekend house up here for longer than I've lived here.

"Follow my fingers with your eyes," I order, lifting a hand.

The blank look stays. "I'm fine."

Great. Want to pretend to be my fake fiancé?

I shake my head and rise, aware that he's tracking my movements as I begin to circle him.

The man could have a concussion. Now is not the time to ask him for a favor.

There's no obvious blood anywhere. Pupils seem fine. Breathing normal.

Good. "What are you doing here?"

He doesn't answer.

"Who was that?"

Again, no answer.

Just him watching me watch him as I pace around him, checking to make sure his movements are normal.

Until he flings an arm out. "Don't step in the coffee."

So I don't fall?

Or so I don't destroy evidence at a crime scene?

Oh my god.

What is even happening right now?

Breathe, Sloane. Breathe. "Who gave you the code to get in here? What are you doing here?"

His eyes slide to the back door again, then to the wide filing cabinet where one of the drawers is cracked, then back to me, like he's saying *following someone else who's not supposed to be here, duh.*

And like that's all the answer I'm going to get.

But more questions are bubbling up.

Who was in here with him? What did they want?

The worktable's crooked. There's the broken coffee mug on the ground. That filing cabinet drawer—it's bent, and there's a crowbar on the floor next to it.

I suppress another shiver and look back at Davis.

"Did you pull any muscles? Strain anything? Twist anything?"

"You're a nurse."

Teenage me squeals in my head. *He remembers who I am!*

I tell her to shut up because when he finds out the other thing I've been doing, he's probably going to have a restraining order filed against me.

Also, why is my imaginary fiancé in a place where a crime just happened? And in a place he shouldn't even know how to get into?

Because you really know how to pick men, Sloane.

Even the imaginary boyfriends have questionable character.

Awesome.

Also, I am never buying another dress without pockets in my entire life.

Ever.

You don't need your phone to be on glitter patrol, Sloane. There will be security people everywhere. Plus, Waverly and Cooper were pretty firm about not wanting people having opportunities to take pictures to slip to the paparazzi.

That's what I told myself.

That I didn't need my phone today. That I didn't have to figure out how to shove it in my cleavage. That it would fall out and I'd lose it.

And now I'd give both of my boobs and all of my cleavage to have my phone on me.

I watch Davis watching me. "That's me. Doc Adamson's nurse. Does anything hurt? Should I go find him too?"

"No."

"You're sure?"

"Yes."

"Who was that?"

Blank stare.

"How did you get in here?"

"Security system needs an upgrade."

"*Why* are you in here?"

"You should change the code on the doors immediately." He rises to his feet with the grace of a cat like he truly didn't bruise, pull, or tear anything when he went down, navigating the slick spot on the floor without issue this time. He's in suit pants and a long-sleeve button-up, definitely dressed for a wedding compared to what he's usually wearing, though his pants are splattered with coffee that also shouldn't have been in here. Hints of the tattoos covering his arms peek out at his wrists as he straightens his cuffs.

He pulls out his phone and starts snapping pictures like *he's* the freaking sheriff.

And he still doesn't answer.

It's pissing me off.

This isn't technically my museum, but after the hours I've spent after work and on the weekends to fundraise for the building, collecting display items from the Rock family and even venturing into enemy territory to get historical artifacts from people in Shipwreck's rival town of Sarcasm just a little north of here, planning the museum's grand opening, gathering volunteers, and volunteering myself now that it's open, I feel an ownership of this place.

I've done a little more than drop a few twenties into the museum fundraising jars around town and stopped by to peruse the exhibits, which are about as much as Davis did.

Though he has been doing other charity work.

Namely, being the subject of secret pictures that I've snapped of him and sent to my grandmother for the past year, telling Grandma that he's my boyfriend, Steve.

Because Grandma started making noises about sending Nigel to get me and bring me home and marry me and fill my belly with babies.

Yes, she actually says it like that.

All of it.

So can you blame me for telling the woman who raised me that I already had a boyfriend?

Slipping yesterday and saying that *Steve* had proposed though—that was probably a mistake.

Especially since Nigel's here.

Calling me out on my lies and demanding that I come home with him.

I won't—clearly—but my life will be infinitely more difficult until he accepts that I'm not moving back to Two Twigs.

"Are you sure you're not hurt?" I ask Davis.

"Yes."

"Good. Don't touch anything. *Quit taking pictures.* No one's supposed to have phones here."

He slides another unreadable look at me.

And unfortunately, I read a crap ton into that look.

You don't get yourself a pretend boyfriend without knowing a little about him when he's a real person.

And I know a little about what people say about him.

And I suspect he likes what people say about him.

But I don't. Not right now.

"Don't freaking start with that *I'm doing my job* thing. I don't believe it. Sarah Ryder told me you work at the nuclear reactor down in Corieville and just like making people think you're a spy. I'm going to get the sheriff. You need to give him a statement about what you were doing here and anything you saw or know."

Once again, the man doesn't answer as he goes back to snapping photos of the workroom.

33

But I do get a different kind of answer.

The kind that comes in the form of a swooshing noise near the front of the museum.

I know that swoosh.

Davis apparently does too.

His head jerks toward the front of the museum, then he grabs me by the arm and pulls me out of the workroom.

But unlike when Nigel grabbed me five minutes ago, this time, I get a full-body shiver at his touch.

The kind of shiver I have actively chosen to not ever get again in my life because I don't want men touching me.

Not because I don't enjoy physical activities between consenting adults—though that took me a few years to embrace after I left Two Twigs too—but because I pick terrible men.

But do I wrench myself out of Davis's grip?

Nope.

Why?

I don't want to talk about it.

"Bathroom," he murmurs so quietly that it's almost like he's not talking. "Hide. Now."

"Excuse you, *no*. If someone knows the code—"

And that's the last thing I say before everything goes from bad to worse.

Because Ray, one of the Rock cousins and fellow museum volunteer, is calling my name.

"Sloane? Sloane, you're never going to believe this. I just found an old friend of yours who got all tied up in that glitter bombing! I saw you come in here, so I offered to bring him. Sloane? You in here?"

Davis stops and looks down at me, and for the first time since I realized who he was when I spotted him on my first trip to Shipwreck, the man makes a face that's not completely straight and unreadable.

I don't know what this face is, but it's not good.

It's full of suspicion.

Worry.

It looks like he's connecting dots.

Like he knows.

He knows what I've been doing.

"Go hide in the bathroom," I hiss at Davis. "Go! Now!"

He looks at me.

Just looks at me.

Doesn't narrow his eyes, doesn't scowl, doesn't make an *are you out of your mind? That's what I just told* you *to do* look.

Simply stares at me, straight-faced.

And I'm pretty sure this straight-faced look is saying *fuck no*, even though it's not saying anything at all.

Possibly I took this pretend boyfriend thing a little too seriously if I think I can read this man's mind.

Or possibly that's the only thing a rational human being would think in this situation.

Footsteps come closer.

"*Please* go hide in the bathroom, and I'll explain later," I hiss at Davis.

The man folds his arms over his chest and looks at me, and this look, for once, is incredibly expressive.

There's no mistaking the *fuck no* on his face now too. "You knew the blond caveman was here?"

The blond—oh, crap.

Seriously?

He wants to talk about *that* ex-boyfriend?

The one who used to date Davis's friend Ellie?

The one who was still dating Davis's friend Ellie when he started dating me, making me *the other woman*?

The one I still can't think about without flushing with shame at knowing what I did to Ellie?

"What does Patrick have to do with this?"

Davis blinks.

This one's actually a startled blink.

And we're running out of time.

I need to come clean.

But more importantly, I need to get the damn sheriff because *someone broke into my museum.*

Except Nigel's *right here.*

Even if he hasn't said anything, I can feel him here, making my skin crawl and guilt and shame eke out of my pores, and that's enough to make me shiver.

And that's the shiver that tells me what I have to do next.

The footsteps get closer.

Nigel's voice answers Ray, confirming I'm not shivering for nothing, and I shiver harder.

And then I take my life into my own hands—apparently *again* today—and I fling myself at Davis.

I can explain the Steve thing away.

Nigel apparently already knows who Davis really is, so I'll tell Nigel I couldn't tell Grandma that I was dating a guy who was in the boy band Bro Code fifteen years ago. That it was hard enough to tell her that I was dating a guy with tattoos and thick facial hair and a manbun, because Grandma doesn't approve of any of those things.

I'll say I made up a fake name for Davis to keep Grandma from having a complete heart attack, since we all know those boy band guys go around sleeping with everything on two legs and sometimes sheep too—yes, also Grandma's words—and an innocent thing like me deserves someone who's only had sex for practice with those loose women and not farm animals.

Also Grandma's words.

As grateful as I'll always be that Grandma stepped in very early in my childhood to raise my brother and me, I'm horrified that I used to think sentences like that were normal.

And I'm taking a special delight in what I'm doing now because it's complete rebellion against the things she taught me to be afraid of.

I'm not *just* flinging my arms around Davis.

I'm also pressing my lips to his, squeezing the hug tighter than I should, waiting for him to shove me away—at least I'll have a great breakup story and an excuse to tell Grandma that I've decided to go live in a convent or something—but he doesn't.

That by itself is shocking enough.

But what he does next?

The man—my pretend boyfriend who doesn't know he's my pretend boyfriend—slips his arms around my waist, angles his head, and kisses me back.

Soft mustache and beard tickle my mouth and chin.

37

Warm, firm lips suckle at my lower lip.

I taste toasted marshmallow and smell pine needles.

One of his hands lifts to tangle in my hair.

My belly drops.

My nipples contract.

My vagina does too.

Oh my god.

I'm kissing Davis Remington.

I'm kissing Davis Remington.

I let one of my hands drift up into his hair too.

Davis's hair is so soft.

Like, *crazy* soft.

No wonder he keeps it long.

Hair this soft shouldn't be cut short. It should be long. Luxurious. Pettable.

Pettable?

Fuck.

I go two years without dating, kissing, or even having recreational sex with a man, and the first time I need to kiss one just to keep up appearances of a fake boyfriend, I'm fantasizing about his hair and calling him pettable.

But also—

God, I miss kissing.

The lights flash on around me, but I can only tell by the shift behind my eyelids.

"There you—*oh*. Oh, my. I—"

Another unexpected voice joins us. "Ray, the museum's —*oh my god*. Out. *Out!*"

Tillie Jean.

Tillie Jean to the rescue.

Am I still kissing Davis?

I am.

I'm still kissing Davis.

And he's still kissing me back, his tongue swiping over the seam of my lips, and *oh my god*, I haven't been wet this fast when kissing a guy in—well, ever.

All because the boy band crush of my teenage years licked my lips.

"*Sloane,*" Nigel's deep, chiding voice says, and that does it.

That jerks me back to reality.

I break the kiss, but keep my hand in Davis's hair because apparently my hormones are still half in control of this situation now.

I blink around the room.

Tillie Jean is gaping at me, but it's like a smile-gape.

She knows.

She knows all about my fake boyfriend situation.

She and another of our friends helped me learn to use photo manipulation software. They helped me take the pictures. They egged me on.

And we kept it a secret from the entire town—naturally, because it's flirting the line of being against the unspoken town rule of being safe for celebrities—which is why Ray's lip is curled up in confusion.

I mean, Ray's a sweet guy, young but sweet, so he'd probably be confused no matter what, but this is extra confusing.

Until he starts to grin, like he thinks we're perfect together.

He's such a romantic.

He'd totally instantly go to shipping us.

But Nigel—

Nigel is staring at me like I'll be covered in a true crime podcast very, very soon.

Yes, her murderer says she had it coming. That saving her from herself was the only way to save her eternal soul.

I risk a glance at Davis.

And it's official.

I'm fucked.

3

Sloane

I DON'T KNOW how to silently communicate *just go with it, I'll explain later, holy shit, was that kiss real?*, so I settle for making a face that I hope says *sorry*, and I turn to my friends and whatever Nigel is.

And that's when I see my salvation.

"Oh my god, *out!*" I shriek at Nigel. "You're getting glitter all over the museum!"

Nigel's glittered up like a Christmas snow globe gone wrong. There's the big spray of glitter on his chest that was my fault, but he also has it all down his arms and pants. In his hair. On his face.

He folds his arms over his overly-glittered chest. "Oh my *god*? What's happened to your language?"

Dammit.

Might as well have said *fuck me sideways, you won't believe this goddamn shit.*

"Nigel, meet Davis. My fiancé. Yes, yes, I lied to Grandma and told her his name was Steve because you know how she is about former musicians who fuck—have carnal relations with sheep, but we're madly in love and we're getting married next weekend because the ol' ovaries aren't getting any younger, and if we're going to have six kids, we have to get on it and pray *super* hard for triplets."

Davis stares at me.

Nigel growls.

And Tillie Jean—god bless Tillie Jean, who's also glittery, though less so—lunges for Davis and smothers him in a hug. "Oh my god, Davis, *finally*," she says. "I thought you'd never pop the question. You two are going to be so happy together. Ray, go get Max, and *do not* spoil this for Sloane. *Do not even tell your boyfriend*. She gets to tell the whole town, *not you*, or I'll empty every last glitter bomb that the glitter squad collected today and use that glitter to make sure that you fart glitter for the next fifty years. *Do you understand me?*"

"How does a woman get *two* men that hot in her lifetime?" Ray mutters.

Tillie Jean releases Davis and spins to face Ray again, backing up against us until both Davis and I are forced to also step back toward the workroom.

"Sloane hasn't had any other hot boyfriends."

"There was that guy she was dating who was cheating on Ellie Ryder—"

Davis clears his throat.

Lava replaces the blood in my face.

I don't know what that noise meant from Davis.

Nigel clears his throat too, but this one, I can interpret.

This one means *sex before marriage is a sin, Sloane, and I'm going to punish you for the rest of your natural life.*

It would be so much sexier if a hero from one of my friend Henri's romance novels said that than it is when Nigel implies it.

"*Go get Max,*" Tillie Jean orders again. "And so help me, if you ruin this announcement for Sloane... I know things, Ray, and I *will* repeat them."

"Okay! Okay! I'm going. I'll be back with Max in two minutes, I swear."

"Stupid dresses without pockets," Tillie Jean mutters. "I need my damn phone."

"*Right?*" I gasp.

Gasping is pretty much all I'm capable of now that I've spilled the CliffsNotes version of our story to my fake boyfriend.

Especially with Nigel glaring at me.

And that pisses me off too.

We were friends once.

Friends should be happy for friends when they have good news.

Not that my good news is real, but I haven't seen Nigel in far too long for him to know I'm lying.

Especially since Davis has an arm wrapped around my waist and is holding me close to his body.

He smells like camping in a forest. Like a starry sky next to a campfire. S'mores in the middle of summer.

And his arm—my god.

The man's lean, but he's strong.

So strong.

Stop it stop it stop it, Sloane.

I owe him an explanation.

Also some undying gratitude.

But wait—*why* is he going along with this?

Does he...? I gasp again, this one more of a croaking gasp.

Does he *like* me?

Oh, fuck.

Is this going to get complicated and ugly?

Of fucking course it is, dumbass. You made up a fake boyfriend who was just snooping around in your museum while someone else was here apparently trying to rob the place.

I shiver again.

Then remember that Davis was also unauthorized to be in here and that we need the sheriff, and *this is too complicated.*

Can I please have one emergency at a time?

"So you actually know each other," Nigel says as Ray's shoes slap over the wooden floor and back toward the door.

"They've been dating for at least a year, and saw each other around town more or less since Sloane moved here like five years ago, so why would they not know each other?" Tillie Jean gives Nigel a once-over. "Who are you?"

"I'm Sloane's fiancé."

"*Oh my god*, shut *up*," I snap.

He rears back.

Davis makes a noise that might actually be a laugh.

And wouldn't that be something?

I don't think I've ever heard him laugh.

Or even seen him smile.

Anytime he's in a bar or restaurant in town with his friends, he's just so straight-laced.

Like something terrible happened in his past and it made him forget how to smile.

I don't even remember him smiling the night we played darts, and I was hella funny that night. I think.

See again, that night was a little hazy. I more have vibes than actual memories.

Focus, Sloane.

"Tillie Jean, this is Nigel Hipplewait. I grew up with him. Our grandparents thought we were adorable together, but we never dated, and we are *not* engaged."

Nigel pulls himself up to his full six-foot, four-inch height. "We did too, and it's an arranged marriage."

Tillie Jean looks him up and down again. "Oh, I'm pretty sure I would've heard about it if Sloane was arranged to be married to a guy who looks like you."

I sigh.

It's incredibly annoying that Nigel is, by all objective and subjective standards, completely gorgeous.

He was born with thick black hair that has always fallen in the most perfect way possible over his broad forehead. His eyebrows aren't too bushy or too skinny. His blue eyes are set not too deep and not too shallow. His nose is the right kind of prominent without being too big. His jaw square, his lips scandalously thick. He even has handsome ears.

Handsome ears.

What are handsome ears?

They're what Nigel has, along with the build of a quarterback—which, again, he was in high school—the hands of a sculptor, and even handsome fingernails.

And to top it all off, all of his features are perfectly symmetrical.

If Michelangelo were alive today, he'd use Nigel as his one and only model for eternity. If we lived in Regency England, he'd be a duke. If Nigel had gone to Hollywood instead of following in his grandfather's footsteps, *People* would've retired the "Sexiest Man Alive" feature because Nigel would've won every single year for his whole entire life.

And I fucking hate Nigel.

I'm not sure I realized just how much I hated him until right now, and there's a large chunk of guilt and shame swelling up in my chest over acknowledging to myself that I hate him—*hate is for the wicked, Sloane*—but I do.

I. Hate. Him.

"Welp, now that you've seen that Davis and I are happy and engaged, you can leave," I tell Nigel.

"I need to hear it from him," Nigel says.

Tillie Jean makes a choking noise. "Because you don't believe a woman?"

"Because I know how Sloane can be."

Davis's grip on me tightens. "Watch yourself."

The quiet authority in his warning makes me shiver.

The good kind of shiver.

The kind of shiver that I'm never supposed to shiver for a man again because if I shiver this way over a man, and we fall into the sack, and we start dating, I'll discover he's secretly taking pictures of my feet to sell on that GrippaPeen video-on-demand subscription site, or he'll give me a sob story about how his mother's dying of cancer and he needs five thousand dollars to pay her bills and I'll be the dummy who gives it to him even though he's already told me before that his mother's dead, or he'll convince me that my apartment smells like pickles and we have to move, only to find that he's somehow removed me from the lease, thus leaving me homeless when we break up.

I shake my head while Davis and Nigel have a staring match. "Can we please focus on what's important right now?"

"You mean this lie?" Nigel says.

Once again, it's Davis to the rescue. "It's not a lie."

I suppress another shiver and look up at him.

And my belly drops.

He stares straight into my eyes, and for a guy who keeps a pretty straight expression most of the time, he's being very expressive right now.

I owe him an explanation.

This isn't a small favor.

I'm going to pay for this.

He wants something in return.

And I need to quit thinking I can read anything at all in Davis's expression because *who does that?*

We're practically strangers.

"And as you said, my love, we have bigger issues." Davis breaks eye contact and looks at Nigel. "Were you invited?"

Oh, I can answer that. "No, he was *not.*"

"How did you get past security?"

"That's an *excellent* question." Tillie Jean turns to Nigel again. "How *did* you get past security?"

Nigel quirks a brow, which makes him look like a dark-haired Prince Charming from the Shrek movies. "I'm hardly a threat to anyone."

"You walk in here trying to break up my best friend and her fiancé, and I'm going to classify you as a threat."

"I'm a preacher."

"That's not the flex you think it is."

Nigel rolls his eyes.

One of my hands curls into a fist.

Davis tightens his grasp on me even harder. "Tillie Jean, we need the sheriff."

She squints one eye at him. "I don't think the sheriff is the one ordained in town to do impromptu weddings, and as much as I love you both, you're not upstaging my sister-in-law's wedding day."

I freaking love Tillie Jean.

I would give her a kidney. I would sell pictures of my feet for her. I would move out of a pickle-scented house that wasn't actually pickle-scented for her.

That's how much I love her.

"There was a break-in," I say.

My friend's eyebrows meet her hairline. "What? When? Where?"

"Sheriff first, details later," Davis says.

"*Here?*" TJ looks down at Davis's pants like she's just realizing something more is off than me kissing him and him going along with this fake fiancé ruse. "*Today?* Dammit. I have to sober up, don't I?"

Davis doesn't answer her directly, but he does answer.

48

And it's oddly calming to have him issuing orders. "Everyone needs to leave."

Tillie Jean looks at Nigel. "You. Out. Now."

"Sloane—" Nigel starts.

I growl at him.

He draws back, clearly shocked.

Probably thinking I need an exorcism.

"You can talk to Sloane later." Tillie Jean pulls a move I've seen her do on each of her brothers and forces Nigel to step backward merely by walking at him in the right way. "But right now, you're talking to my brother's security detail about how you got into town when you weren't on the guest list. Sloane, Davis, I'll be back with the sheriff in the next five minutes. Please keep your clothes on."

Nigel bristles. "I'm not leaving Sloane alone with this—"

"If you want to keep your ball sack intact, you won't finish that sentence," Tillie Jean says. "Move."

Davis gives the subtlest of subtle headshakes as we watch Tillie Jean back Nigel all the way out of the room.

"Five minutes. Clothes on," she calls to us.

The museum door closes, and silence settles around us.

I try to pull away from Davis, but he doesn't release me.

So I look up at him again.

Big mistake.

Big mistake.

The full intensity of his gaze lands on me in a way that makes me want to confess everything.

Probably more than everything.

I'd take the blame for every glitter bomb ever launched in Shipwreck. I'd own up to being the one who taped a kazoo to Waverly's armored SUV's tailpipe a year ago in an incident that shut down the entire town for three hours. And I'd claim credit for the goats that got loose during my first trip to Shipwreck and still are all over town, along with their offspring now.

None of which I've done or had anything to do with, but I *want* to confess to everything when he stares at me like that.

You know the way.

Like he's figuring out that he's been my secret pretend boyfriend for the past year.

And I'm still unprepared for his first statement on the situation.

"You named me Steve?"

I force a bright smile that probably looks like the expression a panicked goat would make when it comes face-to-face with a lion. "Haha, yeah, probably should've gone with Colt or Steel or Aiden. Actually, I don't know why I would've thought you looked like an Aiden. But there was an Aiden that my grandmother hated when I was growing up, and I don't mean my brother, I mean the other Aiden. The one who used to draw penises on my arm in math class. Although sometimes I hated my brother too, but you know how it goes with siblings."

He's not saying a word.

Not interrupting me.

In fact, his gaze is dipping to my lips.

That kiss recreates itself in my mind, and the only

reason I don't shiver again is that I've decided I'm done shivering today. Possibly for the rest of my life.

I'm all shivered out, and I'm in control of my body.

My eyes dip to his lips, and my nipples, vagina, belly, knees, and heart demonstrate that I'm full of shit if I think I'm in control of anything right now.

"My grandmother's the type who thinks a woman's job is to get married and have babies, and I have a pretty crappy track record with men, so I've decided I'm never getting married, and I'm not interested in doing the single mother thing, but she wouldn't stop asking who I was dating, no matter how many times I told her I like being single and that my life is fulfilling all on its own. It used to be funny, like, haha, of course that's what older generations think, but the past two or three years, she's gotten… harder? Yeah, harder about it, so I just kinda…snapped… one day, and the next thing I knew, I was sending her a picture of you and making up stories about us dating so that she'd leave me the ever-loving *fuck* alone about it."

He keeps watching me, not saying anything, and my mouth keeps verbally vomiting when I should probably shut up. "I swear on my honor as a human being whose life has mostly been guided by guilt and shame, even if I'm working on getting over that, that I never once imagined that we were actually dating. I didn't tell anyone else we were dating. I mean, Tillie Jean was in on it, but it's Tillie Jean. If there's mischief, she's in, you know? But she knows the truth. She knows why. I didn't send pictures to anyone else. I didn't fantasize about actually dating you, and I have never masturbated to thoughts of you."

Crap.

Craaaaap.

The minute you say you haven't done anything, that's like saying you *have* done it, even if I *haven't*, but I certainly will now after kissing him, and unlike Mr. Straight Face, I have a face so expressive that outer space aliens could probably translate everything that's going through my brain right now.

Davis continues to stare at me in silence.

Heat floods my entire body, including my eyeballs.

No.

No no nope nope nope.

I will not cry.

I won't.

Even in absolute mortified embarrassment.

"Okay," he says.

I suck in a breath so fast that I choke.

He releases his grip on me and lets me cough myself out.

You know what's dumb?

It's so dumb that I'm worried about what he thinks about this whole situation when we're not even really friends.

We're people who know a little bit about each other who once played a game of darts and then today shared a kiss during a very stressful time, and that's it. That's the end.

"Okay?" I manage to say through my coughs.

"Okay," he repeats.

"You're not mad?"

"Anger serves no purpose."

I slide a look back at the workroom. "What were you doing here?"

"Being the good guy."

"Good guys don't say things like that."

He doesn't reply out loud.

But I hear myself in my own head claiming to have never masturbated while thinking about him.

Which is the truth.

It is.

So maybe he's telling the truth.

"You want to get married?" he says.

"*Want?* God, no. I have awful taste in men. But I wouldn't mind if my grandmother believed I was married."

He looks back at the workroom too.

Then at me once more. "Okay."

"Okay? What does that even mean, *okay?*"

"I'll marry you. Next weekend. Like you said."

If I were capable of breathing, I'd be choking again.

But I'm beyond bodily functions working like they're automatically supposed to.

"Staged," he adds. "Not for real."

"Why would you agree to fake marry me?"

"Family's gonna family. Have to occasionally out-family them."

That's a bullshit answer and we both know it. "Do you have a secret X-rated comic book collection? Do you bet on illegal hamster races? Is your long-term life plan to cozy up to rich old ladies to get yourself countless inheritances while keeping people like me on the side for fun and sex? Wait. Am I the old lady? *Am I the old lady?*"

He doesn't answer.

I suck in a long breath through my nose and look up at the ceiling tiles. "He's not saying anything. Of course he's not answering."

"Have my own money, rarely think about hamsters, and for the comic books—is yes or no the right answer? Could see that going either way."

"Any other time and place, I'd agree with you. Today, no is the right answer."

He shrugs a shoulder the barest amount. "Then no."

"Are you just saying that to make me happy?"

Once again, all I get is a straight-faced stare.

"Right. Right. It's pretend, so it doesn't matter if you have secrets."

"Everyone has secrets."

"Yes, but I need to know that no one in my hometown will see *Steve* on the local news for having murdered a man."

"You have an ex who made the news for murdering someone?"

"No, but there's always a first time, isn't there?"

"Could be justifiable homicide."

"*Oh my god*. Are you marrying me to get an alibi?" I flap my hand toward the workroom. "Was that your accomplice? Are you trying to steal something from my museum? Are you involved in some kind of extortion scheme?"

"Pretend marrying. No. I don't steal and I don't help criminals."

But what's he doing here? Who was in the workroom? And where's the sheriff? "Why would you do this?"

"I like helping people."

"So you just go around agreeing to fake marry women to get their grandmothers off their backs?"

He looks me straight in the eye. "World's been good to me. Why not be good back?"

"Again, that's not an answer."

"It's true."

"Is it the full truth?"

"No."

"What's the full truth?"

"I'm offering fake marriage. That's it."

This is too easy. *Entirely* too easy. "Is this the first time you've offered to fake marry someone?"

"No."

It says something about this conversation that I'm not actually surprised, and I think I believe him. "Were there pictures?"

"Yes."

"Just one wedding?"

"No."

"How many times have you fake-married women to help them out?"

"Fewer than five."

I squeeze my eyes shut.

For as much as I think I believe him, I also can't believe anyone would subject themselves to more than one fake wedding. "You've fake-married women four times?"

"Legally, I'm not allowed to say anything else."

Fucker. "How many of them thought fake marrying you was a path to romance and a real forever?"

"Just my sister."

Speechless.

I'm actually speechless.

In all of the dozens of times I've seen this man in Shipwreck, I've never once witnessed him crack a joke.

I'm sure he has before. I mean, what human being hasn't? I've even heard Nigel crack jokes.

But Davis's reply is so dry and straightforward that I believe him.

"That was a joke," he says.

And *now* I don't believe him.

I think he did marry his sister once. And I don't know if I want to hear the full story or not.

I shake my head. "You'd agree to fake-marry me simply because you're a nice guy?"

"Are you always this suspicious?"

"Around men? Yes."

His gaze once more lingers on the door to the workroom, then slowly peruses the displays here in Thorny Rock's wardrobe room.

The door swooshes again, telling us that Tillie Jean is likely back with the sheriff.

"You grew up with that guy?" Davis says, looking toward the front of the museum where Tillie Jean pushed Nigel out a few minutes ago, leaving a trail of glitter that'll be hell to get rid of.

"Yes."

"You were friends?"

My history with Nigel is so much more complex than just *friends*. "I thought so."

"He know what *friend* means?"

56

"I was raised to not speak ill of preachers."

Once again, he looks at me like he's reading my soul.

Like he knows how much work it's taken for me to not feel guilty for breathing, to embrace my body as a gift and sex as something that's not shameful, to sometimes choose myself over the expectations of the people I grew up with and the woman who raised me when no one else would take me and my brother in.

But I have no intention of getting any closer to Davis than I have to in order to finish pulling off this ruse. "Thank you for your help. If there's anything I can do to make it up to you, I will."

While I'd make the offer to anyone, and I mean it, there's something about the way Davis has been watching me that's put me at ease.

That's led me into a false sense of security.

I'm doing it *again*.

I'm believing the best in people.

But as I watch him, something shifts in his expression, and I know I'm going to pay for this.

Probably dearly.

Of course I will.

I have terrible taste in men.

Before he even opens his mouth, my stomach is already dropping. My shoulders are already bunching. My breath is getting shallower and shallower, and my pulse is pretending to be a cheetah.

His deep brown eyes connect with mine, and I feel his words more than I hear them.

"Appreciate that. Because I need a favor."

4

Davis Remington, aka a quiet man of mystery who is being very difficult right now

<REDACTED>

5

Sloane

You'd think two days would be enough to work through the stress of my new reality, but Monday night, as I'm on my way to fulfill my end of a bargain that I made with a devil, my pulse won't slow down.

I'm okay.

Nobody's hurt.

Everything's fine.

But my body is on an adrenaline high, and I can't decide if I love it or hate it.

Everything's been wrong since Nigel showed up at the wedding on Saturday. Since I found Davis and a mystery person in what was supposed to be an empty museum.

We gave our statements to the sheriff, who thinks that it's likely someone at the wedding was playing a game to practice for an upcoming Hollywood role. While he took photos of the workroom and dusted for prints, he says he's not expecting to find anything. Only the coffee cup was broken, with prints on it belonging to one of our volunteers who forgot they'd taken their coffee with them to the museum the day before the wedding, and nothing was stolen. The sheriff and the rest of Waverly's security team are convinced no one other than Nigel had gotten into town to crash the wedding, so the sheriff agreed to add extra patrols around the museum, but otherwise, they say it was the dumbest time to commit a crime, so it's likely it was just a joy break-in.

After what Davis asked for his favor, I don't agree.

And after I agreed to do the favor for him in exchange for him playing my pretend fiancé, including having a fake wedding with Nigel as a witness this coming weekend, my entire life is spinning out of control.

And it's my own fault.

Approaching the house Davis told me to meet him at after I was finished with work today isn't helping.

Not just because all of my patients wanted to talk today about how I kept my relationship with Davis a secret the past year, and I was already frazzled before my errand that's the favor that I owe Davis.

I'm also keyed up because Davis's house isn't actually a house.

It's a camper trailer hidden in the woods. Like the kind you'd pull behind a truck. A *big* truck—this is one of the largest campers I've ever seen, like the kind that's an inch short of being a tour-bus-type RV—but still not a permanent structure here.

Probably.

With the fall leaves half-off the trees as dusk settles two days after the wedding, it's even more eerie.

Especially since between the Shipwreck gossip chain and my work at the museum, I know all about this little piece of land, even if it's the first time I've visited in person. There's a run-down cabin sitting a little ways behind the camper with an ancient outhouse leaning in the slight breeze just beyond it, and lots of clumps of scraggly bushes all around it too. The cabin's porch has caved in, and the roof is half blown away. It was condemned years ago, supposedly owned by a now long-deceased descendant of the founder of Sarcasm who didn't fully fit in Sarcasm but was never accepted into Shipwreck either.

Rumor has it the former owner of the cabin died without any heirs, but I don't actually know how long ago that was. I also don't know if he lived here when he died or if he'd lived out his last days in a nursing home.

Rumor mill says both.

I wonder how many people in town know that Davis is staying in a trailer up here.

Gonna guess not many. If they did, I would've heard about it today at the very least, sooner with the company I keep.

Not only is Tillie Jean, who knows everything, one of my best friends, but I've also made friends with other people who know everything about everyone in Shipwreck and the surrounding areas. After my last breakup, I dove headfirst into volunteering with the historical society, and there were two things I quickly learned about my fellow volunteers.

One, if something happened in a five-mile radius of Shipwreck, they'd hear about it. And two, the townspeople here have a *lot* of historical data about Shipwreck.

Including maps.

Apparently I'm more fascinated by historical artifacts than I ever knew before. Participating with the historical society in getting the Thorny Rock Historical Museum opened just off the square in town has felt like finding my purpose, even more than helping patients every day as a nurse.

And I've stared at this lot on the map more than I'm comfortable with now that I know Davis is here. At least for tonight.

For our clandestine meeting where I'll fulfill my half of our bargain so that he does his half.

Cheating and divorce are both bad, so having a fake husband really will get my grandmother and Nigel off my back.

I park my car on a leaf-littered gravel parking pad next to the trailer, consciously aware of the fact that there's not another car here. No motorcycle either.

So where did Davis park?

Do I get cell signal here?

I check, and—yep.

There's signal.

I climb out of my car and approach the trailer door. Knock once. Then twice.

Wait a bit.

Knock a third time.

When he doesn't answer, I back down the steps.

Maybe there's another entrance? I start circling the trailer, leaves crunching beneath my feet, suddenly unsure if I'm in the right place.

I'm reaching for my phone when I feel it.

I'm not alone.

I am so serious when I say my heart cannot take much more. It's hammering like I'm doing one of Tillie Jean's senior aerobics classes.

Don't knock how hard she makes us work.

There's a reason all of our senior citizens are in tip-top shape.

I wish one of them were here with me now.

Nana Rock has some biceps.

She could help with whatever I'm about to find as I turn around, expecting a bear or a grizzled mountain hermit, and instead—

"You're early," Davis says.

Did *he* make noise when he was stepping on the leaves?

No, he did not.

Is *he* panting like he just ran a marathon?

Also no.

He's standing there holding five firewood logs under one arm—*how?*—and catching me inspecting his camper.

"I was efficient." I almost manage to not stutter at all.

Now that I've committed a crime for this man, I'm feeling less sure of myself than I did two nights ago when I convinced myself this could be a harmless trade to get myself a fake husband.

He doesn't answer.

No, the man simply sets his firewood down, then walks up the steps and opens the door.

Opens it.

Not locked.

I've never seen his former bandmates without a security detail—and yes, I've seen all four of them in Shipwreck, including two days ago at Cooper and Waverly's wedding—and here Davis is, staying in an unlocked camper just outside of a town with residents nosy enough to break in and have a look around.

Or is he the one breaking into someone else's camper?

He didn't have any problems breaking into the museum the other night, did he?

This *is* the real Davis Remington...isn't it?

I shake my head and follow him.

Of course this is the real Davis Remington. An entire town of people wouldn't have gaslit me about that.

I don't think, anyway.

Would they?

No. Absolutely not. I don't matter enough to gaslight about something like this, and if it was a prank on the newbie when I moved here, they would've cracked by now.

Plus, I *know* it's him.

The first time I ever saw him was that week I was here for the other wedding. I was supposed to be digging for buried treasure in the town square with the wedding party, including my boyfriend at the time—the one Davis called the blond caveman the other day, the one who had a girlfriend he didn't tell me about when we started dating, the wedding where my boyfriend's ex-girlfriend was maid of honor to his best man—and I looked up, and there Davis was.

The notoriously reclusive fifth member of my favorite boy band from my teenage years.

My secret crush.

The guy whose posters I hid beneath my old school workbooks and piles of papers that I told my grandmother I kept because I wanted to make sure I never forgot everything I'd learned.

The guy whose concert I finally got tickets to while I was in nursing school in Copper Valley but never got to attend because the band called it off a week before they were supposed to do the show that I was going to.

When I saw Davis that day, I second-guessed myself.

What was the likelihood that he'd just be strolling down the main drag in a small town an hour north of the city where he grew up without security or anyone else with him? I'd just seen a tall, slender, tattooed, bearded, man-bunned man, and my brain made the connection without any real evidence.

Not like pictures of him were still all over the tabloids so I could see how much he'd changed in the decade or so since the band split up. How he'd aged. How many new tattoos he had. What he'd done with his hair.

I heard a bit about him here and there, since the guys in the band all grew up in Copper Valley and you can't spend two weeks in the city without someone mentioning its most famous residents, but I'd never seen him in person.

Yet I was still so sure it was him.

And then I saw him on the balcony of the restaurant across the way, talking to his friends, and I knew.

I knew that it was him because he was with Ellie Ryder, his former bandmate's sister, and my boyfriend's ex-girlfriend.

The sun hit him just right on that balcony, and I *knew.*

Much like I have this gut feeling that I can trust him.

That he *is* the good guy in this situation.

Problem is, my gut has steered me wrong so many times that I don't trust it anymore.

So why did I commit a minor crime in exchange for him pretending to be my fiancé?

Because the sheriff isn't taking the break-in seriously.

Davis is the closest thing I have to answers.

He pauses in the doorway without letting me in. "You have it?"

I straighten and smile. "I have something even *better.*"

The look he gives me suggests he doubts that whatever I've done, it's *better.* And he manages to do that without twitching any of his facial muscles.

Huh.

Maybe he's more expressive than I gave him credit for. Maybe you just have to watch him closely.

I wiggle my phone at him. "I didn't steal it. I took pictures instead. So no one has to know."

Oh, that is *definitely* a look. "You took pictures."

"Yep."

"With your phone."

He asks a lot of questions that sound like statements. "Don't usually take my Polaroid with me."

"Is your phone backed up to a cloud?"

"Is there anyone who's ever had to upgrade a phone these days who doesn't back it up to a cloud?"

He purses his lips together.

Davis.

Davis Remington.

The man who straight-faces everything.

He's pursing his lips together.

Visibly swallowing too.

Definitely displeased with my ingenuity.

I'd call this a *him* problem, except I'd still like him to fake marry me.

Some to get my grandmother off my back.

Some because it'll give me the joy of a lifetime to make Nigel watch me marry my teenage boy band crush when Nigel didn't even believe Davis knew who I was.

Davis holds his hand out. "Give me your phone."

"I can transfer them to you over Bluetooth."

"Do you know how to fully delete files so that the internet as a whole has no record of their existence?"

Would you look at that?

He's fully frustrated.

I didn't think that could happen. In all of the pictures I've snuck of him over the past year, he's always wearing the same expression.

Always.

But I have managed to visibly exasperate him.

Guess this answers a lingering question I've had for a while.

I am, in fact, the reason all of my past relationships haven't worked.

Or possibly every last man on this planet simply sucks.

Actually, thinking about my history with men—Nigel, the boyfriend I was dating the first time I came to Shipwreck, the gaslighters, the thieves, and the narcissists— yeah, I'm pretty sure every man on this planet simply sucks.

"Please give me your phone." Davis's words are slow and calm, not unlike how I speak to irrational patients at work sometimes.

"Will I get it back?"

"Yes."

"Before or after you get a copy of the pictures so that I don't have to go make another excuse to see Pop?"

He doesn't answer.

I'm starting to get used to that.

It's starting to annoy me too.

"Tell me why, again, you wanted to see Thorny Rock's —*aah umph.*"

Huh.

I'm inside the camper now, and the door's shut. "Well. This isn't getting weirder by the minute. Also—hey! How did you get my phone?"

He lifts it over his head, and since he has a few inches on me, I can't reach it as I stand there, going up on my tiptoes on the creaky vinyl flooring inside the small, enclosed space that smells vaguely like curry chicken.

He swipes to unlock my phone with it angled just right for face ID, and then opens my photo app.

Okay, that takes talent.

Anytime my friends ask me to take a picture, their

camera and photo apps are always in different places and I have to search for a while.

Not Davis.

He just *knew*.

"Are you actually a spy? I've heard the rumors. The job at the nuclear reactor is a cover story, isn't it? It makes sense. You being there when someone was breaking into my museum despite me not seeing you at all the rest of the wedding, fake weddings with an untold number of women—including your sister—clandestine meetings at secret trailers in the woods, abnormal abilities with electronics, you never smile, no one knows if you're dating anyone—*oh my god*, that's what your previous fake weddings were about, weren't they? You were on missions."

The man doesn't acknowledge me.

Heat creeps up my chest.

I hate how much I've been second-guessing everything I know since Saturday.

And now I'm wondering if I've accidentally put myself in danger by believing I know Davis because I developed a parasocial relationship with him in my teenage years, then saw him as a real person—but still mostly out of my sphere of existence—once I moved to Shipwreck.

One game of darts does not make a friendship.

Nor does a year of telling lies about him being my boyfriend.

I sneak a glance around the interior of the camper, looking for any evidence of blood or dead bodies while telling myself I'm being overly paranoid.

There's a galley kitchen with 1990s-style oak cabinets

and ivory Formica countertops. No food on the counters. Across from the kitchen, a closed computer sits on the beige dining table with built-in brown benches on either side. No stickers on the lid, very much unlike my small laptop, which I've decorated with stickers from all over Shipwreck and Copper Valley.

Beyond that is a door that I assume leads to a bedroom. To my other side, there's a small sitting area with a tan leather couch along the side wall of the trailer.

Maybe it's not a bedroom back past the kitchen.

Maybe it's a special operations spy center.

Am I breathing heavily?

Or am I breathing too light?

Davis shoots me a look. "Do you need a paper bag?"

"Are you going to murder me?"

No answer.

I do get *quite* the look though.

This one involves his eyebrows and his mouth and a little tic high on his cheek, high enough to see it over the beard, not high enough to impact his eyelids.

And a small part of me dies a little.

I had such a crush on this man when I was a lost and lonely teenager feeling like everything I did was wrong and that I was definitely never going to be a good enough person to escape the pits of hell.

And I could have a crush on him again if I wasn't over men and if he wasn't clearly as annoyed with me as every other man I've ever dated has ultimately been.

"That wasn't a no," I point out.

He hands my phone back without a word, but I get the

feeling if he *were* to use his words, he'd say something like, *Thanks for coming, get the hell out now.*

I open the photo app.

The pictures of Thorny Rock's diary are gone. All sixty-four of them.

I got every page that he wrote on.

And I made sure they were clear too.

None of my other photos appear to be missing.

Not even the photos that I took at the wedding and realized later that Davis was in.

"Are we still getting fake married?" I ask.

He's head down over his own phone. "I don't back out of my promises."

"You didn't ask about wedding plans."

"Tillie Jean's on it."

He's not wrong. Tillie Jean and her other sister-in-law, Annika, got us a room at the winery just outside of Sarcasm, and TJ's working on picking someone who can be a fake minister with real-looking paperwork.

She has no shortage of options. Because she's Tillie Jean.

I lean against the countertop and keep watching him mostly ignore me. "You're very well-informed."

"Not difficult."

"I saw Nigel today."

"Condolences."

Freaking Nigel. "He's taken a short-term pastoring gig in Copper Valley because he knew that I'd be stubborn about accepting what's best for me and that it might take me some time to come to my senses."

71

Davis lifts his head and gives me another blank look that's not quite blank.

This one either means *truly, you can go,* or *I'd like to put my boot through Nigel's head.*

"Those were basically his exact words," I say. "Also, I'm sorry about what I said the other day about you fornicating with sheep. I don't believe that. My grandmother has lived...a peculiar life...and she's not entirely in touch with reality. Really, it was funny and cute when I was growing up. But I don't know if she's changed or if I have, but it's not funny anymore."

"Far from the worst thing I've ever heard."

"Nigel can't get away again to come up here for a few days, so neither of us needs to worry about him surprising us anywhere."

Intense brown eyes study me like he's deciding if I'm stupid for believing that, or if he's having second thoughts about getting involved and fake marrying me now that he has what he wants.

Truth?

I didn't bring all of what Davis wanted in the format he wanted it because I was afraid he'd back out of the wedding.

I'm dangling little bits so that he doesn't have a reason to bolt before I get my fake husband.

"Plus, he's still super glittery, so you see him coming a mile away," I add.

"Heard you started that."

"I'm not always at my brightest when I'm panicking. You are *exceptionally* well-informed. Are you sure you're not a spy?"

After one lingering look that I'm almost positive means *this conversation is about over*, he resumes studying the pictures on his phone.

"Does your phone back up to the cloud?"

"No."

"Just out of curiosity—"

"Only people who bring me what I actually asked for get a hint of a real answer to that question."

I'd ask how he could read my mind, but who wouldn't be in this situation and desperately want to know why he wants a centuries-old pirate diary that said pirate's descendant adamantly refused to let us put in the town museum about the pirate?

While living on a curious piece of land near Shipwreck?

And that circles me back to the one obvious answer to my question that I've been avoiding acknowledging to myself since Saturday night.

Davis is hunting for Thorny Rock's treasure, and he thinks there's a clue in the diary.

And if my hunch is right, then I also think that Pop Rock, Tillie Jean's grandfather, *knows* there's a clue in the diary.

Why else would Pop have given us so many Thorny Rock artifacts but refused to let the museum hold the diary?

Thorny Rock died over two hundred years ago.

Pop never would've met him.

Pop doesn't have any grandparents or great-aunts or great-uncles that he would remember from even his youngest childhood days who would've ever met Thorny Rock either.

There's something in the diary.

And these people think it has to do with a treasure.

"What are you going to do with it if you find it?" I whisper.

He once again looks up from his phone to study me. "What would *you* do with it?"

I bite my lower lip.

What would I do with it?

There's likely not a person in Shipwreck who hasn't asked themselves that question.

What if I was planting a flower garden and I found Thorny Rock's treasure chest?

Rumors say it's buried somewhere in Shipwreck. It's a fairly normal question to ask yourself.

Except every time I ask myself that question, right after acknowledging that I'd turn it over to the Shipwreck historical society because I'd feel guilty for the rest of my life if I kept anything that I didn't deserve for myself, I come back to the logical answer.

"That's kind of a pointless question since it doesn't exist."

He watches me a moment longer, then goes back to his phone. "What time's the wedding?"

"Two p.m. on Saturday. You think the treasure exists."

"Its existence is irrelevant. Do you need money for a dress or catering?"

"I thrifted a bright pink prom dress a few weeks ago that'll give Nigel a coronary, and Annika's insisting that we let Grady bake wedding cookies, which is also so beautifully nontraditional that if the coronary doesn't do Nigel in, the aneurysm will. Especially if we do sugar cookies in unfortunate shapes, which I'm considering asking for but probably won't because I'll have regrets, but Grady would do it anyway to be funny. The only thing I really need to complete the day is for you to show up in jeans and a leather jacket, and for us to ride off on a motorcycle, but only for like a block. Just far enough for Nigel to not see when I get off of it and let you go about your life. If the treasure's existence is irrelevant, why did you want the diary?"

He pins me with another look, this one mostly the neutral expression I've come to expect from him with the barest hint of lingering frustration. "Have you heard of the Fenn treasure?"

"The one buried by some guy out west that a med student found in Wyoming? Yes. Of course. Pirate town, duh. We hear about treasures. Plus, we're working on an interactive display in the last wing of the museum, and parts of it are about treasures that have been found around the world."

"Do you know how many people died looking for it?"

"Not an exact number."

"More than one. That's what matters. How many people are coming to Shipwreck right now looking for the treasure that you don't think exists?"

"So you're going to find it so no one dies looking for it? Even if it doesn't exist?"

I've clearly used up my quota of answers from him for the day because once again, he doesn't answer.

Awesome.

And once more, I am never, ever, ever getting married.

For real, I mean.

I don't even want to date anymore.

Men are fucking awful.

All of them.

I pocket my phone. "Could you do me a favor and not die looking for a treasure before we get fake married so that I didn't steal photos of that diary in vain? I have this thing where I feel an absurd amount of guilt and responsibility for things that aren't my fault, and while I recognize that I was gifted with that guilt and shame in childhood as a control and manipulation tactic, my emotions don't always get the logic message to overcome the guilt and shame. Also, in this case, since I basically committed a crime for you to get you information that you might use to hurt yourself, I feel premature remorse and shame over your demise while looking for it too."

"I won't die."

Men.

Freaking *men* and their egos. And their ability to only comprehend the slightest bit of what a woman says, and only the parts that concern them.

"So you know, if you do die, I'll be under a ton of pressure all over again to marry Nigel so that he can take care of me since being a widow would turn me into a helpless ninny."

Flat brown eyes lift to mine once more.

And somehow, he keeps a straight face while also silently asking me if I really just used the word *ninny*.

I stifle a sigh. "That's what they'd say. My grandmother and her friends and the people I grew up with."

"Ever thought about simply disappointing them?"

"Tried that once and have the exorcism videos to show for it."

I'm joking.

I say it like I'm joking.

But the way he keeps staring at me—

It's like he can read my soul, and he knows it has scars, and he knows that me telling them to fuck off and let me live my own life won't work.

"Nigel fucking *moved* from Iowa to try to claim what he thinks is his right. My grandmother and the people who helped her raise me—they view the world one way, and I used to see it the same, but I don't anymore. They think I'm damning my eternal soul while I'm happier and healthier and more at peace and grateful to just have this life to live than I've ever been. I know they think they're trying to save me, I know they believe they have my best interests at heart, but they're just…"

I shake my head.

Davis doesn't care.

This is transactional. He wants my help so he can go find a treasure. I want his help so that I have a buffer between my family and their misplaced worry about me.

You don't try to control and manipulate people if you don't care about them, right?

"Anyway. Thank you. Again. Even Nigel won't try to break the sacred bonds of marriage, so having a fake husband will go a long way toward me continuing to keep my peace. I'll just send photos every once in a while like I did before, except this time you'll know it. Yay. Hooray. Everyone will be happy."

Everyone will not be happy.

Davis glances up at me once more. "Is he coming again before Saturday?"

"That's not the plan."

"Does he follow plans?"

I wince. "I mean, lunch wasn't exactly in the plans today…"

Swear on my old poster of him, Davis looks like he's considering making some plans of his own that I definitely need to know nothing about.

And his quiet "Call me if he shows up" makes me even more convinced there's danger simmering beneath his surface.

I suddenly have an old song that Waverly played for us once back in my head. A song about a guy named Earl.

"I—I don't have your number."

He sets his phone down, pulls a notepad out of a drawer, scribbles a number, and hands me the paper. "That'll work. Use it if *anyone* you don't want to see shows up."

That'll work.

Not *that's my number.*

And *use it if anyone you don't want to see shows up?*

What does that mean?

Aside from the fact that it makes him fascinating and dangerous.

And aside from the fact that if my gut says I can trust him, which it's actively telling me right now, I absolutely should not.

"Thank you. Again. I know you don't have to do this. I

should handle my own problems." *Shut up, Sloane. Don't be an overly apologetic ninny.*

He nods once more.

And that's that.

Davis Remington and I will see each other again only when necessary until we get fake married in five days and convince Nigel to go back to Iowa, and then I'll go back to therapy to discuss my first crush on a guy since I gave up on men.

Yippee.

6

Davis Remington, aka a man finally ready to do a little bit of talking, if he must

MOST OF SHIPWRECK is still sleeping when I swing my leg off my bike, softly stride down the alley, and then climb into the passenger seat of the black SUV parked behind the Thorny Rock Historical Museum after a long night of trying to ignore my own hero complex while studying the pictures of the journal that Sloane took for me.

Not the same as holding the real journal.

Not even close.

And that's what I'm focusing on.

Not on the haunted expression in her bright blue eyes when she talked about the expectations her grandmother and other people from her past have of her, or the way she kept twirling her copper locks while she talked too fast, like I made her nervous.

I don't want to make her nervous.

I want for her what I want for everyone—that she be safe and happy and healthy.

The end.

I don't ever let myself want anything more because it will inevitably end in hurt, because it always does.

She's a project. That's it.

A project unfortunately related to the reason I'm climbing into this SUV in the pre-dawn hours, which means that no matter how much I want to not think about her, I'm going to think about her.

"Anyone see you?" I ask the woman in the driver's seat.

Even in the dim pre-dawn light, I know she's pinning me with a look that she's been perfecting since before we were born. "You know this is why people ask you if you're a spy, right?"

Says the spook herself.

Everything I learned about being mysterious, I learned from my twin sister.

Everything I learned about hacking, the internet, and all the reasons cloud backup is a bad idea for things you don't want people to know you know, though, I taught myself.

Mostly.

I ignore Vanessa's question. "Did you bring it?"

"No. I told you. We're staying out of this."

"You're publicly staying out of this. I publicly stay out of everything."

"Davis."

"Someone's gonna get hurt."

"That is not your responsibility."

Not even 6:00 a.m., and she's hitting me with the phrase she usually reserves for much further into our conversations.

"Patrick Dixon's looking for the treasure," I tell her.

I feel her shoulders tighten as if my own were tightening for her.

Feel her suck in a breath too. Engine's not running, so yes, I hear it, but I *feel* it also.

She turns in her seat to face me more fully. "I'm still not helping you with this."

"This is the smallest favor I've ever asked for."

She stares at me.

"In the last decade," I add.

"This is not a small favor."

"Do you know what happens to this town if they find out what we know?"

"Once again, not your responsibility."

Except this one is.

If I'd kept my nosy ass out of my own business, I wouldn't know what I don't want to know.

But I do know what I don't want to know, and thanks to Cooper Rock's wedding here, all of the national attention on Shipwreck and Thorny Rock and the fucking treasure means someone else could figure it out too.

Someone like Patrick Dixon, who *would* use the information to hurt people.

People like the Rocks.

Vanessa.

Beck's sister, Ellie.

And now Sloane, who I shouldn't have any allegiance

to whatsoever, but the same could be said about my lack of allegiance to any number of the other people that I've quietly helped in the past decade.

Often with my sister's help, because she knows things.

Even things she denies knowing.

Like what random federal agencies might know about an old pirate and his crew.

"Nobody cares anymore once a treasure's found," I say. "It can go in a museum—one with actual security—and the legend will live on. But if Dixon finds it—"

"He won't find it."

"He's been in Shipwreck every day for the past two weeks. Including Saturday, when security had the entire town locked down for the wedding. He's been dodging another of his ex-girlfriends while visiting the museum every single day. Nearly certain he's the guy who broke in Saturday night too."

"Sort of like you?"

"I'm the good guy. He's a fucking fucknugget."

Vanessa rolls her eyes.

We were the youngest of the crew growing up in our neighborhood. The other kids included us, but sometimes it felt like just barely.

That changed for me in late middle school and continued more when our parents agreed to let me drop out of high school and tour with the band, but Vanessa never joined in the neighborhood shenanigans.

Partially because she was uninterested in keeping up with the guys—there were only two other girls in the group besides her, both a couple years older—and partially because while we were playing basketball and getting in trouble, she liked reading and doing her math homework.

So when my sister realized that Ellie Ryder—Ellie Morgan now—was dating the same guy who'd dumped Vanessa for a woman in his office a couple years before that, she didn't say anything.

Not even to me.

Not until the fucker cheated on Ellie with Sloane, who, as far as we can all tell, was completely clueless that he was dating someone else when they met.

When a dude has dated three women in my circles and none of them have anything good to say about him, he's trash, and I'm gonna treat him as such.

"How much longer are you off work before you have to get back to the reactor?" Vanessa asks.

"I quit."

"*Davis.*"

"Got bored. They hired new staff. Younger kids. Next-level smart. They'll be fine."

She stares at me harder.

Not squirming is far harder in front of my sister than it is in front of anyone else.

"Is this Denver all over again?" she asks.

Denver.

Where Bro Code fell apart.

Because of me.

And because of something none of the five of us in the band have ever told anyone, but Vanessa knows.

She talked it out of me one night about four years ago.

I roll my shoulders. "Not if you tell me what the CIA knows about where Thorny Rock's treasure is buried so I can get it and give it to the Rocks and pretend that's the end of this."

"The CIA doesn't work on American soil."

"Doesn't mean you don't know things."

"We don't know things. Even if we did, I don't have any need to know what we know. And what's next? What's next for you after you find a mythical treasure and need something new?"

I look out the passenger window at the back of the concession stand inside the water park on the other side of the alley.

Good question, *what next?*

And I don't know.

Which is exactly what led to the disaster in Denver that made the band call it quits. Me not knowing what I'd do if my life fell apart.

And then I went and made it fall apart.

Probably because I didn't actually like eighty percent of what I was doing. My every move being dissected by the tabloids. Interviews where people asked intrusive questions about our private lives. The inability to even come home without having reporters and gossips camped out around the old neighborhood.

The band? The band was great. Performing? Yeah, I liked the rush. Being with the guys? With the men I will call my brothers until my dying day?

Fantastic.

The rest of it?

I knew I'd break. I just didn't know when.

It's been fifteen years since Denver.

I've grown a lot since then.

Matured.

Found coping mechanisms. A purpose in life with my job.

Learned to deal with my feelings.

But I'm *feeling* the same restlessness that led to Denver, and Vanessa is the one person in the world I can't lie to about it.

Doesn't mean I can't deflect though. "You busy this weekend? I told a friend I'd fake-marry her to get her grandmother off her back."

"Again?"

"First time in this half of the country."

"Are you going as yourself?"

"Yes."

She snorts.

"What?"

"How are you going to explain that to all of your other fake wives' families?"

"Most of them were very small ceremonies to appease dying grandparents who are no longer with us."

"Is your *friend*'s grandma dying?"

I don't miss her emphasis on the word *friend*.

It's not a word I use often when referring to anyone outside of the circle we grew up in.

"No idea. I'm just along for the ride until she's ready to tell her family to fuck off. Bonus points to her if she also tells them that she hates men and will forever."

Vanessa snorts again.

My sister already actively, publicly hates men forever. Probably partially due to one of the same men who sent Sloane down that path as well.

I'm occasionally an exception.

Probably not today though.

For either of them.

Sloane wasn't happy when she left last night.

Can't blame her.

I was a dick.

Easier to be a dick than to let her get close. And my dick wanted her to be close.

Fucking basic body part.

"Did you really drive down from DC in the middle of the night to tell me you won't help me?" I ask her.

"No, I drove down from DC in the middle of the night to find out what's wrong with you before you get yourself in trouble. And it's worse than I was afraid of. Go back to school, Davis. Get another degree. Philosophy will keep you busy for a while. Learn a new foreign language. Travel. When's the last time you left the country? What's Cash up to? Isn't he touring with Aspen? Join them. See something new. Get away from here."

Ten years ago, it would've been *what are Beck and Cash and Tripp and Levi up to? Go travel with one of them.*

Now, all of my best buddies are married or on their way to marriage.

Hooked up.

None looking for a third wheel.

Only Cash is still traveling.

Levi's home in Copper Valley all the time, raising his stepkids with his wife.

Beck's home in Copper Valley or Shipwreck all the time, raising his kids with his wife, occasionally visiting his in-laws in LA.

Tripp's home in Copper Valley all the time, raising his kids and running Copper Valley's baseball team with his wife.

The Fireballs—Cooper Rock's team—should've belonged to all of us in the band, but things didn't end up happening that way, for reasons.

And that one still smarts.

The Fireballs should've been my *what's next*.

I could ask Tripp for a job, but it's not the same.

It's not all five of us together again.

Like it used to be before we got famous.

"Cash and Aspen are in Copper Valley in two weeks. That'll get me far."

Vanessa sighs. "You know the CIA didn't exist during the pirate age, right?"

"Like that would stop them from having information about historical events from before their time."

"And also, there are these things called *security clearances*."

"Yeah, a guy who got paid as a white hat hacker to look for vulnerabilities in nuclear power plant security systems definitely can't be trusted."

"You quit."

"Maybe I should come work for the CIA."

"I will actively recommend against that. And not to you. To them. I will actively recommend that they not hire you."

As she should.

I'd be a shitty spy.

Can't keep a straight face for anything.

Kidding.

THE PRETEND FIANCÉ FIASCO

But also, I don't want the commitment and pressure of being a spy.

Have a few issues with boundaries when I believe in a cause.

Clearly.

I'm asking my sister to give me random info a government agency might have stumbled across and kept secret, aren't I?

And I broke another rule when I asked Sloane for a favor.

I do favors for people. I don't ask for favors. Not from people outside my tight, close-knit circle of friends.

Ask for favors from people you don't trust with your life, and it gets complicated.

Like when they bring you pictures of the thing that you need to put your hands on and inspect for yourself.

Vanessa goes still.

Eerily still.

I look at her, and she reaches across me to hold me in my seat the way Mom used to when she'd brake too hard.

Except we're not moving.

Vanessa might not be breathing.

I look at her, then out the car in the direction she's looking.

And—

Ah, fuck.

Sloane.

She's coming down the alley, chatting on her phone. Undoubtedly coming to check on the museum before her day shift.

She does that a lot, which I shouldn't know, but I do.

She's not the only one in our fake relationship who's been watching the other.

She makes a frustrated face at the phone that I feel in my soul, and my heart does that annoying thing it's done every time I've seen her since she kissed me where it flutters like I'm a fucking teenager.

I breathe through it.

Just because I'm as interested as Sloane is in never dating or getting married doesn't mean I've fully mind-over-bodied my biological instincts yet to convince myself women in general aren't inherently attractive, some more than others.

And it's not like I'd never noticed her before.

Who wouldn't notice a curvy redhead who's always smiling? Especially one who wasn't as subtle as she thought she was about taking my picture anytime I've seen her in Shipwreck lately.

That pretend boyfriend thing?

Wasn't my first guess as to what she was doing, but it was on the list. And it was a short list.

"That her?" Vanessa says so softly I almost don't hear it.

Shit.

I'm wearing my puppy dog eyes.

I scowl at my sister.

She takes that for the *yes* that it is. "And how long have you had a crush on her?"

"I do not have a crush on her."

"Then what are the moon eyes all about?"

"She told me once she hated me because she finally got

tickets to see one of our shows, but the band broke up before her ticket date. I feel guilty."

Predictably, Vanessa snorts again. "You're not even trying to lie effectively now."

"It's the truth. She was tipsy at a bar and challenged me to a game of darts. I don't know if she even remembers. Tillie Jean told me she'd had a bad day. Got yelled at a bunch at work by people who were too ungrateful or something."

Vanessa sucks in another breath and her eyes narrow. "No."

"Everyone has a bad day now and—oh, fuck."

She's not objecting to my explanation.

She's objecting to what's happening in the alley.

And as soon as I see it too, I'm in motion.

Sloane isn't alone.

And it's unlikely that she knows she's not alone.

I know she's not alone.

Vanessa knows she's not alone.

We both know who's trailing Sloane in the shadows.

And while I'm flying out of the SUV as Sloane slips inside the back entrance of the museum, my sister's staying put.

Because she doesn't want Patrick Dixon to see her?

Or because she doesn't want to be seen in general?

Motherfucker.

Is Vanessa working a Thorny Rock case? Is she here because the CIA wants Thorny Rock's treasure and she knows something about what Dixon's up to?

Problem for later.

My boots hit the ground with a crunch.

Vanessa turns on the SUV lights, illuminating the fucking blond caveman mere feet from the rear museum door.

He throws his hands in front of his face as Sloane swings the door open and sticks her head back outside. "Hello? Whoever's there, you should know I have bear spray and I can scream loud enough to wake the dead, so —oh. It's you."

With the direction the door opened, she's staring straight at me, and she can't see Dixon, who's also made me, and is now turning on his heel to sprint back down the alley.

Sloane frowns and turns her head in his direction— shoes on gravel aren't quiet—as Vanessa's engine roars to life.

Her SUV glides past me while Sloane looks between me and my sister in her getaway car, chasing Patrick down the alley and around the corner.

I'm gonna get a cryptic text about this later.

Be epic if she ran him over. Doubt she does though.

Not her style.

Plus, she'd get put on administrative leave while the incident was investigated, and she likes her job.

Sloane blinks at me. "What's going on?"

"Let's go inside."

"Are you spying on me?"

"No."

"Who was that?"

"Who?"

"*Oh my god*, you have a girlfriend, don't you? Was that your girlfriend? Were you telling her about us? The fake us. Not the real us. *Oh my god*. I am so over men. Over. Men."

She ducks back into the museum.

The door slams behind her.

I slowly count to five, then punch in the code and follow her into the museum.

She and I need to talk.

7

Sloane

CAN a woman not visit her favorite spot in town before work in the morning without having her pretend fiancé follow her around?

This is getting creepy. Especially the part where someone else was in the alley and another someone else was driving a car, and that person looked weirdly like Davis when they drove past, right down to the manbun.

And that weird feeling has taken firm hold even before Davis strolls through the back entrance like he owns the freaking place.

"What are you doing?" I hiss as he tests that the door is shut and locked. "How did you do that? We changed the code. We're changing the code *daily*. How did you know the code?"

I don't know why I'm hissing.

I could yell.

We're alone.

No one to hear me.

Probably.

I think.

"You didn't lock the door behind you."

I blink. Did I—

I *did too*. And on top of that, we upgraded the locks yesterday so that they lock automatically.

He knows the code.

He knows the freaking code.

"Who are you working with? Why are you following me?"

He doesn't answer.

Naturally.

But he *is* staring rather intently at the two maps that one of the volunteers left laid out last night when she closed up.

"Are you spying on me?" I ask again. Or— "Oh my god, are you *guarding* me?"

His face freezes.

You'd think I couldn't tell with Mr. Poker Face, but I'm paying close enough attention that I see the shift.

His face has gone as still as the eye of a hurricane.

"You *are*."

"Prefer not to."

"Why are you guarding me?"

"What I do for my pretend fiancées."

I'm not a growler. I'm truly not.

But for the second time in just a few days, I'm growling at a man.

He holds eye contact briefly, and I swear his lips twitch up.

Just the teensiest bit, but it's enough for me to be certain he's amused by me.

And that annoys the shit out of me. "I could call the sheriff and have you removed."

"Someone broke in here three days ago and one of your staff left maps out overnight? That normal?"

I shiver.

I don't want to, but I do.

Fine. I'm not here because I like to visit before work, or because it's my favorite place in Shipwreck.

I'm here to make sure everything's in order.

And he's right.

It's not normal for maps to be left out overnight. I hadn't noticed before the hairs on the back of my neck stood up and I ducked my head outside to see why I was suddenly freaking out as soon as I got in the building.

"You know the code," I remind him. "I don't know how you keep knowing the code, but you know the code. So *you* could've been in here causing problems."

"I haven't been here since Saturday."

"How do I know I can trust you?"

Dammit.

Heat floods my face. I'm fake marrying him, and I don't know if I can trust him. He's doing me a favor, and I'm calling him suspicious.

Am I overreacting?

Stop it, Sloane, I order myself. *You have every right to be suspicious. Including about why a guy like Davis would even agree to pretend to be your fiancé.*

And don't tell me it was because he wanted a favor.

He could've asked a favor from anyone in town. Or he could've snuck into Pop's house the same way he snuck into my museum and gotten it for himself.

But he didn't.

He asked me to get involved with him.

So yes, I'll continue to be suspicious about what else he's getting out of fake marrying me.

He watches me like he knows every thought flitting through my mind.

And then he shrugs. "You don't know that you can trust me."

Dammit.

Dammit.

That weirdly makes me trust him more.

And also less.

He shifts his gaze to take in the workroom again. The coffee spill and broken mug from Saturday have been cleaned. The wide filing cabinet has been repaired. Aside from some marring on the metal, there's no sign left that anything went wrong in here the other day.

"You know everything in here," he says.

Ah.

It's about the treasure hunt again. Of course. "Maybe."

"More than anyone else in Shipwreck."

"Not more than the Rocks do. They know everything."

"You know things you probably don't realize you know."

"Like what?"

Instead of answering, he crosses the room to study one of the two old maps that we haven't put out on display and which shouldn't have been left out overnight.

It's old—*old* old—and crumbling at the edges.

The museum is one of those projects that we started locally, all on volunteer power, without fully realizing what we had on our hands. We've had a few consultations with preservationists and archivists and curators, so we're keeping with best practices as much as we can, given funding and time constraints.

Yes, yes, we could ask Cooper and Waverly for help, but they already do so much. And it makes me proud that we were able to rally everyone in town to support this without having to ask for major donor assistance.

It's probably time though.

Because someone left two maps out overnight.

That's unusual.

Everyone on staff pays close attention to proper handling and storage.

Not for the first time in the past few days, a shiver slinks from my scalp to my tailbone.

Tillie Jean says the treasure isn't real.

Cooper and their other brother, Grady, both say the treasure isn't real.

Grady's wife, Annika, told me she thinks it might've been real at one point, but also that it was found years ago —before the internet—and that we'll never know what happened to it.

But is that what the Rock family is supposed to say?

Or is it the truth?

And what does Davis know?

If he was trying to find a treasure to make people quit

looking for a treasure that doesn't exist, he could use his resources to fake-find it instead, pay off the experts who'd authenticate it, and that would be the end of it.

But he's actually looking for it.

And I don't think it's because he's worried other people will hurt themselves doing the same.

"The treasure... It's not real," I say.

He doesn't answer.

He's bent over the map, studying it. "You got this from Sarcasm."

"How do you know that?"

"Only reason it wouldn't be on display."

He's lying.

I mean, yes, I think all men are lying on a regular basis, and I'm well aware Davis has to have his own reasons that he's not sharing for ninety percent of everything he's done since Saturday, but I swear on Thorny Rock's maybe-not-so-imaginary treasure, Davis Remington is outright lying to me right now.

He knows the map was donated by a citizen of Shipwreck's rival town, and he doesn't want me to know how he knows it.

Does he know who donated it?

Or just where it came from?

"Say the treasure is real." Are these words actually coming out of my mouth? Tillie Jean had better be prepared for lunch with me today because I have so many questions for her too. "How do you know it's still where it was buried? How do you know someone else didn't find it years ago? How do you know it's not hidden between the walls in some gazillionaire's house for his

99

heirs to find six generations from now when they do heavy renovations?"

Davis slides a look at me. "For someone who doesn't believe the treasure's real, you have interesting ideas for where it might be located."

"My grandma used to show us the Muppets version of *Treasure Island* all the time. Knowing pirate lore and believing there's a treasure in Shipwreck are two different things."

Davis isn't touching the map.

He's studying it intently, bent over, eyes roaming over every inch like it's the missing piece to the puzzle.

It reminds me of how he kissed me Saturday night.

Intently.

With purpose.

I shiver again and add a mental head slap.

Who cares how Davis kisses women?

Not me.

Definitely not me.

I'll kiss him again this coming Saturday at our fake wedding, possibly once or twice more if Nigel comes to town and Davis hears about it and shows up before Nigel leaves again, and that will be it.

And in the meantime, I have a drawer full of toys to help me do for myself what very few men have ever done for me, and I'm quite content with that.

"Why does it matter where the map came from?" I ask him.

"How much do you know about Sarcasm?"

"Founded by a guy named Walter Bombeck, supposedly a distant relative of Thorny Rock—who once tried to poison Walter. The two towns have been at war ever since."

He straightens and stares directly into my soul again. Can the man do anything less intensely today? Please?

"Who told you that?"

And I'll add Annika to the list of people I need to talk to today.

Grady's wife is from Sarcasm.

That little intel came directly from her.

"Do you know how many people I've talked to while we've been putting this museum together? And you think I remember who told me what about who?"

He folds his arms. "Yep."

I shrug with my eyebrows.

He watches me.

I fold my arms and watch him back.

Hello, my name is Sloane Pearce, and I'm a thirty-five-year-old nurse who has staring contests with men who have agreed to fake marry me.

Because even when it's fake, *they're still fucking annoying*.

He blinks first. "You need better security here."

He's not wrong.

"To protect it from people like you?" I ask.

That gets me a nostril flare, and his brown eyes go flat.

We're so gonna sell this fake marriage thing.

Look at how well we annoy each other already.

"Are you working here today?" he asks.

"Nope. Day job calls."

"Tell whoever's working that your security system's getting an upgrade today. And don't walk to work alone."

101

I bite back a snippy answer, mostly because I'm here this early only partially because I've been having trouble sleeping since Saturday night.

The other part is that my grandmother called to tell me she's lonely and worried about my safety in a pirate town and having heartburn over how old my ovaries are getting.

Oh, and also that Nigel told her I've been lying to her about the man I'm engaged to, and if I don't love him enough to tell her his real name, then I shouldn't be marrying him.

That was a reasonable point which she unfortunately ruined by adding that he probably has sex with barn animals and that you should never trust men who cover their sins with ink on their arms.

Yep. That's what has my grandmother out of bed and making phone calls before five a.m. her time.

I get it. She's lonely and worried about who will take care of her as she gets older. It's been worse since my brother left Two Twigs to work for a different airline, but it feels like it's worse for other reasons too.

Like she's not entirely in touch with reality at all sometimes.

I've stayed in touch with a couple of her friends as much as I can tolerate to make sure she's not completely alone—and she's not, they tell me she has a very active social life—but I'm stuck between wanting to live my own life and worrying she's right, that I'm the only person who'll be able to take care of her when she can no longer take care of herself.

It's a hard spot to be in, and between the extra guilt

and the dating nonsense she throws at me every time, I just don't enjoy talking to her much anymore.

So I opted to head here while we were on the phone so I'd have to make an excuse to go when I got here.

And now on top of planning a fake wedding to a man that my family has written off because of his former job and his tattoos, my fake groom is convinced an imaginary treasure is real and that my museum isn't as safe as the sheriff thinks it is.

"The museum can't afford—" I start, but I stop when Davis tilts his head.

It's subtle.

You have to watch this man carefully to notice.

But that little head tilt makes his eyes go even flatter.

Like he's offended that I'd think he'd order an upgraded security system for anyone and expect them to pay for it themselves.

I suppress a shiver at the idea that a man would spend thousands of dollars even before rush job fees to keep me safe.

This isn't about me.

It's about guarding evidence about where his precious treasure is.

Also, the money is nothing to him.

He's a former famous person.

Probably has plenty of cash to throw around at little projects. Even if he didn't, we both know with one call to Cooper, an upgraded security system would instantly be funded.

And Cooper's reachable. He and Waverly aren't taking

their honeymoon until after the holidays, so they're hanging out up on his mountain.

Not that anyone wants to bother the newlyweds.

But I think Davis would if he needed to.

For me.

No.

No.

This *isn't about me.*

He doesn't actually care about me.

"Don't you have a day job?" I ask him.

"Sure."

Yep.

It's becoming more and more clear why he agreed to the fake engagement.

It's because he thinks I have information he can use for his own purposes.

Honestly, that makes him the best fake groom for me.

So very fitting.

And I'm going to throttle him before our fake wedding is over.

8

Davis

IT'S BEEN a while since I've wanted to crawl out of my own skin.

About since Bro Code broke up, matter of fact.

But today, I can't sit still.

I could go hunt for the treasure, but I don't know where it fucking *is*. I need hands on the journal to see how the pages fit together, to fold them where they've been folded before, to inspect the binding and see if there's anything hidden in the covers.

But after Saturday's break-in, with me present for it, I can't go talk to Pop Rock again about anything having to do with the treasure without him accusing me of trying to steal things.

So I'm stuck.

Worthless.

Useless.

And going fucking nuts.

It *does* feel like Denver.

Like I'm on the cusp of a new life that I'm not ready for, but my old life doesn't fit me anymore and I can't bend it and snap it back into place the way I want to.

Working out doesn't help.

Meditating doesn't help.

Complex logic puzzles don't help.

Reviewing all the pictures Sloane took of the journal doesn't help.

Keeping up over text with the upgrades to the Thorny Rock Museum's security system doesn't help.

Wondering if Sloane's going to walk home alone after work doesn't help.

Thinking about how she was clearly pissed at me when I refused to leave and wouldn't let her walk to work by herself this morning doesn't help.

Contemplating that she might dump me before we get fake married, which leaves an unusual sensation in the pit of my stomach, doesn't help.

My inability to suppress the memory of kissing her Saturday doesn't help.

Wanting to jack off and refusing to because that will only make things worse doesn't help.

Wondering if she's actually masturbated to thoughts of me doesn't help.

And Beck showing up in the early afternoon doesn't help either.

When the band split, Beck went into modeling underwear, then later launched a fashion empire. He's mostly out of the game now while he and his wife, Sarah, raise their two babies.

Dude's the best.

Annoyingly happy, but also the best.

He's the original reason any of us knew Shipwreck existed. He got a weekend house up here years and years ago, and he's hosted parties and get-togethers and he lets us all use his house anytime it's free.

He has me by a couple inches, and he enjoys the metabolism—and appetite—of a goat. He has Ava, his oldest, who just turned two, with him.

They find me splitting wood outside the camper I drove up here when I quit my job after I realized how much attention Shipwreck and the treasure were getting because of Cooper's wedding.

And how solving this treasure hunt needed to become my full-time job.

Beck takes one look at me, then does a double take. "Whoa. You're up in some shi—shitake mushrooms, aren't you?"

"Mush-ooms!" Ava yells from his arms.

Beck winces. "Whoops."

"Whoops?" I ask.

"Mush-ooms!" Ava yells again.

"You just ate twenty minutes ago," Beck says to her. "Peas and carrots and a banana and turkey rolls and a big grilled cheese sandwich. You ate, we changed your diaper, and then we left. Remember?"

She glares at him. "Mush-ooms."

He looks at me. "Ah, you got any portabellas? She's having a growth spurt. I packed applesauce and cheese sticks and toast and grapes and Cheerios and this really great bean salad we had for dinner last night, and she really did eat a big lunch just twenty minutes ago, and—"

"Mush-ooms!" Ava interrupts.

"You had leftovers from dinner last night?" I ask. Beck doesn't leave leftovers.

Ever.

It was one of the things that both amused me and annoyed me most when we were traveling together as a band. Sometimes a guy just wants leftovers.

He grins. "It was our fourth side dish."

Of course.

Four side dishes are one too many for even Beck in a single sitting.

Apparently.

I jerk my thumb at the door. "Help yourself."

"Seriously? You have mushrooms?"

Ava wiggles and dives for the ground. Beck does some gymnastics trick that should be physically impossible to keep her from landing on her head, and he comes up holding her upside down by one foot.

She giggles.

Then she growls at me, reminding me of Sloane, which makes my heart do that pitter-patter fucking annoying thing again.

Mind over emotions.

Mind over hormones.

Mind over wanting to be her hero.

I need to find this goddamn treasure and then figure out what's next in my entire life.

And a woman will never be *what's next.*

I do this thing where I get bored with something and move on. Not doing that in a relationship, so I just don't do relationships.

Also, I'd have to trust a stranger with some of my deepest, darkest secrets.

Not happening. The end.

"Mush-ooms," Ava says.

I bend over and look the toddler right in her blue eyes. "Life lesson, kiddo. Uncle Davis hears all, and he will always stock mushrooms for you."

"You uggy," she says.

Beck chokes and lifts her so her face is up near his face. "*Ava.* Where did you learn that word? We don't like that word. That word is ug—oh. That's where you learned that word."

She flaps her arms, still upside down. "I fwy! Mush-ooms!"

I toss my axe aside and lead them inside, where I dig mushrooms out of my fridge and hand them over to my honorary niece, who's shoved my computer out of the way at my small kitchenette table.

I open the blinds on the window over the table so she can look out at the colorful fall trees too.

Vanessa's never having kids.

I'm never having kids.

So my buddies' kids are our nieces and nephews.

Like it this way.

Ava pounces on the mushrooms like she hasn't eaten in four days.

I slide a look at Beck.

He grins again. "Yeah, good thing I have a little cash saved up. Both of the girls got my appetite."

"Vanessa sent you."

He pulls a milk box out of the diaper bag on his shoulder and hands it to Ava, who's kneeling on the bench, one elbow on the table while she uses her other hand to shovel mushrooms into her mouth.

Then he looks back at me. "She said the Denver word. I didn't know she knew the Denver word, but she said it."

"Who else is coming?"

"Cash tomorrow, Levi this weekend, and Tripp next week. Wyatt and Ellie whenever they can clear their schedules. But I swear they still don't know what Denver actually means. They just know, you know, the general Denver thing."

"I won't *Denver* again."

Probably.

I learned my lesson.

And this is a completely different situation.

Beck hands Ava a stick of string cheese from the diaper bag that he's set on the bench on the other side of the table.

"Mo mush-oom," she says.

"But the cheese is yummy."

She death-glares at him.

I suck in a smile. "Think your kid just called you a liar."

"Cheese is *delicious*. Don't insult cheese. It's the pinnacle of all food groups."

"Maybe brie. Some high-quality blue. Goat. Honey

goat. Sarah's magic cheeseball recipe that she perfected for you. But not that crap you're trying to give her."

"Not dat cwap," Ava agrees.

"Mommy's gonna love all of your new words," he says to her with another wince.

She grins.

I grin too, knowing he's wrong. Sarah's pretty chill.

Not much better in life than watching your buddies fall in love and have kids who will grow up to be just like them.

We had a fuck ton of fun as kids.

Even when I felt like I was on the fringes, it was fun.

Love to see that legacy live on.

I squat next to the table and poke her in the foot. "Hey, Ava, you know what's better than mushrooms?"

Big blue eyes turn to stare at me while she nibbles on a piece of a portabella.

"Dragon fruit."

"Eat dwagon?"

"It has scales like a dragon, and it tastes like a dragon."

Her gaze jumps between me and Beck.

"You better have dragon fruit too," Beck mutters to me.

Like I'd torture his kid—or myself—by making her cry.

"Dwagon taste wike cookie?" Ava asks.

"Psh. Cookies are trash compared to dragon fruit."

Beck's already digging into my compact fridge, pulling out the dragon fruit.

He's also giving me a look that's pretty unusual on him.

It's a serious look.

Beck doesn't do serious.

He does funny. He does happy. He does *oh, fuck, I screwed up*.

But he doesn't do serious.

"I know you're distracting me," he tells me while he starts cutting the dragon fruit.

"So easy to do."

"Look, I don't care what you do, so long as you don't end up in jail. Jail is bad. We don't want jail."

"Your vocabulary is adorable."

"We also don't want me to throw this dragon fruit at you, because it's food, and it smells good—"

"Wike dwagon!" Ava yells.

"Yeah. It smells like a delicious dragon. Ava, please tell Uncle Davis we don't want him to go to jail."

She squints at me. "Uggy in jay-ah?"

"*Ava.* Seriously. Not the ugly word. Uncle Davis isn't ugly. He's...hairy."

Huh.

I suddenly want a two-year-old's opinion on something. And not because I care that she thinks I'm ugly.

This is a new development.

I squat down to her level and stroke my beard. "Is this why you think I'm ugly?"

"No."

"My hair?" I touch the top of my head where I've tied my long hair up into its usual bun.

"No."

"My eyes?"

She nods. "You eyes uggy. An' nose."

If Beck cringes any harder, he's gonna turn his face inside out.

"So I should grow the beard over my eyes and nose?" I ask.

"Wike Wed?"

I squint. "Wed?"

"Red," Beck says. "Red, the new panda on *Panda Bananda*. And again, Ava, *not nice.*"

Didn't know there was a new panda. Apparently I need to brush up on my kid shows.

"You not nice," Ava says.

"Are you sure you're only two?" I ask her.

"I Ava," she says.

She wolfs down all of the mushrooms that I have in the house, two string cheeses, and two dragon fruits before she announces she wants to play.

Beck bundles her in a little vest, and we head back outside so she can run.

"She gonna puke?" I ask Beck.

"Unlikely. You gonna puke?"

I glance at him.

He grins. "Or get yourself arrested?"

"I'm not going to get myself arrested."

"You're searching for Thorny Rock's treasure."

"Patrick Dixon is too."

That thing where Beck's always happy?

It stops when his sister's ex-boyfriend is mentioned.

Fucker dumped Ellie at Christmas, which set off a string of events that led to her having a car accident where we almost lost her.

She's good now—she married Wyatt Morgan, one of

the few guys from the neighborhood who didn't have any interest in joining Bro Code, and who's always been tightest with Beck—but Dixon is one of maybe two people I don't expect Beck will ever forgive and forget in his lifetime.

"The fuck?" he mutters, eyes on Ava—probably to make sure she's too far away to hear him—while his expression turns grim.

Maybe a little pissed off too.

"Dude's been in town for two weeks," I tell him. "Caught him trying to break into the new museum this morning. Pretty sure he's the guy who was in there Saturday night too."

Beck slides a glance at me, then looks back at Ava again. She's chasing leaves in the light breeze. "That's all? You're not gonna pull a Denver again? You're just trying to beat him to the treasure?"

This is what I like most about Beck.

He's not gonna question that I'm hunting for a treasure.

He's not running a museum *about the fucking treasure* while pretending it doesn't exist.

He's not suspicious about why I know where a map came from and about how it shouldn't be in Shipwreck.

He just says, *oh, there's a treasure and you want to find it? Cool.*

"Just trying to beat him to the treasure," I agree.

And also stop him from learning anything else he shouldn't know about this area.

Some things are better kept quiet.

"And then what?" Beck asks.

My shoulders twitch.

"Don't know yet."

He slides another look at me.

I don't heave the sigh that I want to heave. I don't give him the *knock it off, I'm fine* eyeball of *shut up*.

"Is this a spy mission?" he asks out of the corner of his mouth. "Like, dude, I won't tell anybody if it is. But also, can I help? In a safe way? So Sarah doesn't get worried? Especially if I get to punch the blond caveman in the face?"

"I'm not a fucking spy."

Ava's head whips around.

"I said ducking," I call to her. "I'm ducking the sky. It's falling."

She looks up as a bright red leaf floats down from one of the maples. "I catch sky!"

"Good job, Ava! Keep catching the sky," Beck says.

Another leaf drifts down, and she chases after it.

Beck goes back to talking out of the corner of his mouth. "I never told anyone what happened in Denver. Even Sarah, and I tell her everything. If I haven't told Sarah about Denver, you know I can keep a secret. We can all keep a secret."

"You ducking know I'm not a spy. You visited me in college when I was getting my degrees. I gave you a reactor tour when I started my job. You know what I've done with my life for the last ten years."

"Cover story. Plus, you quit the reactor. Vanessa told me so."

"You know *she* works for the CIA, right?" It's not actually a secret. She's an analyst, not a spy who goes out and does spy things in the field.

Or so she says.

Which I believe about sixty percent of the time.

"See, I think you both tell us she works for the CIA, but in actuality, she's your doppelgänger for when you do missions. You have matching buns, and paste-on beards are a thing."

I stare at him.

He pulls a pack of Goldfish out of his pocket and rips it open. "Dammit. Giving you shit about being a spy makes me hungry. So. You dating anyone? Vanessa also said you're getting married."

"She did not."

"She did. You should've seen our other group text—the one you're not in—when she dropped that bomb. Who's the lucky lady?"

"You're right. I'm a spy."

He cackles, then chokes on a Goldfish.

"Dada o-tay?" Ava asks.

I pound him on the back.

"Daddy made a poor decision," I call to her. "He'll be fine."

He's coughing and sputtering.

He won't die.

I get him a glass of water from inside, along with a full-size bag of chips.

If giving me shit about being a spy makes him hungry, the Goldfish won't cut it.

He gulps the full glass and is still coughing a little after he's done. And then he looks at the chips.

"Wheat germ and flax chips? Wha—what *is* this? Is this real food? I eat just about anything, but this—this looks suspicious. This looks like you're trying to distract me from asking about your lady and your wedding."

"Doing a friend a favor. That's it."

"What friend? You don't have friends except us."

If Beck had spent five minutes in town, he'd know the answer to that. So he's clearly been holed up at his house and hasn't seen a single solitary soul in Shipwreck since Cooper and Waverly's wedding.

Tillie Jean did a good job of keeping that gossip quiet until the wedding was over.

She was fucking serious about not upstaging her brother.

I shrug at Beck. "It's a generalized term for *someone I know who needs a favor.*"

"And a wedding is a favor?"

"You remember when Ms. Wilson didn't want Tripp and Levi to know she was dating the Fireballs' manager?"

He grins. "And you told them she was dating the car guy."

"Car guy was in on it. He did Ms. Wilson a favor being the fall guy until she was ready to tell them the truth. My *lady* and my *wedding* are just a favor."

"With or without benefits?"

Fuck me, now I'm thinking about the way Sloane kissed me again.

Her soft curves pressed against me. The scent of

cinnamon in her hair. Soft lips that tasted like a top-shelf margarita.

Been a while since I kissed a woman.

Been longer since I kissed a woman and didn't want to stop.

And now I'm in danger of being indecent in front of a toddler. "Your daughter's eating dirt."

"Probably tastes better than these chips. Hey, Ava, want to try something gross? Uncle Davis thinks these are real chips. Also, he's getting married. Want to be a flower girl?"

"That's low, man," I mutter while Ava comes running.

"What a fower-grr?" she asks.

"It's when you wear a pretty dress at a wedding."

Her nose wrinkles. "Ew. No dwess."

Good answer.

The fewer wedding guests, the less likely someone will let it slip that the whole wedding is staged.

I don't want to make more trouble for Sloane.

Her situation seems complicated as hell.

Know a thing or two about that too.

And it's bothering me that I want to know very specifically what all of her complications are. Not just the ones I've put together with context clues, but *all* of them.

How I can help.

What more I can do to keep her out of harm's way.

What's next? my sister asked.

We know how this goes.

I get obsessed with something, I achieve it, I move on.

I won't do that to a woman.

She won't be the next obsession.

Because I won't hurt her when I move on if I don't let her in in the first place.

Even if the way that Nigel fucker has treated her makes me want to do things that would result in jail time.

Which I won't do.

Came close enough to jail once before. Not interested in needing another cover-up.

I hold out a fist to Ava. "You know what's up, don't you?"

She stares at my fist like she doesn't know she's supposed to bump it. "You uggy."

"That's what my lady friend says too."

Beck sighs. "How about we say *that's not for me* instead of calling things ugly?"

"Dat uggy," Ava replies.

"*That's not for me* is a lot of words," I agree.

"It's four words," Beck says. "One syllable each. Only one R in the whole bunch, and no L's at all."

"One of those words is a contraction. It's like five words. Very confusing."

Ava looks between us.

Beck offers her a piece of a chip.

"Dat dirt?" she asks.

Okay, yes.

Beck visiting is helping me feel a little more comfortable in my own skin. Especially since he's easily distractible.

It's like a game.

But he and Ava can't stay forever.

And I need to make sure the security system at the museum is good.

So when the two of them pass out for an impromptu nap on my couch, I climb onto my bike, put on my helmet, and head down the mountainside and into Shipwreck.

Sloane isn't my responsibility.

But no matter how many times I tell myself that, I can't help but arguing back.

Yes, she is.

9

Sloane

The best-worst thing about working in the local family practitioner's office as his lead nurse is that my hours are consistent in the nine-to-five sense, but also sometimes topsy-turvy within the day itself.

Like today.

And unlike yesterday, today's problem isn't just that every patient I see wants to talk about my surprise secret boyfriend and our wedding. Today, I work through my lunch because of three last-minute appointments—strep throat, a stomach bug, and a late-season poison ivy rash— and only manage to get out for a bite to eat because Doc orders me to.

Not that I'm interested in eating.

Even if I do head straight to Crow's Nest, Shipwreck's bakery.

Grady, Tillie Jean and Cooper's older brother, owns it. And I need to talk to his wife.

Again.

This time not about wedding plans.

I've already texted Annika, who's six months pregnant with their second baby, and she's promised to meet me here.

But the look I get from the dark-haired, green-eyed baker when I burst into the shop, making the door bells jingle wildly, tells me I'm not playing these new developments in my life as chill as I like to think I am.

The L-shaped bakery cases are nearly empty, with only a few pastries and muffins and cookies remaining. No one else is sitting in the booths lining one wall or the café tables scattered around the space either.

"How's the bride of the week today?" he asks me.

I slow my pace and smile at him. "Hey, Grady. Any sandwiches left?"

"You're carrying a lunch bag."

Oh.

Right.

I am *definitely* not as collected as I'd like to be. "I felt like a bear claw but didn't want to admit it, so I had a brain fart and asked for a sandwich when I meant I want sugary goodness."

"Sorry, Sloane. All sold out for today."

I make an effort to pull a face. "The universe is saving me from myself."

"Is this a fitting into a wedding dress thing?"

I grimace harder, then try to smile. All of the questions

about my secret romance with Davis and our super-fast wedding ceremony are making my head hurt.

Does Grady know it's fake? Tillie Jean knows it's fake. Annika was in on the fake boyfriend part, so while she hasn't said as much, I'm pretty sure she knows the wedding is fake too.

So Grady must know.

They don't keep secrets.

Or would she tell him it's real because both of them run their own businesses and they have a toddler of their own and baby brain is a thing?

But I haven't expressly told Annika it's fake.

Not that I won't tell her eventually, but I haven't yet since the fewer people who know it's fake, the better.

Is it better to ask a friend to keep a secret from the world for you, or to apologize later for not telling the whole truth?

They're both bad, and I feel like a complete asshole either way.

And Grady might already know.

He also might not.

Gah.

This was a terrible idea, and my brain hurts thinking about all of the ways it's a bad idea.

But then I think about Nigel, and I would fake-marry Davis ten times over, even with his Mr. Mysterious routine, if it gives me an excuse to send Nigel back to Iowa.

I'd probably even marry Davis for real to give me an excuse to send Nigel back to Iowa.

Marriage of convenience is a real thing. Why not be

real fake married if you're only doing it because you're never dating and you don't intend to live together?

Aren't there tax benefits?

"If you think any harder, you're going to burn the cookies I have in the oven," Grady says.

I shake my head. "Right. Sorry. Lot on my mind. If you're gonna get married, do it fast so you don't have time to worry about dieting. Thank you for baking wedding cookies. We're both honored and grateful. Is Annika around?"

"Not yet. She's—"

The bells on the door jingle again, and I don't have to turn around to know that my friend has arrived.

I can see it in Grady's smile.

They're adorable. And disgusting. And adorable.

It's a disgusting sandwich made with adorable bread.

Pretty much like all of the couples around my age in town.

"Dada muffin?" a little voice says.

"Hi, Miles, nice to see you too," Grady replies. "How was naptime?"

"No nap," the dark-haired little boy replies.

"Mommy had a nap," Annika murmurs. "Miles did not."

As Miles tears past me to race behind the counter toward Grady—for muffins, not out of excitement to see his dad, let's be real here—Annika greets me with a hug. "What's up? You sounded frazzled. Wedding plans go awry?"

I glance at Grady.

Then at his wife.

Annika grew up in Sarcasm.

I didn't move to Copper Valley until college, and I didn't make the hour trek from the city to Shipwreck until I was almost thirty, so all of the stories I've heard about the rivalry between Shipwreck and Sarcasm are secondhand. But I know these two were semi-forbidden friends in high school, that they had a friend breakup when Grady wanted more after they graduated, but Annika left for the army while Grady went to culinary school.

They reconnected a few years back when a family emergency brought her home.

I *was* here for that.

And then I *did* witness the town rivalry firsthand.

There's been a reluctant truce in public for Annika and Grady's sake, but I know behind the scenes, there's still a lot of name-calling and suspicion.

Which is why Davis was correct in wondering how I would've gotten a map from Sarcasm, even if he shouldn't know where it came from.

"Can we talk outside?" I ask Annika.

Annika's brows lift. She's roughly my height, with brown hair and brown eyes and a no-nonsense vibe. She'll tell Grady everything I'm about to tell and ask her.

It's what all of the couples in town do.

You tell one, you tell the other.

But I don't want to ask Grady what I need to know.

I want to ask Annika.

I need to see *her* instant reaction to the question without any Grady influence.

"Outside," I repeat.

125

Her lips twitch. "Sure."

"In back?"

She glances at Grady, who's lifted Miles up onto his shoulders while he finishes wiping the tables off.

"Sloane and I are taking a snack break outside."

"Saved you a special snack in the kitchen," he tells her.

Her smile lights up the entire bakery as she rubs her swelling belly. "My favorite?"

"Of course."

"Thank you. You can come home tonight and you don't have to sleep on the couch."

He chuckles the chuckle of a man who was never concerned he'd be sleeping on the couch. "Grab a snack for Sue too. He's hanging out back there."

Clearly good men exist in the world.

But not for me.

Annika pulls me behind the counter, rescues a donut from above the fridge and then a few carrots from inside the fridge, offers me anything I want from the trays of cookies on a rolling cart, and when I decline, she leads me out back where there's a one-horned goat staring forlornly at the dumpster by the back door.

If she weren't six months pregnant, I'd ask if we could climb the ladder up to the literal crow's nest decorating the roof of the building, but she *is* six months pregnant, so I settle for huddling against the wall while she tosses Sue the goat some carrots.

"Remember that map you got me?" I whisper. "For the museum?"

All of her cheerfulness dies a quick death. "What about it?"

"Davis knows it came from Sarcasm."

You know those times when you tell a friend something and it doesn't quite compute for them and they take one long, slow blink at you, like they're trying to reboot their brain to understand what those things have in common?

That's Annika right now.

Which is understandable. I'm coming at her from left field.

Even Sue pauses in his munching to give me a side-eye.

Annika tilts her head and studies me while she slowly chews a bite of her donut.

I curl my toes in my shoes and try not to squirm.

Or blurt out more of the story.

She swallows. "That's not on display, is it? When did he see it?"

"Not important. What's important is that I think he thinks the treasure is real, and I swear, he was looking at that map like it's an actual treasure map."

She glances up and down the alley. "Does this have anything to do with why you're getting married? Tillie Jean wouldn't give me any details."

I hate lying to my friends.

Hate it.

Especially when my friends feel more like family than my grandma and my brother some days.

I'll tell them everything once Nigel's gone. I swear I will.

So instead of answering, I rush ahead with my own question.

"I have fifteen minutes before I have to get back to work, and I have to ask you something, and I need you to be so for real with me right now. Is the treasure real? I've heard Grady and TJ and Cooper all say it's not, but is that just the Rock family story? Like so the tourists aren't disappointed when they don't find it and so people don't bring actual backhoes and dirt-digging things out here to tear up Blackbeard Avenue in search of it? Does it exist and they found it and it's hidden like Pop's been hiding Thorny Rock's diary? *Is it real*, Annika? Is it?"

She takes another bite of her donut, then puts a hand in front of her mouth while she chews and talks. "You're really worked up about this."

"Davis is upgrading the museum's security system and acting like it has secrets about where to find the treasure."

"Oh, I saw the work trucks."

"This is weird, right?"

"Is anything about your fiancé not weird?"

That's a very valid point.

And it's also not answering my question.

"If the treasure's real and any of the Rocks know about it, now would be a very good time for any of you to tell me or for one of them to talk to him."

"If it's real, Grady doesn't know anything about it." She frowns and glances down the alley past me again, then shakes her head and makes eye contact with me once more. Sue's finished with his carrots and is eyeballing the last bit of donut in her hand. "We've talked about it a lot with the museum opening. He thinks there could have been *something*, but who knows if it was gold or silver or jewels or even something more obscure, like historical documents or the 1800s version of his enemy's favorite sneakers. Maybe he stole the wrong pirate's scabbard."

"So there's no secret knowledge in the family?"

She purses her lips together, clearly trying not to smile, as she shakes her head.

"And no rumors about where it would've been hidden if there was something?"

"We both fully believe that *if* the treasure existed, it's either been found, or it's forever lost."

"Or you've been sitting on a map of where to find it in Sarcasm for years and didn't know it."

She pops the last bite of donut into her mouth and shrugs at me.

Sue bleats mournfully and flops to the ground.

"Does your mama know anything else about Thorny Rock and Walter Bombeck?"

Annika's mother was the source of all of my knowledge of Sarcasm's side of the old pirate tale. She also told me Sarcasm's version of the original reason for the feud between the two towns.

"Maybe? I don't know. Do you want to talk to her? She loves it when Shipwreck shitheads—ah, residents—need things from her." Her eyes twinkle as she grins at me. "Oops. Don't tell Grady I slipped."

As if she won't tell him herself.

And as if she didn't do it on purpose.

"I would love to visit your mama."

"Me too," a voice says behind me.

I shriek.

Annika shrieks.

Sue leaps to his hooves, bleats in terror, and takes off running down the alley.

And Davis stands there stone-faced, looking for all the world like he has no idea why we'd be shrieking about being snuck up on from behind a dumpster.

I press a hand to my hammering heart. "Where the hell did you come from, and how long have you been standing there?"

"You are *so* not my favorite boy bander anymore," Annika says. "Dammit. I have to pee. You scared the pee out of me, and I was having a good pee day. The baby's not sitting on my bladder for once, but now I have to pee."

Davis gestures to the bakery back door. "Apologies. Don't let me stop you."

"No, no, I can hold it for a minute. What are you doing here?"

"Taking a walk."

"Down an alley instead of on the main roads?" I ask.

"More private."

Or he was spying on me again.

Or guarding me.

My stomach flutters, but it's also growling a bit.

"Why do you think Thorny Rock's treasure is real?" Annika asks him.

He studies her briefly before looking back at me. "Do you have any museum artifacts stored at your house?"

"Rude," Annika mutters.

"Agreed."

He flicks a glance back at her. "Real or not real is irrelevant when perception is reality. The public believes it exists. The perception is that someone can find it."

Annika's no longer amused.

She's former military. And both risk-aware and risk-averse, which means she's likely now thinking about how many people could get hurt looking for the treasure.

She's mentioned it before a time or two as well.

"Sloane?" she says. "*Do* you?"

I don't want to answer that question. Mostly because there's not a good answer to it.

The bakery back door opens, and Grady sticks his head out, Miles still on his shoulders. "Everything okay? I heard almost screaming."

"Shipwreck's next most important groom scared us," Annika says. "Scared your goat too. One of us should head home and let Sue inside. I think that's where he was headed."

Grady looks at Davis.

Davis nods.

"Heard you're getting married," Grady says.

"Yep."

"Gonna treat her right?"

"As right as she wants me to."

"Don't be a dick."

"Sometimes necessary."

"Not for a fake wedding."

I choke on air. "You guys. *Quiet.*" If Davis snuck up on us, who else is listening?

"Isn't a fake wedding a dick move by default?" Davis's brown eyes cut to me. "No judgment. Guilting someone into a fake wedding is also a dick move."

"You could've said no," I sputter.

"Meant your family."

131

I blink.

He just called my family dicks.

And I think I like it.

"Don't piss off your bride in front of the guy who's making your wedding cookies," Grady says.

I shake my head. "I'm not pissed. I'm grateful. And annoyed, but grateful."

Davis is still watching me like he knows I'm finally putting into words that my family is full of dicks.

And I feel a little guilty for that, but also, they are.

"How many people know this is fake?" I whisper to Annika.

"*Know*? A very small handful. *Suspect*? Most of the town. But also, they're well-trained."

My face is getting hot. "I know I should've told you—"

"That guy who crashed the wedding? The hot one?" Annika interrupts.

"He wasn't that hot," Grady mutters.

"Grady. We're happily married, not blind. He got past all of security because he's Hollywood hot."

"With a terrible personality," Davis adds.

"*Exactly*," Annika says. "If I were you, I wouldn't risk anyone spilling the beans to a guy with that kind of personality. Especially when all of your best friends are pregnant and/or keeping up with toddlers. *We're tired.* We love you, and we get it. We wouldn't tell us either if we didn't have to, and the fact that I didn't even wonder why you never told me you were dating is very much a statement about my mental capacity to handle complex information right now."

"Or it's a testament to how much you know some

people who are main characters in this wedding are very secretive and private," Grady says.

"No, this is definitely pregnancy and mother-to-a-toddler brain. Talk to me in about four years, and I'll have a different take on things. Probably. Also, I get to be a bridesmaid if you ever have a real wedding, right?"

I'm so relieved, I could cry.

Who handles secret fake weddings like this?

And how do I deserve them as friends?

I hug her tight. "Of course. No question. Real weddings get best friends for bridesmaids."

Davis shifts beside me. "Can we go talk to her mother now?"

The right answer is *no*.

That there's no *we*, there's *me*.

Except he knows something, and I want to know what he knows.

"Would it be a total inconvenience to talk to your mama sometime soon?" I ask Annika.

"Are you sure you want him to go along?"

"I have to learn to pretend to be in love with him in person and not just in photoshopped pictures, and I have to do it in four days. Practice is probably good."

"Don't the ladies usually find you irresistible?" Grady says to Davis.

"No." He looks at me. "Let's go. Now's good."

At least he's aware of the fact that he's annoying. "I have this thing called work," I say.

"When are you off?"

"Five."

"I'll pick you up."

I look at Annika.

She's grinning.

So is Grady.

Miles is drooping up on Grady's shoulders, bent over Grady's head like not napping is catching up with him.

"Is there anything you want to tell us about Thorny Rock's treasure?" I ask Grady.

If I had any doubts that he was hiding something, the utter confusion wrinkling his face clears that up. "What's with you talking about the treasure again? There isn't a treasure."

Davis gives a subtle headshake, which I interpret to mean *this guy's dumb.*

Or possibly *this guy's hiding something.*

Or maybe he's used up all of his words for the day and doesn't know what to do with himself now.

"We're playing a game," I tell Grady. "He fake-marries me, and I humor his insistence that the treasure is real and we have to find it."

Grady slowly nods, making Miles tilt more precariously up there. "Well. Good luck with that."

I nod back. "If you're gonna be in a lose-lose situation, might as well do it right."

And Davis—

The man smirks.

"Also," I tell my pretend fiancé, "I told my grandmother that you'd video call with her soon. I forgot to mention that this morning."

His expression goes flat again. "This for that? You take me to see Annika's mother and then I talk to your grandmother?"

I could come up with a story about how Davis got busy seeing if he preferred fucking goats to fucking sheep and is so sorry to miss her, but what's the fun in that?

I'm never getting married.

And this back-and-forth, I'll-do-this-for-you-if-you-do-this-for-me thing is almost fun in a weird way. "It's what we're doing, isn't it? And she won't talk to you solo. She's heard things about you and also made up a whole lot worse in her mind."

He holds eye contact for an uncomfortably long while, like he's calling me on the lie, but I don't blink, and I don't look away either.

Finally, he gives the barest of nods. "It's what we're doing."

10

Davis

To no one's surprise, Sloane gives me the *I'm not getting on that thing* look when she walks out the back door of the local doctor's office shortly after five.

She's in light-blue scrubs with little bears all over them, but *I'm not dressed for this* isn't her first argument.

Her first argument shouldn't be a surprise, given what she asked about our getaway from our wedding, yet it still makes me want to twitch.

And it involves the look she's giving my motorcycle as I hold out the spare helmet for her.

"I'm not getting on a death trap at dusk, and especially not to go thirty minutes away. A block and out of sight after our wedding, fine. Here, now? No."

"Rawk! Death traps blow glitter! Rawk!"

I cut a look at the parrot, whom I haven't seen since

the wedding, then back at Sloane. "You're very suspicious of everything."

"I worked in an emergency room when I lived in Copper Valley."

Fine.

She wins.

This round.

And it's more disappointing than I want to acknowledge.

Was I looking forward to a thirty-minute ride, each way, with her arms wrapped around me?

Unfortunately.

There's something about an overly suspicious woman who doesn't fall to the ground in appreciation of my mere existence that appeals to me.

Don't like being worshipped.

Not my thing.

Been there, done that, with letting people down before. Not too keen to do it again.

Especially not the way I did it fifteen years ago.

Much prefer when expectations are kept low.

So this thing where I like Sloane?

It's just about knowing that she's tempering her expectations of me so I won't let her down, or at least so she'll be expecting it when I do.

It's probably not about actually liking her.

I'm merely appreciating that she doesn't treat me like I must be infallible since I was once in a boy band. One that I know she liked.

Big difference.

She walked to work after walking to the museum this morning, so we make our way through the residential neighborhood north of downtown toward her house with the parrot trailing us and making occasional vulgar suggestions.

When we reach her house, she asks if I want to come inside the red brick cottage while she changes.

Fully expected her to tell me to wait outside.

That whole *I don't trust you* vibe and all, even if we need to sell our relationship to anyone who might be watching. For her sake more than mine.

But that feeling is also short-lived.

I grab her arm at the wooden door with three small windows making an arch at about my eye level. She has a porch the width of the house, with yellow and orange fall flowers in pots on either side of the door, but something's not right here.

"Did you leave this open?"

The door's cracked.

Not a lot, but enough that I notice.

She freezes and takes a half step back, right into me, giving me a whiff of antiseptic mingling with a softer cinnamon scent in her hair. "No."

"Stay here."

"Or maybe I did," she adds.

"Do you usually leave your door cracked?"

"No, but everyone makes mistakes. I'm a little off these days."

"Rawk! Intruder alert! Rawk!"

"Get lost, Long Beak Silver," she says to the bird, but her voice is high and uneven.

I peer down at her. "Do you leave your porch

light on?"

It's off. In my experience, when people know they're getting home after dark—and it gets dark early these days —they leave their porch light on.

She visibly shivers as she answers me in a small voice. "Yes. Usually."

"Stay here," I repeat. I tug her back so I can go in first.

"Oh my god. Peggy."

She lunges for the door, but I grab her arm to keep her from going in. "Peggy?"

"My cat. *My cat.*"

I'm not the buffest guy in the world, but I'm not a weakling either. Lift weights regularly. Use my punching bags to manage stress. Keep up with martial arts practice too. So when Sloane wrenches herself out of my grasp and darts inside before me, I'm mildly startled.

She's either surprisingly strong herself, or she's running on straight adrenaline.

"Peggy?" The name barely makes it out of her mouth before she gasps.

And since I'm right on her heels, I can see exactly what has her startled.

An oak foyer table is lying on its side. There's crushed glass and water and flower bits scattered across the wide-plank wood floor.

"Oh my god," she whispers.

"Stay here."

"*I need to make sure my goddamn cat is okay, okay?*"

I turn on my phone's flashlight and aim it beyond the foyer.

"Peggy?" she whispers. There's a tremor in her voice

that turns into an audible inhalation as I light up the entryway to her little house.

I want to pull her into my arms, drag her out of here, take her somewhere safe, and then hunt down whoever did this and make sure they will never, ever, *ever* cause harm again.

However necessary.

After finding her cat for her.

But I breathe through the anger and focus on the immediate problem. "Where would it be?"

"She. She'd be in my bedroom."

She takes two steps, then freezes, and I hear the distinct sound of teeth chattering.

Fuck.

Fuck.

"What does she look like?" I ask Sloane. "Short hair? Long? What color? How big is she?"

She doesn't answer.

I push past her, carefully avoiding the water and broken glass while I head in the direction I assume is her bedroom, but I don't make it three steps before a soft meow stops me.

"*Peggy!*" Sloane drops to her knees, giving me half a heart attack at the thought that she might be kneeling in broken glass, and a three-legged gray tabby dashes to her. "Oh my god, you're okay. My precious baby. You're okay."

A sob wrenches out of her chest.

A lump forms in my own throat.

Later, I tell myself. Feel it later. "Can she go outside?"

Sloane buries her face in the cat's fur. "No."

"Just for now? With you holding her? I'll make a call. Make sure the parrot's gone."

She growls softly while another sob racks her body. Seems like she's trying to hold it in.

I get that.

Held in a few too many things of my own over the years.

I squat down beside her, my entire body alert. "Sloane. I need to check the house, and you should wait outside."

"We should call Chester." Two sobs, but no more. She's clearly fighting for control of her emotions.

"Who's Chester?"

"Sheriff's deputy. He's Tillie Jean's cousin." She sucks in a deep breath, her face still buried in the cat. "If the goats aren't causing trouble anywhere, he can probably be here in five minutes. Probably."

That's another thing about Shipwreck.

Someone let goats loose here a few years back, and they wander everywhere. Tillie Jean campaigned for mayor with the pledge of catch-and-release after fixing all of them so they quit procreating.

If anyone in Shipwreck leaves a door open, a goat gets in.

It's the way of the town.

Surprised me they weren't all over everywhere at the wedding on Sunday. Must've been a hell of a roundup campaign.

Which isn't important.

What's important is making sure whoever did this isn't still here and didn't leave any surprises.

I rise and head deeper into the house.

"Seriously, I'm calling Chester," Sloane says. "*Wait.* He can deal with—I said *wait.*"

"Call him and wait outside."

"*Davis.*"

"If I get murdered, do me one last favor and tell Nigel to fuck all the way off and let you live your life the way you want to live it."

I'm not going to get murdered.

If whoever did this was still here when we arrived, they had to have heard us coming.

But more likely, they knew when Sloane would be at work and cleared out long before now.

"You're an a—asshole sometimes, you know that?" She sounds farther behind me, like she's moving herself and the cat out onto the porch.

"Do my best."

I stride carefully deeper into the house as I hear her talking on her phone. "Ch-Chester. It's Sloane. S-someone broke into m-my house."

I turn left into her living room and text my sister.

Someone broke into a museum volunteer's house.

I don't mention that it's the same volunteer we saw this morning behind the museum.

Vanessa's already suspicious, and I don't need her crap, even if I want her help.

A small-town sheriff's deputy is fine, but I want better resources. Especially since the sheriff's office didn't take Saturday's break-in at the museum seriously.

Naturally, Vanessa doesn't answer.

Doesn't mean she's ignoring me.

Could mean she's busy.

More likely means she's doing whatever she'll do her own way without telling me because she's annoyed that I'm involving myself in what's going on here in Shipwreck.

My friends think *I'm* secretive.

I have nothing on my twin.

Not that they'd know since she wasn't really a part of the crew growing up.

I step carefully around the couch cushions—lavender with a funky circle pattern on them—and the overturned white distressed wood end tables and coffee table. The large-screen TV hung on the wall over a gas fireplace is shattered.

I pass through a small dining room with wall hangings littering the table and three of the six chairs overturned, then into the kitchen.

All of the drawers are pulled out, their contents spilled everywhere. Cabinets ransacked. Two oak cabinet doors hanging off their hinges. The oven's open. So is the microwave.

"Davis?" Sloane calls from the front of the house.

"Stay outside."

"I didn't mean to call you an asshole. You're annoying, but you're not an asshole, and I'd really like you to not get murdered."

"All good."

"Seriously? Is that how you react every time someone calls you names?"

"Not my problem what people think of me."

"That's very enlightened, but enlightenment won't keep you from being murdered."

Dammit. She almost made me smile. And this is not a smiling situation. "Stay outside."

I take a side door from the kitchen into the laundry room, which leads into a closet scattered with more scrubs, sweaters, jeans still on hangers, and boxes of pictures overturned all over the floor. I pick my way around the mess and into a modern primary bathroom with a claw-foot tub, large tile floor, and marble double sinks.

Whoever did this left no cabinet unsearched. They pulled the shower door off its hinges too.

And the bedroom attached to the bathroom is as messy as the rest of the house.

"Who—*why*?" Sloane says from the main bedroom doorway.

She's hugging her cat tight enough that it yowls while her gaze sweeps around the room.

The queen-size mattress crookedly hangs off the rustic wood frame. A floral quilt and ivory sheets and blankets are tossed about. Her underwear is everywhere.

So is an impressive collection of dildos and vibrators.

Some of them...quite large. All of them in different colors.

Ignore them ignore them ignore them.

I picture Sloane spread out on the bed, toy between her legs, eyes glossy, thinking about me—

Stop it.

Breathe.

Focus.

There's a framed painting haphazardly tossed across a

tipped-over rocking chair, with one armrest poking through the canvas.

I bite my tongue to keep from asking if she believes me now.

It's more productive to make two phone calls to get security on her house and someone in for cleanup.

Tomorrow.

Maybe the next day.

After I call Vanessa and ask her to have someone do a more thorough search of the scene once the local sheriff's done with it.

She has connections everywhere.

She can get the best. And I'll return any favors that need returning for it.

Don't like asking for favors, especially outside of my small, trusted circle.

But I'll offer my sister anything she wants to help find who did this, including making it up to whoever can get her the information I want.

"Anything valuable here?" I ask Sloane, pretending I can't see any of the various dildos in all sizes and colors of the rainbow.

Her eyes are shiny as she points to the torn painting. "Tillie Jean did that for—"

She breaks off as her voice cracks again.

My fingers curl into fists.

If the blond caveman did this, it's the last thing he'll do on this earth.

And I'm battling the desire to destroy him with a desperate need to hug Sloane.

Much like I don't ask for favors, I don't hug people outside my group.

They're not safe.

Not trustworthy.

But *fuck*, I want to hug her.

Instead, I shove my fists into my pockets. "She'll fix it or make another one. Let's wait outside."

She sweeps a glance around the room, and her face goes beet red.

Like she, too, is noticing that all of her adult toys are on display.

Focus. Focus. Focus.

"Can I—" she starts, then shakes her head, tossing her long copper hair as something new takes hold.

Confidence.

Rebellion.

Fuck-it-ness.

Probably some anger too.

Good.

She's gonna need that.

I manage to steer her toward the front of the house without touching her. "Do you have any enemies? Or were you storing museum artifacts here?"

Her shoulders visibly tighten, then sag, and her breath comes out in a quick *whoosh*.

"Sloane?"

She visibly shivers as she walks through the front door onto the porch.

Sniffles again too.

Fuck.

I curl my fingers so tightly into my palms that my short nails dig into my skin to keep from reaching for her.

"So you're right." Her voice is dull. "Someone's taking this treasure hunt very seriously."

Her gaze swings sharply to me as she abruptly halts halfway down the porch stairs. "Or someone wants it to look like someone's taking this treasure hunt very seriously."

I probably deserve that kind of suspicion. "Spent the morning at my place. Beck came out. He left. Saw you at the bakery. Spent the rest of the afternoon at Crusty Nut."

"Quick alibi."

"You ever been in trouble?"

She blinks.

I watch her, waiting, wondering what has her surprised by the question.

Or if she relates to it.

Huh. Is she a recovering troublemaker too? I repeat my question, softer. "*Have* you been in trouble?"

"Have you?" she fires back.

"Yep."

"Real trouble, or you just did something normal and human that people had a bad reaction to because it wasn't what they wanted you to do, so you just *felt* like you were always in trouble?"

"That's a very specific question."

"I've lived a very specific life. How much trouble have you been in? Do you have a criminal record?"

"No, but only because I had money."

Usually I'm the one watching someone until they crack.

Not right now.

And right now, the back of my neck is getting hot.

I'm not normally that forward with practical strangers.

It's sympathy for her being in a shitty situation that likely isn't her fault and nearly certainly is related to Thorny Rock's treasure.

Tell me what you had in your house.

She had something here.

Her body language is incredibly easy to read, and I hit a nerve when I asked her if she was storing something for the museum here.

I look at her, silently telegraphing the demand that I know better than to put into words.

Don't need to look like a dick by ordering her to confess it to me out loud.

"Rawk! Eat a bag of dicks! Rawk!" The parrot's voice is farther away.

Good thing.

I don't want to see the parrot meet the cat.

Sloane looks out across the street like she's thinking the same thing, then resumes walking down the four steps to her well-trimmed but browning lawn, still holding her cat. "I can't decide if that means you're more or less likely to have done this yourself."

"What I want is at someone else's house."

She eyes me again.

Did I say having a woman suspicious of me was enjoyable?

I was mistaken.

This is too far.

A sheriff's car pulls to the curb, and Sloane lets out a heavy breath.

I let out a slower breath as a familiar face pops out of the car.

So that's Chester.

He was shooting me looks all afternoon at Crusty Nut. Alibi verified.

He hitches his uniform pants up, goes ruddy in the cheeks, and looks at Sloane. "Someone did a B and E on you, huh? That hasn't happened around here in at least four years."

Fantastic.

"Except for Saturday night at the museum," I remind him.

He shifts another look at me but doesn't answer.

"You have a forensics crew?" I press.

He ignores me and talks directly to Sloane. "Welp, let's go have a look-see."

I suck in a deep breath so I don't mutter anything I'll regret later.

Like *Fuck on a platter, have a fucking look-see?*

"A *look-see*?" Sloane's voice gets higher. "Davis is right. Where's the forensics crew? *Someone tossed my house,* Chester. That's not worthy of a *look-see.*"

"He makes me nervous, okay?" Chester blurts. "He was my favorite. And now he's—"

The deputy gestures to me, as if to say *now he's right here.*

"Oh my god," Sloane mutters again.

If I squeeze my fists any harder, I'll draw blood. "I'll go take a walk."

"You're a witness," Chester says.

"Happy to give a statement after you have your look-see."

I stroll down the center walk from Sloane's house to the sidewalk, ignore the images of her sex toys that keep popping into my head unbidden, then hang a right, without him stopping me.

"Shouldn't you wear gloves?" Sloane says to him as I'm walking away.

"*Psst*," someone else says.

I pause.

"Over here," they whisper.

The neighbor to Sloane's right has her door cracked and is gesturing to me. She's maybe four foot ten if she's an inch, with tight white curls on her head, more wrinkles than an elephant, and the combination of her large glasses and the porch light makes her eyes seem larger.

I head up her walkway to her front door in the rapidly darkening evening. "Yes, ma'am?"

"Are you the guy marrying Sloane on Saturday?"

"Yes. Why?"

"I saw another guy at her house earlier, and—"

Thank fuck for small towns and retired people. "What did he look like?"

She squints at me with watery brown eyes like she's debating if she wants to tell me.

I actively suppress a frustrated sigh and pull my phone out. One quick search later, I hold it out to her. "That him?"

"It *is!*"

Fuck.

"You know him?" she asks. "Ohhh, I've been reading these why choose romances where the woman hooks up with multiple guys. Is Sloane having the time of her life? Is she actually marrying two or three of you on Saturday, but they're telling me it's just one because they think I'm too old to handle how young people do things these days? I'm so jealous. These old bones can't even handle my vibrator anymore."

Sloane has at least four vibrators. Which I need to not remember, ever. "Maybe try a lower setting."

She snorts. "Oh, you think I haven't tried that? Almost broke my wrist even then. Take it from me, young man. Take your calcium and keep lifting weights."

"Will do. Thanks. You willing to tell the deputy over there about who you saw?"

She squints at me through her glasses, then peers past me to Sloane's house. "Is that the single deputy?"

"Is Chester single?"

She gasps. *"Chester's her third?* I'm telling his wife. I'm telling his wife *right now.*"

"Sloane's house was broken into sometime today."

She gasps again. "While she was having a threesome with all of her fiancés?"

I look over at Sloane's house.

Can't see as much now.

No porch light on.

But there's a flashlight bouncing around the living room windows from the inside.

"Sloane," I say.

"What?" comes the short reply from her porch.

I almost smile. That's more like the normal cranky I appreciate out of her. "Your neighbor saw someone."

"Convenient," she mutters loudly enough for her voice to carry.

"Are you having a why choose romance next door?" the older lady calls. "Are you actually marrying more than one man on Saturday?"

"No, Mrs. Kapinski, but someone did break into my house," Sloane calls back.

"He was breaking into your house?" a guy calls from somewhere else on the street. "I saw a dude hanging out when I got home for lunch. I thought it was weird since you're engaged to the lost Bro Code guy, but like Mrs. K. says, if we didn't even know you were dating him, how many other fiancés are you keeping from us?"

"Are you serious right now? Someone *broke into my house*, and you want to know if I'm living out one of our book club books?"

"Somebody has to be," Mrs. Kapinski says. "We want it to be you."

Chester's flashlight bobs in the doorway, lighting up the electrician's van across the street. "You saw someone, Vinnie?"

"Yeah, guy looked familiar," Vinnie calls back. "But I can't place him."

"This young man knows who he is," Mrs. Kapinski yells. "I think they're having a polyamorous lover's quarrel over who gets to say vows first."

They'd be hilarious if Sloane's house hadn't been trashed.

"Can you ask him who it is?" Chester says to Sloane. "I, ah, need to go call in for backup."

"It's your *freaking job*," Sloane says.

"Yeah, and…"

Whatever he mutters doesn't carry over the yard.

Doesn't matter.

Pretty sure I know what he's saying.

And he's the missing Bro Code guy.

Basic gist of it.

So fun, being the *missing Bro Code guy.*

Never been missing. Anyone who's needed to know where I am has always known.

And I'm in Shipwreck often enough that the deputy fucking knows I'm not missing.

"Also, you can't stay here tonight," Chester adds. "It's a crime scene. Like, a real one. Not the kind where Tillie Jean calls and complains that Cooper left a crime scene at her house."

I don't hear Sloane answer, but I feel a shiver ripple the air.

Highly doubt she'd want to stay there tonight.

I wait until Chester's at his car, then I bid Mrs. Kapinski a good night with whatever she needs to make it a good night, and cross the lawn back to Sloane's house.

She's sitting on the front step, shoulders sagging.

The cat's audibly purring.

No coat, so I shrug out of mine and drape it over her shoulders. "Go ask Vinnie if it was Patrick Dixon."

That's a look.

Lucky I'm not shriveling up into the crusted remains of a dead toad right now.

"Why the *hell*—"

"He was outside the museum this morning."

She stares at me.

I stare back.

She doesn't crack, but after one of the longest games of *don't blink* I've ever played, she looks away and pulls my coat tighter around her while balancing the cat.

"Why?" she says quietly.

"Why was he there?" I clarify.

"Why *all of this*?"

"Human nature to want to find a treasure. Even if it doesn't exist."

She slides another look at me. "Blow through all of your boy band money?"

I snort in amusement before I can stop myself. That also doesn't usually happen with people I haven't known my whole life either. "No."

"So you just want to find a treasure for the fun of it."

There's no right answer to that question.

No, Sloane, I want to find the treasure to end the curiosity about it so no one else finds out the secret I know that could end Shipwreck as you know it.

"Yep," I say.

"I don't believe you."

That makes two of us. "You have a place to stay tonight?"

She's still staring at me, but a visible shiver makes her shoulders twitch. "I can find a place."

"Mine's away from all of this."

"Are you offering me a place to stay, or are you bragging?"

"Offering."

"Why would you do that?"

"Good picture opportunity for Nigel and your grandmother. We're getting married Saturday. We should be living together."

"And?"

"And I'll be sitting outside wherever you go anyway to make sure your ex doesn't try any more shit."

"*Why?*"

"He hurt Ellie, and now he's doing bad shit."

She flinches.

I watch her, but she doesn't look back at me this time.

"Wasn't your fault he was a cheat," I add on a hunch.

"It *feels* like it was my fault."

"Why?"

"Because—because it does, okay?"

"Stupid answer."

"When you grow up being told everything's your fault and you need to do better and be perfect, it's fucking hard to forgive yourself when your decisions hurt good people." Her whole body freezes, and she pinches her eyes shut. "Never mind. Forget I said that."

Not a fucking chance.

I lift my phone again and hit *call* on Ellie's number.

She picks up on the second ring, and in very Ellie-like fashion, she doesn't bother with a *hello*. "What the *fuck*, Davis?" she hisses, which probably means she's far enough away from her kids that they can't hear her dropping the f-bomb. "Everyone's worried sick about you, and this feels like when no one would talk about why you all—"

"You remember Sloane Pearce?" I interrupt.

There's a long pause. "Yes. Why?"

"She's here. You're on speaker."

"Seriously?"

It's official. The rumor mill that I'm marrying Sloane hasn't reached all of my friends yet.

I nudge my pretend bride and wave my phone at her so she can see the name on the screen.

"Hi, Ellie," Sloane says hesitantly.

"Is he giving you shit? Tell me if he's giving you shit. My brother's out there in Shipwreck right now, and I can be there in an hour if I need to kick his ass."

"Kick…whose…ass?"

"Davis's. I'd kick Beck's ass too if you needed me to, but I suspect he's too busy to give you shit. Also, giving people shit isn't his style. Not that giving people shit is Davis's style, but I hear he's had…a day."

"Davis is only giving me mild shit. It's more like indigestion."

Ellie snorts. "That's how we all feel."

"Sitting right here," I remind her.

"It is," she says. "You go off and do your secret-secret stuff, and then you show up and you're all, *hey, Wyatt, can you get me four VIP tickets to the air show?*, and you don't say why, and you don't show up for the air show, and then the next thing I know, Beck's reporting you're about to do something stupid. Including *getting married*, even if he doesn't know *to whom*."

"She's very blunt," I say to Sloane.

I almost get a smile.

"Ellie, are you mad at Sloane for what Patrick Dixon did to you?"

"*What?* No. I'm pissed at him for what he did to both of us. I mean, I was. I don't think about him at all anymore. Oh my god. Sloane. Tell me you're not dating him again. I mean, if you are and you're happy, I'll...be...happy for you? As happy as I can be? I really think you can do better."

"That's not the problem," Davis says. "She's smarter than that."

"Oh." Ellie pauses but only briefly. "*Ohh.* Oh, no. Oh, no no no. Sloane, you aren't holding yourself responsible for a shithead man's actions, are you? It's not your fault. I was never mad at you. Jealous because you're gorgeous, yes, but I'm only human. I think you're awesome."

Sloane eyes me.

Then the phone.

She presses one palm into an eye socket while clinging to the cat with her other hand. "Thank you," she whispers.

"We're coming out this weekend with Levi and Ingrid and their kids, and I'm buying you a beer at the Grog," Ellie says. "Badasses stick together. Don't waste one more minute feeling like that asswipe was your fault. Seriously. He's not worth it. Why do the men never feel as guilty as we do?"

Sloane hugs her cat tighter and huddles into herself as much as she can. "Thank you," she says again.

"Uh-oh. I think one of the kids just got Wyatt in the bathtub. Gotta go. Davis. *Do not be stupid.* I'll call your sister. Don't think I won't."

"Good luck with that," I reply.

"Don't underestimate me."

"Wouldn't dream of it. Have fun with bath time."

157

I disconnect.

Sloane sucks in a shaky, audible breath.

"Backup's on the way," Chester calls. "We're gonna need to get statements from everyone."

Vinnie's wandered over from across the street. "I saw someone. You want me to describe him? I'm real good at drawing too. I can take a stab at it. Also, I called the mayor. The new mayor. She's freaking out and coming over too. Gotta have everyone involved when there's a crime around here, you know? All hands on deck."

Sloane sighs again.

I feel that one.

It's gonna be a long night.

And that's before the next car that comes screeching to a halt in front of Sloane's house.

11

Davis

I DON'T NEED to see who's climbing out of the Audi to know I'm not going to like it.

First, very few people in Shipwreck drive Audis.

Second, even fewer would drive across town for this. Most would walk.

With snacks and drinks.

Bet even Tillie Jean's walking. Even if she wasn't mayor, she's one of Sloane's tightest friends.

But this car?

This car holds a dude.

A tall, built, thinks-he's-a-god dude.

"Sloane? What the hell's going on here?"

She flinches beside me. "Hello, Nigel."

I scoot closer to her and slip an arm around her.

Gotta play the part.

Ignore the *zing* racing over my skin from touching her.

Not real.

This is adrenaline, and the wedding is a favor.

Nigel stalks up her front walk. "What happened?"

I hate the concern in his voice.

It almost sounds sincere.

Don't mind that the streetlight flickering on illuminates a couple sparkles of glitter still in his hair though.

Sloane huddles closer to me. "Small break-in. It's fine."

"You had a break-in and you think it's *fine*? What the hell's wrong with this town? You're not safe here. We're leaving. Now."

Peggy the cat yowls while I make myself stay still. "She'll decide for herself what she wants and needs."

"She needs people who've known her forever, not you stupid asshat musicians."

I would enjoy the shit out of putting a fist through this guy's face.

Peggy yowls louder.

"Shh," Sloane whispers. "It's okay, sweet girl. It's okay."

"Now, now, let's not get name-cally," Chester says. "Everyone here's good people."

"Sloane. It's time to go somewhere safe," Nigel says.

I look at the woman I'm pretending to be engaged to. "Sloane, you want to go with him?"

"No, thank you."

I look back at the fucker.

Don't say anything.

Just look at him.

He has me by a few inches. Definitely by fifty or so pounds too.

THE PRETEND FIANCÉ FIASCO

But he's mistaken if he thinks that means he can force his way through me to get to her.

Don't mistake muscle for strength.

"Don't be stubborn, Sloane." Fucker sounds bored now. "The sooner you accept what's best—"

"For who?" I interrupt.

His eyes flicker to me in the dim light. He leans toward Sloane, and I rise and get in his way.

"What are you doing here?" I ask.

"I'm here to take care of my...friend."

"Where were you all day today?"

He lifts himself to his full height and glares down at me. "I don't like your tone."

He's smart there, at least.

And I don't think he did this. I just want him to think I think he did this.

Don't be a dick, I tell myself.

And then I tell myself to fuck off.

I'll be whatever Sloane needs me to be.

"Now, gentlemen." Chester shoots a quick look at me before focusing on Nigel again. "Crime can make tempers run high, but we're all on the same team here."

Sloane snorts softly.

So does her cat.

"We are *not* on the same team," Nigel says.

"Who's that now?" Mrs. Kapinski calls from next door. "Is that that hottie who crashed Cooper's wedding?"

Sloane sighs.

The cat meows loudly.

And Nigel puffs his chest up. "I was blessed by God, ma'am."

161

"In all the ways?" she calls back. "How big is your penis?"

He visibly chokes. "Excuse you, ma'am—"

"Welp, that's disappointing. If you're not willing to answer the question, we know what that means."

"Sloane, this town—"

"Is my home," she says quietly.

"Davis, how's your penis?" Mrs. Kapinski calls.

Do not answer. Do not answer. Do not— "Formally classified as a biological weapon, ma'am."

Silence falls over the street.

Silence except for a very small squeak coming from Sloane's direction, and the sound of quick footsteps rushing toward us on the street.

"Mrs. Kapinski, the tabloid rules are still firmly in effect, and I will quadruple your punishment if you leak that to the press," Tillie Jean says. "Go back inside. All of you. Chester, what's going on? Where's the crime scene tape? Why haven't you put that up yet? Excuse me, sir, you need to be at least fifty feet from the house."

Nigel glares at Tillie Jean.

"Wouldn't challenge her if I were you," I murmur.

"Shut your fucking face," Nigel snaps back.

"You sure you're a man of God?"

Remarkable how little it takes to make someone's temper blow.

Good thing Chester's apparently well-trained too because the minute Nigel swings at me, Chester's in motion.

I let the two of them tussle it out while I back up and

hold out a hand to Sloane. "We should also get away from the crime scene."

She gapes at me. "*Oh my god*, how did you duck that?"

"Just did."

"It's like you didn't even move. Did you teleport? Did you teleport yourself away from his fist? Oh my god, are you okay?"

My biological weapon isn't the only part of me enjoying her being impressed, and I need to tamp that down. "Martial arts are good for anger management."

She stares at me for a brief moment longer, then she's on her feet, glaring at her...whatever he is. "*What the hell*, Nigel? *We don't hit people.*"

He grunts from the ground, where Chester has him pinned. "Watch your language."

"You watch *your* fucking language," she fires back. "*Don't punch my fiancé.* Do you want to be uninvited from the wedding?"

"He doesn't deserve you."

"He's not wrong," I tell Sloane.

"God, he's so swoony," Chester says. Then he grunts as Nigel twists under him. "*Stay still.* I'll get my taser out if I think you're gonna try to punch someone again. Mr. Remington's right. I'm gonna need to know where you were all day today."

Peggy meows loudly.

And Tillie Jean crushes Sloane and the cat both with a hug. "You okay?"

Sloane's muffled *no* makes my heart crack in two.

"What do you need?" TJ asks her quietly.

It's what I should be asking, but instead, I issued orders.

Same as fucking *Nigel*.

"To wake up from this nightmare?" Sloane whispers.

Tillie Jean shoots me a look while she hugs Sloane tighter.

That look could mean any number of things.

Is this your fault?

Are you doing anything about it?

How will you fix this?

Can you keep her safe?

Do you want me to tell Chester to accidentally knee Nigel in the gonads?

If you're going to be her pretend fiancé, you damn well better take good care of her.

There's one appropriate response regardless of what Tillie Jean's look means.

I nod.

I've got Sloane.

I won't let anything happen to her.

Anything *else*.

I won't let anything *else* happen to her.

We have to find the fucking treasure. I have to find the fucking blond caveman. And I have to make sure Nigel knows that Sloane is completely off-limits. Not just starting Saturday, at our wedding, but from this moment on.

Fake.

Fake wedding.

I meant to think *fake wedding*.

Shit.

"Get off of me, you buffoon. Do you know who I am?" Nigel says.

"Nobody punches former Bro Code members in my town and gets away with it," Chester replies.

"I didn't *punch* him. I *scared* him."

"You didn't do either," Chester says. "He dodged you like he's the wind, and the only person any of us are afraid of in this town is Tillie Jean."

"He's mistreating my fiancée."

"Uh, last I heard, *he's* her fiancé."

"But he might not be the only one!" Mrs. Kapinski calls.

Sloane sighs.

Tillie Jean sighs.

I stifle a sigh.

"Chester, what do you need from Sloane?" Tillie Jean says.

"Just her statement."

"Great. Get off the hot preacher dude and come take her statement so she and Davis can go home and rest."

There's no mistaking the look Tillie Jean gives me now.

It's *you're fucking lucky I'm willing to keep up this ruse, or I'd be taking Sloane home to my house right now.*

"Peggy," Sloane whispers.

"Got everything she needs," I tell her.

And I will.

Just need to send one quick text message.

"You heard her," Nigel says. "*Get the fuck off me.*"

"Your language is atrocious, Nigel," Sloane says.

165

"Maybe try saying *please* so that Chester knows you're not going to try to take out my fiancé again."

"He started it."

"Do you know what's sexy, Nigel? Taking responsibility is sexy."

I've spent fifteen years practicing daily meditation. Impulse control. Mind over body.

And a redheaded nurse whom I barely know saying *responsibility is sexy* has me completely losing my shit.

Internally.

And in my biological weapon.

Because all my brain sees are those dildos and vibrators scattered all over Sloane's bedroom while I kneel in front of her and tell her everything I've ever taken responsibility for in my life.

"I think you might have to sit on him for a while so I can go take their statements," Chester says to Tillie Jean.

"Ew. I'm not touching him," she replies. "Let me call Max."

"Get *off* me," Nigel says again.

"Let him go," Sloane says. "If he tries to hurt Davis again, I'll take him down myself."

Chester and Tillie Jean share a look.

Tillie Jean grins.

Chester shrugs, then lets Nigel go.

Nigel climbs to his feet, glaring at all of us. "Sloane. *Let's go.*"

She heaves another sigh. "If you want to be helpful, Nigel, you can go find a cat carrier for Peggy. I can't go back in my house to get any of my things, because it's a fucking crime scene, and I can't transport my cat without a cat carrier."

Nigel stares at Sloane.

Then he looks at me. "Go get Sloane a cat carrier."

I don't reply.

Not worth the breath.

Instead, I slip my arm around Sloane. "Chester. Can we give you statements from Tillie Jean's house?"

He looks at me, and even lit only by the glow of house-lights and headlights, I can see him going red again.

He answers me by speaking to Sloane. "That's a really good idea. Sloane, you two head over to Tillie Jean's house." He points down the street. "Backup's here. I'll have one of them give you a ride. Stay close. We'll have some questions."

Nigel takes a step toward Sloane.

The cat hisses, and Nigel leaps back.

"This is not the way," Sloane says quietly to him.

His jaw muscles tic while he stares at her.

He probably knows.

He knows he's losing her. Might even be realizing he never had her in the first place.

And that makes him one more loose thread in her life that needs to be tied up.

Tomorrow problem.

Or Saturday problem.

At the moment, though, getting Sloane and her cat out of the rapidly cooling night air and away from her house is what matters most.

12

Sloane

THEY WON'T LET me have my car.

They won't freaking let me have my car.

I knew I wouldn't get my clothes. I knew I wouldn't get my cat carrier.

But I didn't expect that they wouldn't let me have my car.

That's what finally breaks me, and that's why I'm now clinging to Davis's back for dear life as he steers his motorcycle up the side of Anchor Mountain, with Peggy in a backpack carrier that Tillie Jean found for me.

There are fewer houses out here than on Thorny Rock Mountain, Cooper's mountain, which is exactly what I want tonight.

I just need to be *away*.

Once Nigel texted that he was arranging to stay at the inn tonight, it was clear that I couldn't crash on Tillie

Jean's couch, or at Annika and Grady's house, or at anyone else's house so that I wouldn't have to actually go home with Davis.

And part of me is relieved that I can't stay with any of them.

I don't want my friends to see just how rattled I am.

I know.

I know, okay?

Your friends are exactly who you should turn to when you're rattled.

But it's complicated.

Especially since I realized what's missing at my house.

Thorny Rock's coat.

It's gone.

Tillie Jean's aunt Bea had dropped it off with me the day before the wedding last week. I was supposed to take it in over the weekend, but I've been enjoying the last few days of warm enough weather to comfortably walk to work.

It felt like one of those things that should be driven and not exposed to the elements. Even warm elements.

And after the break-in on Saturday night, I thought anything new would be safer at my house than at the museum.

Because no one knew it was there.

Stupid stupid stupid.

Someone knew it was there.

I grip Davis tighter and lean my helmeted head against his back as he slows for a sharp switchback curve, taking comfort in the weight of Peggy and her carrier on my back, breathing in the chilly night air and the scent of pine and leather, unsure which is coming from nature, and which is coming from the man I'm wrapped around and his coat, which I'm still wearing.

It's warm.

Enveloping me like a hug.

Giving me the sensation of safety no matter how much I don't trust *safety* right now.

It's not long before we arrive at the trailer deep in the woods.

There's a single light on inside and no other cars.

He parks next to a pile of what looks like fresh-cut firewood and helps me off the bike.

"You okay?" he asks.

I nod and hand over the helmet.

He's bare-armed with all of his tattoos visible. And he drove us up here like that, despite the fifty-degree weather.

He leads us inside and goes directly to the thermostat, then leaves the camper again.

And that's when I see it.

Cat litter and a litter box under the kitchenette table. A bag of the cat kibble that I feed Peggy. Two pet bowls on the table beside a pile of cat toys.

My eyes sting.

He said he'd take care of Peggy's supplies when he offered to let me stay here.

He didn't say they'd magically appear out of thin air without me needing to make a list and sending him back down to the store.

I set the backpack carrier down on the couch and unzip it so Peggy can explore at her leisure. Once I have her litter box set up and food out for her, I take a minute to escape to the teensy-tiny starkly white bathroom. While I'm in there, I pause to stare at myself in the mirror over the sink.

"You've got this," I whisper to my reflection. "You've been through worse. You're okay now. You'll keep being okay."

My reflection stares back dubiously.

Clearly I don't believe myself.

And have I been through worse?

Have I?

I remember Oliver, the boyfriend who stole half my life savings with that lie about his mom a couple years after I graduated nursing school, and I decide I don't care to contemplate if this is worse or not.

When I leave the bathroom, Davis is back inside. He's set a bottle of some kind of alcohol on the compact coffee table in front of the tan leather couch.

And that's when it hits me that we're in a camper trailer.

With likely a single bedroom.

And a single bed.

My stomach dips.

This was a bad idea.

I'm definitely sleeping on the couch.

Peggy is hopping from the living room area into the kitchen, eyeing both of us warily. She came to me missing her front right leg, and she hops more than she walks, and she's my favorite cat that I've ever had. The cuddliest, sweetest cat ever.

Not that I've had many.

Grandma didn't do pets. The two older cats I got in college were my first pets.

They both left me not long after half my life savings went to California with Oliver the ex.

"How did you get supplies here?" I ask Davis. "I mean, thank you, but *how*?"

"Sarah has a cat."

Sarah.

Ava's mom. Beck Ryder's wife.

He called his friends to help.

My eyes get hot again. "Thank you."

He nods.

I step into the living room and perch on the edge of the couch, watching Peggy explore.

Davis is watching me.

"What did he take?"

That's a question I'd rather not answer, but I have a feeling my face isn't nearly as good as his right now at hiding how I feel about that.

It's also a question Chester didn't ask while I was giving him my statement.

I should've offered the information, and I didn't.

He crosses the living room and sits on the other end of the couch. "That bad?"

Worse.

Because I know what it means.

I finally look back at him, and I actively squirm under the intensity of his gaze. "You know Bea? She runs the Grog?"

He nods.

"She gave me a coat that she said was Thorny Rock's. It

wasn't where I left it. It was this old leather thing, like a trench coat."

He doesn't say a word.

"I know. *I know*, okay? I know I should've taken it to the museum sooner, but the museum had the break-in, and you started acting weird, and I thought I should drive it instead of walking it. I had it by the back door. The one closest to my carport. And I only had it for four days. But it was—it was in near plain sight. He didn't have to wreck my entire house to find it."

Dammit.

The shivers are back.

They're making my teeth clack together as Davis watches me ramble while my cat leaps onto the bench at the kitchenette table, sniffing out the cat toys.

I force my jaw shut, trying to stop my teeth from betraying me.

"Tequila?" he says.

I look at the bottle again.

Clase Azul.

I'm unfamiliar with the brand, but the fact that he'd offer tequila instead of vodka or whiskey or rum—

Has he watched me? Has he quietly paid attention to me when I wasn't looking?

I clamp down on my inner teenager swooning before she gets a chance to start, and I eye him again. "How did you know I like tequila?"

"You order a shot of the shitty kind every time I'm at the Grog. And if you have three shots instead of just one, you might tell me again that I ruined your life."

I freeze. "What?"

173

He smirks. "Never mind."

"No, not *never mind*. What are you talking about?"

He shakes his head.

And a little teeny tiny memory of him doing that motion in the Grog knocks something loose in my head. "Oh my god, I said that to you the night that we played darts."

"In vino veritas."

In wine, there is truth.

Or in my case, tequila and a bad day make for weakened verbal filters and suppressed memories.

"Sorry," I mutter. "I didn't mean it."

His eyes smile. "Heard a lot worse."

Like tonight.

With Nigel insulting him while he stood between me and my ransacked house.

I shiver harder.

Someone—no, not *someone*.

My *ex-boyfriend* broke into my house, completely trashed it, and stole a historical artifact that was supposed to go to the Thorny Rock Historical Museum.

Dammit. My teeth are chattering again. "Dita Kapinski told me the new security system is up and running at the museum. Thank you."

"Kapinski—your neighbor?"

I shake my head. "My neighbor is Dita's mother-in-law. Dita lives closer to Tillie Jean's parents."

Davis scoots closer to me, pops the top on the bottle, and pours a shot into each of two rocks glasses.

He hands me one.

I down it.

He refills me, then leans back on the couch.

But he doesn't shoot his tequila.

He sips it.

I sniff my glass.

I've never had a tequila that I've wanted to sip.

Much like I've never had a vodka that I've wanted to sip.

Tillie Jean told me once it's because we only drink the cheap stuff. She's been to parties in Hollywood because of Cooper, and I get the feeling she's tried things that are way out of my income bracket.

Probably like this tequila.

I slide a look at Davis as warmth finally takes hold in my belly. "Is this your land now, or are you squatting because you know no one else is using it?"

"Mine. For now."

"Until you find the treasure."

"Sure."

I try a little sip of the tequila, and *oh my god*.

Not asking.

Definitely not asking how much this cost.

But it's good.

Smooth. Minimal burn.

I sip again.

After a third sip, I have the courage to ask the question that's suddenly niggling at me. "If the treasure doesn't exist, it can't be found. If it can't be found, when will people stop looking for it? How long do I have to worry that people will perpetually be trying to take things from the museum, thinking it's some kind of clue?"

"It exists."

I shift on the couch until I'm leaning one shoulder against the back cushions and stare at him. "How do you *know*?"

"Just do."

"Because you feel it?"

"Have proof."

"What proof?"

The fucker doesn't answer.

Not that I thought he would.

Maybe if I get more tequila in him, he will.

The corners of his lips lift behind his beard.

Just a little, but a little's enough.

"Are you laughing at my plans to get this information out of you?" I ask him.

He wasn't in my head. He can't know what I was thinking.

Except he might.

"Were there any hidden pockets in Thorny Rock's jacket?" he asks me.

"Why? Do you think there were? Have you seen it? Have you inspected it? If you did, why didn't you look for hidden pockets yourself?"

The man has the audacity to smile.

Actually *smile*.

"You're very suspicious," he says.

"You're stalking me after agreeing to fake-marry me because you think I'll be useful in a treasure hunt for a treasure that might not exist. You almost got into a fistfight with my grandma's preacher's grandson, who's being an even bigger dick than I remember him as. Also, my ex-boyfriend broke into my house and

176

stole a pirate coat. I think I have a right to be suspicious."

"The last time I did a fake wedding, the bride was more grateful."

I roll my eyes, which is likely the tequila's doing. It's making me mouthy.

And I think he knew it would.

"Excuse me. My humblest apologies for not worshipping at your feet for your magnanimous gesture in *insisting* that you help me. You are *such* a man."

Is his—it is.

His smile's getting bigger.

His eyes are even twinkling.

I point my glass at him. "Stop it. Do not twinkle. You don't get to twinkle."

Shit.

I'm getting toasty.

But I'm not shivering anymore.

Actually—I shrug out of his leather jacket, but not before I sniff it one last time.

It smells like campfire and tequila. Like fresh pine logs and s'mores with a hint of smoke.

When I miss men, I miss how they smell.

But I don't often miss men.

I hand the jacket to him. "Thank you, oh benevolent king, for the undeserved gift of warmth."

Fucker smiles *even bigger*.

And it makes him look twenty years younger.

I used to watch all of the YouTube videos I could find of Bro Code performing, especially after I left Grandma's house and moved to Copper Valley for nursing school.

Davis smiled like that when he was performing. Regularly in photo shoots that went along with tabloid interviews. On the billboards around Copper Valley advertising the hometown band.

He was far less hairy then, but that smile—that smile was why he was my favorite. It spoke to my soul.

In a parasocial *I'm never going to meet this guy and he has no idea I exist* kind of way, but it did. It made me believe I wasn't going to hell.

It made me believe that not only would there always be good in the world, but that I was part of the good in the world.

Now, you don't see it on him when he's out in town.

But here he is.

Smiling.

At me.

"Are we in an alternate dimension? Because you don't do *this*. This *happy* thing. What's going on here?"

"It's an honor to have your suspicion, my lady."

I snort. "Sure it is."

"I like to earn respect."

"Been a long time since a man's earned that from me."

He watches me.

Doesn't say anything.

Doesn't drink more of his tequila.

I drink more of mine.

I shouldn't, but the tequila is in control of my decisions now. And honestly, I could go for some nice, solid, alcohol-induced amnesia about tonight.

"Do you have food?" I ask.

"Yes. Unless you want mushrooms."

I don't know what my eyes are doing, but there's horror coming from everything I was taught growing up, and intrigue from every part of me that I suppressed in an effort to be a good girl who wouldn't burn in the pits of hell for all eternity.

"I've never done mushrooms."

Is that my voice?

That husky, intrigued voice?

"Portabellas," he says. "Two-year-old cleaned me out."

"Oh."

"Dragon fruit's gone too."

"You have a two-year-old?"

"Beck's two-year-old."

"Ava."

"You know Ava?"

"Doc's seen her occasionally when they've been out here. Toddlers get sick all the time."

"She called me ugly."

"You're having quite the day."

He smiles again, and then he's in motion.

It's not chaotic motion though.

Just smooth, slow movements taking him where he needs to be. "Hope you like grilled cheese."

"Like popcorn better."

"Buttered?"

"With garlic and parm. Sometimes cinnamon sugar. But not together."

I feel mildly like I'm being an ass, but every time I get snippy or mouthy, he smiles.

Davis Remington.

Smiling.

Because of me being an ass.

My entire body mellows as I watch Peggy while she continues sniffing out her new surroundings, and then I feel left out because they're both in the kitchen and I'm not.

When I stumble into sitting at the table, Peggy leaps into my lap and rubs her head all over my boobs.

Davis is quiet while he slices a sourdough bread round on a thick wooden cutting board over the small Formica countertop next to the small sink.

No marble or porcelain in sight.

The floor is a tan patterned vinyl meant to simulate tile. Not some kind of fancy, exotic porcelain that I'm sure some rich people would put into an RV to feel more at home.

Or even budget floor store tiles that normal people might put in their often-used camper.

He drops a pat of butter into a hot stainless-steel skillet, swirls it, then sets two slices of bread down, and tops each with a single slice of deli cheese.

One's cheddar.

The other—Havarti maybe? Provolone? Not gouda. It's not yellow enough to be gouda.

I sip my tequila again and glance at the counter. I recognize the butter—it's from a local farm.

But it's the popcorn he pulls out of a cabinet that makes me straighten.

That's not microwave popcorn.

That's a jar of fresh popcorn kernels.

Be still my heart. The man stocks fresh popcorn kernels in his remote mountain camper.

He has limited cabinet space.

How does he have everything I want?

I count the cabinet doors, all of them painted brown with dull silver knobs, and since this space is tiny, it doesn't take me long to finish.

We don't even reach double-digits. Me and my counting fingers.

There's no way he has a popcorn popper in here.

But he has a cast-iron skillet. With a lid.

"Do you have someone who buys and stocks houses for you?" I ask.

He shakes his head.

"You got everything for the kitchen yourself?"

"Usually do."

"When don't you?"

"When Vanessa or Ellie or June get the opportunity to decide I'm doing it wrong."

I know Ellie. Clearly. I stole her boyfriend from her and she's kind enough to not blame me for it.

I think June is related to Cash Rivers. I saw a news article that mentioned her as part of the coverage of Cooper and Waverly's wedding.

But Vanessa—I don't know who Vanessa is. "Is Vanessa your sister?"

"One and only."

"I forgot you have a sister. Even though you told me you married her. Which I don't believe, by the way."

He shifts a look at me.

And this one isn't blank.

This one is *something*.

"What?" I say.

He lights the burner beneath the cast-iron skillet. "You don't trust me."

Huh. I have the perfect view of Davis's ass. Which shouldn't matter, because Smart Sloane knows that Teenage Sloane's crushes are still men, and men are bad. Men lie, steal, and cheat.

"I don't trust most men anymore, but honestly, with the Mr. Mysterious routine you have going, I trust you a little less. And a little more at the same time since I know I can't trust you."

"Smart."

"At least I don't have to worry about you stealing my savings before you disappear into the night."

He doesn't blink, which makes me wonder if he knows about that one too.

I don't talk about it often.

Don't like to.

When I do, I usually play it off like I'm joking.

But I don't usually talk about it after tequila.

He switches his attention back to the grilled cheese. "The blond caveman fucked over Vanessa before he met Ellie. Ellie doesn't know. None of them know. So I'm lying when I say I'm fighting to find the treasure before him just for Ellie. I'm doing it for my sister too. And now *you* know."

Did the tequila just say that, or did he?

"Ellie doesn't need to know either," he adds. "But you do."

"Because I don't trust you."

"Because I need things from you, so I know I have to give things to you."

"I don't *like* being suspicious. But even when I've dated people in Shipwreck with Tillie Jean's seal of approval, they still did things that were red flags in my world."

"Not wrong to be suspicious."

"What if I want to talk to your sister?"

He pulls his phone out and thumbs over the screen, then pockets it again. "If she wants to talk to you, she'll call."

"So this *man of mystery* thing is hereditary."

He doesn't smile again, which is disappointing. "Ever been famous?"

"No."

"Had a famous sibling?"

"Aiden's biggest claim to fame is that he was the pilot on that transatlantic flight where a B-lister went into labor and a vet on board delivered the baby before they landed."

Davis slides me a look. "That's a stretch."

I grin. "He's still pissed that the local news crews interviewed his copilot but didn't talk to him. So no. Neither of us are famous or have even had a brush with fame."

"I was seventeen when we signed our first record deal. Two years later, my parents got divorced. My father took most of my early money for what he claimed were management fees. Vanessa had to switch colleges twice because of the attention and ended up at a school where she was finally left alone but didn't fit in either. My grandma leaked our hotel schedule to the press once. Had an uncle who wrote a tell-all. *I* don't trust people. That's the mystery. The whole mystery."

"That sounds lonely."

"Still have the family I made before we got famous."

And I have the family I made after I ran away from home.

We're the exact opposite.

With every passing year, it's harder and harder to make myself go visit my grandma, even though I know she has limited time left. While with every passing year, he apparently clings harder to the people from his past.

I wonder if he hopes they don't move on and forget him.

I would if I were him.

Aren't they all married with kids now?

No, wait, only most of his friends are married with kids. Not all of them.

I stare at my tequila while I swirl it in my glass. *Focus, Sloane.* "And the only reason you care about Thorny Rock's treasure is because you don't want Patrick to get it?"

He doesn't answer.

I'm sure he'd say it's because he's concentrating on flipping the two halves of the grilled cheese sandwich together, or because the other skillet is hot enough to put in the popcorn kernels now, or something else.

Except I wouldn't believe him.

A revenge treasure hunt to beat someone who hurt his sister years ago—probably close to a decade ago, given what I know about how long Patrick dated Ellie before he asked me out, which was—stupid math—ah, yes, about seven years ago.

Anyway, doing a revenge treasure hunt a decade later

doesn't make sense. "Why else do you care so much about the treasure?"

Serious brown eyes bore into mine. "I don't trust you enough yet for that."

"*Yet* implies you think you might. Or that you think I want to earn your trust. Or you want to earn mine. Wait. The tequila's confusing me. Which way is this supposed to go?"

But even with the tequila, I'm starting to realize just how much he says without moving a single facial muscle.

Like right now.

Right now, he's saying *I just gave you gossip no one else has, so I'm going to find out very soon if we're doing the next level of this trust thing.*

"Why didn't you tell Ellie that your sister had dated Patrick too? Or your sister? Vanessa? Why didn't she ell Tellie—*tell Ellie* what Patrick had done?" I ask.

"We're tight, but we're not *tell you everything every day* tight. I was busy. Vanessa moved out of the neighborhood and made her own life. Ellie was busy. I heard she was dating someone. Didn't meet him for almost a year."

"He didn't know who you were?"

"He didn't know Vanessa was related to me."

"*How can you not know that?* You're famous. Everyone should know everything about you."

He's smiling as my phone buzzes in my scrubs pocket, and I jump.

I pull it out and stare at a number I don't recognize.

"Probably your only chance," Davis murmurs.

Oh shit.

It's his sister.

"I have her number now."

That gets me a full-on snort of laughter as my phone keeps buzzing in my hand. "No, you don't."

"What does that mean?"

He shakes his head, grinning as he pulls the sandwich off the skillet and plates it on a yellow Fiesta plate.

"How do I know this is your sister?"

"You don't."

"How do *you* know it's your sister?"

"Because I know my sister."

Fuck it.

I might be a little tipsy, but I can do this.

I can figure out if it's really his sister.

I swipe to answer, and before I can say *hello?* a woman's voice is saying, "This is Vanessa Remington. Am I speaking with Sloane Pearce?"

"I—yes. How do I know you're who you say you are?"

Davis is grinning as he bites into the grilled cheese, so I don't hear what his sister says, because I'm distracted by my surprise. "*Oh my god*, I thought you were making that for *me*," I say to him.

"Didn't say you wanted one."

"What's he cooking?" the woman on the phone who's claiming to be Vanessa and who weirdly sounds like Davis —but in a less-deep voice kind of way—says.

And that opinion about her voice is definitely my tequila talking. "Grilled cheese."

"Cheddar and Havarti on sourdough?"

"How did you know that?"

"He's predictable. Why did he let you into his trailer? He never lets anyone new into his trailer. And please

186

don't lie to me. I've had a *very* long day, and I have no interest in having you investigated."

I look at Davis, then at his grilled cheese, then at the popcorn he's pouring into the cast-iron skillet. "Do you really never let anyone in your trailer? What about your house? Do you have a house somewhere? Have your friends even seen it? Also, may I please have a grilled cheese? The tequila isn't settling too well and I don't know if popcorn will be enough to help. *Oh my god.* That wasn't tequila, was it? Was that some kind of weird truth serum?"

"Are you talking to me or him?" maybe-Vanessa says.

"Him. But I'm back to talk to you because clearly he won't answer a simple question."

"Why are you there?" she repeats.

"Because you and I have a mutual ex who broke into my house and trashed it probably as part of his hunt for a treasure that doesn't exist, and your brother feels a sense of responsibility about it. What's his name? Our mutual ex, I mean. Not your brother. We both know *his* name."

There's a long stretch of silence on the other end of the phone.

"*Oh my god* again. Are you looking it up? Are you texting Davis for the answer? This isn't really Vanessa, is it?"

"Tell him I'm smiling."

"Why? Do you smile as rarely as he does?"

Davis slides a look at me, then lifts a middle finger.

The woman on the other end of the phone cracks up. "He's flipping me off, isn't he?"

"He's flipping one of us off."

187

Vanessa cackles again.

"Why do you sound so gleeful about that? What the *fuck* is going on? I know this isn't just the tequila."

"Patrick Dixon," she says. "Our mutual ex is Patrick Dixon. And he wants Thorny Rock's treasure because he thinks it's going to destroy our family when he finds it."

"It's been—" I pause and count on my fingers, staring at the ceiling, where there's a butterfly-shaped crack in whatever material makes up the ceiling of a camper trailer, which is weirdly pretty.

When I get cracks in my plaster, it's always in the shape of a penis.

I have crack envy.

Wait.

Focus.

"Six years," I finish. "It's been six and a half years since I dumped him, which means it's been six—no, almost seven years since he cheated on Ellie with me, which means, if *someone* is telling me the truth, it's been at least eight years since he dated you. So why *now*? Why does he care *now*?"

"Put me on speaker."

I fumble with my phone and put maybe-Vanessa on speaker. My cat doesn't help.

The tequila doesn't either.

"Did that work?" I ask.

"Yes," she says, her voice echoing through the kitchen as the first bits of popcorn start to pop in the skillet.

"Good. Sometimes I hang up on people when I'm drinking."

"Davis?" she says.

"Yep," he replies.

"Show her the family tree."

"No."

"If you don't, I will."

"You were here this morning. You're not coming back for at least another month."

"I have her number," Vanessa replies.

"Is this your real number?" I ask.

"No," they both answer together.

"How?"

"Magic tricks," she replies, which is so very Davis that I believe she's his sister.

"Who *are* you?"

"That's classified. But our family tree isn't."

"Did you find out Patrick's related to you?"

"Yes," she says at the same time Davis says, "No."

I gasp.

"Fourth cousins thrice removed," she says.

"Practically no DNA in common at that point," Davis says. "It's like saying we're all related to the king of England."

My head is spinning.

The popcorn is popping.

Maybe-Vanessa says something else, but I don't hear it over the popcorn.

I head back to the living room, which smells like campfire and melted cheese.

Why doesn't my house smell like campfire and melted cheese? In the good way, I mean.

I think about my house, then I think about it being ransacked, and I shiver again.

"Why now?" I repeat to Vanessa. "Why's he searching for the treasure *now*?"

"He's had a string of bad luck personally and professionally, and he could use a treasure," she replies.

"Davis?"

She snorts again. "No. Patrick."

"Oh. Was it…your fault…he had a string of bad luck?"

"No," she says as Davis says, "Probably."

Okay.

Yes.

I am fully convinced, no questions, that these two are siblings.

"Did you really fake-marry Davis once?" I ask.

"Yes."

"Why?"

"You've used up your quota of questions for the day, and I have to go. Davis, show her the family tree or I'm sending the mothers."

He's shaking the cast-iron skillet over the stovetop, but the way his head whips toward me—he heard.

And he's not happy.

"Who are the mothers?" I ask, but my phone screen flashes. She's hung up.

"Rude," I mutter.

Not too surprising though.

She's Davis's sister.

It's probably hereditary.

"What's with your family tree?" I ask.

He scowls and takes a massive bite out of his sandwich while he keeps shaking the skillet.

Mr. No Expressions is very expressiony today.

Fascinating.

Also—how freaking strong does he have to be to do that with a cast-iron skillet?

He's not bulky.

But he's clearly strong.

And I'm getting a stirring down south that I don't appreciate, which is made worse when I check out his ass again, and then remember how it felt when he kissed me, and then how it felt to cling to him on the motorcycle ride up the mountain to get here.

He's on the bad list.

But maybe not as high up as he was when we started the day.

"What's with your family tree?" I repeat.

"You like your friends in town?" he says.

"Very much."

"For their sake, you don't want to know."

13

Davis

"YOU THINK I can't keep a secret?" Sloane asks as her phone rings again.

"I have trust issues."

"That's the lamest—*ugh*."

She's staring at her phone.

I watch her.

"It's my grandmother," she grumbles.

"Answer it."

"I don't *want* to. Nigel probably called her and told her I'm being a petulant child, so she's going to lecture me, and—"

"Answer it." I tip the pan over a bowl, pouring in all of the popcorn. "I want to speak with my grandmother-in-law-to-be."

She blinks at me.

Then at the phone.

Then back at me.

"It's a video call."

"Even better."

The phone's still ringing.

She's still staring at it.

I grab my garlic salt and a small container of grated parm from my fridge, toss both into the popcorn, and reach her before the phone stops.

"Ooh, *popcorn*," she breathes.

Taking her phone is like taking candy from a sleeping baby.

I swipe to answer and am instantly grateful for the things that I've already seen in my life.

Because I'm not prepared for the face staring back at me on the video call.

No idea how old Sloane's grandmother is, but she was clearly a beauty in her day, and her day isn't over.

Her silver hair is neatly framing her face. Minimal wrinkles. Bright blue eyes. Cheekbones still prominent.

I don't know what's in the water in Two Twigs, Iowa, but whatever it is, it's working.

"Who are you?" she says to me.

"Davis Remington, ma'am. Your granddaughter's fiancé."

The pretty disappears behind a scowl. "Over my dead body."

Sloane pauses in shoveling a massive handful of popcorn into her mouth and looks up at me with wide eyes.

They're getting bloodshot, and I don't think it's the tequila.

I think the day's catching up with her.

"Strong words," I say to Granny Grumpy. "Want to get to know me before you judge me?"

"Oh ma gah," Sloane says around her mouthful of popcorn.

She's fucking gorgeous.

Completely real.

Unfiltered.

I like her.

Fuuuuck.

I *appreciate* her. I can appreciate someone's realness and the way realness lends itself to attraction.

"Where is my granddaughter?" Granny Grumpy says.

I turn so she can see Sloane behind me.

Sloane finger-waves and shoves another full handful of popcorn into her mouth.

She moans like it's the best thing she's ever tasted, then cuts herself off mid-moan to stare at the phone like she just got caught masturbating in public.

To thoughts of me, my brain adds.

I flip it off.

"Sloane's had a long day. We're having a late dinner," I tell Granny Grumpy.

"Let me talk to my granddaughter."

I back up three steps so Sloane's larger in the camera view. "She's right here."

"Alone."

"Sloane, you want to talk to your grandmother alone?"

Her eyes say no.

Her frozen body says *please don't make me answer that.*

"I didn't ask if she wants to," Granny Grumpy snaps. "I said to do it."

The cat yowls, then hisses.

Relatable, Peggy. "Last I checked, your granddaughter is a grown woman capable of making her own decisions."

"Clearly not, if she's marrying you. Which she won't be. Sloane, Nigel's ready to bring you home."

Sloane visibly swallows, then makes the *come closer* gesture to me.

I don't want to, but I obey, sitting on the couch next to her.

Because someone needs to respect her damn wishes.

And I swear I'm only so close that our thighs are touching because we have to sell this fake engagement.

She leans toward the phone, the focus in her eyes telling me she's all here. "Grandma, I'm marrying Davis. Saturday. Whether you're there or not. Because I love him, and he loves me, and it would mean the world to me to have your support. But I'll do it with or without your support."

Granny Grumpy's jaw shifts back and forth. Her blue eyes are on fire. "I didn't take you on to raise you to use that kind of sass with your elders."

A buzzing starts in my ears.

I don't like where this is going.

Sloane digs into the popcorn bowl again. "You raised me to be strong and independent and think for myself."

"I raised you to not be a dummy, and look what you're doing now. Is this the gratitude you show me for taking you in when I'd already done my part and raised your father? Now you're defying me when I'm getting closer and closer to heaven's gates with every passing day?"

Sloane flinches.

I curl my empty hand into a fist, order it to relax, and don't listen to myself. "How old were you?" I ask Sloane.

"What?"

"How old were you when your grandmother took you in?"

She's watching me like she doesn't trust me.

Smart woman.

My fuse has been lit. There's a fire in my soul, and I'm ready to burn the fucking world down to prove a point.

"Three," she says quietly.

I twist the phone so Granny Grumpy can only see me.

I can see me too, and the heat reflected back in my own eyes is telling me I need to calm the fuck down.

But I don't want to. "How much agency does a three-year-old have over their life?"

"Oh, we're using fancy words to be better than other people, are we?"

"Can a three-year-old take care of herself?"

"Of course not."

"Can a three-year-old clearly in need of a parent be the one who determines who that parent will be?"

"What kind of stupid question is that?"

The kind of question that she should've asked herself before raising two more kids.

I fucking hate when parents blame kids for existing.

I fucking hate when adults manipulate their children into believing they're shitty when the truth is, kids are just fucking hard because it's fucking hard being a kid.

196

I can barely hear myself over the roar of fury in my own ears. *Breathe. Breathe. Breathe.* "Stop. Blaming. Sloane. For. Your. Life."

Sloane sucks in a breath beside me.

Granny Grumpy leans into the phone until all I can see are her eyes and nose. "Do not tell an old lady what to do."

Breathe. Breathe. Breathe. "The day you can prove to me that a kid asked to be put on this earth, that a kid manipulated you into taking care of her, that a kid is born inherently evil and that every decision they make throughout their life is merely to spite you, that's the day I'll quit telling manipulative old ladies to leave my fiancée the fuck alone."

I need fresh air.

Need to take a hike. Meditate. Stare at a campfire. Touch a few fallen leaves.

Find my center.

Find my calm.

Let go of the hero complex.

Go hit a punching bag.

Sloane grabs the phone from me. "Well." Her voice is husky. "That's hero material for you, isn't it? Bye, Grandma. I need to go."

She hangs up.

I suck in air through my nose, aware that both of my hands are balled into fists now, aware that I need to not be here.

I need to not lose my shit.

Sloane rests a hesitant hand on my back. "Are you okay?"

I blow out a slow breath.

Her house was broken into. She's being attacked by the woman who raised her and a man who doesn't give the first fuck about what's best for her.

And she's asking if I'm okay.

I blow out another slow breath. "I don't like parents using *I raised you* as a control tactic."

"Did your parents—"

"My father did."

I start to move, but her voice stops me. "I didn't realize that's what it was until a couple years ago. That *I raised you* was one more tool in the guilt kit. Now, I watch Libby and Clay Rock with Tillie Jean, and with Grady and Cooper, and I watch how they enjoy letting their kids live their own lives and make their own choices, how they trust their kids to be good people without the constant insistence that what they want is best, and I just—I want that. But I'll never have it."

"You have them though. They're the family you chose."

She doesn't have what I have.

She doesn't have the tight-knit group of friends that she grew up with. The ride-or-die buddies that you can trust with everything because you always have.

She had to start over from scratch to build her family.

What if she'd started somewhere else?

What if she'd started somewhere with more people just like her grandmother and Nigel instead of people like the Rocks?

She blinks quickly. "Sometimes when I'm with them, I almost feel like I could do it. Like I could be the parent I didn't have. The one who doesn't use guilt and shame and manipulation. But I don't know if I ever really wanted kids of my own, or if they were just the expectation. But I still love my grandmother. She *did* raise me. She *did* save me. I just...don't...like her right now."

I realize I've gone from clenching my fists to rubbing my hands down my thighs, and I bolt to standing. "Can't control other people's choices. She can't control yours, and you can't control hers. Can only control how you react to it. You want a grilled cheese?"

I don't wait for her to answer.

Easier to keep my hands busy and make a sandwich neither of us eats than it is to sit there with her, wanting to wrap her in a hug and not let go.

Keep her safe.

Safe from the entire goddamn fucking world.

From the shitstorm coming at her from all sides.

And to get a hug back.

To have someone I don't know who's been through shit and come out on the other side hug me tight and tell me that I'm okay too.

That my temper doesn't define who I am.

That I do good in the world.

That my scales will be tipped to the right side when my time's up.

Not because I need to believe in eternal salvation. But because I need to know that I've done my part to make the world better before I go.

The cat dashes in front of me, skids to a stop, looks up at me, and meows.

I toss it one of the cat toys Beck and Sarah left on the table, and it crouches down, wiggles its butt, and attacks.

Sloane's eating the popcorn again.

She's watching me.

It's like it was Saturday night when I slipped on the coffee at the museum.

She's making sure I'm okay.

It's not as foreign and wrong of a feeling as it should be.

I take care of me. When I struggle, I call Vanessa or one of the guys from the neighborhood.

Don't always say I need help.

Don't need to.

Not with them.

Feels almost the same with Sloane right now, and that has me off-kilter enough that I burn her grilled cheese.

She eats it anyway.

Insists on it, actually.

Once she's eaten, her eyelids begin to droop.

I don't ask if she wants the bed.

Instead, I rise and hold a hand out to her, and I take her there. Toss a clean shirt and sweatpants on the bed for her, since all she has is her scrubs.

And then I leave her alone.

Tomorrow's Wednesday. She still has to work.

And it's not like I'll sleep well even in the bed.

She should have it.

She face-plants onto the quilt covering the mattress, and I retreat outside for the fresh air I've needed since that phone call then start a campfire.

Check my phone.

No messages from Vanessa, but it's blowing up with texts from everyone else. On the group text.

Naturally.

So if anyone didn't know before, they do now. I scroll. And scroll. And scroll.

And I finally get to the beginning.

Ellie: What the HELL is going on in Shipwreck? Davis, we need an update RIGHT NOW. Is Sloane okay?

Beck: Did we bring the right kind of litter for her cat? We can go back out if the cat's picky. Our cat's picky. We get it.

Sarah: Our cat is not picky. You simply spoil her. Davis, Ellie's not the only one who wants to know. How's Sloane?

Cash: You're not hosting a woman at that tour bus-wannabe thing you've got out there in the mountains, are you? My dude. You can spring for a hotel room. A fancy one at that. Spoil her. Don't make her stay in the camper if you want to keep her in your life.

Tripp: Let the man have some peace. We all know he doesn't date, even if he's marrying her on Saturday, and we need to respect that.

Cash: Speak for yourself. I don't know that he doesn't date. I just know he doesn't talk about his dates. And I know you're all saying this wedding is another one of his fake weddings to do someone a favor, but this is above and beyond for a fake fiancée. Is there something going on with you and Sloane that we need to know about? I have an entire catalog of songs in a secret folder called "Davis's wedding album" because they seemed right for the moment that you'd finally fall, but I didn't expect it to be now. With Shipwreck's favorite nurse. My brain is so blown.

Ellie: Are you all serious? A WOMAN'S HOUSE WAS BROKEN INTO, PROBABLY BY OUR MUTUAL EX-BOYFRIEND. And you're worried about who's getting into her pants and if this fake wedding is real? I'm so disgusted right now.

Beck: Dude's in his own honeymoon phase, El. He probably didn't think about how that would sound before he said it. And I'm sure he's sorry.

Aspen: I've taken his phone away. Yes, he's sorry. Also, can someone fill me in? Who's Sloane?

Ellie: Got you on a side text, Aspen. Davis, not kidding. IS SHE OKAY? What does she need? What can we do?

Sarah: I'm going over first thing in the morning. Hoping she's sleeping now. I don't know if I could sleep if I were her. I barely slept the night after I thought Beck was breaking into my house, even though I figured out he wasn't actually a threat.

Levi: Do you need security? I can send some people up.

Tripp: Good idea since he feels the same about security as he does about dating, but in the security case, I don't support honoring his wishes.

Beck: So… you do or you don't support Davis having some security now? I'm confused.

Tripp: Go eat a sandwich. I support having security on Davis whether he likes it or not.

Wyatt: I'd just like to point out that Davis can take out the blond caveman with a flick of his wrist. Dude doesn't need security. After the years of martial arts he's done, he *is* security.

Ellie: But if Levi sends a team, we get reports.

Beck: Okay. Got a sandwich. Brain's thinking clearer now. And I think we should respect his privacy.

Ingrid: Speaking as a regular nobody and one of the newer members of this group text… I thought we were supposed to be most worried about the fact that he quit his job. I mean, yes, worried about Sloane too, but our concern for Davis was him having too much time on his hands. Right?

Levi: We're easing into it so he doesn't change his number and flee the country instead of answering us.

Ingrid: Oh. Crap. Sorry. Has he done that before?

Tripp: We're still not sure.

Lila: Uncle Guido says no.

Levi: Oh shit. You called Uncle Guido?

Beck: Whoa. I think I just got not hungry in fear.

Sarah: He's still eating his sandwich. He's fine. Also, ditto to Levi's Oh shit.

Beck: Habit. Not hunger. What else—wait, do I want to ask that?

Wyatt: What else did Uncle Guido say, Lila?

Ellie: It's so hot when you're not afraid of the retired CIA guy. Wanna leave this group chat?

Beck: Ew. I've definitely lost my appetite now.

Sarah: He finished his sandwich. And now I'm echoing Wyatt—what else did Uncle Guido say?

Lila: He says the treasure's real and Shipwreck is fucked if the wrong person finds it.

Beck: Oh shit. I like Shipwreck.

Sarah: How can a treasure fuck a town?

Lila: Actually, I read a book once where that happened, but it was…a thing.

Tripp: Lila's reading habits are sometimes scarier than her having an uncle Guido. I didn't know the depth and breadth of the romance genre until I met her, and I'm still horrified that my kids might one day find the same books.

Ingrid: Is Davis actually on this group chat? And can any of you focus? Do I have to pull out my mom voice?

Levi: He's on the chat, and yes, please, use your mom voice. I like your mom voice.

Ingrid: Davis Remington, get your ass into this group chat and explain yourself right now, or I'm returning every one of the books you ordered from my store last week and telling all of my bookseller friends to make you track them down in a library instead. And then I'm telling the librarians you're coming and not to help you either.

Aspen: Treasures and jobs aside, getting in on this group chat is possibly the second- or third-best thing that's ever happened in my entire life. Maybe fourth. Definitely top five.

Wyatt: My kid might have a crush on you, but we all need to be quiet while we wait to see if Ingrid's mom voice worked to get Davis in the chat.

Beck: Unless he's getting laid if this wedding thing is more real than he's making it out to be. Or finding a treasure. Can't deny it—finding a treasure would actually be fucking cool. Like, how often does a guy get to be in a boy band, then be an underwear model, then marry the love of his life, then get the best babies ever, AND find a treasure, all while living in a world where the food is incredible?

Ellie: Cash, how far are you from Davis's place? Beck's in happy land. We need someone who'll be a little harder on him.

Sarah: I'm ten minutes away too. And I still have the taser that convinced Beck I was the love of his life.

Ellie: Sarah, I love you, and I will never not love what you've done with your taser, but as Wyatt pointed out, Davis has been in martial arts classes since he was like three.

Beck: So has Sarah. She just doesn't talk about it so that if it's necessary, nobody sees her coming.

Aspen: Top four. Definitely top four things to ever happen in my life. Cash and I are on the tarmac in New York. Taking off soon to head back to Copper Valley since we don't actually have to be in New York until this weekend, but it'll still be a few hours before we can be there.

Sarah: I'm on it. Davis, see you in ten minutes.

Davis: *picture of a campfire* Bring marshmallows and stay silent. She's sleeping.

Tripp: We're gonna need that picture with proof of time and date in it too.

Wyatt: You know he probably has a stash of time-date photos that he can crop to make us believe anything he wants to within minutes, right?

I LET MYSELF HEAVE A SIGH, then focus on the campfire again as my phone keeps buzzing with incoming texts.

My friends are the best.

And also the worst.

But usually the best.

I start a response.

I don't want anyone coming, and I know Sarah well enough to know she won't take me up on the toasted marshmallows offer. She doesn't like to leave the kids at night, and Beck loves her more than he loves food, so there's not much danger that he'll show up again either.

But before I can finish telling them thanks for their concern, but I'm fine, a muffled scream explodes inside my trailer.

14

Sloane

Nigel's eating the treasure.

He's eating the treasure and telling me I have to go back to Two Twigs and give him as many babies as the number of gold pieces he eats, and he's eaten *eighteen*, and now he's saying that his new sex ritual involves me sticking emeralds up my nose to guarantee triplets for the first round, and he's taking off his clothes, and—

Oh my god, his penis is a hippopotamus.

I sit straight up and scream.

An unfamiliar darkness surrounds me. I'm on a mattress that's harder than I'm used to. Peggy isn't in bed with me. These sheets are flannel, I'm sweating in a T-shirt that smells like my grandma's cedar chest, and I don't know where it came from.

"Sloane?"

I scream again as a man throws open the doorway. "No hippo dick! *Back, hippo dick!*"

He freezes.

Peggy meows.

My eyes adjust, and even with my heart pounding this fast and my blood pressure making dots dance in my vision, I remember who I am.

Where I am.

Why I am.

Maybe not *all* why I am, but definitely why I'm here. Specifically in this trailer.

Maybe not on earth.

And the T-shirt.

I'm wearing one of Davis's T-shirts that he pulled out for me because I didn't want to sleep in my scrubs and I wasn't allowed to take anything but my cat from my house and I didn't think to ask Tillie Jean for any clothes before we left her house.

I drop my head to my knees and pant for breath.

The floor creaks, and a moment later, the mattress sags next to me. I'm in the middle of the queen-size bed because I live alone, so I sleep alone, and I practice taking up space by taking up space when I'm subconscious.

"Bad dream?" Davis asks quietly.

Peggy leaps onto the bed and hops over to rub her face against my quilt-covered legs.

"Yeah." I gulp more air. "I'm fine."

He falls quiet while Peggy meows until I pull her against me and concentrate on slowing my breathing.

It was a bad dream.

Nigel can't make me do anything.

He's not eating treasure and sticking it up my nose.

If he has a hippo-sized penis, I will hopefully never know.

But also, in my dream—Nigel had Patrick's face.

"Always fucking with me," I mutter to myself as I exhale slowly to control my breathing.

"In your nightmares?"

I snort softly. "Sometimes in real life too. He showed up tonight, didn't he?"

I don't expect him to say anything—let's be real here, it's Davis—but after a moment, his voice rumbles softly in the darkness. "This isn't the first time Nigel's tried to hurt you."

Peggy purrs, and I bury my face into her body. "People hurt people. It's what we do."

"Not always."

"Do you date?"

"No."

"Because you have trust issues."

"Yes."

"But not with the people you grew up with?"

"Not most days."

There's a light on in the kitchen area, streaming in through the open door and illuminating the twisted quilt and sheets, the utilitarian nightstand with a single lamp which is currently dark.

It's not bright in here, but it's not cave-dark either.

And knowing that Davis doesn't trust people—that weirdly makes me trust him more.

Like he gets it.

He'll continue to get it.

He's not secretive because he wants to hurt people. He's secretive because he doesn't want people to hurt him.

This isn't a scary dark room.

It's a still night and he's here, and no matter what I don't know about him, no matter how much I've fucked with my own instincts to the point that I don't trust them anymore, I trust Davis.

I don't think he's stalking me.

I think he really is protecting me.

Or trying to in whatever capacity he can.

"Did you ever have a crush on any of them? The people in your neighborhood?" I ask.

He shifts on the bed, his eyes dropping away from my face for the first time since he came in here.

"One more thing I don't get to know, hmm?"

Velvety brown eyes collide with mine. "Ellie. I had a crush on Ellie early in high school."

Is he freaking serious right now?

What am I, a magnet for Ellie's leftovers?

He lifts a shoulder. "Weren't many girls in the neighborhood. Cash's sister didn't hang with us as much. Wyatt picked on Ellie, and I thought I could defend her."

"Do you still—"

"No. She's not my type."

"That's the only reason?"

"Also grew out of it when I realized the world was bigger than our neighborhood."

"I fell in love with Nigel in middle school."

You know that feeling when you realize someone's paying closer attention?

That's me right now.

Davis hasn't moved, but again, I feel like he's watching me far closer than he was a moment ago.

Also, I've never confessed this to a soul.

But if anyone's going to know, shouldn't it be my pretend fiancé who's been standing between me and Nigel for the past few days?

"I got up the courage one day to ask him if he liked anyone because he sometimes chased me on the playground, and I was dumb—no, naïve and inexperienced in the world enough to believe the stupid line about how boys pick on girls to show that they like them."

Davis doesn't make a noise, but I swear he tenses.

Or maybe I'm projecting.

I'm probably projecting.

"He told me then that he liked one of my friends. It was a little crushing, but none of us were allowed to date —too young, concentrate on school, don't open your legs for boys until you're married, all of that. But then I found out that they were secretly going together. I tried so hard to get over it because what kind of a monster has a crush on her friend's boyfriend? Especially when I wasn't supposed to have feelings for boys at all because I was too young, and boys were dangerous and they could get you pregnant and ruin your life and God would be so disappointed in you if you slept with a boy, even if no one ever said God would be so disappointed in *him* because boys *had needs* and God understood that."

Davis stays silent.

I know he's listening though. It's this unique sensation like being wrapped in the warmest blanket on the coldest night of winter.

"I secretly started going with this other guy early in high school, and Nigel asked me to break up with him. Because Nigel said he'd realized then that he liked me. So I did, but after I wasn't passing notes and having secret phone calls with that boy anymore, Nigel told me we had to be even more super secretive about it than I'd been with the first boy because his parents didn't approve of me and we needed to give it space so I could heal from my breakup."

Still no sounds from the man sitting on the edge of the bed.

But he puts a hand on my forearm and squeezes.

"I wasn't upset about the breakup. I just wanted to be with Nigel. Except we only talked at school. No notes passed. He didn't text me or call me on nights or weekends. He'd say hi, I'd say hi and blush like crazy, and at lunch he'd sit with the guys on the basketball team so we wouldn't tip anyone off. And then I heard one day that he was dating—*dating*-dating—one of the cheerleaders. He was all *it just happened, Sloane, but you know we weren't meant to be together.*"

"He strung you along."

"Three times," I whisper. "Three times before the end of high school, and because he was the grandson of the local preacher, I thought it was God's will. That I'd done something wrong to deserve the hurt and the pain. That it was my fault for not being good enough. That it was punishment for the sin of having a crush on a boy too young. I wasn't today years old when I realized the first boy I ever loved made a sport of gaslighting me, but it truly wasn't until Patrick that I could see it clearly. And I just… Now Patrick's back and Grandma sent Nigel and I feel like—I feel like all of this work I've done to let go of the guilt and shame that's haunted me since childhood just for *being born* is all crashing back. I've worked through all of this shit already. I don't want to do it again, but clearly, I have to."

Davis shifts on the bed.

One arm slips around my back.

The other circles me, pulling me against him.

He rests his chin on my hair, his beard scratchy against my scalp, and he hugs me tightly.

A shuddery breath leaves my lungs as warmth and safety and comfort envelop me and Peggy.

"You're a good person, Sloane."

Heat slides down my face, from my hairline, over my forehead, down to my brows and eyelids. "I was taught that I'd never be good enough."

"We are all enough."

"I know they love me. They mean well. They're coming from a place of caring, but they just—" Another shuddery breath ripples through me.

He hugs me tighter, and my nostrils fill with the scents of campfire smoke and pine needles and safety. "Love isn't love when it's used as a weapon."

Peggy purrs loudly.

I think she agrees.

"It's fine. I'm fine. It's stress. Who wouldn't be stressed in my shoes right now? I just—I just need some sleep, and then I'll have the strength to deal with it. I can handle this. I can. Just…tomorrow. Not today."

He doesn't answer.

Not with words, anyway.

Instead, he strokes my back with his thumb while he keeps holding me.

Davis Remington.

My secret teenage crush.

My *shameful* secret teenage crush.

Holding my world together with a hug while giving me a safe space away from the horror of what happened to my house today at the hands of another man I never should've trusted.

I shouldn't trust Davis.

But old habits die hard. All it takes is a little kindness, and I fold.

Like right now.

When I close my eyes and breathe in his scent again.

Any minute now, he'll let go.

But he hasn't yet.

So I keep breathing in his scent.

Keep soaking in the warmth and strength and comfort from his arms around me. Feel the distant beat of his heart as my head droops against his chest.

Even if it's fake, even if he hurts me later, right now, I feel safe.

I've learned a lot about living for *right now*.

"I'll get you the journal," I whisper.

"I'll get it."

"Pop doesn't like you."

"Deserve that."

"Why?"

"It's complicated." He bends his head over mine, scratching his beard into my hair, and is he—

215

Is Davis kissing my head?

Is he?

Or isn't he?

I should be able to tell, shouldn't I?

My voice is higher than it should be when I speak again. "What's complicated about it?"

"Your family thinks they know what's best for you, but they can't honor your own wishes for how you want to live your life."

"What does that have to do with Pop?"

"He and I have a disagreement about what's best for someone. Neither's right. Neither's wrong. And neither of us will fully honor the other's wishes."

"How does that even work?"

"It doesn't, and that's why he doesn't like me."

He kisses my head.

He does.

He kisses my head.

I'm not imagining that. It's not the tequila. It's not a dream.

My pretend fiancé is taking care of me.

"Go back to sleep. You're safe."

I don't want to sleep.

Sleep is where the bad dreams come.

"You're safe here," he repeats.

He releases his hold, and chilly air envelops me.

I shiver.

"I don't—I don't want to be alone."

The words linger in the air while I wince.

I've taught myself to be strong. I've taught myself to be independent.

And I just don't fucking want to be tonight.

But I also don't want to have just said that.

It's too dim to read his expression, but after a moment's pause, he leans over, off the side of the bed.

There's a *thump*, then a second one, and then he straightens just long enough to release his hair from its bun before stretching out on the bed.

Peggy stares at him.

I got her after my last breakup, so she's never slept with a man in her bed.

And it's been well over two years since I've slept with a man in my bed either.

He's not a man, I tell myself. *He's a friend.*

Liar, my nipples reply.

"I'll stay on this side," I stutter. "I just—I'm normally—I'm always—I don't usually need to not be alone. Today's…different."

He looks at me.

I suppress a sigh and settle back under the covers, huddling closer to the opposite side of the bed than I was when I had it all to myself.

Shouldn't have expected an answer just because he talked more while he was cooking for me and giving me free rein with his tequila.

Peggy steps off me, standing between us, and she purrs.

Then purrs louder.

He settles his large hand over her back and strokes her, then does it again, until she's running the show, telling him exactly where to pet her. She sprawls out, lying down between us but still closer to him so she can arch her head into his hand and do that thing where she stretches out her one front paw like she's kneading biscuits.

I wonder if cats experience phantom limbs like humans do. Does she feel like she has both front paws right now?

The light's still on in the kitchen area, filtering in here through the open door.

"Do you always sleep with the lights on?" I whisper to Davis.

"No."

"Do you want me to—"

"No."

"Is that for my sake?"

"Yes."

"If you'd rather it was dark—"

"I can sleep anywhere. It's fine. Can you sleep?"

I suck in a breath through my nose and look at the man who's still so full of secrets, but who's starting to make sense.

He's not telling me he loves me.

He's not telling me we're in this together.

He's just saying he'll pretend to be my fiancé because he's done it before and it doesn't mean anything, and he's giving me a place to stay tonight that's safe.

I'm a mess.

But I'm not alone.

And for tonight—for *right now*—that's enough.

"I think I can sleep," I whisper.

"Good."

"Thank you."

He watches me watching him while he pets my cat.

And then he pulls in a long, quiet breath. "You may not ever be in my close circle, but you can trust that I mean you no harm. I've hurt enough people in my life already. Don't want to do it again. You truly are safe here."

My eyes sting.

I squeeze them closed so he won't see, and I lie there, feeling my own heartbeat, listening to his slow, rhythmic breaths that don't mean he's sleeping but are still a little hypnotic, and I wonder if either of us will sleep tonight.

15

Davis

I WAIT until Sloane's breathing has settled into a steady rhythm, and then I sneak out of the bed.

Fire's still going outside.

Need to put it out.

Also need to breathe in the cold night air to try to get a grip on my body.

I've been around people having a difficult time before. Been around women having a difficult time.

And I've never wanted so badly to be the shield protecting them from all of it.

Has to be because it's my fault.

If I wasn't looking for the treasure, Dixon wouldn't be looking for the treasure, and he'd be leaving Sloane alone.

If I hadn't let her take photos of me to tell her grandma that I was her fake boyfriend, we wouldn't be fake engaged, getting fake-married, and—

And the two have nothing to do with each other. I didn't ask her family to be controlling, manipulative dicks.

I blow out a slow breath in the chilly evening.

Then another.

And a third.

My phone rings.

I move as far from the trailer as I can before I answer. "Hey."

"I always assumed that the day you got in over your head with a woman, it would be with someone who had a criminal record for trespassing and being a public nuisance. An activist type. Maybe a hacker who robbed from the rich to give to the poor. But you have managed to find the squeakiest-clean woman on the entire planet."

"I'm not in over my head," I tell my sister.

I am completely over my head.

And as much as I want to blame seeing those dildos—I can't.

I was already in over my head.

Sloane smiles, and the world gets a little brighter. *My* world gets a little brighter. That's not supposed to happen with strangers.

Vanessa makes an amused noise on the other end of the line. "Keep lying to yourself. That's a fabulous tactic that's always ended well for you."

It has never ended well for me, and we both know it. "Where's Dixon?"

"Ah, the distraction so we don't talk about how you wanted me to call a woman to vouch for you for the first time in a decade."

"Yes."

"Thank you for your honesty. Refreshing change in this conversation."

"My pleasure."

"And I suppose you want a reward of information for that honesty?"

"Yes."

"Fine. I lost Dixon south of Shipwreck, which feels off. He shouldn't have been going south."

"You on this officially?"

"Something about this entire situation is off. I'm missing a vital piece of a puzzle, and I don't like it."

"That wasn't a no."

"It's a no."

I fill a bucket from the water pump between the old cabin and the old outhouse while we talk. Don't want to leave Sloane alone too long, so I need to get the campfire handled.

"You sure?" I ask my sister.

"My organization doesn't work on American soil. I just happen to live here and like puzzles. I'm personally curious. That's it."

"But you checked to see if Sloane had a record."

"Yeah. Duh. Not the first time for any of you yahoos, and I'd like it known it took immense self-control to let Tripp figure out Lila's secrets on his own, but I did it, and I'm proud of myself. So. Patrick Dixon. He went south of town this morning, circled back, ransacked Sloane's house, and then disappeared into the ether again. How good are the witnesses?"

"Four total. Three of them picked him out of a random

group of pictures."

"Gotta love small towns."

"Only if you don't love boundaries."

She snickers. "You really tell an old lady your dick's a biological weapon?"

And people think I hear everything. How the fuck did she know that? "Not my finest moment."

"I'm looking into this Nigel guy too. What do you know about him?"

"He's a dick."

"What else?"

What else matters? I pour the water slowly over the fire while I continue filling Vanessa in on anything she might be able to use to find dirt on him. "Pastor at a small church in a town called Two Twigs, Iowa."

"What's he doing in Shipwreck?"

"Tormenting Sloane."

"Why now?"

"She told her grandmother we're getting married and Grandma doesn't like me."

"What did you do to Grandma?"

"Breathe."

She snorts.

"Didn't even talk to her until tonight."

There's a pause.

And then— "Tell me you didn't verbally eviscerate an old lady."

That's not happening. I keep emptying the bucket. The fire sizzles and smokes, just like it should. And when I breathe through my irritation with Sloane's grandma, I know I'm on even ground again. That my temper has been locked back up where it belongs, and I'm in control.

"I need more information on this Nigel guy," I say. "I don't like him."

"He's a preacher, Davis."

"He gives off Uncle Gerry vibes."

I feel my twin shiver on the other side of the phone.

Creepy old dude always telling us we were wrong for breathing. Best thing about not doing family shit with our father anymore is not having to see Uncle Gerry.

Or think about him.

Until now.

"Thanks, asshole," Vanessa mutters. "It had been at least eighteen months since I last thought about that guy."

"Same."

Something creaks in the night.

I pause and make a slow turn, listening and watching in the darkness.

Leaves rustle in a cold breeze. Clouds are moving in. No stars, minimal moonlight.

Fire's nearly out.

No more creaking noises.

But I still don't like it.

"If you know where the *thing* that I'm looking for is…" I trail off, cocking my head again.

Doesn't feel like anyone's out here, but something's moving.

Likely a small animal. Squirrel. Chipmunk. Skunk. Something.

Vanessa sighs. "Told you already, that's before our

time, and even if I knew something, I'm not telling you. What's going on there? You got quiet."

I turn in one more slow circle.

Gonna lock the trailer door tonight.

"Animals making noise," I tell Vanessa.

"You sure?"

"Mostly."

"Stay safe, okay?"

"You too."

"It would be helpful to have a last name for Nigel."

"I'll text it to you. Gotta go. Left a burner on inside."

I didn't, but she knows what I mean.

I need to get off the phone and don't want to say why.

I want to go check on the woman sleeping in my trailer, and I don't want to tell you that's what I want to do, because you already know I'm in over my head with her.

I slip inside as silently as I left and lock the door.

Then check again that the door is locked.

And a second time for good measure.

When I'm satisfied that I've locked the fucking door, I duck into the bathroom and change into cotton shorts and a T-shirt, moving as quietly as possible, with little light.

Even then, Sloane's sitting up, rubbing her eyes when I step into the bedroom. "What's wrong? What happened? Did you hear something? Is someone here?"

The way I have to restrain myself to keep from hugging her and kissing her and promising her she's safe… "Had to put out the campfire."

"You had a campfire?"

Her voice holds a yearning that hits me in the gut. "You like camping?"

"I like campfires. And s'mores." Her voice gets softer. "And friends. Tillie Jean took me to a campfire at Beck's house once. It was nice."

I sit on the edge of the bed. "Unlimited s'mores at Beck's house."

"Unlimited fun. Friendly people. Very entertaining."

"That too."

I missed a campfire at Beck's house that Sloane was at. That sucks.

But is probably a good thing.

Peggy meows at me.

I stretch out on my side of the bed, wishing I had this room arranged so I could be closer to the door than Sloane is instead of having the door at our feet, where if someone or something broke in, it would have to go through me first.

I locked the door.

I made very certain to lock the door.

Dixon's a coward. He wouldn't break into an occupied home.

But I still triple-checked that I locked the door.

"You can get under the covers if you want," she says quietly. "We're both adults. And Peggy always sleeps with me, and she likes you, so she'll probably sleep in the middle of the bed. She'll be like a self-appointed barrier. And, it's your bed. Very important detail. I could go sleep on the couch."

The cat meows again.

"You're not sleeping on the couch." I hesitate briefly, then climb under the quilt.

The sweatpants I left out are on the floor next to her side of the bed, right next to her scrubs, which means she's in nothing but a T-shirt and probably her panties.

One of my T-shirts.

Mind over body. Mind over body.

She's here because she needs help.

Not because it's playtime.

And now I'm thinking about her toys. That one dildo —it was ungodly large. Not the largest I've ever seen—or nearly been hit with—but larger than necessary. I think. My dick's not really a biological weapon, but it's healthy. I'm *blessed*, as the fucking gaslighter from Sloane's past would say.

And that vibrator—I haven't dated in a very long time.

A *very* long time.

I have no business knowing anything about vibrators.

But I want to know if she uses it on her clit, or if it's for internal use. If she sticks it up her—

Stop it, you dumbass.

It's fucking hot under this quilt.

"Davis?" Sloane whispers.

I almost jump out of my skin. "Yeah?"

"Are you okay?"

Shit.

I'm breathing hard. "Yes."

"Are you sure?"

Not. At. All.

I roll onto my side and look at her in the dim light still

coming in from the kitchen. She's shadows and curves, rolled onto her side so she's looking back at me.

And I give her an excuse for why I won't be sleeping tonight. "Been over a decade since I had anyone else in my bed."

The silence is exactly what I expect.

What's anyone supposed to say to that?

I'd wonder if she's wondering if I mean that's how long it's been since I've had sex with anyone either, but I doubt she's thinking about the state of my dick.

"Two years for me," she whispers. "If you don't count Peggy."

Fuck.

Now I'm wondering if she means two years since *she's* had sex.

Given what I saw in her bedroom—probably.

"Do you…miss…having someone else in your bed?"

I swallow hard.

My cock gets harder.

"No," I lie.

It's not a full lie.

There's only a handful of days in any given year when I'm lonely. When I stare at the ceiling, unable to mind-over-body myself to sleep, wishing there was someone to talk to.

Someone to touch.

Someone to kiss.

Usually happens around the holidays, when I'm more likely to hang out with my friends and family. Noticeably when spring training hits for the Fireballs and we all get together at their training facility in Florida because why wouldn't we?

We get together when they make it all the way in the playoffs too.

Any excuse for some of our old favorite things to bring us back together.

"I like stretching out and keeping the room at whatever temperature I want it, and I like no one else complaining about my cat being on the bed or that my décor is too feminine, but sometimes when I'm hanging out with Tillie Jean and Max, or with Annika and Grady, or with Ray and Jacob, or with Georgia and Francisco, or take your pick of any of the rest of the Fireballs and their significant others, I wonder if I'll ever have enough therapy and life experience to want to take a chance at dating again. I like kissing. I miss it."

I didn't.

Not until she kissed me on Saturday.

"I'm not asking you to—" she starts in a rush, cutting herself off when her cat meows loudly.

Like the cat's saying *you don't have to explain yourself to that dumbass.*

"Sorry. Right. Sorry. I'll go to sleep. We should both go to sleep. *All.* We should all go to sleep. You too, Peggy."

Neither one of us is sleeping tonight.

For all that I don't know Sloane well, I can *feel* it.

She's hyped up now.

Peggy meows again, rises, climbs over me, and settles in the crook behind my knees.

Like the cat's saying *leave me out of this, I'm not interested in being your barrier.*

Sloane stares at me.

I stare back.

Had a staring contest like this once with Tripp's oldest kid. I'd crashed at his place and woke up to James standing six inches from my nose. He was probably three.

I don't startle easily, but I was so startled that I almost fell out of the bed.

And while I was telling myself to breathe, that it was a kid standing there, he leaned into my face, whispered *ooga-booga*, turned, and left the room.

Definitely not the right tactic here.

"You're not closing your eyes," she whispers.

I inch closer to her to give the cat more room, and our legs touch.

Her bare skin against mine.

I swallow again. "Peggy needed more room."

"She's a crotch sleeper. If you lay on your back, she'll curl up on your crotch. Or more likely mine. She likes my —I'm going to stop talking now."

"I'm making you nervous."

"Life makes me nervous today."

"I'll go—"

"*No.*"

She sucks in an audible breath, and I hear her teeth chatter again.

My heart squeezes.

I hate that she's afraid.

I hate that it's my fault she's afraid.

That I can't fully and completely protect her from what's out there.

"I'll quit talking," she whispers.

Fuck this.

Fuck all of this.

She's scared, but she doesn't have to feel alone too.

She's not alone.

I'm here.

I slide one arm under her pillow, the other around her back, and I tug her against me. "You're safe," I murmur.

Her breath rattles out of her, and she loops an arm around my waist and scoots closer.

And closer.

And closer.

Until she freezes as her hip connects with my raging boner.

I don't move.

Don't breathe.

I stay still as I can make myself while my heart's still beating, waiting for her to relax.

But she doesn't relax.

And my heart doesn't slow.

It speeds up.

It launches faster when she lifts her head to look at me.

And when she whispers, "Thank you for trusting me," it hits the stratosphere.

I can't do this.

I cannot lie here with her, holding her, my cock against her body, and not kiss her.

And so that's exactly what I do.

16

Sloane

OH MY GOD, I miss kissing.

And this—this kiss—with no one watching, in the dark, my hands itching to stroke his thick, hard, unexpectedly large erection—it's everything I need.

Want.

Everything I *want.*

I don't *need* kissing.

I just *want* it.

With Davis.

His beard tickling my mouth. His lips suckling mine. His hand curling into my hair.

His hard-on getting harder as I roll to line up our bodies, kissing him back.

He smells stronger of campfire and pine, and he tastes like tequila, and when his tongue touches mine, it takes everything in me to not moan.

Cannot moan.

Absolutely cannot.

This isn't about moaning.

It's about—

Actually, I don't know what it's about.

Do I care?

He adjusts his grip on my hair, massaging my scalp and curling harder into my locks, and nope.

Don't care.

I hug him harder around the waist, pulling him closer while his breath goes ragged. "Sloane—"

"Practice," I gasp. "Sell it. Wedding. Practice."

At least, I think that's what I say.

Whatever it is that actually comes out of my mouth convinces him that kissing is good.

Kissing is right.

Kissing is necessary.

He rolls so he's mostly on top of me, freeing my other arm to wrap around him too while our lips and tongues clash in my favorite dance of all humanity.

His leg slides against mine, parting my thighs.

I find the hemline of his T-shirt and slide my hand under it, tracing along hot, smooth skin.

I wonder if he has tattoos all over his back like he does on his arms.

If I'll get to see them.

Study them.

His arms are fascinating. Some people get intricate patterns. Davis has *things*, all woven together like a puzzle. A basketball. A guitar. A turtle. A volcano.

I'm kissing the ultimate man of mystery, and on Saturday, I get to marry him.

For pretend.

This is fake. Imaginary.

I slide my other hand under his shirt too, and he angles his mouth harder against mine, then shifts his hand from my hair to my neck, fingertips barely brushing my sensitive skin, making me gasp.

His fingers drift lower, over my collarbone, and my vagina clenches.

Touch my breasts. Touch my breasts. Touch my breasts.

"Tell me to stop," he says against my lips.

"Nuh-uh."

The light's dim, but I swear he smiles.

Davis.

Mr. Straight Face.

Smiling while he's kissing me.

While he's—

Oh my god.

I arch into his hand as he scrapes his fingers down my breast.

His breath catches and his hand stills, barely touching my pebbled nipple.

Don't stop don't stop don't stop.

I squeeze my eyes shut and push my breast harder into his hand, arching my back as far as it will go, but he stays completely still.

Don't stop don't stop don't stop.

"Please—touch me. I miss—touching."

God, I do.

I miss kissing. Touching. Sex.

Physical intimacy.

He studies me briefly, and then he's in motion. Smooth, controlled, easy motion.

Sliding down my body.

Pushing my shirt up.

Lowering his mouth to my chest.

His beard tickling my breast.

His tongue swirling around the tight bud of my nipple.

I gasp as he sucks, the sensation rocketing a jolt of pleasure straight to my clit. My hips reflexively pump against his leg, and he sucks harder on my nipple.

"Oh god, yes," I whimper.

Shouldn't be doing this.

We shouldn't.

But how can something that feels so right be wrong?

He shifts his mouth to my other breast while he rubs my wet nipple with his thumb, and I almost jerk off the bed at the sensations ruling my body.

I'm not in control of my hands as I grip his hair, long and soft and perfect, while I hold his head to my breast and my hips jerk against his leg. Swear his hard-on has doubled in size, and that's making me hot and wet too.

"I want—" I gasp, but the lingering guilt and shame stop me from saying it out loud.

I want to have sex.

With Davis.

Now.

Here.

Go all the way.

Lick his tattoos. Grab his ass while he's balls-deep inside me.

Do all of the things that *I know I can do*.

That *I should not be ashamed of.*

"What do you want, Sloane?" he says softly, rubbing his beard over my bare breast while he watches me.

I feel so exposed, and it's not because he's eye level with my nipples.

"I want to shut my brain off and just *be.*"

"Here?" He thumbs my nipple again.

"Yes."

"Here?" He licks me low between my breasts.

"*Yes.*"

"Here?" He presses a line of kisses down, and down, and down, until his mouth hovers over my belly button. His body is pushing my legs wider apart, and I can't feel his erection anymore.

My pulse beats in my vagina, the steady drum making my clit ache to be touched too.

"Lower," I breathe out. "Just—just touch me. Please. Or I can do it. I just want—make my—make my brain be quiet."

"Show me."

"Show you?"

"Show me how you like to touch yourself."

My belly dips and my toes curl.

I enjoy sex, but I've always done it in the dark. No peeking.

Ridiculous, right? I'm a nurse. I know naked bodies are natural.

Except there will always be that little voice in the back of my head telling me it's shameful to enjoy myself with a man.

"That's...hard."

He kisses my belly button again. "Why?"

I huff out a breath and stare up at the ceiling. Not enough light to see if there are any cracks in here. "Years of being lectured about being a good girl."

"You *are* a good girl, Sloane. And good girls get to be happy."

"It feels like—"

I'm lying here, in the dark, my pussy hot and bothered, my breasts heavy and aching, a sexy bad boy between my legs, hard *for me*, and I'm ruining the mood.

He brushes his thumb over my hip, just above my panties. "It feels like what?"

"Like Patrick breaking into my house was my punishment for lying to my grandmother about you."

I squeeze my eyes shut.

Why am I like this?

Why do I say the wrong thing at the wrong time?

Why can't I just enjoy a good thing?

He's not saying anything.

Just lying there.

Probably watching me.

Thinking I have issues.

"Never mind. Forget I said that. I—"

"Sloane."

"What?"

"Having met your grandmother, the only thing I can feel about you telling her I was your boyfriend is honored. You should've picked someone hotter."

I lift my head and stare at him.

Even in the dim light, I can tell he's not smiling.

Not joking.

Not digging for compliments.

"Are you for real right now?"

"Yes."

I snort. "There is no one hotter."

And then I hear what I just said, and my entire body flushes.

"I—I don't date," I stammer. "I can recognize that some men—like you—are hot and still not want to date anyone."

His teeth flash.

He's smiling *now*.

"Good. Show me how you like to touch yourself."

My heart pounds, and my panties get wetter. "Now?"

"Whenever you're ready."

"With or without my underwear?"

"However you like it."

Fuck the voices shaming me in my head.

I'll deal with them tomorrow.

Or never.

I pull one leg up and reach between my thighs. He shifts to give me room, his eyes following my hand.

"I don't usually—use—just my fingers," I whisper as I stroke myself lightly over my soaked panties.

He knows. He saw.

My entire collection of personal satisfaction tools was scattered across my room.

My bedroom flashes in my mind, everything wrecked and tossed, and I shiver again.

Davis's voice penetrates the memory. "What do you use?"

Never. *Ever.* Ever, in the history of me dating, has a man asked me what adult toy I use to masturbate.

Probably because of how I pick—*picked* men.

I slip my finger under my panties and stroke the slick skin, up to my clit. "Depends—on my mood."

"What are you in the mood for now?"

You.

Not letting that one slip.

Not a chance.

But the question makes my vagina ache harder.

So does the timbre of his voice in the darkness. "Is your own hand enough, or would you like assistance?"

I shiver again, but this is pure hormones.

Have I ever been this turned on in my life?

I don't think so.

And every time he speaks, I get wound a little tighter.

"I—would love—assistance."

"How?"

I tickle my clit and look up at the ceiling, my breath coming fast. "Take—my panties—off."

"Like this?" He hooks a thumb under my waistband and tugs gently, and I instinctively lift my hips.

"Yes."

He bends over my pelvis and kisses my hip bone as he exposes it to the air. "And this?"

"Yes."

There's a shuffling on the bed, and then he tugs down the other side of my panties, kissing my other hip bone as he peels my underwear away. "And this?"

"Yes."

He slides the first side down more, and kisses the side of my ass, then does the same on the other side. "You smell delicious."

"Please just tear them off." I bend my legs again, helping with the process, and I only shiver a little as Davis pushes one of my legs to the side so he can settle between my thighs again, looking straight at my pussy.

I'm very exposed.

Very exposed.

And that little part of me that wants to shame me for showing a man who's not my husband my most private parts can fuck off.

Because I've also never felt more safe in my life.

"Show me again," he says.

"Give me your hand."

He slides it up my thigh. "All yours."

Like his body, his hand and fingers are long and lean. I guide it to the slick, swollen skin nestled in my pubic hair, and I stroke his hand up my pussy until my breath catches as his knuckle hits my clit.

"There," I breathe out. "Tease me there."

He flicks my clit, and all of my breath leaves my lungs as my hips leave the bed.

"So there," he murmurs.

Very studious.

Very serious.

He flicks my clit again.

"There," I gasp in agreement.

"Thank you. It's been a while. I needed a refresher."

His fingers stroke down the seam of my vulva, almost to my asshole, then back up again.

My legs fall open wider, and I arch into his touch, my eyes crossing when he teases my clit, then strokes me up and down again.

"May I try something?" he asks while he plays with all of my lady bits.

"Yes."

"Do you want to know what it is?"

"Trust—you."

He lifts his gaze to my face, nods once, and then shifts on the bed again.

Until his face is between my thighs.

He licks my pussy, and once again, my hips shoot off the mattress. "*Oh my god.*"

"Good or bad?" he murmurs against my clit.

"Good."

"A little good, or a lot good?"

"Do it again."

My fingers tangle in his hair again as he obeys orders, licking all the way up my pussy until he gets to my clit.

He flicks his tongue.

I grip his hair harder while my hips pump against his face.

He stops asking questions.

Good thing.

I don't even know what words are right now.

Just know the heavy, tight sensation coiling hard and fast low in my belly. The tickle of his beard between my thighs, the rub of his mustache against my clit as he explores every inch of my pussy with his mouth, the slow, studious licks and sucks getting faster and faster as he uses his mouth and his hands on my thighs to urge me closer and closer.

I think I'm whimpering.

I want to orgasm and I don't want this to stop.

But if I come, then it stops.

My hips buck harder. I can't catch my breath.

And then I'm coming with a scream as everything inside me breaks free.

Shame floats away on the wind.

Modesty flies with it.

My legs go straight.

My toes curl again.

My eyelids squeeze shut.

My hands ball into fists and I'm likely pulling out some of his hair.

I'm coming so hard, my inner walls clamping fast and tight, over and over, ecstasy pulsing between my thighs.

He makes a soft rumble of appreciation while I come all over his bearded face.

The kind of sound you make when you take the first bite of the most delicious chocolate caramel dessert you've ever had in your life.

That's what Davis sounds like.

Like I'm the best chocolate caramel dessert he's ever had in his mouth.

Like my pleasure is his pleasure.

My eyes flood with heat.

It's been longer than since my last boyfriend that I felt this cared for.

My body slowly comes back to earth and melts into a puddle of boneless satisfaction.

Davis props his chin on my lower belly, and when I finally open my eyes, he's watching me.

What do you say in a moment like this?

Thank you?

That seems insufficient.

But as my body melts, my brain is melting too.

My breath slowing.

My eyelids drooping.

Crap. Crap crap crap.

I masturbate to fall asleep.

I've trained myself for this.

A hint of a smile touches his lips.

I think.

Everything's getting blurry.

"Sleep tight, Sloane. You're safe here."

Did he drug my orgasm?

Wait.

That's not possible.

Is it?

I don't answer myself.

Because I'm doing what I've trained myself to do, and I'm falling fast, fast asleep.

17

Davis

SUNLIGHT IS PEEKING through the metal blinds on the small windows in the bedroom of my camper when I pull myself out of a deep slumber.

There's cold, wet drool on my arm and the scent of cinnamon tickling my nose.

Cinnamon.

Sloane smells like cinnamon, but more.

Like a chai latte.

And she's clinging to my arm, her mouth gaping open as she snores softly, her copper red hair curled in every direction but tame.

She snorts once, opens her eyes, and stares at me, but doesn't seem to *see* me, and blurts, "The map is a lie."

Her eyes close, she lets out the heaviest of heavy sighs, and burrows harder against my arm.

She's fucking gorgeous, and I have a boner the size of a hundred-year-old blue spruce.

It's been with me since I fucked up and touched her last night, then couldn't stop touching her.

My balls feel like they've been used as a punching bag. If my cock doesn't cool it, I'm gonna have to call a doctor.

Not good.

I close my eyes and breathe deeply. I can control this.

I can work through this.

I've done it before. I will do it again.

Yep.

I'll feast on her pussy without getting any relief of my own again if that's what it takes to put her to sleep.

No.

No.

I'll get over the boner. That's what I meant.

This is a false situation that's making me feel attracted to her because I'm still a biological, heterosexual male whose body doesn't always agree that the best course for my life is being single forever.

And I like to take care of people.

She needs care right now.

I orgasmed her to sleep because she needed it.

This isn't actual attraction.

It's a disconnect between my body and my brain.

My boner isn't going away.

Wait.

Goddammit.

She said *the map is a lie.*

Is she dreaming about Thorny Rock?

The question can wait.

It can effing wait.

She needs her sleep, and she's getting it, and that's enough for right now.

For this moment.

For all morning, if need be.

The cat's snoozing between my thighs. Sloane's snoring softly again with her face plastered to me.

And I feel...peace.

Fuck.

Not peace.

I'm having a reaction to properly using my hero complex to help a woman in need.

I'm mistaking pride in a job well done for peace.

I inhale another deep breath, ordering the boner to remember we're a loner, and that's when I smell something else.

Coffee.

I sniff again.

The coffee scent gets stronger.

I sniff Sloane's hair again—definitely cinnamon.

But then—then I hear it.

The sound of my tea kettle getting hot enough to shake.

Someone's *inside my trailer*. Using my kitchen.

When I double-triple-checked that the door was locked.

I bolt upright.

The cat yowls and goes flying, thumps weird on the ground, and yowls again.

Fuck.

Three-legged cat.

Shit shit shit.

But I see a shadow move beyond the door, and the cat doesn't matter.

Neither does Sloane, who's gasping, "Who saved the chicken?" as I spin out of my bedroom in a crouch, ready to take on whoever's—

Mother.

Fucking.

Fucker.

In less than a heartbeat, I identify my intruder.

She's about five six. Brown hair. Approaching fifty, though you wouldn't know it to look at her.

And she's smirking at me as she holds a to-go coffee cup of her own that she must've brought, which explains the coffee smell before the tea kettle's hot. "Oh, doesn't feel so good when the shoe's on the other foot, does it?"

Levi will die.

"Oh my god, is this your girlfriend?" Sloane shrieks behind me.

She's in one of my RYDE T-shirts—Beck's clothing line, fabric's soft as hell—but nothing else.

Just a T-shirt hanging down to her upper thighs.

Hiding that sweet pussy that I devoured last night like a starving man.

Been ten years.

I probably am starving. And I have fucked myself over much harder than my dick will ever be.

My intruder turns her smirk to Sloane. "He wishes," she says dryly.

Sloane's copper hair is a swirly mass of chaos and her

eyes have thick bags beneath them. She's gripping the lamp from beside my bed, holding it like a bat.

And then I jerk my thumb toward the intruder. "Levi sent security. This is Giselle. She'll follow you to work and hang out keeping an eye on things for a few days. You said *the map is a lie* a minute ago. What were you dreaming about?"

She blinks at me, then winces.

Dammit.

No *good morning, beautiful, hope you slept well.*

And we've both noticed.

Welcome to awkward land.

I fucking hate awkward, and I don't do awkward.

Until today.

"If I was dreaming, I don't remember it." She slides a gaze back to Giselle, lamp still clutched like a weapon in her hand. "Why does she look scary?"

"Because she is. But she's on your side."

"How do I know that?"

Giselle helps herself to one of the three mugs in my camper cabinets. "First cup black, second two cups cut with almond milk and one of those stevia packets, but it has to be organic since those are the ones without any artificial sweeteners added."

"That's not creepier than anything else that's happened in the past few days," Sloane mutters, and I can't tell if she's being sarcastic or not, but it makes me want to smile.

"I work for people who have people who do research so that we, as security, can be as seamless of an addition to their lives as possible," Giselle replies. "I can tell you how half of the pop stars in the industry took their coffee three years ago."

Sloane creeps behind me, still watching Giselle. "You work for Levi Wilson."

"Yes."

"You're familiar. But why am I picturing you in my head next to Waverly? And not like, in a wedding dress last weekend. Something longer ago."

"Levi and Waverly are friends."

"Giselle was called in when Waverly ditched her own security detail to come see Cooper when they were first dating," I tell her. "She came out here to Shipwreck with them."

Sloane blinks at me. "That was a long time ago. Do you have one of those brains that are magic with details and recall?"

"No." Mostly. "Was at the top of my head because a few people mentioned it at the wedding. Locals. Excited to see Cooper get married to a woman who ditched her security detail for him."

"Oh." She glances at Giselle again. "Okay. Okay. I think this will be okay. I mean, clearly *not* okay, but as okayish as okay can be in the given circumstances."

"You can trust her."

"Will she actually answer my questions?"

"Depends on the question," Giselle says. "I stopped by the sheriff's office on my way here. They can't locate Patrick Dixon and they're looking closer at the evidence from the museum break-in on Saturday night."

Sloane shivers, and it takes everything in me to not turn around and hug her.

Tell her we'll move the camper somewhere more remote.

Hide from him—well, hide *her* from him while I go hunt the fucker—and keep her safe and her cat safe with all of the popcorn and tequila and coffee she needs.

Take care of her.

Guard her.

Smell her hair again.

Cinnamon. That's a new one.

Fucking hell.

I'm falling for her.

These are situational emotions, I remind myself. Not real.

And I need to *not* touch her again.

If I touch her, I won't stop touching her.

As evidenced by last night.

She eyes me, and her cheeks pinken, like she's thinking about last night too.

Thank fuck, someone bangs on the door before I have to say anything, making Sloane jump and lift the lamp again like she's ready to swing.

"Open up, Davis," Cash calls. "We need proof of life. And Aspen wrote you a song about getting a new job. You're gonna love it."

I take the lamp. "You don't need this. They're friendly."

"Are they?"

"Yes."

"If you don't open the door, I'm sending a squirrel in through the window to unlock the door. Pretty sure Levi's old pet is one of these guys staring at us," Cash yells.

"These are the people you actually trust?" Sloane says to me.

Fuck me.

My dick's still half hard, I'm pissed at Levi for sending Giselle, Cash is being an intentional asshole, I haven't meditated or worked out or had breakfast or my own coffee, there are undoubtedly four hundred more messages waiting for me on the group chat that I abandoned last night when I heard Sloane scream, and I'm smiling.

At a woman.

Who made a joke and might just understand exactly how funny it really is.

Not a crush. Not a crush. Not a crush.

"They're consistent," I tell her.

She eyes the door again. "Huh. I can almost appreciate that."

"Do me a favor," Giselle says as she heads to the door to let them in without consulting me first. "Freak out about how much you love Aspen and make Cash think you're going to attack her while I stand by and do nothing. Bonus points if you attack-hug her. Levi's wife is the only reason I'm still around, and I like these men to remember to not take me for granted."

"I think I love her," Sloane whispers to me.

"Most of us do."

Giselle swings the door open, and Aspen steps through first.

She has a new hairdo—dark brown and short today—and she's dressed down in casual jeans and a purplish sweater.

Cash follows. His light brown hair is flopping all over, his nose is big as ever, and he's wearing the look of a lumberjack still on his honeymoon between the flannel and the happy love glow.

He held out a long time, but now the last one of our group has fallen.

Except me.

"*Ooh*, are you Sloane?" Aspen squeals and beelines around me before Sloane can utter a word, throwing her arms around the redhead who just climbed out of my bed. "Ellie told me how you publicly dumped the shitwaffle who lied to both of you, and Sarah said they might have to move to Shipwreck because Ava loves you more than any of the nurses she's had in Copper Valley or LA. You're a freaking rockstar."

"You have to the count of three to release my client before you find out why I was nicknamed head cheer bitch in high school," Giselle says.

Cash snorts. "It's a hug, G."

Giselle looks him up and down, and then she does the most Giselle thing ever.

She hugs him.

There's no warning. No notice. One minute, she's looking at him, and the next, she has her arms around him.

But she's not just hugging him.

She's so fast, her hug also has his arms trapped right at the elbows, so he can only flap his hands at the wrist as his eyes bulge out and he makes a strangled gulping sound and tries to escape her grasp.

"Is this just a hug?" she asks him.

"Uncle," he gasps. "*Uncle.*"

"Call your girlfriend off my client."

"She let go."

"*No one* touches my client without permission, or I will touch *you* without permission. Is that understood?"

"Fuck. I didn't need to know your hair smells like —*ulp.*"

Aspen's jaw has unhinged and her eyes are comically wide. "I'm not touching her! *I'm not touching her!*"

Giselle gives one more very obvious squeeze to her hug, then releases Cash.

Then she makes a tongue-out face like she's gagging. "The things I do for you people... I'm getting too old for this."

"If you ever need funding so you can retire from body-guarding and go do vigilante shit instead, I've been poor most of my life, and I'd be happy to be poor again in the name of supporting a badass real-life superhero because you seem like the type who could pull that off," Aspen says. "Totally worth it. Can we hire you to take out all of the terrible ex-boyfriends?"

Cash visibly swallows. "Babe? We okay?"

"You took a bodyguard hug for me. We're good. But thank you for remembering that's a good question to keep asking."

"Yes. Good. Okay. Always. Also, you won't be poor for the rest of your life," Cash says. "You're too talented. Also, you can have as much of my money as you want. Not that my money's why you love me. I know that. I do. I'm just saying, no price is too—I'm shutting up now."

"Get gross, and I'll hug you again," Giselle says to Cash.

Sloane keeps looking from me to my friends to Levi's bodyguard.

"You're awake," I tell her, sensing the question that's most likely about to come out of her mouth. "They're always like this."

She starts to nod, then sucks in a breath. "*Oh my god, what time is it? I have to go to work.*"

She turns back toward the bedroom, then freezes.

You can just feel what's coming next.

I don't have clean clothes.

They're all in my house, which is a crime scene.

My fingers curl into fists, not because my temper's been lit once more, but because that's what it takes to keep from touching her again.

To keep from hugging her.

To keep from shielding her from the bad in the world.

She's strong. She's got this. She doesn't need me.

And that fucking sucks.

Even though it shouldn't.

"Tillie Jean sent a care package with clothes that should fit you, and a fresh pair of scrubs on top of it," Giselle says. "She also said she'll never speak to you again if you don't come use her very large bathroom instead of a shithole the size of a grape to get ready today, but in case you want to use a shithole the size of a grape, I do have what you need. Tillie Jean can't tell you what to do."

Sloane turns very, very slowly, straightening and pulling her shoulders back as she does.

Summoning her strength, if I had to guess.

Pisses me off that she needs it today.

Wherever Patrick Dixon is hiding, I will make sure he has the day he deserves.

When I'm not battling the boner from hell over how fucking attractive it is to watch Sloane put on her *I've got this* face.

"Tillie Jean is the best," Sloane says to Giselle. "Are you driving me today? Let me get Peggy and figure out who's watching her today. And thank you. I don't usually— thank you."

"The cat can stay," I say.

Cash smiles out loud.

Aspen does too.

Sloane squints at me. "Are you sure?"

"You calling your family back today and telling them to fuck off so you don't have to fake-marry me on Saturday?"

She grimaces. "That's a little too much for this morning."

Good. "Won't be able to keep pulling this off when the god-complex fucker drops by again if your pet doesn't know me."

Those blue eyes hold my gaze, and they're saying far more than I want them to.

You are my lifeline right now.

I will forever owe you a debt of gratitude.

We need to talk about last night, and I'm not ready for that either.

Or possibly I'm reading entirely too much into that look.

Probably am, considering all she says is a quiet, "Thank you."

She looks down, seems to realize she's just in a T-shirt, and then looks wide-eyed at Cash and Aspen. "Mother trucker," she mutters. And then she disappears into the bedroom, shutting the door softly behind her.

I listen, and—yep.

"Way to be naked in front of everyone, Sloane," she mutters to herself.

There it is.

"Coffee's ready," Giselle calls to her. "Rivers. Go get the bag out of my car, and do not touch anything else, or you'll lose a finger."

"She's more dangerous than the bears," Aspen whispers.

"I'm really pissed Levi has the better protection agents," Cash mutters back.

"Aspen, get out too." Giselle turns her don't-try-me look on me. "Remington. Go pretend you're tent camping outside and let the woman have some privacy."

I hold her gaze while I step around her to shuffle through my cabinets, looking for a few things.

"I'll be outside making breakfast, Sloane," I call through the door.

"Thank you," she calls back.

I almost add *Yell if Giselle makes you uncomfortable* because I *can* take her out if I need to, but I won't need to.

She's good.

She'll make sure Sloane stays safe as long as necessary.

And while she's watching Sloane, I'll be out in the world looking for the reason Sloane feels unsafe.

And I'll take care of it.

For good.

18

Sloane

THE WEIRDEST PART of having a bodyguard is how much I appreciate it.

And how much I'm disappointed that Davis isn't my bodyguard.

Which I need to not be disappointed about.

I fell asleep on him.

I fell asleep on him.

I didn't even bother offering to help him take care of his hard-on. Just fell asleep. After he ate me out.

We probably need to talk about that.

But not now. Because now, I get to pretend everything is normal while I go to work.

With a bodyguard.

Doc doesn't blink when I tell him I need Giselle to hang out in the records room all day. He tells me to take the day off if I need to. Apparently he thinks planning a wedding the same week that my house is destroyed is a lot.

I don't take the day off—working is easier than figuring out what I'm going to say to Davis when I go back to get my cat—but I do ask for a long lunch hour.

And that's when I take advantage of having a security person with me.

Or try to, anyway.

Because there's definitely a second-weirdest part, and that part is that I actually need a few minutes alone somewhere.

I haven't spent a large portion of my adult years catching up on movies like *Pirates of the Caribbean* and *Jumanji* and *The Lost City* to not realize that I made a tactical error in not getting Thorny Rock's actual journal for Davis.

What's written on the pages sometimes isn't enough.

Sometimes, you have to see how the pages fit together or if there's something secret hidden in the cover or if there's a page missing.

"What are your boundaries?" I ask Giselle over lunch as she drives me downtown to pick up a gyro before going to the next place on my list.

She slides me a look. "Repeat the question with more details."

"Do your clients ever have to commit small, petty crimes that you know about but can't talk about because of confidentiality and because you know that the crime will be fixed and everything will be put right again before it's actually a problem?"

"Once again, repeat the question with more details."

"If there were, say, a historical artifact that should be on display at a museum, and someone who's like a museum curator were to...quietly and temporarily acquire that historical artifact for the greater good of the world..."

"Let Davis steal Thorny Rock's journal on his own. Keep your nose clean. Especially while the sheriff's still investigating what happened with *your* house last night."

Welp, that *does* answer my question. "Why would you think Davis wants Thorny Rock's journal?"

"It's my job to know."

"So he talks to his friends about what he's up to?"

No answer.

"So he doesn't talk to his friends about what he's up to, but they send spies for updates?"

No answer again.

"You think he's a bad influence on Levi?"

That earns me a dark smile, but just like Davis, once more, she doesn't answer.

I snort softly and sink back into my seat.

Nice car. The leather's buttery soft, the engine's quiet, and the windows are tinted so that no one can see inside.

And I'm in it because there are people in this world doing nice things for me when they barely even know me.

Guilt that I can't repay them starts to well up in my chest, and I order it away.

Be grateful, not guilty, I chant in my head.

"Thank you for being here with me today," I say to Giselle. "It's nice to feel less afraid than I was expecting to after last night."

She nods.

"Can you please tell Levi thank you too?"

She nods again.

I don't know if he intended his security agent to watch me or to watch Davis—I could honestly see the intentions going either way—but I'm grateful nonetheless.

Also, I suppose it's possible there are other bodyguards out there watching Davis.

Like Cash and Aspen's security team.

I noticed them hovering while all of us had eggs and pancakes and sausages over the campfire before I left to shower fast at Tillie Jean's house and head to work.

"Have you heard any more about Patrick?" I ask.

"No."

Giselle and I take out gyros for lunch at Yiannis's deli, and she drives me to the museum, parking in the one spot on the street marked with a giant *No Parking* sign.

I slide her a look.

I didn't ask to come to the museum to eat. I asked to go see Tillie Jean.

So is Tillie Jean at the museum?

She ignores my look—curiosity, I swear, I'm not being judgy about how very kind people see fit to take care of me—and hustles me to the back door, where she hits the right security codes to let me in the building.

"We change those codes *every day*," I say.

"My job to know them."

Jealousy bites me in the ass.

She's just like Davis.

They'd make a great pair.

Whereas I'm not dating. Ever again.

No matter how much my lady parts are still chilling in satisfaction after—nope.

Not thinking about that.

That memory goes in the *to be dealt with a lot later if we actually have to* box.

Inside the workroom, there's no Tillie Jean.

But there *is* an Annika.

She's sitting at the worktable with her mom and her mom's long-term boyfriend, Roger. All three of them have sandwiches that look like they came from Crusty Nut.

My heart is beating overtime in anticipation.

So I *do* get to do some detective work today.

Except— "Where are the maps?"

"Safely tucked away." Annika points to the large filing cabinet with extra-wide drawers. "We didn't want to get food on them when they're not the important part."

"Is that Sloane?" her mom says.

Maria Williams went unexpectedly blind several years back, right as she was opening her own bakery over in Sarcasm, which is what led to Annika coming home and reuniting with Grady.

"It's the pretty nurse lady with the red hair who put all this work into the shitheads' ancestor's museum," Roger says to her.

Maria's in dark sunglasses, as always, so I only see her smile touch her mouth and not her full face. "Oh, I didn't know she had red hair. Copper or carrot?"

"Copper," Annika supplies.

"Is she alone, or did that mysterious boy band guy come with her?"

"Hi, Maria," I say. "I'm alone. Except for Giselle. She's my bodyguard for the day."

"Close protection specialist," Giselle corrects.

"I love the word *bodyguard* in my romance audiobooks, but I'll honor your title wishes," Maria says. "Nice to meet you, Giselle. Do you have any loyalty to Shipwreck, or would you like one of the donuts from my shop over in Sarcasm? As much as I love my son-in-law, his donuts can't touch my donuts. I smuggled some into town. Roger, please offer Giselle a superior donut."

Annika's smiling so brightly that her brown eyes are twinkling. "How about we save the trash talk for after we tell Sloane what you both know?"

Roger eyes Giselle. "She gonna tell those boy band guys?"

"I'll be in the museum." Giselle pins me with a no-nonsense, *do not fuck with me* look. "Don't leave this building without me, or I *will* quit, and you'll have to explain that to Ingrid."

I nod. I've met Ingrid, Levi's wife, and she's every bit as awesome as Sarah Ryder. "Understood."

Giselle lets herself into the public part of the museum, but she leaves the door cracked.

Maria tilts her ear toward the door. "Are we alone now?"

"Yes, Mama," Annika says. "It's safe to talk now."

"Good. Sloane, how are you? I heard about your house."

I suppress a shiver. "Better than expected, but I haven't had to look at it yet today. The sheriff's still documenting the scene, and Doc made me take a break this morning to call my insurance company to get *that* paperwork rolling."

"Ew. Paperwork."

"Agreed. Almost the worst part."

It's not, but no one calls me on the lie.

"Annika told me you stayed with that mysterious boy band guy last night."

"I did."

"Did you see him naked?"

"Mama." Annika pinches her lips together, but you can tell she's trying not to smile. "They're getting married on Saturday. I'm sure she's seen him naked."

She also shoots me a look like she, too, wants the answer to that question.

And I do my best not to blush.

I *felt* him, but I didn't *see* him.

Whereas he saw pretty much all of me.

My toes curl inside my shoes while Annika's look gets lookier.

Like she knows there's a story I'm not sharing.

Thank goodness for Roger. He's missing all of the undertones as he squints at me. "That one's Davis, right? Too hairy. You probably couldn't see him through all that hair even if he was naked."

Annika laughs, then cringes. "Dammit."

"Pee break?" I ask.

"Why is it always like this?"

"Do you want the real medical answer, or do you just want me to tell you that nature hates us?"

"Nature hates us works for me." She rises and heads

toward the public area of the museum too. "Don't spill the good gossip without me."

Roger snorts softly. "We're not letting her within a mile of this gossip," he mutters to Maria.

Maria nods back. "I know my girl's strong and capable, but I agree. What we're about to tell you stays with us and *only* us. Understand?"

Forget the gyro.

I want the tea. "Yes, ma'am."

"Are *you* gonna tell that boy bander?" Roger growls at me.

Maria clucks her tongue. "Roger. He probably already knows."

"But he might not."

"But he probably does. Annika said he just *knows* things."

"Doesn't mean we have to hand him even a single word that he might not know. And if she's marrying him…"

Maria turns her face in my direction. Her dark brown hair is tied up in a loose bun that I honestly suspect Roger did for her.

Annika talks about him all the time.

He's the boyfriend we all wish we could have, and he makes me believe there are still good men out there.

"Sloane," Maria says, "we need you to promise that anything you hear in this room stays in this room, and we need to get on with it before Annika gets back."

"You're worried that I'm going to give secrets to a guy who didn't even want me to know what brand of toothpaste he used this morning?" I say.

Which isn't a promise.

But also, he *did* go into the bathroom and move something around in there before I got in to use the toilet after his friends and Giselle scared the crap out of us this morning.

So it's the truth.

Nowhere near the whole truth, clearly.

But in the light of the day, I can almost say that orgasms aren't enough to talk secrets out of me.

Almost.

"You're marrying a man who keeps his toothpaste preferences from you?" Maria asks.

Dammit. "Yes. It keeps the spark of excitement alive. Just like me not telling him what I know about the treasure hunt will."

Maria keeps her face aimed at mine and drops her voice to a whisper. "Okay, then. That's good enough for me. Now, we don't know this for one hundred percent certain—"

"But we know it close enough to certain to believe it's the truth," Roger finishes, also in a whisper.

"We weren't sure we should tell you at all."

"But if people are searching your house because they think you have clues to the treasure, then you need to know so you can protect yourself."

I shake my head. "Why does everyone think that someone ransacked my house looking for things related to the treasure?"

Clearly, they did. But how does everyone else know it?

"Because of what happened at the museum during Cooper's wedding," Maria replies. "The actual audacity, to do that in broad daylight while a wedding was going on just outside."

Oh.

That makes sense.

"Adrenaline junkies." Roger snorts. "I hate people who're that bold. But to answer your question, there's been people over in Sarcasm asking things they shouldn't be asking."

"Things about things that Roger didn't even know until about six months ago himself." Maria reaches for him.

Roger finds her hand with his meaty paw and squeezes it. "Loyalty to Annika is the only reason we're not telling the world. She's happy here. That matters most."

"This sounds ominous," I murmur.

Maria leans further over the table. "The treasure isn't in Shipwreck."

I make a noise between a croak and a gasp. "You think it's real too?"

Crap crap *crap*. That was loud.

I drop my voice to a whisper again and repeat myself. "You think it's real?"

"Oh, it's real," Roger says. "Been real forever. And the reason nobody's ever found it is because it's not here."

"How do you know that?"

He smirks at me. His dark beard has turned nearly pure white since I first met him several years ago, and his balding forehead reaches almost all the way back to the nape of his neck, whereas he had a little more hair on top a few years ago.

But that smirk—that smirk says *I might be getting old, but I'm not getting dumb*.

"You didn't think I'd give you everything I had for a museum *here*, did you?" he says.

I shake my head. "Of course not. Not with the history between—"

I cut myself off with a gasp.

He tilts his head toward me, a *now you're getting it* if I've ever seen one.

"The treasure is the real reason why the towns fight?" I'm having to fight myself to remember to keep my voice low. "*Oh my god*. Is the treasure in Sarcasm?"

His chair creaks as he shifts in it.

"We don't know for sure, but we think so," Maria says. "When Bailey comes home from college for Thanksgiving in a few weeks, the three of us are going to figure it out."

My brain is spinning.

The treasure not being in Shipwreck would explain why it's never been found, which, *duh*.

That's something all of the Rocks said to me recently too. *If it exists, it's not here.*

But to think it could've been somewhere in or near Sarcasm this whole time...

"Annika says Bailey's loving college life," I say while I mull over their suspicions and think back to what I know about the history of the two towns.

"There's not a thing either one of my girls can't do," Maria declares. "She's killing it."

Maria's two daughters are pretty far apart in age, but watching their relationship has made me wish I had a sister.

267

My brother's wife isn't quite it.

Lovely woman. We just have different outlooks and goals for life, and she doesn't always appreciate that about me, and I don't appreciate her judging me for not wanting to be just like her.

Grandma loves her.

Naturally.

She loved Patrick too, which I was thrilled about at the time, but now—*ew*.

Just *ew*.

"Now, what we need to know," Roger says, "is if you're willing to be Team Sarcasm to help us find the treasure. And since people seem to think you know where it is…"

I spread my hands in exasperation. "Until this week, I haven't had the barest belief that it even exists. Why am I going to know where it is if we switch the town name where it's buried?"

"You've lived in this museum for the past year," Maria says. "You know more than you think you do, and everyone around you but you knows it."

Davis said more or less the same thing.

But how am I supposed to know what I don't even know that I know?

"Sarcasm was founded by Thorny Rock's first mate," Roger says. "Thorny Rock tried to poison him."

Right.

Right.

It's well-documented that Thorny Rock tried to poison Walter Bombeck, the founder of Sarcasm.

I've seen enough old letters referencing it to believe it's true.

Probably.

Gossip is as old as time, and all it takes is one person in authority to say something for people to believe it's true, apparently even without evidence.

"But why would Thorny Rock poison the one person who knew where the treasure was?" I ask.

Maria faces me. "Exactly that. Because he knew where the treasure was. We think Thorny was afraid Walter was going to go after it. Even back then, relations weren't great between the two towns."

"Because Thorny refused to let Walter have the better land when they split up," Roger adds.

"That's a pirate captain for you," Maria sniffs.

Roger nods. "Only looking out for himself when his crew is the whole reason he made any pirate coin in the first place. Couldn't have done it without them."

I need time to think about this and figure out what it all means. "Do you have any idea approximately where in Sarcasm it might be?"

"That's where you come in." Roger claps me on the shoulder. "We think Thorny Rock kept a diary, and we think Grady's shithead grandfather's hiding it."

I wasn't allowed to cuss when I was growing up—it was unladylike and would send you to hell to boot—but there's once again a long string of *fuck*s going through my head right now.

"If you can get your hands on it—" Maria starts, but she freezes.

Roger whips his head to the door.

I look too.

Nothing.

I open my mouth, but Roger holds up a thick hand, and a moment later, Annika pops through the door to the front of the museum.

Maria must've caught the noise of her shoes squeaking before Roger and I did.

"My grandmother had another map, but it burned up in a fire at her morgue about thirty years back," Roger says to me.

"We think it was the real original map of Shipwreck," Maria adds.

Yep.

More *fucks*.

Because now I don't know if they're serious or talking in code.

I do know one thing though—my gyro is getting cold.

Annika slides a look at them. "That's it?" she says. "There was a fire in Sarcasm and all you're going to say about it is that the original map of Shipwreck was lost in it? That's the whole secret you wanted to talk to Sloane about?"

"What else is there to say?" Maria asks her.

That a Shipwreck shithead set it.

That's what else there is to say.

Annika's eyes narrow and her mouth goes flat. "What did you tell Sloane while I was in the bathroom?"

Yay, my gyro tastes like sawdust and my stomach feels like its walls are lined with broadswords and it's having a sword fight without my approval.

"We were asking about if she's had any more famous patients at the office, and she was refusing to tell us. Can you imagine?"

Annika looks at me.

"What?" I say around a mouthful of food. "You know I can't tell you either."

"Don't make me tell Grady to only make licorice-flavored cookies for your wedding."

Giselle pokes her head in the door. "Don't threaten my client or your husband won't be baking anything at all. Sloane, what time do you have to be back at work?"

I look at my watch, and my body goes into both relief mode and *fuuuuuccck* mode at the same time. "About four minutes ago."

"Hurry up, buttercup."

Yeah.

I see why Davis loves her.

I definitely do too.

"Next time you're in Sarcasm, you stop by my house, and I'll see if I have anything else in the basement," Roger says to me.

I shove another bite in my mouth and nod.

The people around me are losing their minds.

And I'm starting to buy into the thing where this treasure might be real. I might actually know things I don't know I know.

And Davis knows more than he's telling me.

Which begs the question—

Is he taking care of me because it's the nice thing to do, or is he taking care of me so that I'll be on his side whenever I start to figure out what I know that I don't realize I know?

The question turns my stomach.

But given my history of taste in men...I can't trust the answer that I want to believe.

19

Davis

THIS IS OFFICIALLY the most time I've spent in one go with Aspen since Cash finally got over himself and told her how he felt last Christmas, and one thing is rapidly becoming clear.

I like her more than I like him.

I managed to keep my other buddies' significant others at a distance far longer—Ellie excluded, of course, since we grew up together before she married Wyatt—but Aspen's already wormed her way into a circle of trust.

Not the closest circle of trust.

Not even the circle as close as I'm refusing to acknowledge I've let Sloane into.

But definitely a closer circle, much sooner than the rest of them.

"Look, I get trust issues," she's saying to me as we

weave our way around clumps of overgrown bushes to circle the dilapidated, condemned cabin on the acreage I moved to a month or so ago. We've spent all day trying to track a cell signal that pinged nearby using equipment I'll forever deny I have. "But you can't both have trust issues and also be frustrated when other people have trust issues. Okay. Okay. You *can*. But I'll judge you for it."

Cash nods. "I support judgment for hypocritical behavior. You know what I don't get though? I don't get why you're suddenly obsessed with Thorny Rock's treasure."

He and Aspen are holding hands, more or less in matching flannel and boots now, since Aspen's first outfit of the day wasn't right for hiking in the woods all day.

They're *that* couple. The couple who have to match to walk around in the woods, even if they might not have realized they were doing it.

And I *still* appreciate Aspen more than I appreciate Cash right now.

"Not sudden." I pause at the sound of an engine. Can't see the driveway leading to my camper, just the back of the camper and the electrical hookup, but that's definitely a car.

And it's going in the wrong direction.

Leaving.

Fuck.

I run the last several yards to the edge of the camper, then slow, cautiously peeking around it to see who came to visit while we weren't here.

Sloane's sitting on one of the logs around the fire pit, and she definitely wasn't before.

She glances at me, then back at the road like she doesn't want to look at me right now.

Uh-oh.

Is this because she doesn't want to talk about last night?

Or did something happen in town today?

All's been radio silent. Levi wouldn't even pass on updates from Giselle beyond *we'll only hear something if there's something worth hearing.*

"Giselle's going to check the perimeter," Sloane says. "She said to tell you that if anything happens to me in the five minutes she's making sure you didn't fuck something up today, that you'll wake up with worms in your bed every day for the rest of your natural life."

She's also wearing jeans, flannel, and boots, which means she must've changed since work. And gotten off early if she's here as the sun's setting.

I look back at my friends.

They flash me matching grins as they, too, look at the woman I wasn't sure would come back.

The woman I'm disappointing by not being able to track down her ex-boyfriend.

Dixon's cell signal went dead about two hours ago.

And no, I'm not telling how I'm tracking it.

"Did you dress her too?" I ask my friends.

It's easier than asking why she doesn't want to look at me.

And why that's making my heart crash in my chest.

"Flannel's in, my dude." Cash slaps me on the back and walks past me, Aspen still attached to his hand, and heads to the fire pit. "You want me to get that started for you, Sloane?"

Irritation roars to life in my chest.

I can set the goddamn fire.

"Are you assuming a woman can't start her own fire?" Aspen asks him.

He wiggles his brows at her. "Is that a euphemism?"

"No offense—okay, no, that's wrong. *All* offense intended, you two are making me want to throw up in my mouth," Sloane says.

Huh.

Gloves are off.

"Shitty day?" I ask her while I try to get my breathing under control.

Those pretty blue eyes hit me with a dead-eyed *my house was broken into and I don't feel safe anywhere, so what the fuck do you think?* stare.

And that's the best-case scenario of what that expression might mean.

I nod. "Just making sure you're a normal human being. Cash. Get lost."

"And leave you to wrestle the bears solo? No can do. I'll wait until Giselle gets back."

"What's up with you and bears?" If he's talked about them once today, he's talked about them a dozen times.

He and Aspen grin at each other.

"They're dangerous," she answers for them.

"*They're* dangerous." I point to the three beefy dudes who've been following us all day as we've hunted through the woods for Sloane's ex-boyfriend.

Yep.

That's who I'm tracking.

And yes, we all know it.

Aspen shushes me. "We pretend they don't exist."

Wanna know what really pissed me off today?

My friends put three security officers on me and just one on Sloane.

The best on Sloane, but still only one.

I could've guarded her myself.

And don't tell me security was here for Cash and Aspen. We're secluded. No one knows to look for them here. Even if they did, Cash usually only travels with one security person. Two when he's in more crowded areas.

Not three.

Which means it's possible they're guarding me from myself.

My phone dings, and I glance down to see a confirmation that the locks have been set at the museum.

Final worker of the day has left the building.

And they left one particular light on inside.

A light shining right over a new map that's been put out.

A fake map, naturally.

Haven't been working on this, knowing Dixon was also looking for it, without putting some tricks of my own in motion.

And now the trap's set if he's around and wants more than what he did or didn't find in Thorny Rock's old coat.

Sloane's phone dings too.

She pulls it out, looks at the screen, and heaves the heaviest sigh I've heard in weeks.

I look at Cash.

He ignores me and takes a seat on a log at the fire pit. "Someone bothering you?" he asks Sloane.

"Old friend," she mutters.

Old friend.

Got a guess or two who that might be.

I drop next to her on the log she's sitting on, take her phone from her hand, switch the camera, lift it, and when she looks at it, I kiss her cheek and snap a photo.

Her hand lands on my thigh and squeezes as she sucks in a breath.

I check the photo.

And it pisses me off too.

Because I lifted a camera and she automatically smiled.

No chance she's actually happy, but she performed for the camera like she is, and the damn picture looks perfect.

"Send it to him," I murmur.

"I don't know what's going on here, exactly, but I know that's not a picture you want to send to anyone to prove you're in a solid relationship," Aspen says. "Talk about posed and unnatural. You two are *so* not selling this engaged thing."

Never mind.

Aspen's not in the circle of trust anymore.

I glare at her.

"No, no, she's right," Cash says. "We don't need details, but we can definitely help you take a better picture. Sloane. Give me your phone."

"I—" she starts, then throws her hands up in the air. "Fine. Here. Have my phone."

It dings as she's handing it over to him, and I'm not fast enough to grab it before he looks at it.

I haven't even seen what the dickwad is sending her, but Cash's face says everything.

Whatever she just got, it wasn't a nice message.

"Who's Nigel?" my buddy says.

Her gaze shifts to the dead fire pit. "Old friend."

"That's not a message any old friend of mine would ever send."

"Leave her alone," I growl.

"'Don't be stupid this time?'" Cash says. "'You know we're inevitable. Tell me where you are so we can quit with the fucking games and go home.'"

Her phone dings again.

Aspen gasps as she peeks at it. "Oh, that's low," she whispers.

"'Do you want your grandmother to die knowing that you're sad and lonely and unfulfilled in your life? Or worse, that you abandoned all of your principles for cheap sex with a sheep-fucker? Do you really want to do that to her?'" Cash reads.

Sloane's cheeks have gone bright red.

"I'll make three phone calls and move the wedding to tomorrow," I tell Sloane.

Aspen chokes.

Cash drops the phone, and it clatters to the ground.

Like they don't know the whole story. I took ten minutes to read the *five* hundred text messages that kept going after I went to bed last night, and I know they know everything.

Overdramatic assholes.

"If you want to give him a massive middle finger and

let someone fight in your corner for you on this one," I add. "Not telling you what to do. I'm offering."

She lifts her head and looks at me. "It's not in Shipwreck, is it?" she murmurs.

She's deflecting by asking about the treasure.

Can't blame her.

But the question still catches me off guard, and it's a struggle to both keep a straight face and also level with her. Which I owe her. "Never was."

"Why is that important enough that Annika's family doesn't want her to know?"

And one more question I don't want to answer.

She stares at me while I debate how much I'm willing to say.

"What's happening here?" Aspen whispers to Cash.

"I don't know, but if I can open this phone, I'd be happy to answer those text messages with a voice message explaining what happens to dudes who presume to know what a woman wants better than she knows it herself. I mean, assuming she doesn't want to be with a dicknugget who calls her names and implies she's miserable when I've never seen her anything but happy. And also engaged to one of my best buddies. Who would never order her around like that."

Sloane's lips wobble, and I can't tell if she's going to smile or cry.

Possibly both.

There's a shine coming into her eyes too.

"Did you have to deal with that all day today?" she asks me.

"Yes."

"Was it annoying?"

"Yes."

"Good." She holds a hand out and makes the *give it back* gesture to Cash as the phone dings one more time.

"How many messages has he sent you?" I ask.

"Just these four—five now. All in the last few minutes."

"You see him today?"

"No."

"Did he see you?"

She blinks once.

Then twice. "I…I don't know."

Unlikely, but I have to ask.

I showed Giselle a picture of him this morning before they left. If he was close enough to see Sloane, he would've been close enough for Giselle to spot him.

If Giselle spotted him, she would've taken care of him.

And that would've necessitated an update to Levi, who can be a dick sometimes, but he wouldn't have been the kind of dick to not tell me about it today.

"Seriously, tell us where we're headed, and we can have a half dozen of us teaching him a lesson before dawn," Cash says.

Sloane doesn't answer.

She's staring at her phone.

At the text messages from Nigel.

And that's when it all goes to hell.

It starts with her rolling her shoulders. Then with a mulish expression settling over her features.

She flips off her phone and snaps a selfie, and that's the last thing she does before everything becomes a blur.

"*Noooo*," Aspen gasps. She dives for Sloane, knocking

her off the log and sending her phone flying. "Don't send it!"

I'm instantly moving, shoving Aspen aside and reaching for Sloane.

There's a flash, then another blur, and then Cash's girlfriend is pinned on the ground. More blurs, and three beefy dudes try to pull Giselle off of Aspen, who's arrived out of thin air to pin the pop star to the ground.

"Do *not* touch my client without permission," Giselle says.

"Jesus, where did she even come from?" Cash says. "Did she teleport?"

"She was checking the perimeter." Sloane's eyes are wide too as she scurries out of my grasp.

I straighten and point to a few trees. "Property line's right there on this side. She was close."

"*You need a ring,*" Aspen shouts, still trapped under Giselle. "*Don't send a middle finger picture without a ring sparkling bright on your hand!*"

Giselle freezes.

Aspen and Cash's security detail pause too.

Aspen slides out from beneath Giselle. "My god, you people overreact to everything. Who has a ring? It's been what, four days since you got engaged? And how much money do you have, Davis? Enough to buy a freaking diamond ring, that's for damn sure. Cash, light the campfire. Davis, do you have any wine? What about a flannel blanket? Sloane, what's your favorite meal? If we're doing this, we're doing it right. You're gonna look like the happiest woman on the happiest planet in the happiest universe to show that toadstool what you have without him. While you flip him off."

"Nigel already believes we're engaged," Sloane says. "He knows we don't have rings yet because it was so spontaneous."

Aspen grins. "That's why you need one now. A big, fat, juicy diamond that says there's no price too high for Davis to pay for you. He went on a diamond ring hunt and look what he found. Nigel can't give you that. Can he? Is he the kind of guy who can afford a five-carat diamond?"

"No." Sloane wrinkles her nose. "Probably. Hopefully. Actually, I don't even want to know how much he makes. It might make me sick. His grandfather *did* have one of the largest houses in town, and—you know what? I don't want to think about that anymore."

"Excellent. Let's go get you a ring."

Cash nudges the biggest of his three security guys. "She's brilliant."

"She's giving me a heart attack," the guy mutters back.

"More cardio," Cash says. "That'll help."

And I'm over this. "Cash."

My buddy looks at me. "Yeah?"

"Get fucking lost."

Aspen finally sits up and gapes at me. "Did you just say a fuck word? Wow. I don't think I've ever heard *you* say a fuck word."

"I have," Sloane mutters.

Cash nods. "Same. He uses it all the time. Just not around you. Giselle, you got this?"

She flips him off.

"Good. Davis, don't do stupid shit alone when you

have a dozen of us ready to jump in and have your back. Except this weekend. This weekend, we're booked. Take a lot of pictures of the wedding. Pissed we're missing it."

"I can get laryngitis if we need to be here instead." Aspen fakes a cough. "Oh no. The leaves. The dead leaves are giving me a tickle in my throat. *Cough cough*. How will I ever perform?"

Giselle looks at the other security team.

They grumble, then one of them quietly says something to Cash, who scowls too. "Fine," he mutters.

"If you need a set for a fancy elopement wedding immediately, I know someone shooting a video in LA tomorrow," Aspen says. "Say the word, and we'll get you a plane and I'll get you on set for a few photos too. Crap. Unless this guy is a huge fan of Keisha Kourtney? Would he recognize the set when the video comes out?"

"That dude won't pay that much attention," Cash says.

"And I want him to be there watching me get married," Sloane adds. "It's the only way he'll believe it's real."

Giselle clears her throat and glares at my friends.

Cash rolls his eyes. "*Okay, okay,* we're going. Davis. Call. We'll be here. Or we'll send people who can be here. Tour's almost over for the year. Can you wait to do the rest of your treasure hunting until we're back? I'm with Beck. I always wanted to find a treasure."

Aspen gives me a sympathetic smile. "All of the guys are coming even if you don't call because they're worried about you."

"I'm aware."

They finally shuffle into the black SUV they arrived in this morning, and then pull down my driveway.

THE PRETEND FIANCÉ FIASCO

Dusk is falling rapidly.

"Can your cat come outside?" I ask Sloane.

She sucks in a sharp breath through her nose, then nods.

"You want her?"

Another nod.

I head inside for the cat, and when I get back, Giselle's lighting the campfire.

I sit on the log next to Sloane again and hand her the cat, who purrs so loudly that even the initial crackling of the fire can't drown it out.

Can't drown out the way Sloane's posture changes the minute she's stroking the cat either.

Maybe I should get a pet when this is over.

Stress relief.

Company.

All good things.

"I won't stop you if you want to send that selfie flipping him off," I tell her.

She shakes her head. "Not worth it. He won't change, and he won't take it as anything other than me rebelling against what he believes is best for me."

"Completely serious. We can get married tomorrow."

She looks at me. "They'll hope we get divorced."

"Shitty thing to hope."

She rolls her eyes. "But they would. Even if it's awful, they'd hope for it. I haven't seen Grandma or my brother in person in a year and a half, Nigel even longer until this week, but they definitely know me better than I know myself, and obviously have only my best interest at heart."

Sloane shouldn't be sarcastic.

285

It makes her sound sad, and I don't like it when she's sad.

She deserves to be happy.

"They come visit you? Until now?"

"I moved away. It's my job to go back."

My breathing routine is getting a good workout since she first kissed me on Saturday. "They ever make you happy?"

She stares at the fire.

Giselle has functionally disappeared, but I suspect she's still listening somewhere.

"They're family," Sloane finally says quietly. "My grandma took in both me and my brother and raised us, even though she clearly wasn't excited about it. Nigel's grandfather would stop by dressed up like Santa every Christmas and bring us presents that his congregation had donated for us. Grandma helped me fill out college scholarship applications. She helped Aiden figure out how to get into ROTC in college so he could become a pilot. She sacrificed a lot for us. She did her best. And now—now, it's like I don't fully know them anymore."

I curl my fingers into a fist to keep from hugging her again.

Boundaries.

Have to remember boundaries.

"Felt that when my parents got divorced," I say instead.

"Are they still around?"

"After the money mismanagement thing, I cut my father off. Still have my mom though. She had some rough years. The other moms in the neighborhood got her through it, and she's pretty happy now."

"Does she support you?"

"More than I deserve."

"We all deserve support."

Both of us fall silent while we stare at the fire.

Sloane strokes the cat.

I angle closer to her without realizing I'm doing it until our hips touch.

She doesn't move away.

But she does speak again. "I made a decision this afternoon."

"Yeah?"

"I'm finding the treasure on my own."

I glance at her.

The sun is completely gone, so her face is illuminated by the fire.

But I don't think the light would make any difference in what I see in her expression.

It's pure, stubborn determination.

She's been handed some shitty cards lately, and she's making a plan to get through it.

Got a lot of respect for that.

"So if marrying you isn't enough to convince you to be on my team…"

"I will forever be grateful that you…helped me fall asleep last night, but in case you haven't noticed, I'm not a big fan of men in general. Even less so men who keep secrets. You know the treasure isn't in Shipwreck. You somehow know it's real. You probably have a rough idea where it is. You might even know what it is. You clearly know it has secrets that could hurt people. And if you don't trust me to let me in on those secrets, then I don't know why I should trust you to tell you what I know."

I swallow.

Swallow again.

Focus on taking slow, even breaths.

She rises. "Ball's in your court, Davis. And if this means you bail on the fake fiancé thing...I'll figure out how to deal with that too."

20

Sloane

"WAIT."

My first instinct upon hearing Davis's request is to comply. Especially when my heart is pounding this fast and my mouth is dry and my legs are shaking and when obeying was ingrained in me from early, early, *early* in my childhood.

Someone uses an authoritative voice to tell you to do something, you do it. You're not in charge. They are.

And there are consequences when you're disobedient.

I fight through the urge to comply, through the urge to do what he says, to listen to my body yelling that it's dangerous to disobey, and I don't *wait*.

I keep walking toward the camper. I need to gather my things and ask Giselle if she'll give me a ride into town.

The sheriff told me I can get back into my house

tomorrow or Friday. So I just need to stay with Tillie Jean or Annika for a night.

Maybe longer, depending on how much time it takes to clean my house up.

Which I will *not* be afraid of.

I won't.

I'll be strong while I get through the rest of this.

Leaves rustle behind me, and then Davis is in front of me. "I'll show you my family tree."

"Not interested."

"Sloane—"

"*I am not interested.* I don't want *one part* of your secrets. If you want my help, you have to give me everything you have. The days of me being satisfied with breadcrumbs are over. And don't think I'll settle for a single loaf either. That's not enough. I want the whole fucking bakery. And I don't mean you and me naked. I mean full partner in the treasure hunt. You get me?"

Peggy meows softly, like she's alerting me that my blood pressure is getting dangerously high.

As if I can't tell by the buzzing in my ears and the narrowing in my vision.

I don't do this.

I don't yell at people who help me. I don't tell my boss I'm taking the next two days off of work because finding a treasure is the most important thing in my life.

I smile. I have fun. I make friends. I hide the darker parts of myself and tell myself I don't need to feel guilt or shame for existing, that if God is real, he'll know I did my best.

But my museum was broken into. My house was trashed. I'm getting fake-married to a man who wants my help and is willing to give me orgasms but not willing to give me his real motivations to find what he wants my help finding.

I've hit my breaking point.

I'm finding the damn treasure.

I'm taking care of myself.

I'm putting an end to all of this.

Now.

Davis stares down at me in the darkness, and I hear a joint pop.

Probably a knuckle. Came from the general vicinity of his hands.

I don't bother looking to see if he's clenching them.

The fact that he's breathing heavily is confirmation enough that he's irritated too.

"I get you," he finally says.

I lift my brows at him.

Another knuckle pops.

He breaks eye contact with me to look around. "Giselle?"

"What?" comes a response from much closer than I expected.

"Get lost."

"I don't take orders from you."

So this is what a truly frustrated Davis Remington looks like.

Flaring nostrils.

Flat lips.

Angry eyes.

It's hot.

No.

No.

Angry men aren't hot. They're asshole little babies who need to learn to control their tempers.

Except I'm starting to wonder if that's what Davis does all the time.

I've never encountered anyone quite like him before. Someone whose facial expressions don't give anything away until he's in his natural element, and even then, you wonder if he's only letting you see what he wants to let you see.

Someone who always seems loose-limbed and relaxed, but *not* relaxed at the same time.

Like, alert-relaxed. Ready-relaxed.

Stop it, Sloane.

Men don't get the benefit of the doubt from me anymore.

Especially men with closely guarded secrets that they dangle like carrots to get what they want.

Carrots like orgasms.

I shake my head and step around him while Peggy meows louder. "I'm getting my things, and I'm leaving."

If I can't use my own car tonight, I can borrow Tillie Jean's or Annika's.

I'll head into the city. Get a hotel room as far away as I can from wherever Nigel's working. Be anonymous for the weekend.

Georgia, Grady's former extra baker at Crow's Nest,

moved to the city to live with one of Cooper's teammates last year. I could hang out with her. I miss her.

"Secrets in the wrong hands hurt people," Davis says.

"Everything can hurt people."

I start to step around him, and that's when I realize something's off.

It's not anything I see.

It's just something I sense.

And that's all the warning I have—that one little premonition that *something is wrong*—before sparks explode in the campfire and something thick and hairy and heavy lands on my head.

I scream and drop Peggy.

The thing on my head hisses and clutches my hair as I spin and scream again. "Get off! *Get off!*"

"*Sloane.*" Davis's voice is distant, like I'm in a tunnel.

Where's my cat?

What's on my head?

Does it have teeth?

Oh my god. It has to have teeth.

Something tackles me, and then I'm eating dirt and leaves, all of the air leaving my lungs.

The weight on my head is gone, but there's a body lying on top of me, and its weight is also twisting and heavy.

Davis.

It's Davis.

He's grunting. "*Stop throwing things.*"

"I'm not throwing things!"

"Not—*gah*—you!"

A flashlight spins above us and light off of the fire makes shadows dance around us too, then there's another shower of sparks.

"Giselle?" I gasp.

She doesn't answer.

Nearby, anyway.

She's yelling somewhere else. "Get *lost*, you fucking mangy assholes. Why is it always vermin? *Why is it always vermin?* Swear to god, if I don't get a good bonus this year, I'm taking Aspen up on that offer to fund my vigilante era."

Something hits my cheek.

Something else hits my shoulder.

The weight on me rolls off, and I spot Davis grabbing a firewood log and spinning in a circle, looking for—

Actually, I don't know what he's looking for.

Or what's going on with his hair.

There's something weird about his hair.

And— *"Peggy."*

I start to rise, but he shoves me back down while he circles me. "Under the camper. Neutralize the threat first."

"Neutralize the threat?"

Something whizzes overhead, then more sparks explode in the campfire.

"Where the fuck are you, you little assholes?" Giselle growls somewhere nearby but not nearly close enough.

There's a creak in the night, then skittering like claws on metal, and Davis ducks again while something flies in the night, lands in the campfire, and makes sparks explode again.

"Try that again and you're getting the wrong end of

my Christmas gift from Sarah Ryder, you goddamn punk rodent," Giselle says.

Oh my god.

Oh my god.

We're under attack.

By...rodents?

What is my life? What the actual fuck is my life right now?

I don't know where my cat is.

Davis is trying to pull me away from the fire while I'm barely on my knees and *move, Sloane, goddammit, move.*

There's an odd shriek—definitely not human—and then Giselle's next to Davis. "How many more?"

"Two. Top of the camper. *Fuck.* Sloane. Get inside."

They both duck while *something* throws something at them.

"I'm not fucking leaving my cat out here alone!" I shriek.

"Okay. Okay. She went under the—*goddammit, stop throwing things.*"

Another shower of sparks explodes from the campfire, and this time, they fall all around us even though we're getting farther from the fire.

"What are they?" I manage to flip on my phone's flashlight and aim it under the camper.

Davis answers. "Raccoons. Whole family of them. Get away from the fire. I don't know what they're throwing, but it's flammable."

I don't give two flying fucks about flammable raccoon games.

I give two fucks about—

"Peggy." I spot her huddled against the back tires on the other side of the camper. "Oh, sweet baby, it's okay. Come to Mama, and we'll go inside where it's safe."

She doesn't move.

Can't blame her.

Davis drops to my side. "Did they hurt you? Are you hurt? Scratched? Did the one who jumped on you bite you?"

"My cat. Get my cat." Crap.

Dammit.

I'm crying again.

I hate crying.

No one takes you seriously when you're crying.

"Hold on for a ride. I'm going after the raccoons," Giselle says.

I look at Peggy, then at Davis, whose hair looks weird in the light, almost like it's glowing, and then at Giselle.

And then I shriek again.

Giselle vaults up the camper steps, and now she's swinging herself up onto the camper roof while the entire vehicle shakes. "That's right, you little fucknuggets, who looks bigger now?"

"Peggy. Don't run away. Sweet kitty, don't run away," I sob as I peer under the camper again.

My cat stares back at me, frightened and frozen.

Three screeches and a whole bunch of chittering reverberate from the top of the camper, and then there's silence.

Peggy keeps staring at me.

I keep staring back. "It's okay, love, Mama's here, don't run away."

"I'll get her," Davis says quietly next to me.

And that's when I smell it.

Burning hair.

I sit straight and feel my own head, then look at his, and—

"Oh my god, your bun's on fire!"

There's a thump next to him.

I scream and blindly swing at it, but Giselle catches my arm, squeezes a pressure point just enough to make me yelp, drops my arm, spins somewhere else, and a moment later, the smoldering *thing* is out.

Because Davis is covered in water.

Giselle tosses the bucket aside, drops to her belly, aims her flashlight under the camper, and rises again. "Keep talking to the cat."

I stare at Davis.

Who's staring back at me, soaked.

Something weird is clumped on top of his hair.

Which isn't in the full manbun it was before.

And not because of the water.

"Peggy," I croak out.

"Keep calling for her," Giselle says.

Peggy.

Oh god.

I lean over and aim my flashlight under the camper again, then I sag in relief when I spot her still frozen beside the back wheels. "Okay. You're okay. You're —*aaahh!*"

She's gone.

One minute she was there, and the next—

"Got her," Giselle says. "Get inside. I'm calling the

fucking exterminator and then I'm calling fucking Levi and then I'm booking myself on a month-long cruise somewhere without rodents and campfires and all of you."

Davis pulls me to my feet.

It's dark, the only light coming off a small lamp outside the camper and the fire, but I can tell he's so grim-faced that he might as well be the grim reaper.

Coming to herald the death of his hair.

His wet, soggy hair.

"Get in the camper." His voice is low. Gravelly. Full of suppressed emotion.

He knows.

He knows his hair is toast.

"Cat," Giselle says, handing me Peggy. "Get in the trailer. *Now*."

My body obeys because authority. Of course it does. "I —thank you."

"Apologies for the nerve pinch. Most effective way to get you to do what I needed you to do. How's your head? Manbun—get a first aid kit."

"Manbun?" I stutter.

"That's what they call—" She pauses and looks at him as all three of us hustle inside the camper, and my heart drops to my toes. "Called him. How's your head? Are you scratched? Good thing you have the doc on speed dial if you need rabies shots."

Davis's hair.

His hair.

It's crispy on one side, sticking up maybe three or four inches. When he let it down last night, it came down past his collarbones, and now—now that part won't even reach his chin.

The other side still has something stuck in it.

Something—is that a pine cone?

"Sloane. *Your head*. Sit."

I obey Giselle's orders and drop onto the bench at the table, still clutching Peggy, who hasn't purred once, and I keep staring at Davis.

His shirt is soaked.

His pants are soaked.

And there's a half-singed pine cone stuck in what's left of his manbun.

I got gum in my hair once when I was a kid.

Forbidden gum, of course.

I got lectured about gum being the devil's handiwork the whole time Grandma was rubbing peanut butter into my hair to loosen the gum so we could wash it all out.

As I'm staring at Davis's hair now—

I don't think peanut butter's gonna solve this.

Peggy squeaks in my arms.

I loosen my grip, but she doesn't run away.

Instead, she huddles closer like she, too, is horrified.

"That bad?" he asks me.

Do not change your plans just because he's losing his manbun, I order myself. *You know you have to leave. Especially if there are attack raccoons out here.*

I swallow.

Swallow again.

And then, as Giselle continues inspecting my scalp, I say the last thing I should say. "You're gonna need some help."

I know what I'm implying. He knows what I'm implying.

But this is it.

This is the last time I help him.

Cross my heart.

The very. Last. Time.

21

Davis

I STARE STRAIGHT AHEAD at the closed bedroom door as Sloane approaches me with the scissors while I sit on a folding chair in the kitchen.

Karma.

It's always karma.

And I fucking deserved this.

Can't even be happy that I've figured out what was making the noise last night.

Not when the little fuckers decided to be agents of chaos.

Sloane's expression is bleak as she takes in my appearance again in the full light inside the camper. Her cat is happily licking its own butt on the floor in front of me.

Now that we're all safe inside, no creatures attacking any of us, with me double-checking Giselle's inspection of Sloane to make sure she was okay—and she is, the raccoon who landed on her didn't break any skin—the tension is back.

And not the good tension.

This is the *I'll help you one last time because you were trying to save me and my cat, but then I'm gone until you decide to be an equal player in all things* tension.

And I don't blame her.

She's been put through hell over this treasure. Not her fault.

Also not her fault that a psycho from her past is here making things worse.

"Are you sure you want me to do this?" she asks.

"Yes."

"I'm no hair stylist."

"Giselle would shave symbols into my head, and I wouldn't be able to go out in public for weeks."

"You could if you shaved it all the way off."

"Don't have the head for it."

She doesn't laugh.

Good thing, since it's not a joke. "I shaved my head after our next-to-last tour, then went into hiding for a few months. Didn't leave my house unless I was in a hoodie with the hood up. Every time."

Got several new tats in those few months.

And it's the last time I really cut my hair. Trimmed on occasion, yes. Cut like this, no.

She circles me with the scissors like she's deciding the best way to tackle cutting out the mess in my hair.

I don't look to see if my hair is all that she's studying.

Had to change out of my wet clothes, and now I'm in nothing but a pair of cotton shorts.

THE PRETEND FIANCÉ FIASCO

A pair of cotton shorts and the tattoos covering nearly every inch of my exposed skin.

It's been a while—a *long* while—since I've let anyone new see me shirtless.

Not ashamed.

But my ink isn't for anyone else's amusement or entertainment.

She's blank-faced as she stops in front of me again. "I'll try to keep it as long as I can."

"It'll grow back."

"You sure you don't want a picture for posterity's sake?"

"I'm sure."

"Okay then." She touches my hair, and goosebumps flare across my scalp.

Mind over body. Mind over body.

My mind responds by dishing up images of Sloane in my bed last night, legs spread, stroking her pussy.

"Thank you for helping save Peggy," she says.

I don't answer.

I'm too busy breathing as she tugs at my hair and takes the first snip.

"And I want you to know I'm fighting a lot of guilt when I say this, but I still have to leave. It's not entirely you. It's a long history of people letting me down and me practicing acknowledging that I don't have to always take the short stick. Not that this has been…the short stick. But also, I have a very complicated relationship with feeling like I owe people when they do nice things for me, and I…don't."

Translation: I'm trying to not let one orgasm guilt me

into doing anything you want.

At least, that's how I interpret what she just said.

My body howls in outrage.

I have lost all control of it.

Still try to get some back as I swallow hard. "Don't feel guilty for taking care of yourself."

She snips again and drops a chunk of my hair into a small wastebasket. The chunk with the fucking pine cone that the damn raccoon launched at me.

Giselle's outside setting traps.

That's what she said she was doing anyway.

I didn't ask if she means traps to relocate them, or traps to fling flaming pine cones at them if they try to come close to the camper again.

We're in their territory.

So I don't want to know how she's handling this.

Or how I'm going to break it to Levi that I broke his favorite security agent.

Snip. Snip. Snip.

More hair on the floor.

My hair.

The hair that helped hide me for years. My disguise, even when people figured out it was my disguise.

Sloane inhales softly. "I'll tell Nigel that I'm not interested and to go home."

Nigel's a fucknugget, and when I'm done with Patrick Dixon, I'd like to have a quiet, private discussion with Nigel too. "Will he listen?"

"If he doesn't, I'll call Cooper and tell him I need help. He has resources. And friends."

My blood pressure creeps higher.

She can't leave.

I can't let her leave.

But I don't want to be one more person manipulating her either.

"I'm not saying that as a threat," she adds. "And yes, I realize that saying that I don't mean that as a threat can be interpreted to mean that I mean that as a threat. But I really don't. Cooper's my friend. He can help me handle a problem."

He would.

His methods would probably make the news, and with him married to Waverly now, it would make every gossip site, get inflated on social media, and probably end up getting him a book deal or something.

I have to tell her.

I have to give her *something*.

Something to prove she can trust me.

"We saved an elephant once."

Her hand stills in my hair.

I point to my left shoulder while my heart ramps up its staccato drumbeat of terror.

I don't tell people these things.

Trust the wrong people, they betray you.

But isn't that exactly why I have to tell Sloane?

She's been betrayed too, even if she might not put it in those words.

She trusted people who were supposed to love her, and they used the threat of eternal damnation to make her feel like she was never enough.

She deserves to know that she's enough.

That she can be trusted.

Even if it scares the ever-loving fuck out of me.

"That elephant. We saved it. Levi still gets postcards about once a year from the sanctuary where it lives now."

She doesn't reply.

Her cat pauses in licking its own ass, gives me an *if you think one little story about an elephant will win her trust, you're an idiot* look, and goes back to grooming itself.

Mind over body.

I breathe deeply to try to slow my pulse, then I point to my other shoulder. "Spent hours on the tour bus watching this show about space cowboys. That's the ship. Sometimes Cash would make us reenact the scenes. I was always the lady mechanic. They said it was because I was youngest, but Beck got to be the badass assassin chick who was technically younger in the show. The youngest."

She puts her hand back in my hair and snips again. "I know what you're doing."

Fuck. "I need your help, and my secrets are all I have to offer."

"How do I know they're secrets?"

I suppress a sigh. I could tell her my mother's never seen all of my tattoos. I could tell her I haven't been shirtless in front of a woman who's not my tattoo artist or someone I've known all my life for over a decade. I could tell her to call any of the guys to back me up, but she doesn't know they'd tell the truth before they'd defend me.

It's why I don't tell people things.

Because I don't want my friends to have to stick up for me.

Or call me out when I tell the lies that make it easier

for me to get around in the world without letting people in.

I wouldn't believe me if I were her. "You don't."

"How do I know you're telling the truth?"

"You don't."

She touches the base of my neck. "What's this one?"

My shoulders bunch.

My body is a canvas with one design rolling into the other seamlessly, weaving together all of my favorite and not-so-favorite moments of my life.

The lessons I've learned.

The highs.

The lows.

Life.

And while she could be pointing to two or three different elements, I know what she's asking about.

It's three overlapping triangles with a coin in the middle. "That one's off-limits."

She touches my thigh just above my left knee as she stands in front of me to trim more hair, and it takes every ounce of self-control I possess to not visibly shiver at her touch.

I like her touching me.

I like her touching me entirely too much.

"Is that mistletoe?" she asks. "With an engagement ring?"

"First relationship I had after the band started. I kissed my sister's best friend at Christmas. We dated for three months, the last two months long distance because of tour rehearsals in New York, and she was mad that I didn't send her diamonds for her birthday."

Her fingers move to my ribs. "The Fireballs dragon?"

Keep touching me. Please keep touching me. "Baseball will be my favorite sport until the day I die. Fireballs forever."

"Not martial arts?"

"Peace and clarity. Not a sport. We—the guys—the five of us—we were going to buy the Fireballs before Lila inherited the team. It's what I was supposed to be doing now. Helping run my own baseball team. With the guys. The band. Together. Like we used to be."

I'm sweating.

I'm sweating, and she can probably see it.

I don't talk about how much I sometimes miss being part of the band. How I set my work schedule for the past decade to give me as much flexibility as possible so I could drop in and see my buddies regularly despite living an hour on the other side of Copper Valley. How much I loved knowing we're doing something amazing for the world together.

Not solo.

Together.

"Tripp and Lila wouldn't give you a job?"

"Not the same."

"You don't like to work for other people."

"Spent the last decade working for other people. I wanted a purpose. To do—to be working together with all of us again. It's different."

She falls quiet while she snips at my hair again, dropping more and more into the trash can.

My heart is in a race with itself.

I don't tell people these stories.

It's not safe.

You don't know who'll sell you out to the paps for a quick profit and who you can trust.

But she doesn't trust me and I need her to.

Want her to.

No, *need* her to.

It's not logical. It's not rational.

And I'm well aware that I'm lying to myself when I say that it's situational.

I just—

Life won't be right if Sloane doesn't trust me.

The end.

I close my eyes and picture myself on a beach at sunrise—nothing but me and the seagulls and sand and ocean—and breathe to ground myself.

Trying to calm my panic at the ammunition I'm giving her.

I'm never in the tabloids. Like it that way.

And she has the power to change it now.

Because I have to trust her.

It's the only way.

She touches the back of my right arm. "Which flag is that?"

"Morocco." I keep my eyes closed, picturing sunset over the Atlantic in Morocco now.

"You've been?"

"Hiked the Atlas Mountains between the band breaking up and me starting school."

"What did you go to college for?"

"Dual degree. Nuclear engineering and computer science."

"Why?"

"I get bored easily. Good challenge." I point to my left bicep where there's an atom and a series of ones and zeros that spell *do good* if you know how to read binary. "That was my job. At the nuclear reactor. Keeping people safe by keeping the bad guys out. Virtually."

"The bike?" She touches a bicycle tattoo on my forearm.

"I was eight before I learned to ride. Scared before that. My father tried to bully me into learning, and that made it worse. So Wyatt taught me. Beck's best friend. Ellie's husband. He didn't want to join the band. Him and the other two Rivers brothers. Wyatt was too serious and needed security. Waylon thought we were going to bomb. Hank had two left feet and sang like a pig being butchered."

"Do they know you talk about them like that?"

"Yes."

"What do they say about you?"

"Far better things than they should."

"Because you're a terrible person?"

My jaw clenches, and I actively force it to relax. "Because I'm human. I make mistakes, and when I do, I judge myself harshly."

Snip.

Snip.

Snip.

My head feels lighter.

My hair too.

I'm still squeezing my eyes shut, and when I realize I'm squeezing and not just closing, I force my facial muscles to relax again.

Hair will grow back.

Sloane won't tell anyone my secrets.

We'll find the treasure.

She'll kiss me again like she did last night.

Fuck.

No.

We'll both go about our daily lives again.

I'll find a new obsession.

It'll be her.

Goddammit.

Trick of the moment. Not real.

Learning that she feels guilty for breathing because of how she was raised when I feel guilty for getting away with things I should've been punished for.

That she's actively fighting shame all the time when I never truly had to face the shame I should've for what happened in Denver.

Wanting to carry her burdens for her because she doesn't deserve them while I do.

This is why I show up and ask my buddies for favors and then never say another word about them.

Because I'll hear a coworker's always wanted to take a trip up to the city to see an air show but never got tickets.

Or an old contact has a kid who's been struggling in school and just needs a win, like seeing her favorite former boy bander turned solo artist in concert.

I've caused harm in this life.

I never want to do it again.

I want to balance my scales.

Watching Sloane balance her own scales for things that aren't her fault—how could I not want to help her?

How could I not find that inherently attractive in a fellow human being?

The snipping stops. "You want the good news or the bad news?"

There's no good or bad.

There's only what is. "Both."

"I got the pine cone remnants out. And it looks like a toddler attacked your head in your sleep. We just had a new stylist move to town. She might not know who you are. She's pretty young. But she's good. She can fix this. Or I guess you could just wear hoodies again for a while."

I blink my eyes open. "Thank you."

"So you want me to call—"

"I'll wear hoodies."

She steps back. "Great. Then I'll just get Peggy and we'll get out of your...ahh... I mean, we'll head home."

Dammit. "Wait."

"Thank you for sharing with me, but I need time to think about what I'm going to do next."

My pulse roars in my ears.

I have to tell her.

Shit.

Shit.

She lifts her brows at me. "I don't know what you're thinking, but whatever it is, I'm regretting not bringing my stethoscope and blood pressure cuff. Are you having a stroke?"

Fuck it.

She has to know.

"Thorny Rock and Walter Bombeck switched identities when they left the ship. Thorny Rock founded

Sarcasm. Walter Bombeck founded Shipwreck. If the treasure was hidden safely, if it was protected right against the elements, there's another journal with the gold and jewels documenting their entire history. If anyone else finds that treasure, if anyone else finds out—Shipwreck's fucked. *Please* stay. *Please* help me. Please."

22

Sloane

OH.

No.

He.

Did.

Not.

But he did, didn't he?

He just said that.

And now Davis is staring at me with panic in his eyes while his left leg starts jumping up and down and he rubs his hand down his right thigh over and over and over again.

Mr. Expressionless, Mr. Stillness, is freaking out right now.

I squat and put one hand on his left knee and the other on his right hand, feeling the tingles of my own panic attack starting.

He's wrong.

He has to be wrong.

"Davis—"

"My mom is a direct descendant of the real Thorny Rock. When her mom died two years ago, she inherited a safe-deposit key to a box at the oldest bank in Copper Valley. We didn't know it existed. She had letters. She had maps. She had the captain's log from the ship. He called it the Helter Skelter. Not the Escape Hatch like you have in the museum. Escape Hatch is what Walter Bombeck wanted to call it. The real Walter Bombeck. The real Thorny's cousin and first mate. My grandma also had the manifest of everything that was on the ship when they docked in Norfolk. The handwriting on the map matches. Your map. At the museum. That's how I knew it was from Sarcasm."

Forget helping him calm down.

I plop down on my own butt and stare at him.

His leg bounces again.

He rubs his palms down his tattooed thighs, seems to catch himself, and crosses his arms over his bare chest instead.

Peggy rubs against me, meows, and then leaps into Davis's lap.

I stare at the man while I attempt to process everything he's just said.

If he's right—if this is true—Tillie Jean.

My god.

Tillie Jean would have half of her life ripped out from beneath her. Being mayor of Shipwreck, continuing on the traditions and the folklore—that's what she was born to do.

And Grady being Shipwreck's baker. And Cooper being Shipwreck's public spokesperson.

This is their history.

Their heritage.

Who they are.

And Annika—Annika, who grew up in Sarcasm—what would Annika say?

Fuck history.

That's what Annika would say because she loves Grady more than she loves town feuds and more than she cares which pirate founded which town.

I think.

I hope.

For once, Davis doesn't look at me. "You can't tell your friends."

"Absolutely not. Are you—"

"Yes, I'm serious, and yes, I'm sure."

"How?"

"Research. Tracing genealogical lines. Old paintings. Drawings. Gossip sheets and newspapers from London from before Thorny Rock left on his adventures. His real name was William George. Third son of a baron. Failed military career. Prone to drinking too much and fucking too much and losing his temper too much."

"*Oh my god*, Annika's mom's last name is Williams."

"No relation. But her boyfriend probably is."

"How do you know?"

He sighs and frowns down at Peggy like he doesn't

realize he's been petting her. "Research. Tracing genealogical lines…"

So this is what dumbfounded feels like. "Are you sure?"

"Already been over this."

"But *sure* sure?"

"I like Shipwreck, Sloane. Fun town. Brings good things to the world. People here treat me like a normal guy. They don't take my picture and sell it to the tabloids."

I flinch.

I took his picture and told my family he was my boyfriend.

He ignores my reaction. "Beck's happy when he's here. Ellie and Wyatt fell in love out here. This one?" He points to a frog peeking out from the top of a palm tree on his left pec. "Spent a weekend playing Frogger at Beck's place maybe eight years ago. Best weekend I'd had in ages. All the guys were there. Like old times. I fit here. I have good memories here. I like it here. If this gets out—we can't hurt Shipwreck. I've done—we just can't."

I pull my knees to my chest and look at the tattooed, crazy-haired, tense man on the chair in front of me. "This is a lot."

"Would've preferred to not have to burden you with this, but you needed to know."

"Does Pop know?"

"Likely."

"Does he know you know?"

"He's not stupid."

"And that's why he doesn't like you."

"Partially."

"What are the other parts?"

He stares at me, and then his lips quirk to the side.

Like he's almost smiling.

"He hates my motorcycle and my tattoos."

I squeak.

Pop is my grandma.

Except Pop has *never*— "*Oh my god*, are you making that up?"

"Ever seen Pop on a bike?"

"No. But he has tattoos."

"Mine are cooler."

This is definitely not the full story. "This is why Vanessa told you to show me your family tree."

"Yes."

"She believes it?"

"She's in the information business and also believes I'm correct in my understanding of the real history of this place."

"That's a lot of words that lead to a lot more questions."

"That aren't mine to answer."

"Why can't anything be simple and straightforward?"

"Because people are inherently good, but they're also inherently selfish and greedy."

I can't go back to town tonight.

I need a game face first. There's zero chance I could walk into Tillie Jean's house or Grady and Annika's house or any of the businesses that the Rock family runs around town without one of them asking me what's wrong, and there's no possibility that I could answer that question, even with a lie, tonight.

I growl at Davis.

He doesn't react.

Probably anticipating me coming to the conclusion that I'm trapped here with him if I don't want to betray my friends.

With the truth.

I rise and dust what I can of his hair off of my hands and clothes. "I'll tell Giselle I'm staying," I mutter.

"I'll take the couch."

"If you double-cross me with this treasure stuff—"

"I've already done all of the shitty things I intend to do for the rest of my life. Least harm is the goal."

I believe him.

I don't want to, but I do.

And I'm taking a guilt-inducing amount of delight in knowing that I butchered his hair.

It's not his fault he found a story about the supposed real history of Shipwreck and Sarcasm, but I blame him for the role I suddenly have to play in it.

And then the shame descends too, making me feel like my skin is too tight for my body. "Would you have dragged me into this mess even if I hadn't asked you to pretend to be my fiancé?"

He lifts his gaze to mine and holds it, those velvety brown eyes telegraphing the answer without him saying a word.

Yes.

Yes, he would've.

Because Patrick Dixon was already dragging me into it.

Because I made myself a target when I decided to make the museum my life.

An unwitting target, but a target nonetheless.

There's no other way this ended than with Davis appointing himself my guardian and asking for my help finding the treasure.

I just made it easy for him when I asked him to be the pretend love of my life.

"Does Patrick know? About Thorny Rock and Walter Bombeck and their true identities?"

Davis's eyes tighten. "I think he suspects, but he doesn't *know*."

"Are you really related to him?"

"Very distantly."

"Through Thorny Rock. The real, biological Thorny Rock."

"Yes."

And if there was a clue hidden in Thorny Rock's coat —which might be Walter Bombeck's coat?—then Patrick might be ahead of the game.

Davis and I have to find the treasure.

"Where's your broom? I'll clean up the rest of your hair. You should go shower."

"If it helps, I'm mad at myself for finding all of this out too."

"And now I have to keep this secret from my friends forever."

"Treasure first. Confirm what I think is in there. And then we'll deal with the rest."

He doesn't move.

But he does keep petting Peggy. Scratching behind her ears and making her rub her head up into his hand. Stroking her silky body with his long fingers.

His hands aren't tattooed. The ink stops at his wrists on both arms. But it dips below his waistband on his stomach and chest and rises above the hemline of his navy-blue cotton shorts.

And I realize what he said.

We.

We will deal with the rest.

Do not go there, Sloane. You know better.

There's a knock at the door, and after a brief pause, Giselle's voice comes through the door. "The Rocks sent food. If you don't open the door, I'm eating all of it myself."

Guilt slashes through my abdomen.

They've been my friends.

And now I know something that could destroy them.

"Don't," Davis says quietly. "Don't feel guilty. You aren't a pirate. You didn't try to double-cross your first mate. You haven't done anything wrong besides being in the wrong place at the wrong time. We'll make this right. However we have to, we'll make it right."

"How? How do we make it right?"

"Treasure first. And then the rest will fall into place."

"What will Patrick do if he finds it first?"

He squeezes his eyes shut, and his chest rises like he's taking the heaviest breath he's ever taken in his life. "We still have things he doesn't."

"Like what? What clues do we have that he doesn't?"

"Not clues. Money. Fame. Power." He shakes his head. "But let's hope it doesn't come to that. I don't—that's last resort. I like to do things the right way. Not the privileged way."

I head to the door and open it to find Giselle munching on a fried chicken leg that very likely came from Crusty Nut, Tillie Jean's dad's restaurant.

Giselle side-eyes me like she wants to tell me to come and get it if I don't want her eating any of the food the Rocks sent.

"You more than earned all of it," I tell her.

"Did you butcher the manbun?"

"Like a toddler turned loose with scissors."

"Good job. You can have a breast."

"This career is wearing on you, isn't it?"

"Only some days."

"You should really take that vacation. Everyone needs time off."

"Humph."

"Thank you for keeping me safe."

"*That* is my pleasure. You're a good person. You deserve it." She lifts a large brown paper sack with her free hand and gives it to me. "Eat up. Especially the vegetables. Good food, good fuel. You're gonna need it."

Heat creeps over my face. "Were you listening in?"

"There are certain things I never want to hear, and I avoid them at all costs."

I'm initially relieved enough that I almost miss her implication. "Oh. *Oh*. Oh no, we weren't—"

"Not my business."

"Where do you sleep?"

"Hotel. Relief shift is on its way. I'll be back in the morning." She looks past me. "Nice haircut. Suits you. Don't fuck with Chuck, or he'll fuck you right back."

"I can call in my own security team," Davis mutters.

"But you don't want to, or you would've done it by now." Giselle hands me a card. "Call this number if you need me. Day or night. Vacation or not. I'm ordained to perform weddings too, and I've been known to lose the paperwork. If you need someone like that."

"Can I hug you?"

"No. But I appreciate the sentiment."

She salutes us with the chicken leg as headlights flash on the driveway.

Davis tugs my arm, pulling me back into the trailer.

And for one brief moment in time, my brain fills in an alternate reality where I trust men and this specific man with his terrible haircut courtesy of me and a few rabid raccoons, this man with the story of his life tattooed on his body who wants to do more than just pull me to safety out of a sense of obligation.

Where there aren't pirates and treasures and ex-boyfriends hunting for things that could hurt my adopted hometown and my friends.

Davis shuts the door as Peggy leaps onto the kitchen counter and meows at me.

"Yes, sweet thing, you get chicken too."

I don't want to eat.

I want—

Well.

Once again, it doesn't matter what I want, does it?

Especially when I know I shouldn't want it at all.

23

Davis

THE FIRST TIME I saw Sloane in Shipwreck was the week that Ellie was here for a friend's destination wedding the summer after her car accident. I'd been called up for a Frogger emergency—no, Beck doesn't know anything ever happened to his Frogger arcade game, and he's welcome—and I was headed down Blackbeard Avenue, going to join Wyatt and Ellie and tell them I'd fixed what they'd broken, when I felt someone looking at me.

Not unusual.

But what was unusual was that I noticed.

I watched out of the corner of my eye and behind my sunglasses while a redheaded bombshell gaped at me like she wasn't quite sure what she was seeing.

And that's exactly how she's staring at the papers laid out in front of her now after analyzing them for the last several hours since we ate dinner, looking at the printed pages of Thorny Rock's diary as if she believes in the treasure and also agrees that the diary has clues.

While humming a very familiar melody.

That's "When You See Me."

An old Bro Code song.

One that we never released as a single.

One I helped write.

And I'm reasonably certain she doesn't even realize she's humming it.

There's a bowl of cinnamon sugar popcorn within reach for her, and I've happily reprinted three journal pages after she smudged them with sugary-cinnamony-buttery hands.

I like taking care of Sloane.

And I'm about done denying it to myself.

Until I pulled her into this mess—and I did, regardless of how much she might say she brought it on herself with the fake boyfriend story she fed her grandmother—every time I saw her, she was happy.

I want to do what I can to put the smile back on her face. To give her her laughter back.

Everyone deserves to be happy.

She suddenly sits up with a gasp. "How did I not see this?"

I've showered, changed into jeans and a long-sleeve thermal undershirt, and pulled a beanie over my hair, which doesn't help me feel any less naked, but it's what I've got.

I made the mistake of looking in the mirror at my hair and discovered I do, in fact, have vanity left.

And it's highly offended.

That's all I'm saying about my hair, and it's zero shade to Sloane.

She did what she had to do.

I squat next to her. "See what?"

She wrinkles her nose. "You don't even have to look closely. It's right here. And here. *And here*. He talks about his chicken on every page. *Every page*."

"And?"

"There's a Chicken Rock on that map that came from Sarcasm. I always thought it was what Thorny would've named a pet chicken or where his chickens roosted if he got chickens—did people have chickens back in the late 1700s and early 1800s?"

"Chickens are dinosaurs."

"Oh. Right. Right. We've had chickens forever. But he only talks about his chicken. One chicken. And look. Right here. He says all it does is stare to the south. Who has only one chicken? And what chicken spends its entire life staring to the south?" She checks her watch, then winces. "Can't see Pop, so I can't go get the actual journal until morning. At least tomorrow's not Tuesday."

"What happens Tuesday?"

She snorts. "Like you don't know. You know everything."

"Do I want to know what happens on Tuesdays?"

"Pop and Nana have sex in the shower every Tuesday morning, so no one sees them until at least noon. Apparently it's getting harder as they get older, but they still do it."

I breathe through the mental image. I did not, in fact, want to know what happens on Tuesdays.

Also, thinking about anyone having sex makes me picture Sloane naked.

Which I also don't need to do. "Good for them."

She grins at me. "You're picturing it, aren't you?"

"No."

"Liar. Pack up. We're headed to the museum. I want to look at a map and a couple of the letters that we haven't put on display yet."

That's a plan I can get behind.

I make sure there's enough food for the cat, then head into the bedroom to grab an extra flannel.

I can mind-over-matter being cold on my bike, but I can also wear extra layers to mitigate how much I have to. And Sloane's getting the jacket.

Right thing to do.

But when I duck back out of the bedroom, she has the outside door cracked and she's talking to Chuck, Giselle's relief partner.

So we're getting a ride in a car.

Great.

Fantastic.

Favorite thing ever to be at the mercy of someone else for transportation.

I grunt to myself.

Apparently I kept half of my Zen attitude in my manbun, and that's fucking gone now.

"Anybody watching the camper?" I ask Chuck.

He gives me a look.

It's the *you want security, get it yourself, my orders are to guard the lady* look.

Thought so.

It's basically what the wall of texts that I finally caught up with confirmed for me this morning.

Davis can take care of himself. Sloane deserves to feel safe. Giselle's the best. I'm sending Giselle.

And that was from Ingrid.

Not Levi.

I text Beck and ask to borrow one of his people to guard Sloane's cat. I'm not leaving her alone when we don't know if the raccoons will come back, and they're actually the least of my worries, given what's already been done to Sloane's house.

Then I gather what I need for a treasure hunt.

Trail mix. Water. Compass. Emergency space blankets. Spare flashlight. Pocket knife. Backup pocket knife if I lose the first. Battery for my phone. Backup phone that doesn't connect to Wi-Fi or cell towers anymore, but that has a copy of Thorny Rock's diary.

And it *is* Thorny Rock's diary.

Handwriting matches. Details that only Thorny should've known match.

Which means Pop, descendant of Walter Bombeck, somehow came into possession of the real Thorny Rock's diary.

Or someone up his genealogical line did.

We might be on a wild goose—ahem, wild *chicken*—hunt, but it's a lead I didn't have before.

Sloane watches me loading up my backpack. "You think we're actually going treasure hunting tonight?"

"Ready if we are."

By the time I'm packed, Beck reports that he has a catsitter inbound for us, so Sloane and I climb into Chuck's SUV, and soon, we're pulling into Shipwreck.

Blackbeard Avenue is empty. The Grog's closed. Don't even catch sight of the cussing parrot that's usually flying all around town.

"Where are the goats?" I ask Sloane. It's unusual to be in Shipwreck and not see random goats wandering around.

"Every last one got rounded up before the wedding. They're being sorted to figure out which ones still need to be fixed so that the goat population dies down."

"It's taking this long?"

"Tillie Jean's also trying to get as much glitter cleaned up as possible before letting them loose again so that they don't track it worse all over town."

"Even Grady Rock's goat?"

"Oh, no, Sue's still at Grady and Annika's house. And their house is already glittered, so that part doesn't matter."

That tracks.

Cooper's the reason Tillie Jean outlawed glitter bombs, so it would be surprising if the third Rock sibling didn't also have a glittered house problem.

Chuck pulls up behind the museum. Sloane hops out faster than either Chuck or I would like, and by the time I circle the car to join her, she's already hitting the code to get into the museum.

"Ma'am, if you'll wait a minute—" Chuck says, but Sloane doesn't wait.

She's not used to security details.

And that's a problem.

Especially because the minute she flips on the light, she screams.

I grab her and pull her out of the way, diving into the back room of the museum myself, and when I spot what she's screaming at, my blood pressure threatens to pull a Mount Saint Helens.

I need my goddamn manbun back.

It clearly held my peace and calm.

"What. The fuck." I glare at the intruder who's pushed himself against the side wall, nearly out of sight, but not entirely.

He's balding, in his mid-sixties, with a slightly bigger belly hanging over his belt than he had the last time I saw him.

Lila's *Uncle Guido* grins at me. "Your sister's lying to you."

No shit.

But if this fucker thinks that's gonna offend me or throw me off with that statement, he's wrong. Vanessa and I have been through thick and thin. I know when she's holding information back because she knows I'll use it wrong, and she knows when to hold information back because she knows I'll use it wrong.

I stifle a growl of my own. "Why are you here?"

"Oh my god, you know this guy?" Sloane's voice is high-pitched, and she's breathing hard. Takes everything in me to not pull her into a hug and promise her everything's fine.

There's a no-touching rule with Sloane.

I know where it goes if I let myself touch her, and yes, it went there—my dick, specifically—even when I was trying to save her from the fucking raccoon that jumped on her head.

Maybe it's not the manbun. Maybe it's the treasure hunt, and I need it to be over.

"Yes, I unfortunately know this guy," I tell Sloane.

Chuck's nowhere to be seen.

Likely because nobody in our circle likes dealing with Uncle Guido, but we all know he's harmless.

Mostly.

Scared the ever-loving fuck out of Tripp a time or two when he first hooked up with Lila, and even I don't know why Uncle Guido had to leave the CIA, but he's still mostly harmless.

"Who is he?" she asks.

"This is John." I don't take my eyes off of Uncle Guido. "He's a menace."

"How did you get in here?" Sloane demands.

"I can answer that for you, sweetheart, or I can—*oof.*"

I blink.

Blink again.

Uncle Guido's bent double as my metal water bottle clatters to the floor beneath him.

I look at Sloane.

Unlike me, she doesn't hold back. She growls at Uncle Guido, "Do. Not. Call. Me. Sweetheart."

My backpack is one water bottle lighter, and it happened so fast, I barely noticed. "Did you just maim him with a water bottle?"

Is that reverence in my voice?

I do believe that's reverence in my voice.

She turns a glower on me. "Get rid of him."

"Jesus H. Christ on a salami panini," he pants. "I think you broke a rib."

I grin. "Hope you want lifetime season tickets to the Fireballs," I tell Sloane. "When Tripp hears about this—"

"You want the fucking diary or not?" Guido's still hunched over, panting.

"I want you to *not fucking break into my museum*," Sloane snaps. "Davis, break his fingers."

Huh.

Look at that.

I'm smiling so broadly that my cheeks hurt.

Hasn't happened in a while.

Hence it doesn't take much to make them hurt.

"I'd like the diary, and I'm not sure breaking his fingers is the fastest route to getting it," I tell Sloane.

"How do you know he has it?"

"Wouldn't be here if he didn't."

"How can you be sure?"

"Because he asked if we wanted it, and he knows that if I call my sister and tell her he's breaking into museums for no good reason, he'll disappear for a while."

Sloane turns the growl on me.

And it takes me a minute of breathing through the need to pop another boner to remember something critical about this situation.

She's missing a piece of this puzzle. "John here—a guy most of us call Uncle Guido—got fired from the company my sister works for."

"What company?"

"The CIA, darl—Darlilah. I missed your name. You said it was Darlilah, right?"

"Darlilah is *not* a name you would suspect me of having."

"Why not? You never know someone's history. If you want to throw something else at me because you think I was going to call you a name you don't want to be called, you should know I have fast reflexes when I'm paying attention, and I'm happy to take a lighter to this diary that I picked—*arrggghhhh!*"

Sloane screams again but cuts herself short.

Probably because she's recognized that it's Chuck currently trapping Uncle Guido in a chokehold, and only Uncle Guido is in danger.

"How the fuck did you get in here too?" Sloane says.

I take a step back.

Break the rules.

All of the rules.

And I slip my hand into hers and squeeze. "Uncle Guido—I mean, John's harmless. Especially with you and Chuck on the job."

"Why does he have two names and why is one of them Uncle Guido and how do you know him? And *the CIA?* Are you for fucking real right now? Do you work for the CIA too?"

"Vanessa does. I do not. His real name's supposedly John. John Smith. Hence the supposedly. What I can tell you for certain is that he's Lila's honorary uncle."

"Lila, the owner of the Fireballs? Tripp's wife? That Lila?"

"That Lila. Hence I hope you like the Fireballs because Tripp will love that you maimed Uncle Guido."

She's squeezing my hand back hard enough to cut off circulation. *"How did he get in here?"*

"I hid in the bathroom when they were closing up," he squeaks out.

Sloane's eyes cross.

I jerk my head toward the door. "Get him out," I tell Chuck.

"You want the diary?" Uncle Guido says.

"This diary?" Chuck holds up a very old book with his free hand, and my pulse leaps at the visual confirmation that Uncle Guido wasn't lying.

He fucking stole Thorny Rock's diary from Pop Rock.

He tries to twist and grab it. "How'd you—shit. I'm getting soft."

"Time to retire from retirement," I tell him.

Sloane squints at me. "What does that even mean? Never mind. Chuck, may I please have the diary?"

"Only person I'd give it to," Chuck replies.

He marches Uncle Guido out of the museum, handing the diary off to Sloane on his way, leaving the two of us alone inside.

With Sloane still gripping my hand.

And my cock noticing.

She frowns as she looks at the book in her other hand. "This isn't the diary."

"What do you mean, this isn't the diary?"

"This isn't the same diary that Pop has. It's not Pop's Thorny Rock diary."

I stare at the leather-bound book in her hand. "Are you sure?"

"I'm positive. Pop's cover is blue. This cover is brown.

Pop's cover has a sail burned into the leather on the top corner. This cover doesn't. It's not the same diary." She unclasps her hand from mine so she can flip it open gingerly. "And those aren't the same pages that I copied for you that I've spent the whole night looking at."

Fuck.

So whose diary is it?

And where did it come from?

Gonna have to read this one too. See if the handwriting matches.

Fuck me.

Did someone else find the real treasure?

"Stay here," I tell her.

"What? Why? Where are you going?"

"To check the rest of the museum."

She blinks at me, then grabs my hand again. "How much more security do we need?"

Isn't that the question?

Since she won't let go, she comes with me as I sweep the building, making sure no one else is hiding out in any bathrooms or corners or in any hollow cases beneath any displays.

Chuck joins us, giving me a side-eye.

Yeah, yeah, I know.

Leave security to the security people.

Especially if Sloane insists on checking everything out too.

We all finally agree the museum is empty.

Chuck strategically parks himself with a view of both the front door and the entryway to the bathrooms.

Sloane and I head back to the workroom.

She's still holding my hand.

And my pulse won't slow.

I like her.

She's brave. She's smart. She's compassionate.

She has ghosts, but she's doing her damnedest to live her best life despite the ghosts.

I admire that.

I *like that.*

Situational attraction, I try to tell myself. *You fell off the wagon and licked her pussy, and now you're confused, but this isn't real.*

Unfortunately, I don't believe myself.

As I shouldn't.

She looks up at me when she should be pulling her hand back so that we can get to work. "Do you know what's incredibly stupid about this whole thing?"

I shake my head.

"The pages I copied for you from the journal Pop has —the writer talked all about how he deserves that treasure and he earned that treasure and he can't wait to get his hands on that treasure again, but he stole it. *He stole it.* It shouldn't belong to him. It shouldn't even belong to Shipwreck or Sarcasm. It should belong to its original owners. But people are *still* here, over two hundred years later, committing crimes in the name of getting rich. Just *what the fuck?* You know? No one *deserves* to be rich. Deserve to be loved? Yes. Respected for who they are? Yes. Rich? Fuck right off. I'd rather be a good person and have fewer things but know that I didn't step all over people to get what I have."

Fuuuuuck.

She needs to stop talking, because every time she talks, I like her even more.

And I can't.

Even if it's not situational attraction, once we've located the treasure and gone through with the fake wedding, we're done.

Done.

Because I don't do relationships.

The last time I tried—yeah, I don't talk about that either.

I swallow.

Then swallow again.

She squints at me. "Why are you looking at me like that?"

Do the goddamn job, Remington. Look at the diary. Look at maps. Find the treasure. Do the right thing.

The right thing is not kissing Sloane. Again.

It's not.

Except it is.

This is Denver.

This is obsession.

This is proving to myself that I can do something that I shouldn't do.

This is danger.

I can't stop myself.

And I don't want to.

24

Sloane

I KNOW exactly what Davis is thinking.

Money runs the world, sweetheart.

That's why he's staring at me like he's never seen me before. Like he has no idea who I am. Like I'm a complete and total unworldly idiot.

That's what I'm thinking when he turns so his body lines up with mine, when he tucks our clasped hands behind my back and slants his mouth over mine.

Oh.

Oh.

This is unexpected.

But also—*oh my god.*

His lips—and his beard—and his body—and the way he smells like pine trees and s'mores and tastes like delicious temptation—

Okay, yes.

I'm good with this man kissing me.

I'm—*oooh* god, he's licking the seam of my lips, and I'm opening to him, and *god*, I miss kissing.

I miss kissing a man who knows how to kiss me.

I miss kissing a man that I trust to kiss me.

And it doesn't matter that he was kissing me like this last night and also Saturday night.

That was a long time ago.

Ages.

Eons, even.

Especially when I know this could be the last time he kisses me.

The last time I'm ever kissed.

He pulls me tighter against him and deepens the kiss, his tongue stroking mine, our breaths mingling, his other hand curling into my hair while I cling to him like he's my lifeline.

We're alone.

There's no one here to put on a show for.

I don't think he's trying to shut me up to make me quit talking about the ethics of pirate treasure either.

Not with that bulge pressing into my belly.

Again.

I think—

I think he *likes* me.

And he can't.

He *can't*.

But...maybe he does.

And maybe he doesn't want to, but he can't help himself.

Very relatable, that.

He pushes me backward, still sucking on my tongue, and my butt collides with the worktable.

Yes.

Yes.

Maybe we can not-date but kiss.

Maybe we can have sex.

Fuck.

We can fuck.

Right here. On the worktable.

Be friends with benefits.

Yes.

Yes.

That would work.

I can be suspicious of him but still arch my belly into his hard-on, and devour his mouth like we haven't done this twice in the past five days already, and fantasize about licking every single one of his countless tattoos while he tells me where they all came from and how they fit together so perfectly on his body.

Explore the ink that disappears below his waistband.

I want to see his penis.

Is it tatted too?

My nipples tighten and my panties become wet.

I've never slept with a man with a tatted penis.

Devil's work, I hear Grandma saying.

I tell her to shut the fuck up and worry about her own damn eternity.

Not mine.

I don't want eternity.

I want *now*.

Davis leans me back onto the table.

I let him, parting my legs to circle his hips while he hovers over me, fitting that glorious erection between my thighs.

Oh god.

Oh god.

We haven't even taken our clothes off yet, and I'm hot and wet and ready and floating on hormones and ecstasy.

Probably because my body still acutely remembers how he can make me feel with just his tongue.

He likes me.

He's dangerous.

Mysterious.

He has secrets.

Connections to the CIA.

Pirate ancestors.

This should turn me off, but instead, I'm clawing at his jacket, pushing it off his shoulders while he slides his hands under my shirt, chilly fingers sliding up my belly to caress my breasts over my bra, and *oh my god*, he's pinching my nipples.

He's kissing me and pulsing his pelvis against mine and pinching my nipples and I'm gonna come.

I'm going to orgasm right here, right now, because—

"One last thing—Jesus Tortellini Christ, do you people *ever* not hump each other? Can't go see my niece without the humping, can't break into a goddamn museum without the humping. Fuck. *Christ.*"

I squeak.

Davis freezes.

341

His tongue is still in my mouth, and he freezes.

My eyes fly open.

His do too, and I'm suddenly staring at him too close, which makes it look like he has three fuzzy eyeballs because apparently I'm also *my eyes are losing close-up vision* years old.

He pulls his tongue out of my mouth.

Dammit.

Regrets?

No.

I like kissing.

I like sex.

I've done a lot of work to get over the guilt and shame hang-ups about it, even if I'm never having sex again because I don't trust men, but I trust Davis.

Shit.

I will probably regret trusting Davis.

Correction.

I will definitely regret trusting Davis.

"What. The fuck. Are you doing. Here. *Again?*" he says to John-Guido.

The man that I assume is a retired spy throws his hands in the air. "Fine. *Fine.* I'm retiring from retiring. Tell Lila I'm never seeing her again. I'm done. I'm just fucking *done.*"

"Is that keypad completely worthless?" I ask.

And yes, I sound like I've been riding him and my breath is coming too quickly and my eyes might still be slightly crossed because his thick erection is still nestled between my thighs, and even two layers of denim can't stop my body's reaction to him.

"Your boy left the door cracked," John-Guido says. "And I'm leaving."

"What do you know that you had to come back here for?" Davis still doesn't pull his body away from mine.

We're lying on the table like caught teenagers while he glowers at the old man.

"I know the blond caveman has an accomplice. And that's all I'm saying."

"Who?"

"Don't know."

"I'm calling Vanessa."

John-Guido snorts, then sees himself out the door, slamming it shut as he goes.

Chuck appears in the other doorway.

He gives us a once-over, then turns around and walks away as well.

Davis straightens.

He doesn't look at me while he adjusts his cock. Or while he exhales a long, slow breath out his nose.

Or while he mutters, "Sorry."

For what? I want to ask.

For kissing me?

Or for us being interrupted?

I stare at his beanie-covered head as he crosses to the storage cabinet. I'm not brave enough to ask.

Because I don't want it to be the former.

Even though the latter isn't his fault.

And so he shouldn't be sorry for that.

"Maps in here?"

I take solace in the fact that his voice isn't fully normal. He likes me.

But he doesn't date either.

Trust issues. He told me so.

He probably broke every rule in his personal rulebook by kissing me and touching me and eating me last night.

I broke mine.

The two of us make quite the pair, don't we?

25

Davis

MIND OVER BODY. *Mind over body. Mind over body.*

Nope.

Not working.

Especially when every time Sloane sees something new on the map, she gasps, then squeals, then does a little butt wiggle.

It's the butt wiggle that's killing me.

I want to hold her ass while she wiggles it. I want to hold her ass while she's riding me. I want to hold her ass while I'm kissing her. I want to hold her ass while she's sleeping.

Mind over body. Mind over fucking body.

I should say something.

Something more than *sorry*.

Something like *Sorry I kissed you, it won't happen again, I like you, but I don't do relationships, I know you understand,*

Jesus fuck, your pussy tastes like heaven and that was a good kiss.

Except everything I think to say ends with *Jesus fuck, your pussy tasted like heaven and that was a good kiss.*

And I can't say that to her.

So it's just been awkward silence since.

Well, awkward on my part.

If she's feeling awkward, she's hiding it well.

"*Look*, Davis. *Look*. If this is Chicken Rock, look what's due south. *Your cabin*. I mean, the cabin on your land. The one I wouldn't set foot in if you paid me a pirate's treasure. But it's your cabin."

"Been through the cabin."

She squints at me. "But have you?" She taps the diary Uncle Guido brought, which is not, in fact, the same diary that Sloane took pictures of just a few days ago.

This diary has Walter Bombeck's handwriting.

The real Walter Bombeck. The guy who founded Shipwreck while pretending to be Thorny Rock.

And while I've been looking over Sloane's shoulder as she goes between reading the journal and studying the map, I haven't processed a fucking word, because I'm too distracted by her ass.

"Look," she says. "*This* diary keeps saying *when I finally go to the light, it'll be at sunrise, not dusk*. Does that mean you have to go east from the cabin, or east from Chicken Rock? Was there a clue in the cabin? Did it have writing on the walls? Anything buried behind the walls?"

"It's falling apart."

She suddenly squints at me. "Why did you buy that land?"

Fuck.

I look at the ceiling.

One more lie is about to catch up with me.

In three… two… one…

"Oh my god, you're squatting? And why *that* land? You know that was owned by someone from Sarcasm. *What do you know,* Davis Remington? And don't fucking lie to me."

"My great-grandfather owned it. I didn't buy it. It's been in my family for generations. We just didn't know until the safe-deposit box at the bank."

She makes a choking noise. "I thought he didn't have any heirs."

"Didn't have any heirs and *didn't acknowledge any heirs other than that one line in his will* are two different things."

She leans over the map again, then hops out of her seat and heads into the museum.

I watch her ass again as I follow.

Stop it stop it stop it.

No good comes from obsessing about a woman. Especially a woman who lives in a town that I like to visit.

We need to find this treasure so I can move.

Preferably somewhere halfway around the globe.

I like India. I could go back to India.

Sloane won't be in India.

India fucking sucks.

"Look." She aims her phone's flashlight at a painting on the wall.

I know the painting well. "Tillie Jean painted that, and that's Norfolk. Not Shipwreck or Sarcasm."

"When Pop asked her to paint it, he demanded —*demanded*—that Long Beak Silver be in the picture, and

347

that he be sitting on the Shipwreck town flag with a baseball bat as the flagpole. Tillie Jean was like, 'I'm not
feeding Cooper's ego,' but Pop insisted so much that she
finally caved."

I lift my brows at her.

She dashes across the room to another painting, this
one much older, of Shipwreck from the late eighteen
hundreds. "Look at the tree."

I tilt my head, and I see it.

In the distance, back behind the buildings and nestled
between two mountains, there's some kind of tree that's
too large for its space. It looks like one of its branches is a
baseball bat, with the leaves hanging off of it like a flag,
and there's a crow sitting where Long Beak Silver is
sitting in the other painting.

She dashes to the third wall in the room. "Now look at
this map."

It takes me a minute, but when I see the tree again, this
one in a field, I almost grab her again.

Almost.

But I stop myself.

And I think she notices.

She goes pink in the cheeks and takes a subtle step
away from me before pointing at the painting again, this
time above the tree. "Look. This land? That's where the
high school was eventually built. The county high school."
She points below the tree. "And this is your cabin. I doubt
the tree still exists, but the diary I copied—that one talked
about the curtained oak that the ravens loved. Both men
had to have known where the treasure was buried. It all
makes sense—they spent their lives trying to outsmart

each other so that one of them could steal it out from under the other."

And this is why she's critical.

She *knows* this stuff.

It's natural to want to hug her for putting puzzle pieces together.

I like puzzles.

This is a normal turn-on.

Focus, dumbass. "What's after the curtained oak?"

She bites her lip and looks around the room. "I don't know. You can't tell what direction it's pointing. Actually, I think it's pointing different directions based on which map and painting you look at."

Wait.

Wait.

"Curtained oak," I repeat. "Ravens."

She looks at me expectantly.

Fuck. "The cabin had a name. Raven's Cloak. Curtains. Cloaks. That's a...stretch. But—"

"But pirates."

"Exactly."

"You're sure that's the cabin's name?"

"It was in the papers my mom found in the safe-deposit box. Land history stuff. Letters from my great-grandfather too."

She cringes. "We need to check the cabin."

"It's falling down, and there's nothing in there."

"Are you sure? *Sure* sure?"

Fuck.

No.

I'm not.

"How old is the cabin?"

Originally built in 1799.

Right in the Thorny Rock era. Only still standing because it's been reinforced a few times over the years.

She's right.

There could be clues.

I start to hold out a hand to her, then drop it before she can take it. We're not doing the touching thing. Touching is bad. "Okay. Back to the cabin. Let's go."

26

Sloane

I'D ASK if it's possible to be so horny you want to crawl out of your skin while also being so pissed that you can't act on your horniness that the anger is actually making you hornier, except I'm starting to think that's just how I'll always be whenever I'm around Davis.

We need to find this treasure so he'll leave and I can get back to living at my own house—

After I clean it up.

Dammit.

Patrick violated me. He violated my house. And even when we find the treasure, I still need to deal with that.

Not just the physical cleaning up, but the thing where I suddenly don't want to be alone.

Including in my own house.

Which doesn't feel safe.

At least I'm over being embarrassed that the sheriff and her entire office have likely been documenting my dildos and vibrators as part of their investigation.

But I'm not over wanting Davis to sit closer to me in the SUV as we head back up the mountain.

Not that he can scoot closer.

He took the front seat.

Next to Chuck.

Leaving me all alone in the back.

He still hasn't taken off his beanie, so I can't see just how bad his hair is since he showered. It was pretty bad before that. Sticking up at all angles, uneven lengths—he might actually have to shave it off to fix it.

"You staying up all night?" Chuck asks us.

"Yes," I answer as Davis says, "No."

I don't believe him.

He seems like an all-nighter kind of guy.

Which means he's probably answering what he thinks is right for me.

I snort.

Chuck snorts too, but his is pure amusement, whereas mine is frustration.

"Chuck, can you get me a metal detector?" I ask.

"I have a metal detector," Davis says.

"Two's better than one."

"You're not going in the cabin."

"Watch me."

"I'll make a phone call," Chuck says.

Davis twists in his seat to look back at me, but since it's black as midnight outside, I can't tell much more than that.

"It's falling down, Sloane."

"Then maybe we need to help it along and take it apart from the outside in."

That'll take days.

Possibly weeks.

I don't want to spend days or weeks taking apart an old cabin. I want to go check out the area south of the high school and north of the cabin.

Which will also take weeks unless that old oak tree is still there, which seems unlikely. Good news—if it's there, it would have to be exceptionally large. It would be over two hundred years old. Probably closer to three hundred if it was already that large in the late seventeen hundreds.

So we should be able to spot it.

But aren't pirates supposed to tell you how many paces to go when they leave clues like *look south of Chicken Rock*?

And what if the treasure's there, but it's buried under the parking lot of the high school?

"You know that thing in TV shows where satellites can look underground to find things?" I say.

"Won't help."

"You've tried it?"

"Would've if I could've."

"Why couldn't you? Because it's not real, or because you'd have to hack a system you can't hack? Wait. *Wait.* I just remembered—I saw a pirate hunt documentary that used—what was it called? It was a thing that looked like a lawnmower but it could see underground with lasers— no, not lasers, it was—radar! It was radar. Can't you buy one of those?"

"This conversation is over."

"Are you on a ban list somewhere? Are you like, legally prohibited from buying one because of something you did in the past?"

"*Over*," he repeats.

Somebody's frustrated.

Chuck snorts again like he's enjoying this.

I'd wonder how often he's witnessed Davis being frustrated, and I decide never, since that makes sense, but there's also a possibility that it's all the time. I get the impression Davis sees his friends regularly, which means Chuck would see Davis regularly while working for Levi.

There's also a possibility Chuck doesn't like Davis and is amused anytime someone gets one over on him.

Relatable.

I dislike him right now too.

And I also like him more than I did when I woke up yesterday morning.

Especially after last night.

And you know what he hasn't done?

Not once?

Hasn't even *hinted* at?

He hasn't once implied in even the subtlest of ways that I owe him an orgasm for the orgasm he gave me last night.

And that's not something I could say for *any* of my exes.

C'mon, Sloane, you haven't put out in days. Dudes have needs. You can't just leave me walking around with a boner like this.

And that makes me mad too because it makes me like him even more.

So maybe I'm mad at myself for rekindling a crush on someone I formerly only had a parasocial relationship with but now have a real *I kinda know you and we've traded some secrets and you've kissed me and touched me naked but we're not planning on being friends forever* relationship with.

My fingers itch to touch that tattoo at the base of his neck again.

The one he wouldn't tell me about.

What in the world could three triangles and a coin mean?

Chuck pulls up to the camper, and we all pile out.

"Beck sent someone to watch Peggy," Davis reminds me as we make our way to the door.

"Are you warning me so I won't scream again?"

"Yes."

"What if I want to scream because I enjoy it?"

Am I poking at him?

Yes.

Would I be if he'd just kiss me senseless and strip me naked and have crazy wild sex with me, with his penis and not just his tongue? And make me scream again in the good way?

I refuse to answer that question, even though I'm asking it of myself.

He opens the door while Chuck starts circling the camper.

"Why are you going inside?" I ask Davis. "We have to check the cabin."

"Getting my metal detector. And raccoon deterrent."

"What's the metal detector for?" a familiar feminine voice says inside.

"Are you fucking serious?" Davis mutters as I peek around him.

And I'm instantly squealing. "Sarah!"

Sarah Ryder, Beck's wife, smiles at me. She's stroking Peggy, who's melted into her lap on the couch, and her eyes are sparkling with mischief. "Hey, Sloane. Having fun?"

"Only when I'm not annoyed. Are you alone?"

"In here? Yes. Also, I have a taser and I can take Davis down in a sparring match."

I grin at her.

She grins back. "I needed to see for myself that you're okay, and I didn't know you had a cat until just a couple days ago. I love cats. They're so sweet. Little Miss Peggy has quite the purr-box on her, doesn't she?"

Dammit.

My throat's clogging and my eyes are getting hot. "Thank you for watching out for her."

"Anytime. How goes the treasure hunt?"

"It's a disaster."

"As all good treasure hunts are, I assume."

Peggy opens one eye—just a slit—and looks at me, meows a long, soft, satisfied *mmeeeeeeeeoooooooowww*, and then closes her eyes again and flips to give Sarah her belly.

"Who is such a good kitty? Peggy is such a good kitty," Sarah coos.

The cat stretches luxuriously.

Davis brushes past me, metal detector in hand, and I look between him and Sarah.

"Can you stay a little while longer?" I ask her.

"I'm bound by the laws of the universe to sit here as long as the cat has chosen me for her throne, so it's really not up to me."

Davis sighs audibly behind me.

Sarah's brown eyes twinkle brighter as she smiles. "Must be an exceptionally difficult treasure hunt if you can make *him* sigh like that."

"I'm not the problem. I didn't bury it. Some stupid old pirates did. Excuse me. I have to go fight him over whether or not I'm allowed to also crawl around in a falling-down old cabin."

"Good luck with that. Please don't die."

"Don't fucking jinx it," Davis mutters.

Sarah smiles wider and pulls out her phone.

Davis sighs again.

"Beck's gonna be so mad he lost rock-paper-scissors," Sarah murmurs.

Davis pauses at the door. "You cheated, didn't you?"

"Yep. Put a cheese ball in front of him and then challenged him to see which of us got to come. Rafael's outside, by the way. Beck wouldn't let me come by myself, even if I can handle things just fine. Including raccoons. What's the raccoon story, by the way? Levi and Ingrid both went silent in the group text after she said something cryptic about owing Giselle real Bavarian pretzels to apologize for the raccoon incident. And Rafael said he talked to Chuck and had orders to shoot any raccoons that try shit."

I look at Davis.

His cheek tics. "Nature natures. You coming, Sloane?"

He opens the door, and I dash to follow with a quick, "I'll explain later," tossed over my shoulder to Sarah.

He doesn't sigh again.

He also doesn't hold my hand to help me across the ground past the decrepit outhouse to the back door of the cabin.

Can't go in the front.

Not with the way the porch has collapsed.

This is okay though. We've made it safely to the cabin, so that's something.

I pause and look back at the outhouse. "Is that—"

"Yes," he replies. "Just an outhouse. Yes. I checked. No, I don't plan to do it again."

"Okey-dokey. Good enough for me."

"Lots of spiders inside," he tells me as the hinges squeak ominously while he tugs the back door open.

"Any raccoons?" I ask.

"Unlikely, but we'll handle them if we have to."

"My orders don't cover battling buildings to keep you safe," Chuck says behind us. "You go in there, you're on your own."

"It probably won't collapse tonight," Davis says. "Probably."

"At least they'll have us to dig them out," another voice says.

Rafael, I assume, who I also assume is either one of Sarah and Beck's security guys, or possibly one of their nannies.

I've read a little about celebrity nannies.

They're badasses and can do so much more than just teach a kid their ABCs.

Davis shines a flashlight inside the cabin.

No furniture.

Uneven wood plank floors. And not like today's smooth wood plank floors. More like rough-hewn logs turned into floors.

No visible raccoons, but lots of cobwebs. They're over the lone window in this back room. In the corners. Silver strands crisscrossing the room and lit up by the flashlight.

I gulp.

I can handle a spider or two. But I hate walking into spiderwebs.

Who doesn't?

Even the National Park Service's social media posts tell people to let their friends go first on early-morning walks so said friend takes the spiderweb out with their face.

Davis looks at me.

"You going in, or are you waiting for me to go first?" I ask him.

He sighs again. "Don't get hurt."

"I know first aid."

He doesn't smile.

Just looks at me for a long minute, then shakes his head and gingerly steps through the door.

The floorboards creak under his weight.

I wait until he's several feet inside the room, then follow.

It's not so much a spiderweb thing as it is not wanting both of us balancing on the same floorboards.

"What's under the floor?" I ask Davis.

"Basement."

Dammit.

I was afraid of that.

"You've searched the basement already?" I ask him.

"Yes."

"With a metal detector?"

"No."

He passes through another door, and I follow him into what was clearly the kitchen.

That's an old stove.

An *old* kitchen stove. There's also a fireplace hearth and a large porcelain sink without a faucet.

No refrigerator.

Obviously no dishwasher.

"Is there plumbing in this cabin?" I whisper in case I'm intruding on pirate spirits.

Could Davis's great-grandfather have known Thorny Rock and Walter Bombeck? I try to do math in my head, and I fail. I don't think so? But I don't know.

"No," he says.

"And your great-grandfather lived here in modern times?"

"He died in the 1950s."

So the cabin's been empty for roughly three-quarters of a century.

No wonder it's falling down.

Also?

It's small. Like he didn't have a bedroom. Just a main room and a kitchen and a basement.

No visitors for Great-grandpa, I guess.

Nice cabin for a hermit.

Davis turns into a short doorway, ducks, and shines his flashlight down the stairs. "You sure you want to do this?"

No. No no no no no no no. "Yes."

He stares at me like he knows my brain is protesting, then turns without a word and heads down the stairs.

They creak worse than the floor.

Much, much worse.

I flip on the flashlight on my phone and follow once he's all the way downstairs, feeling the steps sag beneath my weight. As the wall beside me turns from wood to stone, I lean against it to try to take some of the weight off the steps.

No idea if that works, but it makes me feel better.

Davis is sweeping the metal detector over the dirt floor when I join him in the musty-scented basement that reminds me of my grandma's basement back in Iowa.

And that reminds me that I still haven't answered Nigel's text from earlier tonight, which feels like it came in four days ago.

Was that really tonight?

It was.

Well, too bad, Nigel. You don't get a response tonight because I'm hunting for a pirate treasure.

I take a minute to scan the walls with my phone.

They're stone.

Old stones, piled like bricks with cracking mortar around them. I touch the mortar where it's falling away, looking for loose stones that could hide something behind them, but I don't find any loose.

I walk into three different cobwebs and handle it in silence.

Every once in a while, I catch Davis watching me.

"Did you already do this?" I ask him.

"Not as thoroughly."

I don't believe him.

I don't think there's anything the man doesn't do thoroughly.

He kissed me thoroughly a few times, didn't he?

He ate my pussy thoroughly, didn't he?

He went diving in to protect me multiple times in the past two days, also thoroughly, didn't he?

And now he's thoroughly pretending none of it happened while he thoroughly sweeps the dirt floor with his metal detector.

Twice.

He even tests that it's working by tossing a coin on the ground.

I watch him, fascinated not by the test, but by how he's able to do it. "You still carry change?"

"Yes."

"Why?"

"Need it sometimes."

See?

He's even thorough in his preparations for what he might need in case of who knows what?

"Were you a Boy Scout?" I ask him.

"No."

"But you're always prepared now."

"Life lessons."

"Who cleared out your great-grandfather's things?" It

makes zero sense that this basement would be here but empty. If I died all alone—*when* I die alone—someone will have to go through my things and sell my house.

Not that I'll be *alone* alone.

I'll be single.

But not alone.

I'll have friends who will take care of arrangements.

Everything I heard about the last owner of this cabin though—he was alone.

Alone alone.

Even what Davis has implied—*having heirs and not claiming heirs are two different things*—suggests that he was alone.

"Don't know," Davis finally says.

"Someone had to. If he lived here, he would've stored things in the basement and there would be furniture in the room. Even minimal furniture. Like a bed. Something to put a lamp or a candle on. Something to eat on. Or eat with. Maybe he gardened and stored canned vegetables down here. Or he was secretly a Halloween freak and used this space to store all of his skeletons and pumpkins. Everyone has *things*. Where are all of the *things*?"

He stares at me a moment, then shakes his head and starts for the stairs. "I'll ask a few people who might know."

"Your sister?"

He doesn't answer.

I roll my eyes at his back, and he catches me as he glances back. "You go up first."

No point in arguing.

We're done down here.

But about halfway up, there's a more ominous creak than any I've heard before.

And as my brain clicks with the realization that we can't see the underside of the stairs, the wood beneath me gives way.

27

Davis

SLOANE MAKES A NOISE, and then a cloud of dust envelops her as she drops.

No, not drops.

Falls.

Falls through the stairs.

My heart stops beating. My brain pictures her falling sixty feet into the earth below.

I drop the flashlight.

I drop the metal detector.

And I lunge to save her. "*Sloane.*"

"Mother—*auuullkkk*—fucker," she gasps.

She coughs.

I suck in a cloud of dust and cough.

But I have her.

I have my arms around her, and I'm hauling her out by her armpits.

One foot fell in. Not both. She only went down to her thigh. Not all the way.

She's not dead.

She didn't fall sixty feet from the sky.

She fell maybe two feet, even though she could've fallen a few more.

I pull her back down to the basement and set her on the ground next to the stairs. "Are you hurt? Are you cut? Did you twist anything? Break any bones? Do you need a tetanus shot? Fuck. *Fuck*. Say something."

She coughs again.

I grab the flashlight and inspect her legs.

Dust all over her jeans.

Her feet aren't at awkward angles in her sneakers.

I tug up the bottom of her pants, looking at the skin on her legs.

No blood.

"What—*ehlk*—are you doing?" she rasps.

"Are you hurt?"

"*No.*"

Fuck again.

I wrap my arms around her and pull her into a hug.

She's safe.

She's okay.

She barely fell.

"Water," she says.

Shit.

Right.

I dig in my pocket for my phone and text Chuck. *Need a water bottle. Dusty.*

An answer comes immediately. *Boy Scout failure. You're covering my hazard pay if I die in there.*

I stifle a growl of my own.

Sloane keeps coughing.

I keep holding her, knowing full well I need to let her go.

I can't keep doing this. I can't keep touching her, holding her, falling for her—

I can't.

"Look—under—stairs," she says.

Under the stairs.

I haven't looked under the stairs.

Why the fuck didn't I look under the stairs?

I stare at the stone wall beneath the stairs and answer my own question.

Because I assumed if this side of the stairs was walled up, everything under them was solid.

I order myself to let Sloane go, and I disobey my own order to stick my nose in her hair and breathe.

She smells like dusty cinnamon.

Like old, dusty cinnamon.

Living, breathing, heart-beating, coughing, old, dusty cinnamon.

"Are you fucking serious right now?" Chuck says from the top of the stairs.

This time when I order myself to let Sloane go, I also listen.

Chuck's holding a water bottle.

I lift a hand, and he tosses it down.

I crack the lid and hand it to Sloane, who downs half of it without pausing.

When she's done, she sighs in relief. "Thank you, Chuck. Much better."

"Are you hurt?" he asks her.

"Nope. Just annoyed."

"Good. This place is fucking creepy. I'm sending Rafael if you need a rope to get up. And telling Levi you need to hire your own damn security. I like working for him. You make his kids look like angels."

He disappears, and I track his path back out of the house by the sound of the floor creaking above us.

Sloane's already on the move, rising and pointing her phone's flashlight at the stairs.

I grab my bigger flashlight and aim it at the broken stair too.

"Wouldn't it be horribly anti-climactic if the treasure's been buried under a stairwell this entire time?" she says.

No, it would be a goddamn fucking relief. "Sure."

I step gingerly up about three steps, just enough that I can peer into the hole in the seventh step left by the split board. I grab one end of the broken stair and tug, and it practically disintegrates in my hand.

We shouldn't be down here.

No, *she* shouldn't be down here.

I'll be fine. But I don't like putting her in dangerous situations.

Gonna need a rope to get back up.

Or a ladder.

Sloane stops on the step below me, leans over the hole too, and aims her phone's flashlight in. "Uh-oh."

That's worth investigating.

I lean over and aim my flashlight into the gaping hole too.

Motherfucker.

Mother. Fucking. Fucker.

Sloane leans closer.

I grab her by her waistband to keep her from falling in again.

"So...your great-grandpa had enemies, huh?"

My flashlight beam sweeps left to right, then right to left again. "Maybe they're animal bones."

"Yeah, no. Those are human."

Fuuuuuuck. "Are you sure?"

"See the pelvis? And the ribs? They *could* be some kind of animal, but it's highly unlikely. That's a human pelvis. I'm positively certain that's a human pelvis." She angles herself to peer deeper into the hole, and I have to brace my feet harder to keep a solid hold on her.

She makes a frustrated noise. "You can let go. I'm not going to fall in."

"You did once."

"And I'm not going to again. Just—let me look at the walls, okay? The walls are wood under the stairs. Where's your metal detector? It's not disturbing a crime scene if all you do is sweep a metal detector over the walls to see if there's anything hidden in there."

Crime scene.

We found a crime scene.

Shit.

"Chuck?" I say.

He doesn't answer.

"Rafael?"

Still no answer.

"What are you doing?" Sloane hisses. *"Get the metal detector."*

"I'm making sure we're fucking alone," I hiss back.

She straightens and looks at me, and then she does the worst thing she could possibly do.

She grins. "Are you frustrated?"

I blow out a slow breath. "No."

"You sound frustrated."

"I'm not frustrated."

"So it takes finding a crime scene to make you fully and completely frustrated."

"I'm not fucking frustrated."

She smiles so big that it's like her entire body has morphed into one giant smile. "If you say so. Metal detector, please."

Fine.

Fine.

I'm frustrated.

And irritated.

And crawling out of my own skin.

"Get off the stairs. If one more of us is falling in, it's my turn." I grab the metal detector, flip it on, and insert the head into the opening under the stairwell, aiming it at the walls.

Sloane returns to the basement, but I can feel her bouncing on her toes behind me.

We're standing over bones of indeterminate origin, potentially stuck in here until authorities arrive to investigate, and she's swigging water and bouncing on her toes like we're at a tennis match.

Or possibly she's nervous.

People with overdeveloped guilt complexes tend to also have overdeveloped nervous systems.

In my experience.

I reach as far as I can into the opening under the stairs, sweeping the metal detector every which way that I can without disturbing the bones, and—

Nothing.

Absolutely fucking nothing.

Which means either there's nothing here, or there's nothing metal here, and it'll take tearing the cabin apart board by board, rock by rock, to figure out if there's anything else hidden in here.

I should text Vanessa.

But the minute I text Vanessa that I found bones, that's the last minute I get any peace.

"Can you tell how old bones are by looking at them?" I ask Sloane.

"Me? No. I just recognize what they are. It'll take a forensic scientist doing some testing on them to really get an idea. The fact that it's just bones though, hidden under the ricketiest stairwell to ever exist—they've probably been here at least a few decades."

I tilt my head at her as I set the metal detector on the lowest step, and before I can ask if she's also a true crime junkie, the metal detector goes fucking nuts.

We lock eyes in the ambient light of our flashlights.

Sloane acts first.

She stomps onto the first step, then jumps.

"*Stop.*" I grab her by the arm and pull her down. "You're gonna hurt yourself."

371

"We can't pry it up. That'll be super obvious when the sheriff gets out here to investigate."

I look up at the ceiling.

She snickers. "Frustrated," she says in a sing-song voice.

"And that makes you happy?"

"Yes. Because for all of the years that I've lived here, the only expression I ever saw you make was this." She aims her flashlight at herself and goes blank-faced with unfocused eyes.

"That is not the expression I make."

"I only started doing impressions of you right now, so please forgive me for needing to work on it. The point is, you didn't laugh, you didn't smile, you didn't glower, you didn't yell, you just *existed* like you didn't have any emotions at all. So yes, it's nice to verify that you're capable of such human things as frustration." She drops the phone from her face, and her voice softens. "And I appreciate that you let me see it. Like we're friends. Or something."

Friends.

I do not want to be *friends* with this woman.

I want to be much, much more.

I lift my foot, then bring it down with enough force to put it through the first step.

The sound of wood splintering echoes up the stairwell.

"Holy shit," Sloane whispers. "Don't do that to the other stairs, okay? I still have some hope we can get out of here without needing a rescue. Are you okay? Did you hurt anything? Is anything cut?"

"I'm good."

I'm not good.

My heart's swelling at the concern in her voice.

I need a break. I need to get back on even footing.

And I don't mean on these damn stairs.

There's a squeak overhead. "What did you break this time?" Chuck yells.

"Nothing," Sloane calls.

"That didn't sound like nothing."

"We're fine," I tell Chuck.

Then I join Sloane, who's already on her knees, peering into the space under the first board.

"Um, Davis... I'm no expert, but I don't think that's good."

I look at the old, round, dark ball that her flashlight is illuminating.

And my entire body flushes hot, then cold, then hot again.

"Is that...what I think it is? And if it is...are we lucky you still have your leg?"

It's exactly what she thinks it is.

And we're getting out of here.

Now.

28

Sloane

"THANK you again for letting us crash here," I say as Sarah leads us into the basement of their house, where Beck's waiting with a spread of food on the bar beyond a comfy-looking couch and a large-screen TV.

Like I need to speak for Davis.

I don't.

I know that.

He didn't even ride with me in the car on the way here.

He took his bike and followed us.

But manners come first, and I can't exactly leave him out and just thank them for letting me stay here for tonight.

Apparently we didn't find a cannonball.

Chuck and Rafael said that we found a *mortar ball*.

And since they can explode, it was obvious we had to clear out of the camper. It's too close to the cabin, and we don't know how big the blast would be if the cannonball —excuse me, *mortar ball* spontaneously went off.

And this was easiest.

And I'm grateful coming here is an option.

"Are you kidding? I'd be so pissed if I didn't get to help." Beck grabs a chip loaded with dip and gestures to us with it. "Did you really find a bomb? In a cabin? Did Thorny Rock put it there? Or is it some kind of replica and whoever lived in the house set it up to look like a crime scene under the stairs?"

"He's like a gremlin, except when you feed him after midnight, he gets very chatty and embraces his inner child," Davis tells me.

Sarah smiles. "Accurate. Beck. Put the food away. We're all going to bed. The girls will be up in just a few hours."

"But Rafael said they found *bones*."

"No, we didn't."

All of us look at Davis.

He sighs and lifts his gaze to the ceiling. "Three days, okay? Give me three goddamn days before you tell anyone else we found bones."

"He's frustrated," I whisper to Sarah.

"It's so odd," she whispers back.

"*I know.*"

That earns me an unamused look from the frustrated man.

Beck crunches on a chip. "Oh, shit, I haven't seen you look like that since—"

"Don't say it."

"Denver. Not since Denver."

"What happened in Denver?" Sarah asks.

Beck freezes.

Looks at the last bit of chip in his hand.

And then he very unconvincingly says, "Nothing."

Davis shakes his head. "I'm sleeping in the pool house."

I straighten. "I'm going with him."

Beck and Sarah share a look, then they share a grin.

"This house is fucking magic," Beck says.

Davis flips him off. "I'm staying in the pool house." He looks at me. "You can have a guest bed in here."

"You know that thing where the vast majority of my experience with men I've trusted has actually been with psychopaths? Like guys who toss my house, guys who gaslight me, narcissists, thieves, con artists, blah blah blah? How do I know you're not going to go hunting for the treasure without me?"

Davis stares at me.

I stare back.

I don't think he'd go look for the treasure without me, but also, I don't think we're anywhere close to it, and we're already finding skeletons and unexploded mortar balls.

He strikes me as the type who'd sneak out to investigate whatever he thinks he should look at next without me to save me from danger.

Sarah's eyes are sparkling with mischief again. "I'd tell you we're setting the security system and he can't get out of the pool house without us being notified, but I think he could, in fact, bypass the security system without us being notified. So I agree. You two should definitely share the pool house."

Ever been in a room with a trapped animal?

That's the sensation I'm getting as I watch Davis glower at Sarah.

She's clearly not worried though.

She tosses her wavy dark hair, crosses her arms, and smiles at him. "You can be as mad as you want, but I will always take Ava's favorite nurse's side over yours."

"I'm her favorite uncle."

"You gave her that singing computer for Christmas. Just because she thinks you're her favorite uncle doesn't mean the rest of us agree."

"Womp womp," Beck whispers.

Sarah tucks her arm through mine. "Sloane, I'll show you how to booby-trap the pool house so that you'll know if he tries to sneak out too."

"I can hear you," Davis says.

"But that doesn't mean you know all of my tricks."

"I wouldn't challenge him if I were you," Beck murmurs to her.

"He can spend his time trying to un-booby-trap the pool house, or he can spend his time resting so he can treasure hunt better tomorrow. And this is perfect. Peggy can make herself comfortable in the pool house, and we don't need to worry about introducing the cats to each other."

I haven't been inside Sarah and Beck's house before. Cooper's up the way, yes. Sarah and Beck's, no. I've only been here for a campfire. Outside. Where they have a pool house with a bathroom, which is what I used when I needed to use a bathroom.

But I'm getting too tired to be curious, and so I barely

take in the surroundings as Sarah leads me up the stairs, through an open-concept main floor with a large stone fireplace in the middle of the room, and out the back and around the pool.

"It's heated, so you could swim if you want to, but I suspect you just want to be in bed," Sarah says as she punches a code on the door and lets me into the cute little place.

"You do have a bed out here?" I ask as I glance around. The floor is marble, the walls painted a sunset orange, and there's a wicker furniture set with ivory cushions around a glass coffee table strewn with packs of card games. Everything from Uno to Phase Ten to normal playing card decks. The back wall has a galley kitchen, and I spot the familiar door to a bathroom.

Sarah gestures to another door. "My dad scares Beck, so we set it up so that my parents can stay out here when they visit us here in Shipwreck. We get warning when they're coming inside. Unlike Davis, my dad hasn't figured out how to hijack and bypass the security system. Here. Let me get you extra blankets."

"Thank you. Again. For everything. I don't know how I can ever pay you back for—"

"Sloane. It's all good. Sincerely. No repayment necessary. We all need help sometimes, and we all get pulled into situations that aren't entirely in our own control sometimes." She smiles ruefully. "That was basically my whole childhood, in fact. So if I can help someone else for a couple days, I'm happy to do it. Especially when that someone has always been kind to my family."

I'd say I was just doing my job, but I've seen Sarah and

Beck and their kids out to eat and at various festivals in Shipwreck too. I'd call them social acquaintances if I wasn't still somewhat intimidated by Beck's celebrity status and Sarah's celebrity parents.

Beck was my second-favorite in the band.

"Also," she adds in a whisper as she glances at the door, "it's not every day that I see Davis making a new...friend. Actually, in the five years since I met Beck, I've *never* seen Davis make a new...friend."

A girlfriend.

She's implying I'm Davis's girlfriend.

"My family wants me to get married and I'm never getting married, so I took not-so-secret pictures of him and sent them to my family and told them he was my boyfriend. He's playing along. That's why we're getting married on Saturday. It's fake. To get my family off my back. Because he likes to do nice things for people. Or something."

Sarah's grinning as she leads me into the bedroom, her arms full of blankets. The bedroom is pretty. Soft lavender walls that remind me of my own bedroom, a rocking chair in the corner, and a fuzzy blue-gray rug under the queen-size bed, which is draped with a quilt.

"High five to the never getting married club," she says. "Me too."

"You're married."

"It's Beck. He's too fun for this to count as actual marriage."

"That is *not* Davis."

"Davis is fun. He's just too reserved to show strangers

that side of him, and if you're not from the neighborhood, you're a stranger."

"So you're a stranger to him?"

"I'm a level-two stranger. He tolerates me because I'm married to one of the people he'd trust with his life, and he has two more honorary nieces because of me. I've been with Beck for five years, and tonight's the first time I've been at Davis's house. Ever. Except it was a camper. And I'm pretty sure he doesn't live full-time in a camper. I think. But still—first time. Tonight. And you've slept there. That makes you at least a level-three stranger."

I set the backpack carrier with Peggy in it on the bed next to the pile of blankets. "Is that more stranger or less stranger?"

"Less stranger. Level one stranger is all people on the planet that he will never give the time of day to. Level two are those of us who know him by proximity to people he's known his entire life. Level three is new. You're the first level three stranger I've known in his life."

People who like numbers sometimes make my brain fuzzy. Especially this late at night. "But he had a day job for a lot of years. Where he theoretically worked with strangers."

"Level-two strangers. He trusted them as much as he had to." She cocks her head, then grins at me as I hear it too.

Someone's opening the door to the pool house.

"The fridge and cabinets are stocked. The, ah, night-stand is too. Help yourself to anything you find and let us —or Rafael—know if you need anything." She squeezes me in a quick hug. "And I'm glad you're safe. Ava would be heartbroken if she couldn't see you anymore."

It's a nice sentiment, but all I hear is *the nightstand is stocked.*

We have provided condoms for your enjoyment.

It's something Tillie Jean would slip into casual conversation too.

No pressure, just—if you need them, they're there.

We don't need them.

We absolutely don't need them.

There's no more touching and kissing.

There's no sex.

I'm too tired for sex.

Davis stops in the doorway, all long, lean muscles with a tattooed story all over his body, his butchered hair still hidden beneath the beanie, eyes tired but alert, looking like sin on a platter.

The good kind of sin.

My favorite kind of sin.

"Booby traps all set?" he asks dryly.

Yep.

Too tired for sex.

So tired.

I'm going to fall asleep as soon as my head hits the pillow.

I won't even know he's in bed with me.

And I am the worst liar ever.

I have to do something about this.

Before I pile on even more regrets.

29

Davis

SLOANE WATCHES me make a bed on the floor after Sarah leaves and after we've both had separate quick showers, but she doesn't say anything.

Out loud anyway.

Her eyes are saying plenty as she sits there in the middle of the mattress.

So is her tongue.

It keeps darting over her lips.

I flop onto the pile of blankets with my back to her and come face-to-butt with her cat. "You should've stayed inside. I won't go treasure hunting without you."

"If that mortar ball randomly exploded and took out the cabin and your trailer, would you miss it?"

"No. You can shut the light off whenever you want. Or leave it on all night if you sleep better that way. Doesn't matter either way to me."

"What's Denver?"

"Nothing."

"Bro Code was supposed to play in Denver the week before I had my tickets in Charlotte."

Huh.

There is, apparently, something that can solve the boner situation.

I roll over and look at her. "Band broke up in Denver. You remember correctly."

"Why?"

"Off-limits."

"To protect one of your friends?"

"No."

"To protect you then. That's why Sarah doesn't know either."

I don't answer.

What happened in Denver—no one talks about it.

For me.

To protect me.

"You don't have to tell me." She shifts on the bed and flips off the light. I hear shuffling, which I assume is her taking off her pants.

And there goes the boner again.

The bed creaks. "I know you probably have enough information to find the treasure without me now. And I wouldn't hold it against you if you snuck out and went looking for it by yourself. I really wouldn't. Coming face-to-face with bones and an old cannonball—sorry, *mortar ball*...spies hiding in my museum...my ex trashing my house...raccoons launching a terror campaign... This is a little more than I signed up for. I know you like to take care of people. That you're keeping me as safe as you can. Which is very nice. But you don't have to take care of me. Even by letting me come along on the hunt. I'll be okay. I've been hurt before and gotten this far in life pretty happy overall. I'll keep going."

Is she—is she breaking up with me? "What are you talking about?"

"Just—life's weird, and sometimes you end up having to make fast friends with someone that you know won't be around in your life forever, and it would be nice if, after this is all settled, and the sheriff finds Patrick and you find your treasure, if you ever come back to town, if we can just, I don't know, say hi and be normal and maybe play darts or pool again. Not every time. Just every once in a while. Like super casual friends."

Goddammit.

I do not want to be *super casual friends* with Sloane.

I want—

Nope.

Can't want.

Because the bare, undeniable truth is that I don't date because I don't talk about Denver.

If I'm not willing to tell someone what I did when I was at my absolute lowest, then I have no business having relationships.

You don't keep secrets from the people who matter most.

From the people you'd theoretically raise kids with. Share a life with.

It's why my last relationship ended over ten years ago, and why I've never tried another since.

Because I didn't trust her with my darkest secret.

Maybe that's why I like Sloane so much.

She's had the courage to face her demons.

She didn't cause them herself, but she's worked hard to get over them. To live a happy life despite what's likely a constant nagging in her head.

The shit you learn in childhood—it sticks. It gets in there before you're in control of your own brain, and it doesn't let its claws go.

"How did you learn to let the guilt go?" I ask in the darkness.

"The *I'm going to hell for breathing* guilt?"

"Yes."

"Distance from my grandmother. Helping save people's lives at work. Being there for victims' families when we couldn't. Realizing how big the world is and how small I am. Making friends with good people who were happy. Watching them make mistakes and forgive themselves for it. Joining a book club that picked the right nonfiction book about shame exactly when I needed to read it. It wasn't just one thing. It's been many, many things over many, many years."

"Your guilt wasn't your fault."

"The overbearing, soul-crushing guilt? No, it wasn't. I'm not perfect, but when I finally realized that was okay, it made it easier to own up to my own mistakes, ask for forgiveness, and truly forgive myself for them too."

"You still battle the demons?"

"Not as often as I used to. Distance helps. Nigel being here, Grandma being mad at me...that doesn't help. But they're the problem. Even when I don't feel it, I remind myself of that. I don't owe them what they want for me. I owe me what I want for me. Good people aren't perfect people. Good people are imperfect people who do their best and give other people grace and the gift of freedom to be who they were meant to be."

Tell her. Tell her what you did.

I want to.

I want to say it out loud for the first time in fifteen years.

I want to confess. I want her to tell me how *I* can let go of the guilt.

Of the shame.

Of the constant need to do more and more and more good in the world to balance the scales.

I want to let her in.

I want to trust her.

And that has never—*ever*—happened before.

My pulse is riding a rocket ship to terror land. My mouth has gone dry.

What if I let it go?

What if I let go of my own old guilt and shame?

What if I let myself take a chance at being happy with someone instead of insisting I'm happiest alone?

What if I take this leap?

What if I trust her?

"Sloane—"

"Maps. *Maps.*" The lights flicker on, and she stares at me wide-eyed, her legs tucked in under the quilt, her breasts hanging free beneath her T-shirt. "Oh my god, *maps.* On the computer. Technology. Internet maps. *Internet maps! Street view! Street view!* Where's your

THE PRETEND FIANCÉ FIASCO

computer? We don't have to hike out to see Chicken Rock. We can look at it on the computer. We can look at it *right now.*"

She starts to get out of bed, but pauses, shirt riding up, showing off a strip of smooth, bare skin over her panty line.

She tilts her head and frowns at me. "Davis? You okay?"

Nope.

Not even close.

I'm having a panic attack about wanting to confess a very old crime to her, and she's sexy and alluring as a siren, and *I am not okay.*

Rather than answer, I spin to rise, trying to hide how fast I'm breathing, and the cat yowls and takes off under the bed. "Shit. Sorry. Sorry. Usually more aware of my surroundings."

"It's late. We should sleep. We can internet in the morning."

We can sleep after we find the treasure, and we can internet now. "Can't sleep until we look. Check on Peggy."

I retrieve my bag from the front room, spot Rafael lounging in a deck chair with an eye on the pool house door, and I stifle another sigh.

Doesn't help to tell myself he's watching out for Sloane.

Feels like he's watching to make sure I don't leave either.

Not that I want to.

Even if I should.

When I return to the bedroom, Sloane's hanging off

the side of the mattress, legs mostly covered, but her pink panties are peeking out in back as she looks beneath the bed. "Peggy, that's not a kitty toy."

"Need me to—"

"*No.*" Sloane straightens and smiles awkwardly at me. "I'm going to assume Beck and Sarah let all kinds of random people stay here regularly, so that there's zero chance we'll ever know who Peggy's new toy belongs to. Ooooh, computer! Does it connect to the internet? Will someone be spying on what we're doing when we pull up a map? Is that a thing? That's a thing, right? That people can remotely hack into your computer and watch what you're doing on it?"

I peek under the bed despite Sloane's squeak of protest, and I snort softly to myself.

That dildo I actually recognize, which is still not the weirdest thing that's ever happened in my life.

And it's twice the size of Sloane's largest dildo.

And now I'm thinking about Sloane's dildo collection.

Again.

Peggy's gnawing on the tip of this one like she's a dog, and she has to open her mouth wide to do it.

"I told you not to look," Sloane says.

"Ellie used that as a weapon to try to bean me in the head when I came out here to save her ass once."

Sloane looks at me. Then leans over and peers under the bed again. "She attacked you with a dildo?"

I settle onto the side of the bed, telling myself this is just a bench to sit on and that Sloane will want to look too. "Before Sarah, Beck had some…interesting guests. They left things behind."

She swings back up to sitting. "Why did you have to save Ellie's ass?"

I stare at her.

She stares back, but only for a minute before she blinks. "Never mind. Not my business."

"There was a weekend, eight or nine years ago, that all of us got together. Beck—he's very in touch with his inner child, and he has a lot of games. Board games, table games, arcade games. Loves games. All games. He set a record on his Frogger arcade game, and we all—"

I cut myself off as I catch her gaze drifting to my chest.

To where my Frogger tattoo is.

I nod. "Yeah. That weekend. Good weekend. He was fucking proud of his high score. So when Ellie broke the game when she was here for the goat wedding—"

"Patrick's brother's wedding. The one where—the one where I found out I was the other woman."

"You weren't the other woman. The blond caveman's a dick. When Ellie and Wyatt were out here for that wedding, she broke the game. Called me to fix it so Beck wouldn't know."

"Does he know now?"

"No."

"Does anyone else know?"

"Just Wyatt and Ellie."

"How'd you fix it?"

"You want me to geek out right now about circuits and switches and code?"

She grins. "Yes."

"No." I open the laptop, disconnect from the internet, and launch the global map program that's stored on my hard drive. She's not wrong. We're doing this without the possibility of being traced. "We're looking for a chicken-shaped rock."

"Can you geek out about how this program works?"

"Yes."

"Will you?"

I cut another look at her.

She grins bigger and scoots closer, the quilt still covering her legs, then leans into the laptop and points. "Oh, is that Shipwreck?"

I actively ignore my brain filling in all of the details of what her legs look like under that quilt, and I zoom in and move the map until we can see the old cabin—the one neither of us will be going back to until I drop Vanessa a note that'll wreck her entire month—and then pass her the laptop. "You know the maps better than I do."

"How do I do that zoom thing you did? I'm better with people than I am with electronics."

I demonstrate the keypad for her, not at all sad when our hands touch as I'm showing her how to operate the software, and then she's off.

Exploring the Shipwreck-Sarcasm area virtually.

While I keep my arms tucked over my crotch so she can't see the effect she has on me just by breathing.

I have such a fucking problem.

Peggy sticks her head out from under the bed and looks at us.

I cluck my tongue once, getting a look from Sloane as the cat leaps into my lap.

She turns her attention back to the computer. "You're a cat person."

"Watched Sarah with her cats."

"Dog person?"

"Ellie and Wyatt and Tripp and Lila have dogs. Levi's considering one, but their kids can't agree on what kind of dog they'd want. They preferred having a squirrel. Would probably adopt the raccoons that attacked us if it wouldn't make Giselle want to set Levi's hair on fire."

She winces, then gasps. *"Oh my god, it's the chicken!"*

Peggy gives her a death glare.

"Don't even," Sloane tells the cat. "You're that loud half the nights of the week too. Yeah, I hear you singing for the goats in the middle of the night. Davis. Look. *Look*. Doesn't that look like a chicken?"

I follow where her finger is pointing at the screen, and I don't even have to look hard to see the chicken.

That rock is definitely shaped like a chicken. Like a chicken walking somewhere, but on its side.

"That's an overhead view," I point out. "They wouldn't have had overhead views."

"We're in the mountains, and it's in a valley. They could've climbed and looked down on it. But look. *Look*. Its beak isn't pointed south."

I lean in.

Sniff subtly.

Inhale cinnamon.

Fuck, she smells good.

She scrolls, and then she pauses and grabs my forearm. "Davis," she whispers.

"What?" I whisper back.

"It's pointed at the Blue Lagoon Nature Preserve."

I've hiked there before.

"And?"

"Look. *Look*. It's here somewhere... Where is it..." She fidgets with the map, clearly looking for something, and the entire bed shakes when she does that butt wiggle she does when she's excited. "*Yes!*"

I'm staring at a waterfall. "Blue Lagoon Falls?"

"It was formally renamed when the high school opened eighty or ninety years ago. First time the kids from Shipwreck and Sarcasm had to go to school together."

"What does a waterfall have to do with that?"

"It was one more thing the towns argued over, and the county officials were trying to find something everyone could agree on that felt kinda neutral. Everyone from Shipwreck called it Thorny Rock Falls, but everyone from Sarcasm..." She squeals and bounces again. "*They called it Crow's Shade Falls.* And look. *Look*. Those are oak trees. Oak trees all over the top of the waterfall. And the journal talked about the ravens. Remember? Think about it. Crows. Ravens. People get them confused all the time. And shade. Like curtains. Curtains give you shade. And *it's a waterfall*. And *pirates*. Pirates would hide treasure near water. Wouldn't they? Or would they? Crap. Now I'm second-guessing myself. This is crazy. It's too far-fetched."

"It's pirates." I take the computer, holding it out over my knees so I don't disturb the cat, and zoom out. Then out a little more.

Until Chicken Rock is in one corner, its beak pointing directly at the other corner, where the waterfall is.

I zoom in on the waterfall.

The wide waterfall.

That looks like curtains.

Sloane gasps softly like she's realizing it too. "Oh my god, that really is it, isn't it?"

I look up at her again. "You're magnificent, you know that?"

She shakes her head. "I'm just a girl who likes history and sometimes puzzles too."

"You are so much more than that."

Her cheeks go ruddy, and she tucks her hands into her lap, staring at them while she tangles her fingers. "People have been hiking all over those falls for centuries. And the landscape would've changed some in two hundred years. If the treasure's there—I don't know *where* around the falls. Where it could be that someone wouldn't have already found it. You know?"

I set the computer aside.

Lift the cat off my lap.

And I give in to what I've wanted to do again all day.

Sloane excited turns me on. Sloane solving puzzles turns me on. Sloane turns me on.

Kissing her is so fucking easy.

Running my fingers through her hair—bliss.

Tasting her—heaven.

I'm falling, and I don't want anyone to catch me. I just want to fall with this bright, glorious rainbow of a woman.

She doesn't pull away from kissing me. Doesn't tell me to stop.

Doesn't push me away.

She melts into me, looping her arms around my neck and turning into my body until we're both splayed across the bed with our feet hanging off the side. She's half on top of me while I grip her hips like she's every lifeline I'll ever need.

I touch skin.

Soft cotton.

And I know what's under there.

She's tugging my flannel off, and then my thermal over my head. We break the kiss long enough for her to get the job done, and then I'm kissing her again.

No apologies.

No hesitation.

Just everything my body has craved all day long.

I push her shirt up and flick my thumb over her nipple, and she moans in my mouth.

Yes.

She keeps saying she misses kissing. Touching.

Intimacy.

I haven't, but now it's all I want. To be close to her.

She's my missing puzzle piece, and I need to stop. I need to tell her to stay here, stay safe, and go live a happy life.

But I don't want to.

I want to suck on her pretty nipples and stroke her between her legs and curse the fucking day I decided not to carry condoms everywhere with me.

"Davis—" she gasps as I indulge in my fantasies. "Nightstand."

Fuck, yes.

I hope.

Shit.

I haven't done this in a goddamn decade.

What if—

What if she's slapping for the nightstand while she rocks her pelvis against me and I need to shut my mind up and just do what we both want?

What feels so right.

Inevitable.

I roll her beneath me, flip open the drawer and grab a strip of condoms from inside, and then we're kissing again.

I fucking love kissing her.

The way she tastes.

The little noises she makes in the back of her throat.

The way she yanks my beanie off to grip my hair while holding my mouth to hers.

The glide of her tongue over mine.

The press of her hips into my hard-on.

I fumble with the condoms, and she shoves at the waistband of my jeans.

Desperate.

Hungry.

No thinking, just doing.

Touching. Stroking. Stripping.

She reaches under the waistband of my boxer briefs and strokes my cock. My hips flex into her touch.

Jesus.

Fuck.

Angel.

Heaven.

Torture.

I break free of the kiss with a gasp.

"Too much?" she whispers.

"More."

She squeezes me and strokes harder and longer, balls to tip, rolling her fingers over the pre-cum leaking out of me, then circling my head with her thumb and stroking me again.

I bury my face in her neck, breathing through the desperate need to come.

Hold on.

Hold on.

Hold—fuck, her hands are magic.

"Wait," I grunt.

"Sorry. Sorry, I—"

"No sorry. Just—been a while. I don't—I want—"

"This?" she whispers, taking the strip of condoms from me.

"*Yes.*"

Foil rips, and then her hands are on me again, rolling the condom down my length.

"You weren't kidding about that biological weapon thing," she murmurs into my hair.

"Hashtag blessed," I force out, which makes her laugh.

I love her laugh.

And I love that she's laughing as she kisses me again, slower, softer kisses that gradually build to desperate, hungry kisses while she shifts beneath me.

My cock nestles between her thighs, oversensitive already, as she wraps her legs around my hips, tilts her pelvis just right, and my tip brushes against her pussy.

My balls tighten.

Breathe. Breathe. Breathe.

She tightens her legs around me, pulling me into her

depths, and *fuck me fuck me fuck me don't come don't come don't come.*

I can last

I can last.

I can do this.

Her hands glide down my back while her tongue strokes mine and she angles her hips up higher to take me deeper inside her pussy.

So tight.

So hot.

So slick.

Don't come don't come don't come.

I try to breathe and hear my own ragged breath. "Feel —so good."

"So good," she agrees.

I let myself sink fully into her, my eyes crossing as she pumps her hips against me, stroking and squeezing me with her inner walls, and I can't—it's been too long—I just—

"*Fuck*," I groan as I come hard and fast inside her.

There's no stopping it.

No holding back.

Just everything I have, all of it, jerking out of me in one spasm after another after another, because I'm a fucking lightweight when it comes to a woman's touch.

This woman's touch.

She squeezes me tight, holding me with her arms and her legs and her body while I let go.

I'm not even a one-thrust wonder here.

I didn't make it that far.

Probably a good thing.

PIPPA GRANT

She won't be sad to see me go.

Except as the tension from my orgasm leaves my body, she strokes soft fingers down my back and kisses me on the forehead.

Like she's glad I'm here.

Like she did this for me.

Like she knew I wouldn't last, and she wanted it anyway.

Dammit.

Dammit.

My heart's still pounding, yet I feel like a jellyfish.

Completely boneless.

Including the rapidly softening bone still buried inside her.

"Sorry," I mutter into her clavicle.

"For being human?"

I pull air into my lungs. "Yes."

"You don't need to be sorry for that."

It takes more effort than it should, but I shift so I'm not crushing her, then slide a little down her body, my dick flopping out of her, and I nip at the pretty pink bud sitting at the top of her plump breast.

Her breath catches.

I do it again.

Her hips arch into me.

Once more, and this time, I order my heavy-as-fuck arm to move, and I stroke between her wet thighs, looking for that other sweet little bud—

"Oh god," she gasps.

"Hardly," I murmur.

"You—I—*there*," she whimpers.

I swirl my tongue around her nipple and flick at her clit, following the patterns of her gasps and moans, letting her body guide me, until I slip two fingers into her channel and feel it clench hard around me as she throws her head back with a cry.

"Oh god oh god oh god yes yes yes yes yes."

I press on her clit with my thumb while she pumps her hips in my hand, and I watch the glow of her skin and the unfocused way her eyes stare blindly above.

Fucking gorgeous.

I want to make her come every day. Every morning. Every night. In the light. So I can watch.

She shivers a whole-body shiver that I track from her shoulders to her toes, and then her body goes limp. "So good," she murmurs. "Thank you."

I kiss her nipple again.

"Won't—fall—so…"

She trails off, her eyes drifting shut.

"Dammit," she whispers.

And then she's out.

Just like last night.

Her chin dipped to her shoulder. Eyelids peaceful. Copper lashes brushing her cheeks. One deep breath. Then another.

So damn beautiful.

So damn complicated.

And so damn perfect.

Which all leaves me so damn fucked.

30

Sloane

THE SUN'S ALREADY UP, but Davis is still sleeping as I sneak out of bed.

That man.

He would be so easy to fall for.

If I let myself.

Bad, bad idea, Sloane.

And that's why I'm creeping through the pool house, pulling on clothes and hoping to not wake him after I once again completely passed out on him as soon as he gave me a single orgasm.

At least I got him naked too this time.

And not for him.

For me.

I like naked Davis, even if I'm disappointed his penis isn't tattooed.

Which I should not think about.

Ever again.

What I need to think about is getting out and finding a treasure.

Checking in with Tillie Jean to see if she's found us a fake minister and what else I need to do to plan my own pretend wedding.

Figure out how to not fall completely head over heels for my pretend fiancé.

But first—food.

Sex and treasure hunts and finding crime scenes and battling raccoons and arguing with family and planning a fake wedding makes a woman hungry.

Who would've guessed?

I spot Giselle parked on a pool chair just outside the pool house, so after a long, relieved breath that she didn't actually quit, I hit the code Sarah gave me on the keypad, wincing with every beep, and stick my head out of the door.

"Morning," I whisper to her.

She gives me a head-to-toe look-over, then smirks. "You forgot the *good* part."

"Do you think it'll be okay if I have some of the food in the kitchenette? I'll replace it."

"Manbun still sleeping?"

"He was thirty seconds ago."

"Then no. You can't have food in the pool house. Go on inside. Ms. Ryder brought her cinnamon rolls, and I'd be fired if you missed them."

"Why does that answer depend on Davis sleeping?"

She smirks again. "It would give me joy if *he* missed them."

"Why don't you like him?"

The smirk fades into a sigh. "Because he wasn't built to be a lone wolf, but he insists on being one anyway, which means that sooner or later, he'll do something stupid."

Again?

No one will come right out and say it, but in the past few days, I've gotten the impression that Davis has done something stupid before.

I would've had to be voluntarily clueless to have missed it.

"You care about him, but he frustrates you."

"I care about my clients and they care about him, and he frustrates all of us. The thing about ghosts—they haunt you until you fully let them go. That man's lying to himself if he thinks he's let go of his ghosts. And he's the only one who doesn't see it." She blows out a breath. "Go on inside. Nobody will care what you're wearing. Ms. Wilson and Ms. Remington are making eggs and bacon and spoiling the kids too."

Ms. Remington.

Oh my god.

Davis's *mother* is here?

Giselle cocks a brow at me.

"I'm glad you didn't quit," I tell her.

She grunts, then makes a face that tells me I have about three seconds to get my ass inside the house before she has to tell me twice, and she won't enjoy telling me twice.

So I dash across the deck around the pool and head inside.

Beck's feeding Francie, Ava's not-quite-one-year-old

sister, at a table near the back door as I slip inside. He grins at me. "Hey, you woke up! We weren't sure that would happen. When Sarah's parents stay with us, they sleep for hours. They say it's the bed."

Every adult in the dining room, living room, and kitchen peers around whatever they need to peer around to look at him.

"I'm just glad he married someone who knows where babies come from," an older woman murmurs to a second older woman while a third snickers.

He winks at me.

The man might be funny, but I don't think he's stupid. And I don't know how, but he doesn't look tired at all.

He should. He was up at least as late as the rest of us, but he's bright-eyed and radiating with energy.

"You want some cinnamon rolls?" he asks me. "My mom made them. They're famous. And better than Grady Rock's cinnamon rolls. Ask anyone except for the Rocks. And anyone from all of Shipwreck and Copper Valley when the Rocks aren't around. Actually, maybe only talk about it when we're in Copper Valley. Oh, hey, this is my mom, Michelle, and Levi and Tripp's mom, Donna, and Davis's mom, Alice."

I say a soft *hi*, and the next thing I know, the three older women are shoving me into a chair with a plate of scrambled eggs, bacon, cinnamon rolls, and a side bowl of fruit salad in front of me.

Giselle appears with a cup of coffee that she couldn't have had time to make in the thirty seconds since I walked in here, then disappears again.

While I sit here with three of the four women who gave birth to Copper Valley's most famous residents.

Okay then.

Not weird at all.

"It's so good to meet you, Sloane," the one with Levi and Tripp Wilson's eyes says. Donna. Beck said her name is Donna. "Ingrid told me you helped Hudson out when he stuck pirate coins up his nose. That boy. I'm so glad he finally grew out of the things-in-noses stage."

"We all are," I reply.

"And I hear you're—" Michelle Ryder starts, only to be interrupted by her two-year-old granddaughter.

"*Soooooooooaaaaaaaaannnnnnnneee!!!*" Ava barrels into the dining room and dives at me. "You have sucka?"

I catch her and pull her into my lap, fully aware of why I'm her favorite nurse.

I told Doc I'd only work with him if he started stocking better suckers for when we have to give the kids shots.

"I have a strawberry," I tell her as I pick one up off my plate.

She makes a face at me. "Dat not a sucka."

"Hey, Ava, how about you let Sloane eat something?" Beck says. "You know how you get hungry? She gets hungry too. But she hasn't had two bananas and an orange and applesauce and four eggs and six pieces of bacon and two cinnamon rolls yet. She hasn't even had *one*. Of anything."

"Was that your breakfast or hers?" I ask Beck.

"Hers," Sarah supplies.

"We had to take out a loan to feed him when he was a teenager," Michelle Ryder says.

Beck stares at her, clearly horrified. "I paid you back."

I don't actually know if they're joking, so I do my best to suppress a smile until the other two moms crack up.

"Sucka?" Ava asks me again.

I try again with the next piece of fruit on my plate. "I have a blackberry."

Her frown gets frownier.

"Did I hear you like mushrooms?" I ask her.

One minute, she's mad that I'm offering her blackberries, and the next, she's vibrating with what I'm assuming is unrestrained joy. "*Mush-ooms!*"

Beck winces. "Ava—"

"Don't worry, I saved you from your own incompetence," a new voice says.

But still a familiar voice.

Weirdly familiar.

I look around, and it takes me twice to spot the woman lurking in a chair in the corner.

Slender.

Brown eyes.

Serious face.

Brown hair in a bun.

Good thing I haven't eaten anything yet, or I'd be choking.

"You brought mushrooms?" Beck whispers reverently.

"Don't mistake me not being here often for me being ignorant."

"You're Vanessa?" I'm speaking in the same reverent tone.

"All my life," she replies. "Nice to meet you in person when I'm not trying to run over our mutual ex."

"*Vanessa*," Alice Remington says. There's no mistaking her because she's also slender and has her hair tied up in a bun.

"She's joking," Beck says.

Alice sighs. "I would love to believe that, but I know her a little too well."

"*Mush-ooms!*" Ava yells.

"Eat," Vanessa says to me. "Long day ahead of you."

"Don't say anything funny, okay? I don't want to have to Heimlich myself."

"I know the Heimlich," another man says. "Beck, you know you have a shipping crate full of mushrooms on your driveway?"

I register Tripp Wilson strolling into the dining room at the same time the deck door slides open.

Davis steps inside, looks around, and his eyes soften when they meet mine.

Like he's saying *you didn't leave*.

Like he's glad I'm here.

Like he wants to try what we did last night again, even if I don't really care how fast he came.

I kinda owed that one to him.

Also, I would've left him a note, but I made a fatal mistake with that plan when I stopped to talk to Giselle first.

"Hi, uggy," Ava says to Davis.

"Hey, bottomless pit," he replies to her as Beck sighs.

Sarah pokes her head out of the kitchen again. "Did my daughter just call you ugly?"

"Yeah, but she's right. I make an ugly panda."

Sarah winces like that makes sense.

"She wishes I was in her favorite cartoon show," Davis tells me.

"Mush-ooms?" Ava says in my lap.

Michelle Ryder rises and holds out a hand to her. "Here, sweetheart, Grandma will take you to find the mushrooms. And clean them. If we have to. Which we probably will, because Vanessa might not have cavorted with your daddy and his friends when they were younger, but she still has the same sense of humor that fits in with this crowd."

"Gamma, what cavabornded?"

"Cavorted is what you're going to do one day with all of your cousins, and you're going to have the time of your life, and hopefully give your daddy a heart attack or two that he very much deserves."

Ava stares at her for a minute. "Mush-ooms."

"Exactly, sweetie. Let's go find the mushrooms."

While Ava dashes off with Beck's mom, Davis's gaze swings to his sister, and if I'm not mistaken, that's some *oh shit* creeping into his expression.

And are his cheeks turning pink?

What the hell is that about?

She folds her arms. "So you know I know."

"Know what?" Alice asks.

"Who told?" he asks.

"Know *what*?" Alice repeats.

I'd second that question, but I'm not sure I want to attract any more attention.

I eat a bite of eggs instead, wary of the fact that any of

407

these people might say something hilariously funny at any moment, though probably not this moment.

Vanessa keeps staring at Davis. "My dear twin brother found bones and an unexploded mortar ball in that old cabin he's staying next to, and he wasn't going to tell us."

Tripp Wilson takes the last empty seat at the table. "I can't believe I'm about to say this, but I think I'd prefer popcorn to cinnamon rolls."

"Popcorn is delicious," I whisper to him before shoving another large bite of eggs into my mouth.

He grins at me.

"Don't flip your friends off in your head," Alice says to Davis.

"And don't hide *crime scenes* from the authorities," Vanessa adds.

Davis rolls his eyes.

Davis.

The man of no expression.

I bite into a cinnamon roll to hide a smile, and *oh my god*.

Everyone turns to look at me now.

Probably because I'm moaning like I'm coming over a cinnamon roll.

But holy crap. Beck's not kidding. This is better than Grady's. And I will never repeat that out loud so long as I live in Shipwreck.

Also, it suddenly occurs to me that I'm meeting my pretend fiancé's whole family while demonstrating that I can make porn star noises.

What the fuck ever.

If they're prudes, they can fucking get over it too.

"It's good," I say with my mouth full.

"Legendary," Tripp agrees.

"She told me I could only have seven," Beck says. "It's not fair."

"Honey, where's Lila?" Tripp's mom asks. "I thought she was coming too."

"I'm here." Lila, the redheaded owner of the Fireballs, also strolls into the room. Unlike Tripp, it appears she stopped in the kitchen first, because she's holding a plate of food. "Had some weird texts from my uncle."

"He broke into the museum last night and when Sloane caught him, she broke his rib with a water bottle," Davis says.

Vanessa stares at him.

He pops half a grin.

And that's when I realize everyone else is now staring at me.

But once again, I realize I don't actually care what they think of me.

And the guilt? The shame over hurting someone?

Nowhere to be seen.

Huh.

I've apparently hit my limits with bullshit this week.

Or maybe I'm very chill after hard, man-induced-orgasm sleep.

I shrug at all of them. "He wasn't supposed to be there, and I'm getting *very tired* of people invading my safe spaces."

"He says he's going on an extended trip somewhere in Asia and we shouldn't worry if we don't hear from him for five years," Lila says.

"Do you believe him?" Tripp asks her. "He's actually leaving? *Leaving* leaving? He won't randomly be sitting in my office when I walk in the door or jump out of the shower when I walk into the bathroom?"

"I actually think he's leaving. He said he's retiring from retiring, and that it doesn't mean he's going back."

Tripp turns to me. "You like the Fireballs? We can get you tickets. For life. Pick your seat."

"Told you so," Davis says to me.

"You don't get to *told you so* anyone this morning," Vanessa replies.

He rolls his eyes again.

But he's smiling.

Davis.

Full smiling.

So this is what he looks like when he's fully in his element. With the people who love him. The people he feels safe with.

My eyes burn. With happiness for him? Jealousy that he gets to have an awesome family?

Whatever's prompting me to feel emotional about this, the biggest thought in my head is that he looks good.

Right.

Happy.

"What's with the hat?" Vanessa asks, nodding at the beanie he's wearing again.

"Like it," he replies. "Any food left? I'm hungry."

"Crime scene, Davis."

"It's at least a hundred years old," I say. "When the murderer is clearly already dead too, justice can wait a few more days so that we can get *all* of the justice and I can get back to my life."

"Exactly that," Davis agrees.

He takes the seat Michelle Ryder just left, which leaves him sitting next to me.

And that makes my heart pitter-patter.

"Fruit?" I ask him, pushing my bowl closer to him.

"Thank you."

"My pleasure. I worked very hard to make all of breakfast this morning."

His eyes meet mine again, and his take on an amused glow. "Sleep well?"

"Clearly, if this is how I'm behaving while meeting new people."

"New *family*," his mom says. "Was I going to be invited to this wedding? Or was this going to be another thing that I found out about from your annual Christmas letter?"

"You send Christmas letters?" I ask him.

Alice snorts. "No, he doesn't, which makes how I find out about these things even worse."

"I send the Christmas letter detailing all of his exploits," Vanessa says. "And if I don't know, I make it up. Like whatever happened to his hair. I'm thinking he had a mishap when he tried to take up juggling."

I blink at her, then begin to smile. "He started with flaming batons?"

"You know it. Men and their egos. *Eat.* So we can find this fu—dging treasure."

"I brought my see-in-the-dark glasses that you got me for my birthday," Alice says.

"Mom. You're not going."

Tripp grins again and pulls Lila into his lap. "She should go. We should *all* go."

"Who are you, and what did you do with the guy who used to tell us no to everything we wanted to do on the bus?" Beck asks.

Francie shouts in agreement.

Or possibly she's shouting for more food.

She's been in to see Doc too, but only once. The round of colds hasn't hit her yet. Lucky duck.

"Request came through to shut down the preserve for a Fireballs promotional photo shoot," Tripp tells Davis. "No one else will be there. You should let your mom go treasure hunting too if you want to go. It's as safe as hunting treasure can be."

Oh no, this is bad. *Bad* bad. They're taking pictures in the preserve today? "The Fireballs are doing a promotional photo shoot at the preserve?" I ask.

Davis shakes his head. "Cover story to get it closed."

I don't ask when he asked Tripp for help.

I slept like the dead last night.

Again.

For obvious reasons.

"Also, Lila and I are coming on the treasure hunt," Tripp says.

"Ingrid says she and Levi are on their way too," Sarah reports. "And Aspen knows a lot of cuss words. In case anyone needed to know that about her."

"What about Ellie?" Mrs. Wilson says. "And Wyatt. Wyatt's military smart. You should get him out here too."

"Someone say my name?" a woman calls from the front of the house, then a door slams.

"I get bwekfast!" a new little voice yells. "Gamma wolls! Gamma wolls!"

I tense.

And then a hand squeezes my thigh, and my shoulders drop.

Ellie doesn't hate me.

Patrick is the dick.

And I think Davis would fight anyone who tried to say otherwise.

"Thank you," I whisper to him.

"Don't thank me yet. I'm stealing your cinnamon rolls."

I blink at my plate, and then at him.

My second cinnamon roll is gone.

He grins.

Full-on grins.

"Pretend, my ass," Lila murmurs to Tripp loudly enough for me to hear.

"*Aaasssssss!*" Francie yells.

"Wasn't me," Davis says.

"Or me," Beck says. "Sarah, I didn't teach her that word."

"You have the best family," I whisper to Davis.

"I know."

"Do they know you know?"

"Yes."

"Good. This deserves recognition."

He squeezes my thigh again, and then chaos erupts.

Good chaos.

The kind of chaos that comes in a house full of people

who have been friends forever and their mothers and their spouses and their kids.

And for just a little while, I let myself pretend that this is real.

That I belong here for real.

Even when Davis and I go our separate ways after the fake wedding, after we find the treasure, after everything's back to normal—I still get to see these people sometimes.

And that—on top of having a really good found family of my own with the Rocks—will have to be enough.

31

Davis

THERE ARE TOO many of us.

Don't tell me there's no such thing as too many good guys looking for a treasure either.

It's not about the help.

Or even about trusting this many people to keep the secret if we find the treasure and someone other than me or Vanessa sees what's inside of it.

It's about how little time I have alone with Sloane all day.

And how much all of my friends and family are competing for her attention.

Ellie and Sloane have a long talk while standing over a rock, and they hug when Beck calls Ellie to help him look under a different rock.

Tripp offers Sloane baseball tickets six more times.

My mom peppers Sloane with questions about when

she moved to Shipwreck and how she likes it here and when the best time to visit is.

Sloane thanks Levi and Ingrid for sending Giselle, and before I realize it, Ingrid and Sloane are trading phone numbers so Ingrid can help make book recommendations for Sloane's neighborhood book club.

Vanessa asks Sloane if she's ever been arrested.

Sloane asks the same back.

We eat lunch outside in the late afternoon, and I don't get to sit next to Sloane. Beck and Wyatt monopolize her time, with Levi and Ingrid hanging close enough to hear the things I can't.

I'm getting cranky about it.

And worried too.

Is this because I came too early last night?

Is she avoiding me?

Is it really just about the treasure?

Fuck. I don't even know how this is happening. It's been five days since she asked me to pretend to be her boyfriend, and I feel like I've lived five lifetimes in that span.

Good lifetimes.

And today is another lifetime.

A lifetime where we spend the whole day using state-of-the-art equipment, underground detection devices even better than metal detectors, with large digging machinery and extra lights on standby if we need them, but still can't find the damn treasure.

No matter how much we scour the area around the waterfall.

Tripp and Lila do a real photo shoot closer to the lake

in the preserve to sell the cover story. Vanessa doesn't give me shit when she catches me using a device I shouldn't have to keep trying to ping Dixon's cell signal.

Went dead sometime yesterday, nowhere near the preserve.

No cameras have caught him near the museum again.

As the sun dips lower in the late afternoon, everyone but my mom, my sister, and Beck and Sarah leave to head back to Copper Valley to pick up kids from school and go about their normal family routines.

And eventually, with the darkness winning, we call it quits too.

An entire day, spent all around the waterfall that should be where the treasure is, with nothing to show for it.

But it means I get another day with Sloane.

To do what, I don't have a fucking clue.

Clearly won't be finding a goddamn treasure.

Maybe she's right.

Maybe it doesn't exist.

Maybe it was found years ago by someone who doesn't know what they found, or who sold it off to someone else who buried it inside their walls for someone to find centuries from now.

"Half the joy is in the journey," Vanessa says to me as we reach the cars to head back to Beck's place and regroup for the night.

Authorities are crawling all over the cabin behind my trailer, so we can't go back there.

I grunt in return.

And Sloane smiles at me.

417

"What?"

"I know I shouldn't be glad you're frustrated, but honestly, it's not getting old to realize you have actual real emotions and aren't straight-faced all the time."

Vanessa laughs.

"Probably you too," Sloane says to her. "Especially since most of what *you've* done all day is just frown and growl at everyone around you."

"You're very happy for a woman who's still stuck with my brother for another couple days. Or longer."

"Patrick was actually the best of my ex-boyfriends. It doesn't take a lot to impress me or make me happy."

Vanessa's nose wrinkles. "That's very sad."

"Yep. So today was fun. And I'd like to find the fucking treasure and get back to normal too, but since I clearly can't decipher pirate code, and I'm honestly nervous to go back to my house, at least I'm with pleasant people in the meantime."

"I don't think you were wrong with your assessment of where the treasure should've been."

"Agreed," I say.

Sloane wrinkles her nose. "But it wasn't there."

She's not wrong about that either.

"I started looking at the rocks and the trees to see if there was possibly another clue somewhere in there, but I came up empty," she adds. "Which isn't really a surprise. Two hundred years is a long time for a tree to grow and hide its secrets."

"You guys coming for dinner?" Beck calls over the cars. "We should have enough extra food."

"Are you sure?" Sloane calls back. "I saw your snack

backpack today. Also, no one asked, but it's my professional opinion that you should have your metabolism checked if you haven't. How much you eat is abnormal."

Look at that.

Even when I'm irritated and frustrated, she makes me smile.

I'm fucked—I like this woman too much.

And I've done it to myself.

"My obstetrician and then Ava and Francie's pediatrician said the same thing," Sarah says. "We've had him checked three times now. He's fine. Perfect, actually. Which is a relief since the girls take after him."

"*Yes*. She still thinks I'm perfect. High five, world."

"Is he really always like this?" Sloane whispers to me.

"Yes."

"Always," Chuck agrees. He's back on shift.

"Glad you're perfect," Sloane calls to Beck. "Had to ask."

"You're a good person, Nurse Sloane," Beck replies. "It's an honor to have you marrying into the family. See you at my house. Last one there might go hungry."

They duck into their car. Vanessa gets into her car, and Mom opts to go with her. Sloane and I get into the car Levi's team is still providing with Chuck in the driver's seat.

And we all head back to Beck's house.

Sloane's quiet as we drive. She stares out the window and starts humming again.

Same song as before, "When You See Me."

My heart squeezes itself.

I let a lot of people down when I broke up the band. Learned to live with it. Forgive myself too.

But hearing her humming an old tune of ours twice now—this one hurts.

It hurts that I hurt her.

She seems to catch herself, and she goes quiet once more.

"You okay?" I ask her after another few minutes of silence.

"I'm trying to think like an eighteenth-century pirate. What would you do if you'd retired from piracy and were sitting on a treasure?"

I watch her in the dim glow of the dashboard screen up front. "You think he used it?"

"Imagine spending your life filling your treasure chest and then not using it. It doesn't make sense. Even if he had to sell it off, there had to be places that he could've sold a gem here or traded a gold coin there."

"Those would've eventually resurfaced and been recognized somewhere."

"But would they? If it was coins that had already been in circulation before the Revolutionary War, then *would they*?"

"I'd use a treasure if I had it," Chuck says. "Why go to all the trouble of criming if you're not going to enjoy what you stole?"

Sloane leans back in her seat. "Exactly my point. Why bury a treasure somewhere you can't reach it? Why have a treasure and not use it? You can be mostly incognito and still use your wealth."

Both of them slide me a look.

Not hard to understand why. I like to be incognito, and I don't have many spending restrictions.

But there are still logic gaps in their argument. "You can't just use as many gold coins as he recorded having in his captain's log."

"Maybe he lied in his captain's log and that's part of why he and Walter Bombeck had a falling out. Men *do* love to exaggerate their…accomplishments."

Chuck snickers.

"It's out there," I tell Sloane. "Even if his exploits were exaggerated, he made enough to retire, enough to have his first mate wanting what he had, and enough to live on."

She sighs. "My brain and body both need a break."

She's not alone.

I'd say it's a good thing we're going to Beck's, except when we arrive, it's not Beck who greets us.

It's Pop Rock.

In the driveway.

And he's pissed.

Ever seen a pirate angry?

That's Pop right now.

He's shrunk a little in stature since the first time I saw him, but he's in full pirate regalia, from the boots to the sword to the coat to the hat to the bird on his shoulder.

"*You stole my diary,*" he yells at me before we're fully out of the car.

Sloane jumps in front of me like she needs to protect me from the old man's wrath, and my heart does that pitter-patter thing again.

"Whoa, deep breath, Pop. It was me. I took the pictures. Davis doesn't have your diary."

His eyes cross. *"You took pictures of my diary?"*

"Rawk! What do you want on your tombstone, sucker? Rawk!"

I move to get in front of Sloane, but she flings an arm out and holds me back.

And my heart pitter-patters harder.

People don't protect me.

I protect them.

This woman will be the one to break me.

"Someone's going to get hurt looking for the treasure." Sloane's voice is calm and measured, and she doesn't flinch when Pop takes two steps toward her. "Your family will get hurt looking for this treasure. You think the people who are breaking into the museum and into my house will stop with me? They'll target Tillie Jean next. Or Grady and Annika. Or you. Or any of your other kids or grandkids."

Pop growls.

"Rawk! Watch the fucker's blood pressure! Rawk!"

"Good point, Long Beak Silver. Pop, let's go inside and have some food and talk about why we need to find this treasure now."

"Nobody's finding the treasure."

"Because you already found it?"

He snorts.

That's not a good sound.

"Where'd you find it, Pop?" Sloane says.

"I didn't find it," he grumbles. "Been all over that damn nature preserve. My whole damn life. Figured it out without all of that fancy internet stuff you can do nowadays. And I'm telling you, it's not there. And I'm also

telling you, I want my diary back."

"*Rawk! Hand it over and walk the plank! Rawk!*"

"Shouldn't that be *or*?" Sloane says to the parrot.

"*Rawk! Fuck off! Rawk!*"

"Max will be so disappointed in you."

"*Rawk! I love Max! Rawk!*"

"Exactly. Wait. *Wait*. Are you sure the diary's missing, Pop? We don't have the diary. When did it go missing?"

Shit.

Fuck.

Vanessa and Mom step out of the car behind us.

"Been missing since yesterday," Pop says.

Sloane's phone lights up, glowing from her pocket.

She cringes.

I curl my hand into a fist again to keep from pulling her close. "If that's Nigel, I'll be happy to answer him for you. If you want me to."

She's rolling her eyes as she pulls it out, but that's not Nigel texting her.

It's Tillie Jean.

"They found the coat in one of the glitter bomb receptacles from the wedding," she murmurs, showing me the message.

There's a picture of an old pirate coat.

Glittered now.

That'll be something for the museums.

"Is it damaged?" I ask.

"Somebody stole my coat too?" Pop says. "*Why is everyone stealing all of my things?*"

"Maybe because *that's what pirates fucking do*," Sloane snarls back. "You know who's a pirate? You're a pirate.

423

Your ancestors were pirates. You know who's not a pirate? *I'm not a fucking pirate.* But I'm hip-deep in this anyway, so *go inside, sit down, eat something, and quit yelling.* Or I'm calling *all* of your family up here to get you."

"Pop? That you?" Cooper calls.

Cooper.

Of course.

His house is next door.

Next door being a relative term. Lots are big up here on the top of Thorny Rock Mountain.

"Go back to your honeymoon," Pop calls back. "I'm practicing a bit for the Pirate Festival next year."

Cooper angles into view. "Kiva said she saw you pacing down here and thought you got the wrong house."

Pop looks at me.

Then at Sloane, who's still vibrating with irritation.

Then he looks at Cooper. "Yep. Must be getting old. Got confused. Thought I was practicing at your house."

"Rawk! His brain's as saggy as his balls! Rawk!"

Pop eyes me again. "Do not fuck up my family, you hear me?"

"Loud and clear."

Sloane slips her hand into mine and squeezes, and everything inside of me relaxes.

We're okay.

She's okay.

She still trusts me.

I didn't fuck up.

Again.

Yet.

"Which way's your house?" Pop says to Cooper, like he's actually confused, even though we all know he's not.

Cooper eyes me.

Dude's about as serious as Beck usually, so the look I'm getting now—

I don't like it.

It's like he's thinking, and he doesn't like thinking. Probably especially whatever he's thinking about.

"Hope you're having a nice not-honeymoon," Sloane says to him. "Sorry about the glitter at your wedding. Again."

His face relaxes into a grin. "Best part of the day. We love glitter. TJ's gonna regret that no-glitter edict. Because wait until she sees what I'm planning without it."

Cooper steers Pop down Beck's driveway and toward a waiting car.

Sloane looks at me.

She doesn't have to say a word, but I know what she's thinking.

He knows. He definitely knows.

He knows Thorny Rock isn't truly Thorny Rock, and he doesn't want anyone else finding out.

Except that's not what she says.

"Patrick has it. Patrick stole Thorny Rock's diary. I'd bet an entire year's paycheck he has it. So what are we going to do now?"

I mentally crack my knuckles. "Find it first."

"Hope we can."

Gonna have to.

There's no other way.

32

Sloane

THE PAST FEW days are catching up with me, so when Sarah asks if I'd rather take a plate to the pool house, I say yes and escape into the quiet with a burger, fries, green beans, a bean salad, a potato salad, and a leafy green salad, all of which I offer to share with my cat.

Beyond the burger, she doesn't have much use for my food.

Understandable.

Eating takes effort, and who wants to expend more effort today?

Davis isn't far behind me.

And he brings popcorn.

We're both splayed out in the little living room area, our feet propped on the coffee table, legs touching, not saying much as we eat. Peggy sprawls half on my thighs and half on Davis's.

Like she wants us both.

Relatable, kitty.

The man's growing on me in all of the wrong ways for a fake fiancé to grow on a girl.

I leave half my hamburger untouched so I can dig into the popcorn instead.

Salt and butter.

Classic.

Delicious.

"For all that it's frustrating that we didn't find what we were looking for, today was fun," I tell him. "Thank you for letting me borrow your family for a day."

He swings his head around to look at me, and I realize he's just as exhausted as I am. "They're yours whenever you want them."

"Ellie told me she'll be insulted if I don't call her for lunch the next time I'm in Copper Valley."

A smile flirts with his lips. "Good."

"I didn't realize that was still bothering me." I yawn and shift lower on the couch, getting a look from my cat, who clearly doesn't like that I just moved her butt. "It's good to keep letting things go."

He casts a long glance my way, and just when I think he's about to say something profound, he flips on the TV. We watch part of a Thrusters hockey game while being lumps on a log.

"Where did the real Thorny Rock live when he was alive?" I ask.

"His house, you mean?"

"Yes."

"The real Thorny Rock. The one who founded Sarcasm."

"Yes."

"The real Walter Bombeck—the one who founded Shipwreck—lived at the base of Thorny Rock Mountain. Old cabin that was torn down and replaced with the parking fields at the end of Blackbeard Avenue. Why'd they name it Blackbeard Avenue? You'd think it would be Thorny Rock Street."

Is he distracting me? "It was originally Thorny Rock Street. One of his grandkids got pissed at him and changed it, and nobody ever changed it back. And I know he lived on what's now the parking fields. There's an old photo of his house in the museum. But where did the real Thorny Rock—the guy posing as Walter Bombeck— where did he live?"

He frowns at the television as it cuts to a commercial break. "No record. Roger might know."

I debate picking up my phone and texting Annika, and I decide I'm too tired.

And that's the last conscious thought I have until I realize I must've fallen asleep on the couch, because it's suddenly dark in the living room, no television, no cat, but a blanket covering me while I drool all over Davis's arm.

He's flipping through the journal we got from the freaky man in the museum last night, and I can only imagine his eyes have to hurt given that the pages are only illuminated by the outdoor lights filtering in through the gauzy curtains.

I straighten and wipe my chin. "Sorry. Didn't mean

to…" I gesture at the wet spot on his shirt.

"Sleep's important."

"You're not sleeping."

"Mind over body."

That answer doesn't surprise me at all.

I gesture to the book. "Find anything?"

"No. More of what's in the other journal. *My pirate rival ruined my life*. These dudes—not a lot of depth. Just a lot of *gimme gimme gimme*."

"I really thought the treasure would be at the waterfall, but the more I think about it, the less sense that makes. Why hide it by water? The area would be prone to flooding, and that could wash it away or expose it."

He presses a kiss to my forehead. "Go back to sleep. We'll solve it in the morning."

I sigh and snuggle closer to him.

He shifts so he can wrap an arm around me, then kisses my forehead again.

This, my heart whispers. *This is how good relationships are supposed to feel.*

And there I go.

Just like that.

Realizing that I'm falling hard for Davis.

Way to catch up, Sloane, my brain whispers.

Like it didn't start when he kissed me back Saturday night. When he said that soft *watch yourself* when Nigel started being Nigel in the museum.

When he sat with me after my house was tossed.

When he gave me a place to stay.

Made me popcorn.

Told my grandmother off.

Shared the stories behind his tattoos.

Trusted me with what he knows about the real history of Shipwreck and Sarcasm.

Gave me the orgasm of my life to put me to sleep without complaining about getting his too.

Making sure to replace the cinnamon roll he stole off my plate with two more this morning.

Being here.

Just being here.

I'm so screwed.

I'm not falling for Davis.

I've already fallen.

Hard.

When to him, this is all temporary.

For show.

A convenient partnership where both of us get what we want.

My knowledge of the area to help find a treasure for him.

His word that he's my one true love to get my family off my back for me.

I bolt straight up. "Bathroom. Real bed," I mutter.

I don't watch to see if he watches me.

Don't have to. I can feel him watching me.

I do my business in the bathroom, then retreat to the bedroom swiftly, where I promptly face-plant on the bed.

He's right. Sleep's necessary.

But my heart is suddenly pounding out a *there you went and did it again, dummy* rhythm, and I don't know if I can sleep now.

Should've gone back to my house.

After breakfast but before we left for the nature preserve, the sheriff came out to take our statements about what we found in the cabin basement. He told me I could go back to my house.

The house I need to clean up. Face. Make myself feel safe in again.

Daaaaaaammmmmmmitttt.

Definitely not sleeping the rest of the night now.

There's a rustling in the doorway, and I tilt my head enough to watch Davis's shadow. He's pulled off his beanie—first time all day—and his profile looks different with his hair sticking up spiky all over.

Stay still, I order myself. *Pretend you're asleep.*

Davis sits on the edge of the bed. It shakes a little.

Probably taking off his boots.

There's a zip—or an unzip—and then the sound of denim swooshing to the floor.

My heart pounds faster.

So he's just in his underwear now.

I squeeze my eyes tighter, but my mind flashes with images of the hard planes of his lean body beneath his tattoos, the lean limbs, his very prominent hard-on that truly does make him *hashtag blessed*, even if he was…erm… quick about it.

Which I'm telling myself was lack of recent practice.

And that makes me glow a little.

If it's really been a full freaking decade since he slept with someone, and he picked me to be the person to break his sex fast with, that's—

Nope nope nope.

Not thinking about what that is.

The bed sags again. The sheets lift. Can you hear a head hit a pillow? Because I think I hear Davis's head hit the pillow.

And my heart is trying to claw its way out of my throat while beating even more furiously.

Davis rolls over next to me.

I hold my breath.

Is he facing me now? Or facing away from me? Or did he start on his side, and now he's on his back? I don't think he's on his stomach. Getting on your stomach takes far more effort.

Something lands on the bed, and I spin and bolt up with a shriek. "*Off, raccoon!*"

Peggy yowls at my feet, then yowls again, like she's saying *get a grip, crazy lady*.

Fuck.

Just fuck.

"Sloane?" Davis says softly.

"Bad dream."

"You weren't sleeping."

I make a *you weren't sleeping either* face at him in the darkness, and I feel him smile.

I don't want him to *smile* at me.

I want him to pull me into his arms and kiss me and make love to me where we both come at the same time with his penis in my vagina, which will make magic fireworks explode and show me that *this time*, I've found someone who's not a problem who wants to date me for real.

But that's exactly the problem.

Every time I think *this one will be different*, they're not.

432

But what if he really is different, and I don't give him a chance?

I snort softly to myself and flop back onto the bed.

Great theory.

Except he doesn't date either.

He probably does have sex even if he doesn't date.

And he probably comes early every single time.

And that's probably why he doesn't date.

It's very kind of him to give orgasms with his hands and mouth though. Very thoughtful.

Also very unusual in my experience.

Must be something wrong with you, one of my boyfriends said once.

Female orgasms are a myth, another said.

If you wanted it hard enough, you'd work for it like I do, a third told me.

But not Davis.

Davis asked me to show him what I like. He made it his mission to make me come.

So does that mean he's a good guy, or does that mean he knows how to use sex to manipulate me?

You know he's a good guy, my brain whispers.

"Sloane," he says again.

"What?"

He answers by gently tugging on my elbow.

My body responds without my permission, reclining back on the bed until he's spooning me, him under the covers, me on top of them.

His arm draped around my stomach.

Not touching my breasts.

Not touching between my legs.

433

Just resting.

Holding me.

His penis is half hard against my back, but not all the way.

That is definitely *not* all the way hard.

He sticks his nose in my hair and breathes, a slow, steady pattern of deep breath in, deeper breath out.

Deep breath in, deeper breath out.

Slow, deep, in. Slower, deeper, out.

My shoulders relax as I listen to him.

Then my heart.

My eyelids.

This, my heart whispers again.

This is what love is supposed to look like.

I tell it to shut up.

I think.

My brain is getting heavy.

So are my limbs.

Because I'm safe.

I'm safe with someone who cares. Even if he doesn't care, he's doing a damn good job of making me feel like he cares.

And for tonight, that's all I want.

33

Davis

SLEEPING next to Sloane all night—or not sleeping next to her while she slept—is torture.

I want to kiss her.

I want to lick every square inch of her body.

I want her to give me another chance to get it right with making love to her.

And when I realize I'm calling it *making love* and not *screwing around*, that's when I realize it's time to get going for the day.

To get some distance.

To focus on what I can and can't give her.

To quit fantasizing that I *can* give her anything beyond a fake wedding ring and my friendship.

So I'm up before the sun, rolling out of bed with a new guilt sitting on my conscience, leaving Sloane sleeping because she needs it and I need to get a grip on my head and my emotions and my body.

I hit the weight room off Beck's garage and punch the shit out of a bag for a while. Chuck's still on duty. When I pass him on my way back to the pool house, he nods.

I nod back.

No other talking necessary.

Maybe he means *love sucks*.

Maybe he means *you're up early*.

Don't care.

Both are true.

The bedroom door's still closed—good—so I grab a change of clothes and head into the bathroom.

I've just wrapped a towel around my waist after stepping out of the shower when the bathroom door bangs open fast enough to startle me.

Sloane's wide-eyed, fully awake, with my computer in her hand, looking every bit as bright and cheery and excited as I've ever seen her. "Why did your cabin have two outhouses?"

"What?" I shift so she can't see the effect her excitement is having on my biological weapon.

I see her, I get hard.

Every time.

"Two outhouses. Two bathrooms. It's barely a two-room cabin, and it had two outhouses. That's an outhouse, right? And there too? Or they were. That's what all of the other closed but not discarded outhouses looked like on the old satellite imagery we got for the interactive part of the museum that hasn't opened yet."

She sets the computer on the sink and points to two small squares on the cabin property, as zoomed in as she can get the satellite imagery.

I lean over and peer at where she's pointing, grateful that she definitely won't notice the movement in my dick while I'm leaning like this.

Also grateful that she's close enough that our arms are brushing, and the steam still in the bathroom is making her familiar cinnamon scent stronger.

I love the way she smells.

And I need to fucking focus.

I blink at the computer again, identifying the remnants of the outhouse I'm familiar with on the north side of the cabin.

I verified that it was an outhouse when I first arrived here, but she's right.

There's another square that could've been another outhouse tucked in among a thick layer of bushes.

I didn't zoom in this close on the cabin with the maps and satellite views because I was on the ground. I could inspect every inch myself.

Except I didn't go crawling into a big clump of bushes.

"Not unusual to have to dig a second outhouse for a building that old," I say. "Maybe not common, but also not uncommon. Depends on how well the first was dug."

"But is it actually a second outhouse? Or is it something else? Can you tell?"

"No idea from here."

She slaps my ass. "Then get a move on. We might be digging up shit, or we might be digging up *shit*."

Our eyes meet in the mirror, and she freezes.

Then turns pink in the cheeks.

Then looks down.

And not at my towel.

No, she's looking down at her own bare legs under another one of my T-shirts.

"Sorry," she stutters. "Moment. Mood. Called for—I'm going to go get dressed."

Fuck it.

Just fuck it.

I straighten, turn, back her against the door, and kiss her.

I kiss the ever-loving shit out of her.

Like I wanted to all night.

All day yesterday.

Every moment since she asked me to be her fake groom.

Possibly every moment since she told me I ruined her life that night that we were playing darts.

Her hands settle on my chest as she opens her mouth for me, and she sighs.

I know that sigh.

It's a happy, *this is so right* sigh.

She said she missed kissing.

I didn't.

I don't miss physical activity with people who don't matter to me.

But I'll miss kissing her when she's gone.

When this is over.

If we don't find the treasure, it doesn't have to be over.

If we get married for real so that her grandmother and that dickweed can't question it and I can take advantage of a few more legal protections for her, it doesn't have to be over.

We can do that.

We can get married for real. I never intended to marry anyone else, and she's never marrying anyone else either, so why not?

Convenient.

Benefits.

The thought of never having to let her go makes me harder.

The thought of being inside her again turns me into granite.

The way she's kissing me back and scraping her fingernails down my neck and parting her legs and lifting one around my hips—exquisite heaven.

I shove her T-shirt up and find those rosy nipples that I want to feast on.

Sloane gasps as I suck on her nipple. "Oh my god, more."

"Feels good?" I ask against her breast.

"I can feel it in my pussy when you do that."

I suck again.

She gasps again.

I reach between her legs and find her panties soaked.

"Off," she pants.

One quick motion, and they're gone, and there it is.

My treasure.

My real treasure.

I drop to my knees, hook one of her legs over my

shoulder, and lick her, and she grips my hair. "Can't—fall
—asleep—you—sneaky—bastard."

I smile against her pussy, and then I devour it until
she's screaming my name.

I don't want her to fall asleep.

I want her to feel good.

I want her to remember how my mouth feels between
her legs.

I want her to think about me every single time she
touches herself for the rest of her life.

And I don't care how hard my dick is or how much my
balls ache to be inside of her.

I just care that she's coming hard in my mouth.

That she feels good.

That something about this will have been worthwhile
for her.

"Oh my god, Davis," she pants, her hands still tangled
in my hair, her eyelids heavy.

She shakes her head.

Shakes it again. "I'm awake."

I press a kiss to her lower belly. "Guess I did it
wrong."

She huffs out a laugh. "You did *not*. Come here. I want
to kiss you."

Fuck, this woman.

This woman and her gorgeous body and her sweet
pussy and her eager mouth and her hands shoving my
towel away and stroking my cock—

My eyes cross before I can kiss her, and I drop my
head to her shoulder.

"I want you inside me," she whispers.

I slap at air until my hand connects with the sink, then reach lower for a drawer while she keeps stroking me.

My hand connects with another strip of condoms—thank fuck for Beck—and then everything's in motion again.

Sloane taking the condoms from me.

Rolling one down me.

Hooking her leg around my hips again.

Whispering, "Do me against the door."

I'm sliding into her sweet, swollen heat. Feeling her body wrap around me while she grips my hair and holds eye contact.

I pump once slowly.

Don't come don't come don't come.

One more, faster.

Her eyes cross. "Oh god, there."

I thrust again, and she bites her lower lip while her eyelids droop. "More."

"You're so fucking gorgeous."

Don't come don't come don't come.

Four thrusts, and she throws her head back.

"Don't fake it."

She almost smiles. "As if I'd—*oh my god*, more, please, *right there*."

My hips jerk on their own as she squeezes her legs tighter around me, riding me while I plunge deeper and harder into her, my balls getting tight, my cock ready to blow, but I want—

"*Davis*," she gasps, and then she's squeezing my cock harder with her inner walls, tight, hot spasms that finally push me over the edge, to the point of pain as I press as hard as I can, as deep as I can, wanting to float on this ecstasy forever.

She whimpers and writhes as she comes again, every motion spurring my own release thicker and heavier and bigger.

What am I going to do without her?

How the ever-loving fuck will I get over her?

Her body sags while I'm still coming inside her, and she drops her head to my shoulder.

I smell cinnamon and I can still taste her orgasm and I am so completely fucked that I will never be unfucked, nor will I ever be so fucked again, because you cannot get more fucked than I am right now.

In both the good and the bad ways.

The last of my climax fades away in a lingering shudder, and I drop my head to her shoulder too.

"Not—falling—asleep," she whispers. "Holy hell, that was good."

"You're good."

"You're better."

My arms are wrapped around her, one around her waist, one under her ass, and I don't want to let go.

I don't ever want to let go.

I want this moment—both of us catching our breath, our bodies still connected, the scent and taste of her surrounding me—I want to live in this moment forever.

This moment where I believe in love.

In peace.

In clarity.

In us.

Her fingers drift through my hair, still too short, still foreign, but I'm glad she was the one who cut it.

"Davis?" she whispers.

"Hmm?"

"Thank you for being the best part of this insane week."

I hug her tighter.

She hasn't been the best part of this week for me.

She's been the best part of my whole life.

34

Sloane

AFTER THE MOST thorough two-person shower I've ever had in my life, where I miraculously stay awake despite someone using his fingers to give me one more orgasm, we head toward the house for breakfast.

"Nobody else is up yet," Chuck tells us.

"Shocking," Davis says dryly, which cracks both me and Chuck up.

Once we're inside, Davis slides me a look. "Want to be bad?"

"Yes." I slap a hand over my mouth while he grins. "I meant *how*? I didn't mean *yes*. I meant *what are you thinking?*"

He whispers something in my ear that I should definitely say no to.

I've seen enough treasure hunt movies to know this is a bad idea.

But also—fuck it.

The entire state police force is now looking for Patrick. The mortar ball remnants and the skeleton were removed from the cabin yesterday.

What's the worst that will happen?

That's the last rationalization I make to myself before I'm on the back of Davis's motorcycle, speeding away from Beck's house without a security detail in the early dawn light.

As much as one can speed when there are switchbacks every few hundred yards anyway.

We reach his trailer in about fifteen minutes. There's yellow crime scene tape all around the cabin, but no deputies sitting here watching the property. Nothing around the camper either.

He grabs shovels and the metal detector from inside, and we head toward the bushy area that I was looking at from the satellite imagery.

And then we both freeze.

There's a car approaching.

"Get back in the trailer," he says.

I look at him.

Just look at him.

And Davis Remington—the man I used to think was completely expressionless—stares back at me with his entire face twitching like he doesn't know if he wants to smile or scowl at me for refusing to follow his orders.

It's honestly the most beautiful sight in the entire world.

Like he's no longer hiding anything from me.

Logically, I know he has to be, but emotionally—

there's something incredibly special about him letting me *see* him.

He looks past me toward the car, and his shoulders relax, but his cheek twitches.

I glance at it too and instantly understand why.

Giselle has followed us.

She parks, climbs out, and glares at both of us.

"Hi, Giselle." I finger-wave at her. "Isn't it a pretty day? I love your coat. It's very…black."

"You're lucky I know he's a bad influence," she grumbles. "What the fuck are you doing?"

"Treasure hunting," Davis answers for us.

She sighs and rubs her eyes. "Get to it then. I'll keep an eye out."

"Do you like cookies?" I ask her.

"No."

Welp, so much for that idea for a Christmas present.

She'd probably appreciate a new stun gun and some body armor more. I'll have to ask Davis's opinion on what would be best for her.

And I suspect he has one.

He nudges me, and soon we're standing in a bunch of stabby, leafless bushes, staring at a mostly obscured wooden cover to what I assumed was an extra outhouse while he passes me a pair of work gloves.

Once we've cleared away the grass that's grown over the edges and dusted off a few years' worth of fallen leaves, we discover the cover has a lock on it.

And not a modern lock.

This one looks more like the kind of lock a pirate would've used.

Very eighteenth- or nineteenth-century.

Also very rusty.

"Stay here," Davis says on a sigh.

We're out of sight of the camper—it's on the other side of the cabin. I can see the falling-down porch of the cabin better from this side.

"Have you looked under the porch for the treasure?" I ask Davis when he joins me again.

He shakes his head. "It's not supposed to be on this property at all."

"Unless someone moved it."

"Or lied about where it was located."

"Or both. You know what I would've done if I were a pirate? I would've hidden it and not told my family where so that they could all fight over it because that's a dick thing to do, and pirates are dicks. And then if my family were dicks too, if one of them found it, they'd hide it somewhere new so that the rest of the family would never know, and they'd use it the same way dear ol' Thorny or Walter or whoever used it. Huh. I wonder if I'm descended from pirates too because my family is also made of dicks."

His lips twitch again before he drops into a squat and uses bolt cutters to break the lock. When he lifts the wooden cover, there's a creak so loud, they can probably hear it all the way down the mountain.

"What was that?" Giselle calls.

"A hundred years of rust rubbing against itself," Davis calls back.

"Not raccoons?"

"Too bright."

447

"Not for those fuckers."

"She has a point," I murmur.

Davis grunts and shoves the lid the rest of the way open, then shines a flashlight below.

And we both sigh.

"Root cellar," he says.

Definitely a root cellar. It's a square room lined with wood shelves and dust-covered jars, some still on the shelves, some on the ground.

"It's small enough to have been an outhouse," I muse.

He smiles at me, then puts a hand on either side of the opening and swings down into it.

I squat wrong and get a stick almost up my ass— freaking bushes—but readjust until I'm able to peer down too.

"Pass me down the metal detector and a shovel, then sit on the edge," Davis tells me. "I'll help you down from there."

It's not deep—he can barely stand straight—so I do as I'm told, and soon, we're standing in the root cellar with a shovel and the metal detector leaning against one of the shelves. It's so tiny in here that we barely both fit, and I wonder if whoever used this last had to bring a ladder over every time, or if it got so old that it just disintegrated.

Roots poke through the dirt walls behind the uneven, free-standing shelves. There's maybe a foot of dirt over-head, reinforced with a couple beams that look like they're about to give their last hurrah.

We should definitely not stay down here long.

"Why was it locked?" I ask.

For one brief moment, I see the pirate in Davis as he grins at me. Then he shines a light at the shelf that's hardest to see from overhead, and when I'm expecting him to say something like *because people are weird*, he says something else entirely.

Something that makes my heart pound and my muscles tense in excitement.

"Because it's not just a root cellar."

Behind the shelves farthest from the trapdoor, there's another half door, this one built into the wall.

No knob on it, but it does have hinges and a frame.

We trade looks, then move as one to clear the old jars off the shelves blocking the door.

It's tight in here and smells even more like my grandma's basement than the cabin basement did.

Dark and creepy too.

Likely full of worms.

No spiders though.

My heart won't stop pounding.

There's something behind that door, and soon, Davis is pulling the shelves away.

Unlike the top door, this one isn't padlocked.

So maybe we're about to find someone's secret stash of historical sex toys. I heard that happened on a ranch in Wyoming somewhere, and given what I know of the people who live in Sarcasm and Shipwreck today, it truly wouldn't be surprising if their ancestors also had secret sex toy rooms.

I mean, I have one myself, if you call a nightstand drawer a room.

But when Davis pries the door open with the shovel,

with me staying as far out of the way as I can, I tell myself to be prepared for an empty space.

Probably a wall.

Maybe the door was put there to reinforce the structure.

Like the dirt was caving in or something. See again, there are roots poking through the dirt walls down here.

So I'm prepared when the door opens to a rock.

Seriously.

There's a rock on the other side of the door. A big, stone-colored, rough-edged, small boulder of a rock taking up the entire width of the door.

But while it's wide, it's not tall.

In fact, it's only half as high as the half-high door.

Davis shines his flashlight in and squats to look.

I huddle close to him, inhaling his familiar scent of pine and campfire, and peer in too.

He stops breathing.

I can *feel* it.

Or maybe that's me.

Maybe I've stopped breathing.

Probably we've both stopped breathing.

The little hidey-hole beyond the rock isn't empty.

It has something in it.

Something treasure-chest shaped.

"Oh. My. God," I breathe.

I blink.

Blink again.

Rub my eyes and peer harder at the box illuminated by Davis's flashlight.

Holy. Fucking. Shit.

That's a treasure chest.

"You afraid of tight spaces?" he asks.

"Yes. No. No. I mean, sometimes. It depends on the space."

"Hold this."

He hands me his flashlight, and then he crawls over the rock into the even smaller little cutout.

Seeing him in the tight space makes sweat break out on my hairline. "Please don't die," I whisper.

I get a grin in response. "All good here."

He's not just grinning.

He's smiling like a kid who's just been told he gets an entire birthday cake for himself.

"Is that it?" I breathe.

He flips the lid, and while I gasp, he sucks in an audible breath too.

Gold coins.

There are freaking gold coins in that chest.

It's not a huge chest—maybe a foot wide, not nearly as long, and just a couple inches high—but it has gold coins inside.

Davis is still wearing his work gloves as he runs his hands through the coins.

They clink like real coins.

He holds one up, and I gasp again.

I recognize that coin.

It's old.

Old old. Likely British.

If it's real—if it's real, we've just found an actual, honest-to-god pirate treasure.

He pauses, and a moment later, he's pulling a book out from beneath the coins.

It's leather-bound.

With a sail burned into one corner.

"Thorny Rock's other journal," I breathe.

He gingerly opens it. "Handwriting matches the real Thorny Rock."

"Oh my god. We found it."

He grins at me again. "We found it. Now let's get rid of it. Here. Stay there. I'll hand it to you, then climb out."

"Wait. We should get a picture."

He shakes his head. "We weren't here."

Is he serious?

We found a *pirate treasure chest*, and he doesn't want pictures?

"Just for us?" I say. "On your phone? No cloud?"

He hesitates the briefest moment, and then he's passing me his phone. "One picture."

"Don't worry. I'm *very* good at getting your best side."

He dead-eyes me, and then he cracks up.

And that's what I get.

Davis, laughing over a pirate treasure.

His pirate treasure.

I hand back his phone. He passes the chest out to me, and I *urp* when I take it.

It's heavy.

Not too heavy, but probably at least twenty-five or thirty pounds.

More than I was expecting.

He crawls back out into the main area and then hoists himself out of the hole. "Hand it up?"

I'm holding a pirate treasure.

A hidden, buried, lost, previously undiscovered pirate treasure.

History.

Blood.

The reason I have a hometown that I love now.

My throat clogs, and my eyes get hot.

A warm hand touches my hair. "You good?"

I look up at Davis. "This is kinda monumental."

"You did good."

"*We* did good. I can't believe it's real."

"Are you the kind of person who can take a good *I told you so?*"

I laugh. "Yes."

"I'll tuck that information away for future reference."

I look at the rusty metal box, then back up at Davis. "Are you giving it to Pop?"

"Cooper."

"*Just* Cooper?"

"You should probably call Tillie Jean and Grady. Get them out here too. All three of them should know."

I nod, and then I lift the thing so he can take it.

It feels almost anticlimactic.

We spent almost a week looking, we found it, and now it's over.

You did the thing. Now go back to doing real life.

It's Friday.

Once we take it to Cooper, I could go back to work.

Or go pick up my house.

Or—

Giselle makes a noise, and Davis pauses over me.

453

"Stay here." His voice is quiet again. Tense. "Be right back."

Like I'm going anywhere.

I'm in a hole and I don't exactly have the body strength he does to pull myself out.

Giselle makes another noise.

At least, I think that's Giselle.

"Davis?" I whisper.

No answer.

Just bushes rustling.

And then— "I'll take that, you ugly piece of shit."

Oh my god.

That's Patrick.

That's Patrick.

"No," Davis replies.

It's the *over my dead body* kind of no, which is not at all my favorite.

Probably my least favorite, in fact.

I eyeball one of the shelves, decide there's no way I'm testing my weight on it, and try to jump a little to peer out of the root cellar instead.

Nothing.

"I already took out your bodyguard. You think I can't take you out too? Give me the fucking box."

I shiver at the malice in Patrick's voice.

I shiver again at Davis's repeated, "No."

Shit.

Shit shit shit shit shit.

What did he do to Giselle?

What did he do to Giselle?

I jump a little more, but I still can't see anything.

"Hand. It. Over."

"Where've you been hiding, Dixon? Half the state's looking for you."

I look around the root cellar again.

Shovel.

Metal detector.

That's it.

That's all I have, aside from some—

Some jars.

I grab one, and I pull a raccoon, and I throw it as hard as I can out of the hole.

"They can keep—*Jesus fucking Christ, what the hell was that?*"

So I was close.

I throw another one.

Then a third.

A fourth.

"*Stop fucking throwing things,*" Patrick bellows.

"Go to fucking hell," I yell. "The bad hell. The hell where you'll be butt-plugged by spiny-tailed lizards every day for the rest of your life until you start to enjoy it, and then they switch to stabbing you in the heart and the liver and the spleen until you can't fucking stand it." I keep throwing jars. And yelling. And throwing jars. And yelling. And throwing. Until I realize I'm sobbing and everything is silent overhead.

Eerily silent.

Nothing rustling.

No breathing.

All I can hear is the rush of my own heartbeat in my ears and my sobs.

"I hate you," I yell at Patrick while I go back to throwing all of the jars. My arm hurts. My face hurts. My chest hurts. My head hurts. My heart hurts. "I hate you, and I hate you for making me hate you, and I hope you die miserable and alone after a long, miserable life of knowing you're a useless fucking cuntwaffle. The cunti-est, fuckiest of fucknuggets."

I gasp for breath.

Silence.

There's still silence outside.

Until—

Until there's a creak. A long, slow, creaky *crreeeeeaaaaaakkkkk.*

All falls silent again.

"Davis?" I whisper.

"Right here, love," he murmurs above me.

Above and behind me.

And then the most massive crash I've ever heard in my life erupts somewhere just beyond the opening. Wood splinters. Dust billows in the sky.

I shriek.

Davis blinks at the dust cloud.

"What happened?" I whisper.

"Sloane two, Patrick zero, cabin zero."

"What does that mean?"

"You put one of those jars through the roof of the cabin, and it's—well, you're gonna want to see this for yourself."

The man pauses, and he pulls out his phone, and he snaps a picture of something.

"I killed the cabin?" I breathe.

He grins. "You got it good."

"And Patrick?"

"You got him too."

"I—what?"

"You got him. In the head. With a jar of what might've been pickled beets. A long time ago."

I blink up at the sky and the dust cloud still billowing and bare bush branches and the beanie-headed, bearded man peering down at me between snapping pictures of what I assume is the remnants of his great-great-something-grandfather's cabin.

"Giselle?" I ask.

"Stunned. She'll be okay. Mad as hell, I expect, but okay."

"You?"

"Dodged a jar of what might've been okra and will live to see another day."

"Patrick's accomplice?"

"He's fucking dead if I find him," Giselle growls. Her face pops into view too. "Get the fuck out of there before he shows up and you have to see me do things you don't want to see me do."

"Is Patrick—is he dead?"

Davis smiles. "No. He'll get everything you've wished for him and more."

I sag to the dirt floor. "I really hit him?"

"Three times, actually," Davis says. "First jar knocked him in the shoulder. Another one got him in the knee. That one tripped him, and he rolled over in time to see the jar of maybe beets land right on his forehead."

"So fucking mad I didn't see it." Giselle's seething.

Davis holds out another hand. "C'mon, Sloane. Let's go finish the job."

Finish the job.

Finish our time together.

Move on with our lives.

Me to put mine back together.

Him to—well, to do whatever the mysterious Davis Remington does.

I don't ask if we can stay friends.

I know the answer.

He'll disappear into the night, and that will be that.

An epic tale to tell my—my friends' grandkids one day.

I reach up and take his hand, knowing this won't be the last time—we are still getting fake-married tomorrow because I've earned it, dammit, but this will be close to the last time.

Unless I'm brave.

And unless he is too.

35

Davis

COOPER AND WAVERLY'S security detail wave us through as I steer Giselle's SUV up the next driveway after Beck's place. I left my motorcycle at the trailer with Giselle, who looked like she needed a long ride to work out some issues.

And who promised to not beat the shit out of Patrick Dixon before the authorities arrived to pick him up.

Vanessa didn't promise the same.

She didn't answer my text at all when I messaged to let her know that Patrick was currently hog-tied and secured to a beam under my camper.

Little bloody too.

Pretty sure that's the only time in my life I'll ever see Sloane look an injured man in the eye, tell him she hopes he gets a flesh-eating disease on his penis and scurvy and tetanus and that he has to spend the rest of his days shitting through his belly button, then walk away without treating his wounds.

Giselle knows first aid.

We don't know if she'll give him first aid either, but she knows it.

Sloane technically left him in capable hands.

When I hit the top of Cooper's driveway, I roll my window down and tell the security woman there that I need to park in the garage.

She doesn't blink, and five minutes later, I'm following Sloane through Cooper's laundry room and into his open living area, a box of history and confessions and life-altering details in hand.

Cooper, Waverly, Annika, and Tillie Jean are all chilling in Cooper's four massage chairs. Grady's cutting what looks like grapes and cucumbers. Max is entertaining the two toddlers on a rug in front of the massage chairs.

Ah.

Toddler snack time.

For toddlers with normal appetites.

And probably also for the goat standing outside the back door, staring in forlornly.

It will never not amuse me that Grady has a one-horned pet goat. A male goat. Named Sue.

Truly, no wonder Sloane loves it here so much.

Never dull in Shipwreck.

Tillie Jean spots me first.

Or, rather, she spots the box first.

She tries to pop up out of the massage chair, but it must be in one of those cycles where it's squeezing her legs because she trips and takes a header toward the kids on the rug, legs still attached to the chair.

"*Aack!*"

"No more head injuries!" Sloane shrieks.

It's the first thing she's said since we climbed into the SUV.

And that—even more than what I have to do right now —is what has my heart in a knot.

A knot that I'm refusing to acknowledge.

A knot that tells me she's far more to me than just a partner in a treasure hunt who needs a fake groom tomorrow, and I have to let her go.

I don't want to.

Even telling myself she'll be okay—that she's strong, she's capable, she has all of these people here as family— it's not enough.

I want to be her family.

And I don't know if I'm brave enough to do what I need to do to prove it to her.

"What's that?" Cooper says to me. "What the actual you-know-what is that?"

Waverly opens her eyes and glances at him, then at me. She squeaks.

Tillie Jean straightens, pulls herself out of the massage chair, and she squeaks again too.

"You gonna live?" Max asks her.

"That very much depends on what's inside that box," she replies.

Annika's giving me a one-eyed glare. "I swear on my bladder, if you're about to drop news that's going to make me have to pee—"

"You should probably go pee," Sloane says.

"*Dammit.*"

Grady drops his knife and strolls in from the kitchen, leaning against a column holding up the high ceiling between the two rooms. "Tell me that's not real."

Can't do it. "It's real."

"That's not what I asked you to tell me."

"It's not real." Cooper pulls himself out of his massage chair. "It can't be real."

"Real what?" Waverly asks. "Real treasure? *Real treasure?* No."

"It's real," I repeat.

"It's real," Sloane says. "We found it."

"But you *can't*," Cooper says.

"Why not?" she asks.

"Because *I* found it."

All of us—even the kids—gape at him.

"Excuse you, *what?*" Tillie Jean says.

Sloane takes a step back.

I take a step back.

Grady takes a step back.

Max grins.

Cackles a little, even.

Waverly hits a button to stop the cycle on her massage chair, then she straightens. "You found a treasure and you didn't tell your wife?"

Cooper winces. "I made myself forget. Because the more people who know a secret, the more people who know a secret. So that can't be the treasure. Because the treasure's been…safe…for about ten years now."

Sloane leans against the nearest wall, then slides down

it, ending with her legs splayed in front of her. "Oh my god, second treasure."

"Second treasure when *there is no treasure?*" Tillie Jean says. "Give me the chair back. I need to sit down. And then murder my brother for lying to all of us. And then sit down again."

Sloane shakes her head. "No more murder. Today."

"Did you murder someone?"

"Patrick. Almost. But I wasn't looking where I was throwing so it wouldn't be first-degree. Probably even count as self-defense, actually. And he's still alive. And likely has a concussion. Serves the fucker right."

"Fucker?" Tillie Jean's daughter says.

Nobody blinks an eye.

At the kid cussing, anyway. They're still alternating staring at me and Cooper.

"How is there a second treasure when there's not even supposed to be a first?" Annika asks.

I study Cooper.

He stares back at me, and again—he's not amused.

"You know, don't you?" I say.

"How the fuck do you know?" he replies.

I set the treasure down and roll my right sleeve up.

Point to the pirate flag tattoo between the tattoo of Copper Valley's famous fountain in Reynolds Park and the tiger I got in honor of a dream I had once. "You're not the only family with pirate blood in the area."

Tillie Jean squeaks again.

"Where'd you find yours?" I ask.

"Hidden in the walls of one of the cabins up here that I

bought when I started buying everything on the mountain."

Sloane pumps a fist in the air. "I told you it would be in the walls!"

I smile at her. "You did. And you were right."

"Now I'm disappointed we didn't find ours in a toilet."

"Where'd you find yours?" Cooper asks.

"Root cellar on some property that belonged to my great-something-grandfather."

Cooper winces.

I stay straight-faced.

The kind of straight-faced I'm very, very good at.

As Sloane has observed. And mocked me for. Hilariously.

Fuck, I'm going to miss her.

Grady's frowning at me, but he's sharing that frown with Cooper. "What's going on here?"

Sloane sucks in a big breath and says what I should but haven't been able to. "Thorny Rock and Walter Bombeck exchanged identities when they left Norfolk to come inland. The real Thorny founded Sarcasm. The real Walter founded Shipwreck. And if they both had part of the treasure, then the towns probably fight because they each spent their entire lives trying to steal back what they split with the other."

"Yep." Annika's voice is a little hollow as she dances out of her chair and toward the kitchen. "I definitely have to pee. Quit talking until I'm back."

Tillie Jean looks at Cooper. "Tell me that's wrong."

He winces again.

"Now that I've said that out loud, I'm forgetting I ever knew it and never repeating it again," Sloane says.

"I'm peeing with the door open so I can hear all of you," Annika calls from beyond the kitchen. "Don't come back here unless you're my husband."

Tillie Jean's still shaking her head. "That cannot be real. This isn't real—*oh my god, that's real.*"

She gapes at the chest that I've just opened.

Max grabs both toddlers, who've seen toys and want some.

Waverly gapes at all of us.

"It's fucking real," Grady mutters.

"Apparently the second fucking real one," Sloane says.

"Where'd you find it again?" Waverly asks.

"How'd you find it?" Cooper asks.

"What are you going to do with it?" Tillie Jean asks.

"All yours," I tell her. "Mayor of Shipwreck should have it. Do what you want with it." I reach into my coat and pull out the journal that Uncle Guido gave us, and the journal that we reclaimed from Patrick before leaving him with Giselle—the journal that Pop's been hiding—and offer them to her. "These too. And I'll get you everything my family has. I don't want it. I like Shipwreck as it is. Up to you to decide if you want the world to know what you know now."

Annika returns from the bathroom and glances at Grady.

"Don't hate each other now," Sloane whispers to them.

Grady slips an arm around his wife and kisses her forehead. "Who needs gold when you have love?"

"Fuck the treasure bullshit," Annika agrees.

"Fuck da booshee," her son says. "I have tesh-shure??"

"I have tesh-sha!" Tillie Jean and Max's little girl says.

"I can't believe you've known it was real for *ten years*," Tillie Jean says to Cooper.

He holds his hands up. "Look, I can be a dumbass, but even I know the first rule of finding treasure and a diary that tells you your entire heritage is bullshit is that you don't talk about finding a treasure and a diary that tells you your entire heritage is bullshit. I even went to a hypnotist and tried to have them erase my memory so I wouldn't know. But I never thought there'd be two of them. I thought Davis knew I found the only one and he figured out where I hid it."

"Where *did* you hide it?"

"Safe-deposit box in DC at first, but now it's behind a secret door in Waverly's secret second wine cellar in LA."

Tillie Jean gasps and looks at Waverly. "*You have a secret second wine cellar?*"

Sloane giggles.

Fuck me, I love that giggle.

"Clearly the most important detail, TJ," Grady mutters.

"Actually, she has a point," Annika chimes in. "Or she will. When I'm not pregnant anymore. Waverly picks the best wine."

"It's a gift," Waverly says. "Much like Cooper funding the Unicorn Festival since he knew his family benefited from everyone believing he was a descendant of the real Thorny Rock?"

Cooper Rock, the most shameless person I've ever met in my entire life—turns red.

Tillie Jean's about to gasp herself out.

And Annika—Annika bursts into tears. "Dammit, Cooper, I hate it when I appreciate you."

I glance at Max, who's been quiet through all of this.

He just nods at me. "Like your thinking."

"Are you sure you want to give the whole treasure to the family?" Waverly asks. "I mean, I know you're giving it to Tillie Jean, but we all know when you give a treasure to one Rock, you're kinda giving it to all of them."

"It's baggage," I tell her. "Not interested in baggage."

She looks at Sloane. "Do you want it?"

"My house was robbed, my ex-boyfriend attacked my favorite protection specialist, and I had to face some guy named Uncle Guido in the name of finding this treasure. I'll go to therapy for the memories. You keep the gold."

"Are they *all* bad memories?" Tillie Jean asks.

Sloane goes pink. "No."

"Good."

Cooper kneels in front of the chest and picks up one of the gold pieces under the third diary. "It's identical. You're right. They must've split it."

Grady shakes his head and pulls Annika over with him to look at it too. "Two treasures. Pirate nutjobs."

"We'll announce it's been found and put some on display in the museum," Tillie Jean says.

"Tell people it was found at the waterfall," Sloane says. "Don't tell them where it was really found. If you can."

"Will Patrick know the truth?"

"Patrick has a concussion," Sloane reminds her.

Tillie Jean grins.

Sloane grins back. "Courtesy of me," she whispers.

I hold out a hand.

She high-fives me, then looks at the room at large. "You didn't see that."

"This morning isn't happening," Max says. "It's all a figment of everyone's imaginations."

We all look at the two toddlers.

Could be their first lasting memory.

More likely, they won't remember any of it.

"I can't tell my mama and Roger, can I?" Annika says.

Tillie Jean hugs her. "We'll figure it out."

"They already know," Sloane says. "If not, they strongly suspect. They told me things while you were in the bathroom."

"Freaking bathroom," Annika mutters. "I miss everything when I'm in the bathroom."

"We good?" I ask Cooper and Tillie Jean.

Cooper nods. "Always, man. Can't be mad at someone who saved my lucky socks for me all those years ago."

Shit.

Forgot I did that.

"That was gross," I tell him.

"And they weren't actually his real superstition," Waverly says with a grin.

"I, unfortunately, am also now aware of that." I look at Tillie Jean again. "Last chance to ask questions before I forget this ever happened."

She slides a look at Sloane, then back to me. "Will it be the last time I ever see you?"

"No."

"Okay then. Sloane? You okay?"

"She hasn't had coffee," I tell Tillie Jean.

"On it." Cooper jumps back up. "I make the best coffee."

"He really does," Waverly agrees. "Maybe when we're both retired, he'll take over the Muted Parrot."

"This looks worse than *she hasn't had coffee*," Tillie Jean says.

Sloane pulls her knees to her chest and drops her head to them. "Adrenaline crash."

"Been there. Usually after Long Beak Silver makes me fall off a roof." Tillie Jean smiles at her. "You wanna hang out for a while? Official historical society secret business? Or we can take you back to Beck's. Peggy's still at the pool house, right?"

"I want—" Sloane pauses.

Her eyes go shiny.

She darts a look at me, then glances down again.

I want to go home.

That's what she was about to say.

And now I'm feeling myself go ruddy in the cheeks. "I can take you. It's…clean."

She lifts her gaze to me again.

Does one slow blink.

"Your house." Shit. My voice is getting husky. "It's clean. I had a crew come in. They took inventory of everything broken. Replaced what they could. Probably put a few things back wrong in the kitchen, but it's clean."

"When did you have time to do that?"

"Doesn't take much time when you know who to call."

"My house is… It's normal?"

"As normal as they could make it."

"And Patrick's behind bars?"

I check my phone, find a message from Giselle confirming the sheriff has pulled away with him, and I nod to her. "Yep."

Her eyes get shinier. "Thank you."

"Least I could do."

She visibly swallows.

Glances at her friends, who are all watching us entirely too closely with smiles that are entirely too big.

Then back at me. "I'll stay and answer any more questions the mayor has for us. You can...do what you need to do."

Offer to stay. Offer to stay. Offer to stay.

I nod. "Okay. See you tomorrow then. I'll bring rings. Let me know if you need anything else."

She purses her lips together and nods back. "Thank you."

"Anytime."

Cooper interrupts the moment by grinding coffee beans.

Fucker.

I glance around again, and this time, no one's smiling at me.

So I do what I always do.

I leave.

I'll see her tomorrow. We can talk tomorrow.

When everything's calm.

Without an audience.

If I can find my fucking balls and be brave.

36

Sloane

MY HOUSE IS SPOTLESS.

Cleaner than it's ever been, and while I'm far from the messiest person on the planet, I'm also not a neat freak.

But it's nice.

It smells nice.

Like pine and s'mores.

Like Davis himself found time to walk through my house, making sure it was put back together right, leaving behind his scent so I'd know he was here.

Or possibly the cleaning crew used Lysol.

Who knows?

"I'll fix your painting," Tillie Jean says to me as she and Max escort me through, all of us making sure the house is empty from the attic to the basement and everywhere in between. "I saw pictures of what happened. Or I'll make you a new one."

"No rush. And thank you. And seriously, no rush. Not like... cleaning up was a rush."

The crew Davis hired did, indeed, leave a list of what they suspected to be missing and what was clearly broken so that I can submit it to my insurance company.

Except I don't need to.

Davis paid to replace almost all of it himself.

Not that he'd tell me that.

But why else would the broken vase that was scattered on my floor a few days ago now be intact with fall flowers in it on my entryway table? Why else would the television that was cracked be brand new? Why else would I have more glasses and plates than I did when I last slept in my house?

Davis did it.

He fixed it for me. He replaced everything he could for me.

No doubt. No question. And if he didn't do it, he was heavily involved.

"Are you breaking your no-dating rule?" Tillie Jean whispers to me.

I shake my head.

"Are you sure?"

"You can't date someone without them wanting to date you back."

"Do you believe him when he says he'll still show up for your wedding tomorrow?"

"Yes." I think.

"Will you?"

I half laugh, and it almost turns into a sob. "Yes."

"Nigel's been in town a few more times, but Chester's chased him away every time. He started using the stalking words, and apparently even Nigel's smart enough to understand you can't get away with that shit here. You want us to hang out a while?"

"Yes." I freeze.

That was too fast.

"I mean, not if you have other things to do. And it's obvious you have a lot to do. Mayor duties just got mayorier for you. Sorry. And you're welcome. And sorry. *Oh my god*, what did Cooper put in that coffee?"

"Lack of sleep and adrenaline crash powder." Tillie Jean hugs me. "We'll hang out. Look. Max is already using your couch. *Oooh*, when did you get all of the streaming services? I thought you only had two. Now you can watch 'In The Weeds' and get caught up so we can talk about how terrible it is and why people might like it so much."

I blink at the screen.

And then it gets blurry.

Because I definitely didn't pay for those.

Which means someone else likely did.

"I hate men," I whisper to Tillie Jean. Then my eyes fly wide, and I peer around her to Max. "But not you. You're...fine."

I wince.

TJ laughs.

Max takes it all in stride with a smile.

He has to, I suppose, if he's truly happy with Tillie Jean, and I'm sure he is.

You can tell by the way he looks at her.

And he doesn't go around town telling people all of her little faults that annoy him or the things that he thinks she can do better. He went around town while she was running for mayor telling everyone all the good things she'd do for Shipwreck if she was elected. He brags about her paintings. Every time she does something very Tillie-Jean-ish, he smiles, shakes his head, calls her *Trouble Jean*, which makes her smile wider, and then he quietly finds a way to help her.

They don't have a nanny because he's stay-at-home-dadding with Rosie while TJ's doing her mayor duties, though Rosie's hanging out with Grady and Annika and Miles right now.

The last time I was at their house, he was making dinner.

And the Tillie Jean I know today shines brighter than the Tillie Jean I knew when I moved here, which is saying something.

Good men exist.

And I will never have one.

Even if I've found the one I'd want if I were willing to take one more chance.

TJ and Max and I watch TV together for a few hours.

Grady and Annika show up with the kids, and we all watch more TV—the kid-friendly kind this round—and eat the pizza they've brought from Anchovies, the local Rock-family-owned pizza place.

And eventually, they leave.

And Peggy and I are all alone.

In my house.

"I'm safe here," I say in the stillness.

The heater kicks on, and I jump.

The fridge kicks on, and I jump again.

I still have the number Davis gave me. I could text him. Ask him if he'd come over. Just once. Just this last time.

Before we get fake-married tomorrow.

Giselle's officiating.

I'm wearing a pink dress.

Tillie Jean and Annika are re-wearing their bridesmaid dresses from last week's wedding.

Some of the Bro Code guys might show up.

TJ confirmed that the winery's ready, and Grady reported that his afternoon baker has all of our wedding cookies ready to go.

And also that he had no intention of putting together a bill for them, but someone left a tip in his tip jar that would've covered three times as many cookies.

The three Rock siblings still have to figure out what to say to who about the treasure and the real history of Shipwreck and Sarcasm, but they'll get there.

Hard to expect them to immediately know what to do after this many years of believing one thing about their heritage, only to be presented with evidence that it's a two-hundred-plus-year-old lie.

I look around my living room again.

Repeat out loud that I'm safe.

That I can go to bed.

That all is well.

And then I flip the TV back on.

Peggy gives me the stink eye.

And finally, well after midnight, which is entirely too late after the week I've had, when I've streamed as much of "In The Weeds" as I can stomach for one night—this was a terrible choice, it really was—I make myself turn off the television, then turn off my lights like I always do.

I make myself prep my coffee for morning with an upgraded version of my coffeepot and a fresh, unopened bag of my favorite beans from the Muted Parrot that I find in the kitchen.

I triple-check that the new house alarm is set with the instructions that were left for me. And it's the same style alarm that Cooper has, and that Max insisted he and Tillie Jean get when they moved back to Shipwreck for his peace of mind, so I had plenty of help before my friends left with fully understanding the whole thing.

I wash my face with a new bottle of face wash and brush my teeth with a new tube of toothpaste and a new toothbrush head on my new electric toothbrush.

All laid out for me on my sink by someone who would've known I'd want to know they were fresh and new.

And then I flip off the bathroom light. I climb into bed, check the nightstand drawer, find my toy collection basically accounted for, and shut off the lamp.

I pick a vibrator at random in the dark and slip it between my thighs while memory after memory of Davis fills my mind.

Davis kissing my head in his camper when I had a nightmare about Patrick and Nigel.

Davis making popcorn for me.

Davis asking me how I like to touch myself.

THE PRETEND FIANCÉ FIASCO

Davis taking the lamp from me that I was going to use as a weapon to defend us against Giselle before I knew who she was.

Davis stretching during the treasure hunt at the waterfall, his shirt lifting just enough to show off a strip of tattoos on his lean stomach.

Davis being frustrated.

Davis smiling.

Davis fucking me against the bathroom wall.

Davis kissing me.

I come in a flash of pleasure that's nowhere near as satisfying as I want it to be.

Just text him, dumbass, I tell myself after I've put my vibrator away.

I'm going to sleep, I reply to myself.

Except I don't.

I lie there.

And I lie there.

And I lie there.

And I stare at the ceiling.

I toss and turn.

I try counting sheep.

I try naming every body part alphabetically.

And I guess I eventually doze off, because eventually, my eyes drift open.

And that's when I see it.

Them.

Two people.

In my doorway.

Two more goddamn people in my goddamn fucking doorway.

I don't know if anger or fear drives me.

I don't know if this is real.

But I lunge for the nightstand drawer, grab the first dildo I can get my hands on, and I throw it at the figures with all my might while I scream at the top of my lungs.

37

Davis

I'M NOT SUPPOSED to be asleep, but apparently I am, because I jolt awake when the passenger door of my truck slams shut next to me.

I jerk straight in the driver's seat, then twist and pull my arm back, ready to—

"Fuck. It's you."

My sister merely lifts a brow at me, completely unconcerned that I was actually going to hit her.

Or, more likely, fully ready to duck and defend herself since she'd know this is how I'd wake up when I fall asleep on guard duty.

Morning's coming soon.

I glance across the street at Sloane's house.

All quiet.

"Patrick's not talking about his accomplice," she says.

I scrub a hand over my face, then glance at my watch.

Four in the morning.

Roughly eight hours until I pretend-marry Sloane.

Eight hours to get my courage together to ask if I can see her again. Take her to the movies. Cook dinner for her at my place.

I shake my head. *Focus.* "They still interrogating him?"

"I don't think that's the question you need to be asking yourself."

I suck in a frustrated breath, knowing where she's going.

And it's exactly where my head's at.

How am I going to ask Sloane out on a date?

"Can a guy have a few days to recover and think?" I ask her.

"Not what I meant. Your girl has visitors."

I stare at her, then past her, and then—

Fuck me.

Sloane's screaming.

I'm out of my truck and across the street like my feet are made of lightning.

Silent alarm. There's a silent alarm.

Sheriff will be notified.

I barely verify the alarm panel is flashing with the silent alarm as I burst inside.

After that, I follow the noise.

The light in the bedroom.

"Grandma? What the actual fuck are you doing?"

And that stops me almost as effectively as the cat stepping into my path.

"I'm doing what I should've done years ago, and I'm taking you home," a familiar-ish voice replies. Granny

THE PRETEND FIANCÉ FIASCO

Gaslighter. That's who it is. Standing there in Sloane's bedroom doorway. "Nigel. Pick her up. It's time."

"Get the fuck out of my bedroom."

Someone moans.

There's a large figure bent double, groaning.

Sloane's largest dildo is on the floor next to him.

Peggy meows at me.

I slow and bend to pick her up. Not sure I shut the front door. Don't want to let the cat out.

"Put those things down and get off the bed," Granny Gaslighter says. "Nigel, stand up and *go get her*."

Nigel's panting. "She'll come—willingly, Bernice. We— don't need—to kidnap—her."

"That's exactly what we need to do. Listen to her language. And look at those—things—she's holding. She needs to come home and find her soul again."

I suck air in, willing my heart to quit beating quite so fast, and I silently creep the rest of the way down the short hallway to the bedroom.

One word—one look—one signal of any kind—and I will set the cat down and take both of these mother-fuckers out.

Gently with Grandma.

Less so with Nigel.

Though, clearly, Sloane's already half taken him out herself.

That's my girl.

I spot her standing on her bed wearing nothing but a Shipwreck Pirate Festival T-shirt and tiny pink panties, holding dildos in each hand. "*My* language? Do you know how bad Nigel's language is? And you never correct him for it? I am *so sick* of your hypocrisy. Also—I. Am. Not. Going. With. You."

Her grandmother sniffs. "Nonsense. Get dressed and throw those obscene objects away. We're leaving."

"I'm. Getting. Married. Today."

"Over my dead body."

"Well, you're fucking old, so that might happen," Sloane snaps.

I suck in a smile as her eyes meet mine.

Her shoulders dip.

Her grip on the dildos wavers.

She blinks twice, eyes going soft and shiny, and then she's glaring again.

"Nigel. Your private parts can recover later. Be more useful than that other one and pick her up," the old lady orders.

"Over *my* dead body," I growl softly.

Grandma screams.

Nigel screams.

Peggy yowls and hisses and shoots out of my arms, dashing to the bathroom.

I step forward, pushing Granny Gaslighter into Sloane's bedroom. "What do you mean, *the other one?*"

Nigel moves like he's trying to get over the pain in his private parts.

I hold one hand up, and he freezes. "Take one step toward me and Sloane's gonna give you a concussion with one of those dildos next. Don't test her arm. She's gotten fucking good playing softball the past few years."

"Who do you think you are, issuing orders?" Granny Gaslighter says to me.

She's taller than I expected. Almost as tall as Sloane.

Has the same blue eyes, but Granny's are snappy where Sloane's are kind.

"He's my friend, and he's welcome here, and you're not," Sloane says.

Red and blue lights flash against the wall.

Her breath audibly catches.

"You're not marrying my granddaughter today, you sheep-lover," Granny Gaslighter says.

"You're right, he's not," Sloane says. "We're not getting married. I told you we were and he was kind enough to go along with it because I was *so fucking tired* of your absolute bullshit attitudes, thinking you know me better than I know myself, that I can't possibly know that I'm so much goddamn happier thousands of miles away from you."

It should be the best thing I've heard all week.

It is.

But I still freeze, my body flashing hot and cold at the same time.

She doesn't need me anymore.

It's both the most beautiful and the most terrifying thought I've ever had in my life.

She doesn't need me.

She's strong.

She's capable.

This week—it's changed her. And with the right people in her life, ultimately, it'll be for the better.

And she has those people.

She has Tillie Jean and Max. Annika and Grady. Cooper and Waverly. Their parents. Pop and Nana. The bartender at the Grog. Doc. Her patients.

Beck and Sarah.

Sloane's voice wobbles as she continues, but I don't think it's sadness.

I think it's fury.

All aimed at her grandmother.

"Thank you for putting your life on hold to raise me and Aiden. Thank you for what you sacrificed. But you know what? *I didn't ask for that either.* So *stop fucking blaming me*, and *stop fucking trying to run my life.*"

"Enough! That's no way to talk to your elders."

"And that attitude is exactly why I don't want to talk to you at all."

Nigel breathes wrong.

I look at him.

He resumes breathing appropriately without looking like he might fully straighten to take a swing at me.

"Davis?" Sloane says.

"Yes?"

"Please remove them from my house."

I start to answer, but before I can, a stout, furry body pushes past me. "*Maaaaaaaa,*" it yells.

Granny Gaslighter shrieks.

And Sue the goat leads a charge of six other goats into Sloane's bedroom, all of them bleating and snorting and circling the old lady.

"Make it stop!" she yells.

"Sheriff's office, everyone freeze," Chester calls. "We're on our way, Sloane. Somebody finally let the goats back out, and I can't—we're coming! We really are!"

"Back, Satan's handmaidens," Granny Gaslighter shouts.

"Sue, eat her purse," Sloane orders.

Sue's easy to pick out. He's been Grady's pet for as long as Sloane's been in Shipwreck, and he's missing one of his horns.

"Why are you doing this to me?" Granny Gaslighter cries while the goats back her against the wall.

"Because you're a fucking evil old lady and you deserve it," Sloane yells back.

Nigel straightens.

Sloane fires another dildo at him.

He makes a gargled noise and drops, grabbing his chest, and one of the goats backs into him and shits in his lap.

"We're here," Chester says. "We're here. We—*Ahhh! What happened to your beautiful hair?*"

He's staring at me.

Beanie must've fallen off in the car.

Fabulous.

Except I don't really care.

"Get the fucking goats out of my *newly cleaned bedroom* and arrest them, please, Chester," Sloane says. "And once again, yes, I'd like to press charges, and can this please be for the very *fucking last time?*"

"Sloane?" Tillie Jean calls. "Are you in here?"

"My grandmother's trying to kidnap me with Nigel's help and I just called off my wedding because fuck the whole fucking world," Sloane calls back.

Her breath catches.

"You are *not* arresting me," Granny Gaslighter says. "I'm old."

I stride through the goats, grab her purse, and toss it to

485

the other deputy now standing in the bedroom doorway. "The goats want whatever's in here."

Sure enough, they turn and charge him.

He dashes down the hall, and they follow.

Probably chasing candies.

I look at Chester and jerk a hand at Granny Gaslighter, who's gripping her chest like she's thinking of faking a heart attack.

As if any of us will fall for that.

Have to have a heart for it to have an attack.

"She's Dixon's accomplice," I tell Chester. "I'd bet my biological weapon on it."

Sloane chokes.

Not sure if that's a laugh or a sob.

Maybe both.

I step around her grandmother and Nigel and head to her on the bed.

Take one dildo from her.

Then another that she must've grabbed after throwing the second one.

Pull her off the bed.

Into my arms.

"How did you get here so fast?" she says on a gasp.

"Right outside. All night."

I know this sound.

This one's definitely a sob.

"If I'd gotten here before Chester, there'd be bodies on the floor," Tillie Jean says as she wraps her arms around both of us, which isn't as odd and uncomfortable as it should be to have someone outside my circle hugging me too. "You're not staying here alone for the next month. My family's taking turns."

I'll stay with her.

It's all I have to say.

I've got her. I'll keep her safe.

Sloane squeezes me tighter like she wants me to say it too.

But the words are stuck in my chest.

She's the one.

She's my all-or-nothing.

She's the only woman I'll be with for the rest of my life, or she's the reason I will never, ever, for all eternity, have companionship again.

"I almost killed a man," I whisper. "That's what happened in Denver. That's why Bro Code broke up. Because of me. It's my fault."

Sloane squeezes harder.

So does Tillie Jean.

Tillie Jean.

Fuuuuuuck.

Just as quickly as she's squeezing me harder, she lets me go. "Chester. Get these assholes out of here."

"Excuse you, *I am an old lady, not an a*—not what you called me."

"You're an asshole," Sloane says into my chest, still squeezing the hell out of me while my heart tries to claw its way through my ribs. "Nigel, you're a bigger one. Come back here again, and I will self-defense you into your grave."

"*Out,*" Tillie Jean repeats. "You've got them both in cuffs. Quit hoping for a peep show and *get out.*"

Granny Gaslighter keeps yelling. Nigel arrogantly insists that he can't be charged for assisting an old lady, that he was trying to stop her and his balls were caught in the crossfire.

And Sloane keeps holding me tighter and tighter.

Which is good.

I think I might fall apart if she lets go.

"Cat's safe and sound in the living room and I'm closing the door," Tillie Jean calls. "Alarm's set again too."

The door clicks shut.

The alarm beeps.

And Sloane keeps her grip on me. "Tell me more," she whispers.

So I do.

I tell her everything.

All of it.

Nothing held back.

"I was breaking. Being on the road. The fame. The attention. Limitless money to try to ease the anxiety. Too much time too. Started playing a game—I hacked into the AV system everywhere we went. Harmless at first. I'd play that dancing hippo that was like the first meme on the internet. Put the videos up on the scoreboards while the crew was setting up. Did it at every stadium, every arena, but people assumed it was one of our roadies taking over the sound and video systems, or people who heard it happened and wanted to be the next to do it. Nobody suspected me. So I started doing darker and darker and darker shit. Started trying to hack local banks. Local police stations. Prove I could. I'd shut the lights out entirely in arenas and put it in straight darkness while our roadies were setting up."

She presses a kiss to my chest, and my breath shudders out of me.

Spent six years singing my lungs out on a stage. I can run a marathon. I can swim for miles.

And I can barely breathe right now.

But she kisses my chest again, and it gets easier to find my breath.

"There was a guy on the crew. Terrified of horror movies. I knew it. We landed in Denver. They were setting up. And I—I put on *The Exorcist*. He was on the lights. Up about twenty feet. Scared him so badly, he—he fell. Landed on his shoulder. Broke it. Wasn't tethered right. If he'd landed four inches to the left, he would've—"

I shudder, still picturing the thing that's haunted me for fifteen years.

Four inches to the left and his head would've hit the corner of a platform.

He would've been dead.

The imaginary blood that wasn't there haunted me every night for the first two years after the band broke up.

That's the part I still can't say out loud.

"But he didn't," she whispers, like she knows.

Of course she knows.

She worked in an emergency room. She knows it can always get worse. She's seen worse.

"We paid all of his medical bills. Set his kids up for college. Him for retirement. He kept blaming himself for not tethering right, but—it was me. It was my fault. Tripp knew it. He was always the dad. He called it. Took one look at me, one look at my computer, and it was over. He smashed the computer. Only time I've ever seen him do anything remotely violent, and it wasn't enough. Beck knew. Levi knew. Cash—he was half hot mess, but he knew too. And we all just—we did what we needed to do. Moved on how we needed to move on. And I don't—I don't tell people because how the fuck do you trust people when your own flesh and blood are the people who betray you? And the guys who have everything to gain from spilling your secrets are the only ones who protect you? The guys who'd go down with you for being accomplices when they didn't fucking do it. How do you find people who'll do that for you?"

My cheeks are wet. Eyes too.

I can't catch my breath.

Can't find it.

It's gone.

Sloane sucks in a breath, and I follow.

There. There's my oxygen.

She sucks in another breath, and I find more air.

"My tattoo. Three triangles and a coin. Mountains. Money. Problems. Change. That's what it means. Behind me where I'm most vulnerable. Because it's—it's what can break me."

"I won't let it."

"Don't tell," I force out.

"You're safe," she whispers back. "You're safe here."

"I haven't—no one else—"

"Shh. Breathe. No one else will ever know unless you want them to." She strokes my back and breathes for me.

When I should be breathing for her.

My body quakes.

I need to be strong for her.

Fucking assholes invaded her safe space again.

And she's here holding me.

Telling me I'm okay.

"The first step," she whispers, "is accepting that you're human. And you are. A very good human, but still human."

"I should be doing this for you."

"The next step is accepting that there are people who love you for exactly who you are. All of you. The good and the bad and the neutral. And there are, Davis. There are people who love you."

Love me. Love me, Sloane.

Another breath shudders out of me.

"You're worthy," she murmurs. "You're a good person. You take care of your friends. You take care of strangers. You took care of me."

I squeeze her tighter.

I shouldn't, but I can't help myself. I need—I need to be closer.

I need to believe her.

"That's why I've married random women." I suck in another breath, realize I can't breathe because of how tight I'm squeezing her, and relax just enough to reach for a little more oxygen. "Balance the scales. Do more good than harm. Right the world's wrongs."

She strokes my hair. "I don't want to marry you, but I would very much like to date you. Under normal circumstances. Where I don't have to press charges against people every time I turn around and no one's

491

breaking into my house and we're not on a treasure hunt."

Say yes. Say yes. Say yes.

Take the win.

Get the girl.

"Sloane. I'm...I'm untethered. Right now. No purpose. No goal. And I—this is when I hurt people. I don't want to hurt you. I don't ever want to hurt you. Especially you."

"Then let me help you find your way."

I know people aren't perfect.

But she is.

Right now, she's absolutely fucking perfect.

"You deserve—" I start, but she cuts me off with a huff.

"Do *not* tell me what I deserve. I *know* what I deserve. I deserve what we all deserve. Safety. Friends. Happiness. Love. And you do too. I would—god, Davis. I would go to the ends of the earth for you, and I know better. *I know better.* But over and over and over—you're the good guy."

"I'm not."

"*You fucking are.* Let yourself be the good guy. Let yourself be happy. And if that can't be with me—fine. Just tell me. Kinda been through worse. But I'm here. I want to take a chance. With you. Even if it crashes and burns. I want to know if any of this was real. I want to know I tried. I want to know if you're the good man you've shown me this week. I want to know *you.* Your stories and your history and your motivations and your weaknesses. And I don't want to want you, but I can't help myself. Not if—not if this is the real you."

I don't know if she's squeezing me harder than I'm squeezing her, but I know I can't let go.

I need to.

Just to break the spell.

The spell where I think she's right.

That we could—that we could do this.

That I could date her.

Take her to that movie. Have dinner together at the Grog. Come home with her.

Take her to my house.

I've never taken a woman to any of the houses I own.

Vanessa hasn't even been in all of them. Mom either.

But I want Sloane there.

I want to show Sloane everything.

"Can we go slow?" I ask her hair.

Her sweet cinnamon hair. On the strongest, bravest, kindest woman I've ever had the privilege of knowing.

"As slow as we both need."

"I don't want to hurt you."

"My own grandmother just tried to kidnap me. You'd have to try pretty hard to hurt me."

I kiss her hair.

Her forehead.

Her cheek.

And then I'm kissing her lips, those delicious, plump lips, tasting that sweet mouth, and I know.

I'm home.

I'm where I belong.

I'm where I'm loved. And where I will try ten times—a hundred times—a million times harder to love this woman than anyone else has ever tried to hurt her.

She's my beginning and my end.

Fuck the gold.

Sloane—she's the only treasure I will ever want again.

38

Sloane

By the next Saturday, I almost feel human again.

Davis has been in and out of town, with me when he's here, texting when he's not.

With his real phone number. The one that goes straight to his real phone. Not whatever backup system he has in place for less important people.

And yes, that's what he called them.

My grandmother posted bail and flew home to Iowa. I agreed to not press charges provided she never set foot in Shipwreck again, which was truly letting her off light, but she's old.

Old, and in cahoots with Patrick.

Davis was right about that. Grandma was his secret accomplice, feeding him information about me and egging him on.

Once Aiden moved away, she was lonely and scared

about who'd take care of her as she aged. Naturally, I was the only person in consideration, since I "owed" her. But she realized I wouldn't return on my own when I was still as excited as ever about Shipwreck after the museum opened.

Apparently she thought I'd get bored when the project was done, completely give up on the life I'd built here, and go running back to Two Twigs.

When I didn't, she decided it was time for a more active tactic and got in touch with her favorite of my ex-boyfriends. She thought Patrick could do no wrong. Not only was he the first boyfriend I ever brought home after moving away, but he went to church on Christmas and made enough money to support me if we had four or five kids. He'd recently discovered his own history with Thorny Rock and Walter Bombeck and the treasure, and the two of them realized they could both benefit from Patrick getting close to me again.

Grandma was stupid enough to believe Patrick when he promised he'd bring me home to Two Twigs, but also thrilled with the idea that Patrick could ruin Shipwreck for me if he found proof that Thorny Rock and Walter Bombeck had switched identities when they came inland.

Patrick was weirdly susceptible to my grandmother's guilt and manipulation.

Except Patrick was slower than Grandma had anticipated he'd be—likely because he wanted to find the treasure first as both a way to destroy Shipwreck for himself, since he'd never been welcomed back since the wedding where I dumped him, but also as a warped kind of grand gesture to win me back—so Grandma sent Nigel to do what Patrick was taking too long to do.

Nigel wasn't her first choice of men to marry me and drag me back to Two Twigs—she didn't like that I'd be poor if I married a preacher—but she was willing to settle for me settling for Nigel, and also hoping having competition would make Patrick focus back on the plan to win me back.

Nigel posted bail and flew home to Iowa last weekend too. Same deal—no charges provided he never sets foot in Shipwreck again—though I made sure the Two Twigs paper posted a notice that he'd been arrested for breaking into a woman's home.

Do I feel bad that he's likely lost his job?

No.

Pretty sure he sucked at it if the way he treated me was any indication of how he interacts with other people at large.

Patrick has not posted bail and will not be posting bail.

I asked Davis if Levi Wilson had something to do with that, and got a very honest *I haven't asked him because I don't need to know.* But Davis did say it's likely. Levi wasn't happy when he heard what Patrick did to his lead security person.

I like Levi.

He and Ingrid stayed with me at Beck's house one night this past week when I didn't want to stay at home and Beck and Sarah had returned to the city and Davis was handling something with selling his house in Corieville, closer to the Virginia-North Carolina border where he's lived for most of the past ten years.

And he was already selling the house before me since he quit his job to move into a trailer while he looked for the treasure.

So everyone has assured me.

And every time they say it, they can't quite help the wince in their faces or voices.

Which means they've all also added *it's best when Davis has a mission.*

And I think I get it now, so I've nodded every time.

He could go back to work at the reactor, but he says that part of his life is over. So he's looking at college classes.

I stayed at Pop and Nana's house one night too.

Not Monday night.

No risking Tuesday shower sex day.

But I stayed with them Wednesday night, and Pop and I had a long talk about how I won't be spilling the beans, but he owes it to his grandchildren to tell them what he knows so they can make the most informed decision about what to release to the public.

The rest of the nights, I was either at Davis's camper with him, or at Beck and Sarah's pool house with Davis, or staying at Grady and Annika's house with Davis because I fell asleep on their couch and no one wanted to move me.

Tillie Jean brought me lunch one afternoon and told me she'd heard nothing in my bedroom the night Grandma tried to kidnap me, and that even the threat of having to watch her own grandparents having sex in the shower on a Tuesday wasn't enough to drag out of her what she didn't hear.

Davis's secret is safe with her. She doesn't know the details, and the details matter.

I worked all week.

Every single patient old enough to talk and comprehend the words asked if I was dating *the lost Bro Code guy*. If they weren't old enough to talk and comprehend the words, their parents asked for them.

And I told every last one of them that yes, he'd taken me to dinner a time or two, and yes, we were seeing where a real relationship should go.

No one in town believed we were actually engaged, but they all were willing to keep up the ruse because they knew I had to have a good reason for it.

And because it was fun.

I've never loved my adopted hometown more.

But I let Tillie Jean and Annika drag me away from it on Saturday.

"Girls' night," Tillie Jean said very sternly to Davis when he asked yesterday if he could come too.

He rolled his eyes.

She rolled her eyes and stuck out her tongue back. "We're being *normal*," she told him. "Normal is girls' nights for amazing concerts in the city every once in a while."

And now the three of us are sitting inside Mink Arena, waiting for Aspen to take the stage, a full week after I was supposed to fake-marry Davis after the craziest week of my life before that.

"Why can't concerts start earlier?" I mutter to Annika while Tillie Jean's taking pictures of the stage after the opening act.

"Oh my god, right?" she says on a yawn.

Tillie Jean taps my leg. "You guys. Wake up. Waverly says this is the best show on the planet, and she didn't get us front-row seats for us to yawn through it."

"Couldn't Waverly have gotten the time moved up?" Annika says. "Seriously, some of us are pregnant and have toddlers."

"Yeah, and you don't see *me* yawning about it, do you?"

We both stare at her.

And then no one's tired.

We're all shrieking and hugging and hugging and shrieking while Tillie Jean grins so broadly that my cheeks hurt for her.

More babies.

More babies in Shipwreck.

More honorary nieces or nephews or niblings.

Someone behind us asks if we want a picture.

We don't tell them we hang out with tonight's performers on the regular because one, I've only hung out with Aspen for barely an hour total, and two, enough people in Copper Valley already recognize Tillie Jean because of Cooper nearly single-handedly taking the Fireballs from the worst team in baseball to the very best.

And no one sent extra security for us tonight.

It's unsettling, which I'm trying to ignore.

I don't need security.

Yes, I'm dating *the missing Bro Code guy*, but no one harasses him in Shipwreck.

Or Copper Valley, apparently.

He just does his thing with that straight face he's perfected, and people leave him alone.

But he's not straight-faced with me anymore.

Or secretive.

I even know how he knew the codes to the museum every day, and no, I'm not telling.

That's his secret.

As is, apparently, where he lives in Copper Valley. He told me he'd be in the city and that I could stay at his place if I didn't want to go all the way back to Shipwreck after the show tonight, but he very specifically did not extend that invitation to Tillie Jean and Annika.

If I do want to go home, he'll meet me in Shipwreck, and we'll crash at Beck's pool house again.

One of these days, I'll want to sleep in my own house again.

I'm working up to it.

But right now, we're still squealing over Tillie Jean's news and the lights are going down in the arena.

I glance at the structure holding lights up over the stage, and my heart squeezes for the young man Davis was when the band called it quits.

I've seen all of his former bandmates except for Cash since he spilled his heart out early Saturday morning, and all three of them looked at me like I was different.

Like they know I know what happened in Denver.

And that they know I know how monumental it is that I know.

Vanessa stopped by to check on me Sunday afternoon, and while Davis was pulling Peggy out of the cat food bag in the laundry room, she told me the reason he never dated was because he didn't want to trust anyone with all of his secrets.

So this *just dating* thing?

Yeah.

It's serious.

And it has me grinning the goofiest grin of my life as the stage lights come up, illuminating Aspen on the walkway out into the crowd as she immediately belts out a high note in her latest hit.

"We love you, Aspen," Tillie Jean yells.

There's zero chance she heard us—she has those thingies in her ears that I saw videos about on social media that help her stay on beat and protect her hearing at the same time—but she looks down at us and winks before strolling down the rest of the walkway in her opening number.

Annika and Tillie Jean and I sing along to every song, dancing and having the time of our lives, with Annika taking regular pee breaks and Tillie Jean sighing and saying that'll be her again soon enough.

And then it's time for the surprise guest of the night.

It's not actually a surprise though.

It's always Cash.

He finished all of the promo stuff he had to do for his last movies this past year, and he's been on the road with Aspen when he hasn't been working movie premieres.

Davis told me Cash had been missing the road, so when he and Aspen hooked up, it was natural for him to leave Hollywood behind and go with her.

Except that's not Cash being pushed up out of the stage in the center of the walkway.

I gasp.

Annika grabs my hand.

Tillie Jean grabs my other hand.

And Levi Wilson rises out from beneath the stage in white jeans and a tight blue T-shirt while the crowd absolutely loses their shit.

I twist and turn, looking around. Is Ingrid here? Did she know Levi would be performing?

He hasn't performed in public since finishing his last tour shortly after they started dating.

Surely she's here somewhere—

"*Sloane*," Tillie Jean shrieks.

I turn back to the stage, and once again, I'm gasping.

Beck Ryder's rising from below the stage on a separate platform.

Oh my god. Sarah.

Sarah has to be here too.

She—

I quit twisting to look, because the roar of the crowd tells me something else is going on.

And the sudden buzz in my ears and uptick of my pulse and the quake in my knees tell me what's coming.

It doesn't matter that the third man rising onto the stage is Tripp Wilson.

Or that Cash is running out from the back of the stage, mic in hand, saying, "Hold up, hold up, this is my number," with the biggest shit-eating grin to ever eat shit and grin.

We're eye level with the stage. Like I have a straight-on view of Aspen's calves.

And even though I can't see it, I know what's happening.

Another trapdoor is opening.

Another head is coming into sight.

The crowd is screaming so loudly that I can't hear myself think.

And—*oh my god*.

"Oh my god oh my god oh my god oh my god."

I don't know if that's me or Tillie Jean or Annika as a fifth head of brown hair lifts high enough that we can see it.

Davis.

On a stage.

With *the rest of the Bro Code guys*.

Without his manbun.

Without the beanie he's been wearing outside the house.

Showing off a crisp new short haircut.

Aspen taps her mic. "Is this thing on? My stage is malfunctioning. Is my microphone working right?"

"Levi shoved me off my platform," Cash says. "I was about to come up, and then he—"

He cuts himself off as a single drum beats out a rhythm.

Levi grins at Tripp.

Tripp pulls a mic out of his back pocket, looks at it, and shrugs.

Beck pulls a mic out of his back pocket too.

Cash takes Beck's mic and pushes him back on the stage so he's behind the Wilson brothers. "Not you. You can't sing for shit. Just be pretty and dance."

And Davis—

Davis looks straight at me, winks, and lifts a microphone to his lips as the first strains of "America's Sweetheart," the quintessential Bro Code song that made them stars, come from the band.

Davis sings lead.

He always sang lead, so he's singing lead tonight, and his voice—

"*Yes, baby, sing it!*" Tillie Jean yells.

Oh my god, I forgot how much I love his voice.

Rich and smooth and perfect. I read an article once where one of the other guys said Davis had the voice of an angel, and *oh my god*, he does.

He does, and he's singing.

Right there.

Right on the stage in front of me.

Not hiding. Not even hiding his shorter hair.

And the dancing—all five of them—all of them are hitting every step.

"Did you know?" Annika yells at me.

I shake my head.

And I stand there with my eyes getting hot while the five men who were never supposed to play together again move around the stage, in sync and on key, performing the song that took them to the level of superstars when I was a teenager.

When Davis was too. He's a little older than me, but he was a teenager too.

The only one of the group who finished high school on the road instead of walking the stage.

They play the extended version while the crowd roars and Tillie Jean and Annika dance beside me, but me—

I'm sixteen again.

With the most massive parasocial crush of crushes on a guy who doesn't know I exist.

Except he does know I exist.

He spent last night with his body wrapped around mine and his hand resting on my cat while we slept.

Woke me with soft kisses and a *gotta go, I have an appointment in the city, have fun tonight,* entirely too early.

So this was his appointment.

Getting ready to perform with his best friends like they used to.

We were supposed to buy the Fireballs. Be together again.

He's getting his *together again.*

My eyes blur, but I blink back the happy tears and stand there, hands clasped, bouncing on my feet while I watch my boyfriend shake his ass and sing his heart out.

I love him.

I do.

I.

Love.

Him.

That's what I'm thinking as the last beat hits, closing out the song.

That I love him and I will love him forever and there was never a way that my life would go that I couldn't love him.

Cash hands the microphone back to Beck.

Levi and Tripp and Davis all grin at each other, and then Levi—the one guy who went solo after the band broke up—lifts his mic first. "Well. That was fun. You bring a good crowd, Aspen. Look at this."

The crowd roars again.

"Take it off," Tillie Jean yells.

All five of the men and Aspen look at her.

So do the security team lining the stage beyond a rope that we're behind.

She whistles and repeats herself. "Take it all off!"

"Who let Cooper's sister in?" Tripp asks. "Can we get security?"

"Hey, no security, I like Cooper," Beck says. "You guys like Cooper? You know, Cooper Rock? Baseball player? About my height? Big ego? Hot bat? Crazy gymnastics at second base?"

Tillie Jean mock gags while the crowd goes positively nuts.

Tripp snickers.

Davis snickers.

Cash snickers.

"Yeah, that guy," Beck says. "Pretty cool wife too. I hear you guys know her."

The crowd roars.

"You're not saying some baseball player has the better wife, are you?" Levi says to Beck.

"What? No way. My wife is the best. She runs this science blog called Must Love Bees, and it's epic."

"Also, she lives with you," Cash says. "That earns her points for…something."

"She doesn't just live with me, man. She's having our third baby."

Annika screams.

Tillie Jean screams.

The entire arena screams.

My eyes burn hotter.

More babies. More babies in Shipwreck.

"Don't tell my in-laws I told you," Beck adds. "They don't know yet."

"Already got three kids," Levi says. "Way to keep up. You know what's as awesome as a science blog? A bookstore. It can get any science you want in book form. And that's what my wife does. She runs a bookstore. Has romance novels too. Y'all like romance novels?"

I am where I belong, because once again, the crowd loses its mind.

"If we're comparing," Tripp says, "might I point out that my wife runs the most successful baseball team in the world and manages baseball players with big egos."

He doesn't have to say which baseball team.

This is a hometown crowd.

They know.

And the Fireballs might not have brought home top honors this year, but they did each of the two years before.

"And speaking of, did you all hear our favorite newlywed player is staying on for one more year to bring us home another championship?" he adds.

"Gag me," Tillie Jean yells.

"Is that really Cooper's sister?" someone behind us says.

"Yes, but she bites," Annika replies.

"Oh, wow, it is. That's Tillie Jean. Tillie Jean. TJ! Did you bring the goat?"

"Can we get back to bragging on our significant others?" Cash says up on stage. "Because you all wouldn't be here tonight if my girlfriend hadn't let you crash her show. Can we hear it for Aspen?"

Oh, yes.

This crowd is here for Aspen.

We love her.

I'll be hoarse before tonight is over.

And it'll be worth it.

But the buzzing is starting in my ears again, because all four of his bandmates are now looking at Davis.

"Welp, that's what we've been up to," Beck says.

"How about another song?" Levi adds.

"A good one this time," Cash says. "Without the manbun stealing all of the vocals."

"Is he really the manbun anymore though?" Levi says. "I don't see a manbun."

"Neither do I," Tripp adds.

"It's there metaphysically," Beck says.

"Metaphorically?" Tripp corrects.

Beck grins at him. "You and your big words. Maybe we should take a poll from the crowd."

"Can the manbun speak?" Davis says, which is so wrong, since clearly, he doesn't have his manbun anymore.

I suspect it'll come back.

Eventually.

The other four look at each other and shrug.

Like they have an option of telling him no.

I'm wearing hearing protection and the roar of the crowd in this building is making my ears hurt.

This crowd wants to hear what Davis has been up to.

He shakes his head, a performer's smile on his lips.

Every time he tries to talk, they drown him out.

It's beautiful.

And glorious.

And I swear I can feel his heart beating every bit as fast as mine is.

In terror?

Enjoyment?

Both?

It takes all four of the other guys and Aspen shushing the crowd before Davis can finally speak.

And when he does—

Oh, my heart.

My heart faints dead away and my eyes get hot and my cheeks get wet and there's a lump in my throat that won't stop.

He slides me another look. "How about some credit to the woman who inspired our reunion tonight by being brave enough to tell me how disappointed she was that she never got to see us play fifteen years ago?"

Tillie Jean sways into me. "I think I just swooned to death, and I'm a happily married woman," she says.

"Oh my god, *he reunited the band for you*," Annika shrieks on my other side.

"That's a good place to give some credit," Levi says.

"If we're being honest here, that's pretty much the only thing that could've pulled me away from dinner," Beck agrees. "We were having cheeseburgers tonight. You know how good cheeseburgers are?"

"I can't top that," Tripp says. "I only perform in private for my wife these days. Not in front of forty thousand people after spending fifteen years being a hermit."

"Babe, can we have one more song?" Cash says to Aspen. "Since we got the manbun—ah, I mean, Davis out here, we should make the most of this."

"My stage is your stage, but only if you make it a good one," she replies.

The drummer hits a beat, and my breath catches.

I know this song.

I know this song inside and out.

"When You See Me."

I haven't heard it in years—not since I used to listen to Bro Code albums on repeat once I left Two Twigs—but this song—this was my secret favorite.

The song about the boy and the girl and the secrets and the truth and how he sees her, and she sees him, and they know.

They know they're real.

They know they're right.

They know it's love.

Even if their parents don't approve and they have to hide, they know it's love.

It's a slower song. The guys spread out on the stage, singing to the crowd from five places.

Except Davis.

Davis makes his way to me.

Drops to his knees while he sings.

Then squats back and swings his legs forward, sitting on the edge of the stage as close as he can get to me.

I inch closer to the security line.

They let me through.

And the man of my dreams—the man who saved me countless times, the man who's made sure I feel safe every second of every day for the past week, the man who's made love to me and spoiled my cat and opened up to my friends and who strives so hard every day to do the right thing for all of the right reasons, and sometimes even more than the right reasons—he holds eye contact while he sings the song of my heart to me.

In the middle of forty thousand people.

With his best friends singing with him.

I'm crying and I'm laughing and when he flips his microphone to one of the security guards before sliding off the stage and wrapping me in his arms and kissing me soundly, right there while the entire arena watches, I know.

I know he's the one.

He's my reward for every bad relationship. He's my family to make up for the family I was born to. He's my everything.

I pull out of the kiss and wrap my arms around him and hover my lips to his ear, his fresh haircut tickling my nose. "Are we going slow enough if I tell you I love you?"

He shudders, then squeezes me tightly. "A guy doesn't face that stage for a woman he doesn't love back."

We don't stay for the rest of Aspen's show.

Davis assures me she'll forgive us.

Considering all the ways he shows me he loves me once we get to his secret apartment just a few blocks away —I don't think I'd care if she didn't.

Who needs a pop star's forgiveness when I have my favorite retired boy bander's complete love and adoration?

Especially when he's so thorough in showing his love and adoration?

And not just with orgasms.

But with making me coffee. Telling me the stories about all of his tattoos. Keeping my favorite Kangapoo shampoo in his shower in this secret apartment that no one else in his circle knows about.

Answering me honestly even when it's hard.

Not being mad when I answer him honestly even when it's hard.

All of the little things that are healing the wounds I still have on my soul.

The things that show me he's a good man with a good heart who will never be perfect, but who is absolutely perfect to me.

"You looked incredible on that stage," I whisper to him late, late that night as we snuggle in bed together.

He presses a kiss to my temple. "Felt good too. More than I thought it would."

"Will you ever do it again?"

"Only if you asked me to."

I hug him tighter. "I would've loved you even if you hadn't."

His fingers comb through my hair, and he kisses my forehead again. "And that's exactly why I did it."

I kiss his chest.

"I did something else this week," he murmurs.

"What's that?"

"I convinced a certain baseball player with a big ego to sell me one of his cabins."

I lift my head and stare at Davis in the dark.

And then it clicks.

And I laugh. And laugh. And I laugh some more.

He chuckles, and it's the best sound in the world.

"Yeah," he says, his voice husky. "That cabin."

"The one where he found his half of the treasure."

"Wouldn't have asked for any other."

I giggle again. "How much did it take to convince him?"

"One look from his wife and one promise from me to donate some resources to his favorite charity."

"Resources?"

"To be determined if it's time or money or both."

"You'd do it anyway."

"Yep. He's a terrible negotiator." He shifts in the bed and slides a hand down my naked hip. "You can stay there any night you want to. For as long as you need. Starting immediately."

Dammit.

My eyes are getting hot again.

"Thank you," I whisper.

"It will always be my absolute pleasure to keep you safe and happy and loved."

I am.

I'm safe. I'm happy. I'm loved.

And he is too.

I might not be able to buy him a house. I might not be able to find him another treasure.

But I will find every way I can to show him how much he's loved too.

EPILOGUE

Davis

SEVEN MONTHS INTO DATING SLOANE, I can officially say I know what true peace is.

I still don't know what I want to do with my life. Other than love her.

And it doesn't matter.

Because when I'm with her, everything in me stills, and the only thing that matters is loving her.

And it's so easy to love her.

Like right now, as we're sitting on the balcony over Crusty Nut, watching the pirate treasure hunt dig in the town square across the street. I'm toying with her hair, happy to be touching her any way I can, with no other place on earth I'd rather be and nothing else I'd rather be doing.

Levi and Ingrid are with us, watching from overhead as two of their three kids partake in digging for treasure.

"You do this Pirate Festival every single year?" Ingrid's asking Sloane.

Sloane nods. "Every single year."

"What happens to the square after it's all dug up?"

"Landscape crew comes in and fixes it all up. There's new sod every year. It's excessive, but everyone has so much fun with it, and we donate a lot of the profits to Sarah's favorite environmental funds."

"You think I could go dig without getting mobbed?" Levi asks.

"No," Sloane and Ingrid answer together.

Levi slides me a look. "But you could."

Sloane squeezes my thigh. "Not this year."

That's unfortunately true.

I had to hire a security team of my own—temporarily, that's for fucking sure—because it turns out when you crash a concert to tell the world you love a woman after not being seen publicly for fifteen years, the attention comes back.

Has to die down soon.

Not like there aren't other celebrities making bigger news happen.

Ingrid sucks in a breath and sits straighter, and Levi loops an arm around the back of her chair. "Chuck's got him."

She presses a palm into her eye. "I know, but it's Hudson."

Hudson.

Their youngest.

He makes Tillie Jean and Cooper Rock together look like angels.

"Was Giselle better with him?" Sloane asks.

"She was," Ingrid says. "We're still looking for the right fit."

"Sorry about that. Again."

"No, no! Don't be sorry. She's so happy now. Don't ever be sorry someone's happy. Did she send you pictures from her last trip? Look. How fun is this?"

Giselle did, indeed, take a vacation after we found the treasure.

She went home and fell in love.

Nobody saw it coming, probably least of all her.

But it means she didn't come back.

And now Levi's straightening.

I look out over the square too, find Hudson—he's turning eight this summer—and I see what's about to play out the split second before it happens.

One minute, Hudson's bending over to pull a string he's just dug up from the ground, and the next—

"No!" Sloane shrieks.

"Oh, fuck," Levi mutters.

"Cussing jar, Dad," Zoe, their oldest, says without removing her nose from a book at the next table.

And glitter explodes all over Hudson and his sister Piper beside him.

"*Rawk! Contraband glitter! Rawk!*" Long Beak Silver crows.

"*Stinky Booty, you are dead when I get my hands on you,*" Tillie Jean yells beneath us.

"Cooper's here?" Levi asks.

"No," Sloane says. "At least, not physically. Clearly he is in spirit. But the Fireballs are in LA right now."

"*Rawk! Stinky Booty goes to the slammer! Rawk!*"

"I love that bird," Levi says.

"No," Ingrid says as Zoe flips her book shut and says, "Really? Can we get a bird? I want a parrot. We should get a parrot. Mom, wouldn't it be awesome? We could train it to tell us when Hudson's trying to sneak out of his room and onto the roof again."

"No," Ingrid repeats.

"Taking Mom's side," Levi says. "We can visit the bird."

I scoot closer to Sloane, watching her watch them with a soft smile. "Your dad's right," she says to Zoe. "I'll introduce you to Pop. He owns Long Beak Silver, and I'm sure he'd be happy to let you visit anytime you're in town. The first time you get parrot poop on you, you'll change your mind about wanting your own. Or the first time he steals your car keys and puts them on a roof."

Levi and Ingrid's security crew is pulling Hudson and Piper to the side to wipe them off.

The rest of the digging has paused while Tillie Jean stalks into the middle of the square. "Do not pull any strings that you find, people. Not if you don't want to get glittered."

"Did Cooper really invest in biodegradable glitter?" Ingrid asks Sloane.

"Yes," I answer for her. "He wants to change the world one prank at a time."

"And it's truly biodegradable?"

"Confirmed with lab work."

"Huh." Ingrid leans back again and looks down on Shipwreck. "How's the museum doing?"

"It is *so crowded*," Sloane replies, which makes me smile.

The Rocks issued a statement a few months after we found the treasure, and they laid it all out there.

That Shipwreck was founded by Walter Bombeck pretending to be Thorny Rock. That the real Thorny Rock founded Sarcasm. That they'd split the treasure, and both halves have been found and will be on display at the museum.

"Raised ticket prices, and it's still sold out through next March," I tell Ingrid.

"And it's paying for itself, even with the increased security to handle guarding a real pirate treasure."

"Some bigger museums have reached out to ask if they can display parts of it."

Sloane smiles at me, and my heart does what it always does when she smiles at me—it breaks into a happy dance.

Impossible to not smile back at that. "They want some of the canned vegetables Sloane used as weapons to keep the treasure from falling into the wrong hands too."

She laughs. "Shush. They do not."

They do. I'll show her the email later.

"Is Sarcasm doing anything to compete more in the pirate tourism world now?" Ingrid asks.

"Nope. They said fu—eff you all, we're keeping our Unicorn Festival, and we're going to do it bigger and better than the Pirate Festival because we've always been better. Direct quote."

"From Annika's sister," I supply.

"Is the museum displaying the mortar ball?" Ingrid asks.

Sloane's grin grows to epic proportions. "It's been defused and we should get it back in the next few weeks."

"They figure out who was buried under the stairs in that cabin?" Levi asks.

Sloane squeezes my thigh again.

"They did," I confirm. "Thorny Rock's oldest grandson. The real Thorny Rock."

"One of your relatives," Ingrid says.

"Yep."

"Do they know why?"

Sloane and I share a look.

"We have a theory," I finally say.

"It's very logical," Sloane adds.

Levi grins. "Usually is with this guy."

"Spill," Ingrid says. "I'll believe whatever you tell me. *Oh my god.* Davis. You need to write a book. You need to write a book about all of this."

I pull a face as Sloane straightens. "That's what I told him too. But he's not ready to hear it."

I love that phrase.

He's not ready to hear it.

She said it to my mom at Christmas the first time when Mom asked if I was going to do anything with the land my camper's still sitting on, and I said no.

Sloane told her I was going to build a house there someday because heritage is important enough to me that I went on a freaking treasure hunt, but that I wasn't ready to hear it.

She was right.

We'll build a house on that land one day.

It means something. Just like my cabin where Cooper found the first half of the treasure means something.

I'm coming around.

Slowly.

"Thorny Rock—the real Thorny Rock, the one who founded Sarcasm—had four grandkids," I tell Levi and Ingrid. "One died in childhood. One moved to Copper Valley—that would be where my family line came from—and the other two stayed in the area up here. The treasure wasn't where it should've been. Either of them. Sloane came up with a theory that Thorny and Walter never told anyone where they were stashing their halves of the treasure, but each of their families had clues. Same clues we had. So we think at least one of Thorny's grandkids found his half of the treasure, and when the other one found out —she killed him to keep him silent."

"He wasn't well-liked," Sloane adds. "We went back through all of the old letters that Davis's mom inherited, and figured out who was who, and it's very likely no one missed him at all."

"Or a justifiable homicide," Ingrid muses.

Levi cuts her a look, and she grins at him. "I read a lot. I'm very happy in my own real life though. Probably because I'd never have a reason to justifiably homicide you. So long as we never get a bird."

"They're so gross," Zoe mutters. "Uncle Davis, if you write a book, I'll edit it for you. You look like the type who'll use your contractions in the wrong places and leave dangling participles and end sentences with prepositions."

"Rawk! Contraband glitter! Rawk!"

All of us lean over the railing and look at the square again.

Three tourists are now coated in glitter.

Tillie Jean's rubbing her temples, then pausing to rub her pregnant belly, then rubbing her temples again.

She glances up, catches us watching her, and visibly sighs. "My brother will never see hell unleashed like the hell I will release on him when he retires in a few months."

"You sure you want to do that to Waverly?" Levi asks.

They hold eye contact.

It's the *I know something* kind of eye contact that makes both Sloane and Ingrid sit up and gasp.

"You know, don't you?" Tillie Jean says.

"That she's going on tour next year? Yep."

"The *other thing*."

"Babies," Ingrid breathes.

The sharp look Levi gives her—the *do not tell the world Waverly's pregnant* look—confirms what all of us apparently suspect.

Bet that'll be an interesting tour now.

"Babies are so—*oh my god*," Zoe gasps.

I look at her.

She claps a hand over her own mouth. "I don't know anything. Don't look at me like you're doing mind tricks on me. And I didn't mean it about your grammar. Oh my god, *baby*."

Sloane leans over and stares at Tillie Jean, who ducks eye contact and fans herself. "Oof. Gotta get out of this heat. Pop. Pop, get your parrot on glitter patrol. I'm over it. Where's my husband? I want a lemonade."

Sloane smiles, then leans back into me. "I like our home."

I kiss her head. "Me too."

"And our friends."

"Most days."

She snorts with laughter.

I didn't know I was an *everything is my favorite* kind of guy until I started dating Sloane.

But I am.

Her laugh is my favorite. Her smiles are my favorite. Her hands are my favorite. Her mouth is my favorite. Her screaming my name and scraping her nails down my back is my favorite.

Everything about her is my favorite.

"I'm glad you were the fake bride who stuck," I murmur to her.

She laughs again. "Same."

"Maybe we'll do a real ceremony one of these days."

She peers up at me, and there's no *are you seriously proposing randomly in front of your friends?* that you might expect.

Instead, there's a bit of shiny eye going around. "Just tell me where to be and when."

Yeah.

She's my calm.

She's my center.

She's my everything.

My absolute favorite.

And the only woman in the world that I will ever love this much.

For all eternity.

PIPPA GRANT BOOK LIST

The Girl Band Series (Complete)
Mister McHottie
Stud in the Stacks
Rockaway Bride
The Hero and the Hacktivist

The Thrusters Hockey Series
The Pilot and the Puck-Up
Royally Pucked
Beauty and the Beefcake
Charming as Puck
I Pucking Love You

Copper Valley Bro Code Series
Flirting with the Frenemy
America's Geekheart
Liar, Liar, Hearts on Fire
The Hot Mess and the Heartthrob
Snowed in with Mr. Heartbreaker
The Pretend Fiancé Fiasco

Copper Valley Fireballs Series (Complete)
Jock Blocked
Real Fake Love

The Grumpy Player Next Door

Irresistible Trouble

Three BFFs and a Wedding Series (Complete)

The Worst Wedding Date

The Gossip and the Grump

The Bride's Runaway Billionaire

Copper Valley Pounders Series

Until It Was Love

The Roommate Mistake

A Thrusters x Fireballs Mash-Up

The Secret Hook-Up

The Tickled Pink Series

The One Who Loves You

Rich In Your Love

Standalones

The Last Eligible Billionaire

Not My Kind of Hero

Dirty Talking Rival *(Bro Code Spin-Off)*

A Royally Inconvenient Marriage *(Royally Pucked Spin-Off)*

Exes and Ho Ho Hos

The Happy Cat Series (Complete)

Hosed

Hammered

Hitched

Humbugged

Happily Ever Aftered

The Bluewater Billionaires Series *(Complete)*

The Price of Scandal by Lucy Score

The Mogul and the Muscle by Claire Kingsley

Wild Open Hearts by Kathryn Nolan

Crazy for Loving You by Pippa Grant

Pippa Grant writing as Jamie Farrell:

The Misfit Brides Series *(Complete)*

Blissed

Matched

Smittened

Sugared

Married

Spiced

Unhitched

The Officers' Ex-Wives Club Series *(Complete)*

Her Rebel Heart

Southern Fried Blues

ABOUT THE AUTHOR

Pippa Grant wanted to write books, so she did.

Before she became a *USA Today* and #1 Amazon best-selling romantic comedy author, she was a young military spouse who got into writing as self-therapy. That happened around the time she discovered reading romance novels, and the two eventually merged into a career. Today, she has more than 30 knee-slapping Pippa Grant titles and nine published under the name Jamie Farrell.

When she's not writing romantic comedies, she's fumbling through being a mom, wife, and mountain woman, and sometimes tries to find hobbies. Her crowning achievement? Having impeccable timing for telling stories that will make people snort beverages out of their noses. Consider yourself warned.

Find Pippa at...
www.pippagrant.com
pippa@pippagrant.com

Made in the USA
Middletown, DE
16 May 2025